POEMS IN PROSE:
A SHOWCASE ANTHOLOGY

Brian Stableford (1948-2024) was a British science fiction writer, translator, and literary scholar who published over one hundred and twenty volumes of original fiction and over two hundred volumes of translations. He also wrote under the pseudonyms Brian Craig and Francis Amery. His original fiction includes the Hidden Swan series of novels, which began with *Halcyon Drift* (1972) and ended with *Swan Song* (1975), and the novels *The Werewolves of London* (1990) and *The Cassandra Complex* (2001). Among his important translations are *Monsieur de Phocas* by Jean Lorrain and *Mephistophela* by Catulle Mendès. He furthermore published numerous volumes of nonfiction, which include *The Mysteries of Modern Science* (1977) and, in four volumes, *New Atlantis: A Narrative History of Scientific Romance* (2016).

SNUGGLY BOOKS

POEMS IN PROSE:
A SHOWCASE ANTHOLOGY

Edited, Introduced and Translated by
BRIAN STABLEFORD

THIS IS A SNUGGLY BOOK

ISBN: 978-1-64525-162-0

Contents

Introduction / *xiii*

Part One: Precursors / 3

Montesquieu / 3
    The First Canto of *The Temple of Gnide* / 4
Charles Nodier / 13
    Sanchette or, The Oleander / 13
Samuel-Henri Berthoud / 15
    Beauduin Bras-de-Fer /16
Maurice Guérin / 19
    The Bacchante / 19
Louis Bertrand / 30
    Vignettes from *Gaspard de la Nuit*
        My Cottage / 31
        The Viola da Gamba /32
        Messire Jean / 33
        The Mason / 33
        Evening on the Water /34
        The Five Fingers of the Hand / 35

Part Two: Parnassians / 37

Charles Baudelaire / 37
    The Double Room / 38
    Poems in Prose from the *Revue Fantaisiste*
        Evening Twilight / 40
        Solitude / 41
        Projects / 42
        The Clock / 43

Tresses / 44

Invitation to the Voyage / 45

Crowds / 47

Widows / 48

The Old Mountebank / 51

Stéphane Mallarmé / 53

The Poor Pale Child / 54

The Barbary Organ / 55

The Orphan /56

The Pipe / 57

Paul Verlaine / 58

Nevermore / 59

A Clock / 60

Catulle Mendès / 62

The Key to Dreams / 63

For Her and Them

The Perfume Less Sweet / 68

The Lying Snow / 69

The Chemise of the Wayfaring Tree / 69

The Little Corpse / 70

The Good Excuse / 70

The Embarrassment of God the Father after Creating the Sun
and the Moon / 71

Louis de Lyvron / 75

Attila / 76

The Madman's Poem / 92

Henri Cazalis / 97

Pensées / 98

Charles Leconte de Lisle / 99

The Combat of the Kronides and the Titans / 99

Augusta Holmès / 103

The Harp of the Ocean / 104

Arthur Rimbaud / 109

After the Deluge / 109

Mystique / 110

Antique / 111

Lives / 111

City / 112

Conte / 113

Theodore de Banville / 114

The Good God / 115

Monsieur le Soleil / 116

Madame la Lune / 117

Judith Gautier / 119

L'Ile de Chiloë / 119

Forgetfulness / 120

Suicide / 121

Punishment / 121

The Seagull / 123

Villiers de l'Isle Adam / 123

Introduction to *Akedysseril* / 124

The Lovers of Toledo / 126

Emmanuel des Essarts / 130

The Eternity of Don Juan / 130

Anatole France / 131

Amycus and Celestin / 131

Part Three: The Third Republic / 137

Joris-Karl Huysmans / 137

Japanese Rococo / 139

Ritornelle / 139

Declaration of Love / 140

The Kipper / 140

Charles Cros / 141

The Distractress / 142

The Piece of Furniture / 143

Madrigal / 145

The Song of the Aryan Road / 146

Charles de Sivry / 148

The Spinner / 149

Robert Caze / 150

Far, Far Away / 151

Jules-Amédée Barbey d'Aurevilly / 152
    Chameleon Eyes / 152
J. H. Rosny / 156
    Psalms / 156
Charles Vignier / 165
    Morituri / 166
    Undines' Chorus / 167
    The Mage's Daughter / 167
Marie Krysinska / 168
    Ballade / 169
    Windows / 171
    A Romance in the Moon / 174
    Russian Legend / 175
    Amorous Siesta / 176
George Auriol / 177
    The Spider / 178
    The Ballad of Wasted Time / 179
Albert Tinchant / 180
    Empty Heart / 181
Alphonse Allais / 182
    God / 183
Gabriel Mourey / 184
    The Song of the Stars / 185
    Crucifixion / 186

Part Four: Decadent Proses / 189

Leo Trézenik / 189
    The Good God / 190
    Egotisms / 192
    Child's Play / 194
Charles Morice / 195
    Listen, Listen, See if it's Raining / 195
    Interior Testimony / 197
    And I am the one of your souls . . . / 200
    I Know Them . . . / 201

Remy de Gourmont / 202
    Litanies of the Rose / 203
    News of the Unfortunate Isles / 208
    Hell / 211
    The City of the Sphinxes / 213
Pierre Louÿs / 217
    Some Songs of Bilitis
        Psappha / 218
        The Dance of Glottis and Kyse / 219
        Advice / 219
        Uncertainty / 219
        The Encounter / 220
        The Little Terracotta Astarte / 220
        Desire / 221
Marcel Schwob / 221
    The Mirror, the Needle and the Poppy / 222
    Hermes Psychogogos / 223
    The Three Bottles / 224
Gustave Kahn / 225
    The Smoker / 226
    Transitions / 227
Jean Moréas / 229
    Narcissus / 230
Adople Retté / 235
    The Little Goddess / 236
    Hélène / 237
Gaston Danville / 238
    Contes d'Au-delà
        Avant-Propos / 239
        The Valley of Hearts / 239
        Unknown Harmonies / 241
        The Crystal Cup / 242
Jules Renard / 244
    The Lock of Hair / 245
    Glow-Worms / 247
    Grass / 247

Saint-Pol-Roux / 247
    Poplars / 240
    The Malign Statue / 249
Jean Lorrain / 253
    Flower of the Fortifes / 254
    Autumnal Souls / 256
Victor Remouchamps / 259
    Of an Ideal Species / 259
    My Soul is Poor / 260
    Impression on Dreams / 261
    The Féeries of the Shadow / 262
    Future Barbarities / 263
G. Albert Aurier / 265
    The Lover / 265
    Plutus / 266
    The Blue Woman / 268
Ephraim Mikhael / 269
    The Toy Shop / 269
    The Wake / 271
    The Solitary / 271
Bernard Lazare / 278
    The Garden / 279
    The Forest / 281
Henri de Régnier / 284
    Hermogenes / 285
    The Knight who fell asleep in the Snow / 291
Jean Richepin / 295
    Tomorrow / 295
May Armand Blanc / 299
    Neurasthenia / 299
    The Wedding of Time and Death / 303
    Winter Heaths / 305
Jacques Fréhel / 308
    Last Light / 309
    Kemp Owyne / 314
Henry Kistemaeckers / 318
    The Hour of the Last Judgment / 319

Paul Margueritte / 321
   Pierrot Mormon / 322
   The Paradise of Horses /
Francis Jammes / 326
   Paradise / 328
   The Paradise of Animals / 330
Gabriel de Lautrec / 332
   Sad Pride / 332
   Moonlight / 333
   The Mistresses of Poets / 334
   For a Demon / 336
   The Invisible Soul / 337
Frederic Boutet / 338
   The Valley Named Solitude / 338
Alfred Jarry / 345
   The Amorphous Isle / 346
   The Fragrant Isle / 347
   The Isle of Ptyx / 348
   The Isle of Her, the Cyclops and the Great Crystal Swan / 350
Hugues Rebell / 351
   Successive Deaths / 352
   The Virile Robe / 352
   The Noble Pauper / 354
Guillaume Apollinaire / 355
   Poem Read at the Wedding of André Salmon
      on 13 July 1909 / 356
Renée Vivien / 357
   The Black Swan / 358
   The Dead / 359
   Lilith / 361
   The Forest / 362
Maurice Magre / 364
   The Black Serpent that Brings Luck / 364
   The Emperor of China and the Emperor of Japan / 365
   The God of Benevolent Intelligence / 366
Hélène Picard / 367
   Invocation / 368

Introduction

The oxymoronic notion of *poèmes en prose* was popularized in France by Charles Baudelaire and has remained solidly associated with him. This is not to say that *poèmes en prose* did not exist before he produced his key examples, but the label had not been established in public consciousness and, more importantly, no paradigmatic set of illustrative examples had been put forward for imitation and variation.

Oxymoronic combinations are, of course, paradoxical and ironic, but they are not nonsensical and are often rich in significance. The classic example of an English oxymoron, *bittersweet*, is a perfect illustration of the fact that combining contraries, like theses and antitheses, can sometimes synthesize new and useful meanings, intellectually challenging precisely because they defy simple analysis. There is no clear definition of a poem in prose; exemplars advanced by various critics and historians only have, at best, the kind of "family resemblances" that Ludwig Wittgenstein famously credited to the members of the conceptual set of "games." An anthology of poems in prose is therefore bound to contain controversial examples, and could not be appropriate if it did not. Whatever idea particular users of the term might form of the genre, it is bound to have "fuzzy edges," and that is not a bad thing.

Attempts at unpacking the concept of "poems in prose" are, of course, made more problematic by the difficulty of defining the precise range of the term "poem." In crude terms, it seems easy enough to identify poems because they are usually divided up into lines possessed of a rhythmic quality and a rhyme-scheme, but there are forms of poetry that do not possess those attributes, the most familiar example being the Japanese haiku, the formularization of which specifies a number of syllables. A further problem arises when poems are translated from one language into another, when rhyme and scansion are usually lost—or, if they are fetishistically maintained, require more-or-less radical distortions of meaning.

There are entire literary genres that are known in the modern world almost entirely in translation, the most relevant to the present study being the legacies of ancient Greek, Latin and the primary languages of Holy Writ. Anyone in search of possible examples of "poetry in prose" is likely to settle immediately upon modern renditions of Homer, Virgil and the Bible—although, of course, not all the "verses" of the Bible seem equally "poetic" to the modern ear, so the searcher in question is more likely to zero in on the *Song of Songs*, *Ecclesiastes* and *Revelation* than *Isaiah* or the *Acts of the Apostles*. That is because the erotic subject-matter of the *Song of Songs*, the portentous tone of *Ecclesiastes* and the visionary allegory of *Revelation* seem inherently "poetic"—and, unsurprisingly, a great deal of modern poetry in prose is either erotic or portentous, and often both. Although it would be an exaggeration to contend that all poetry in prose consists of footnotes to the three texts cited, it would not be too wide of the mark. Viewed as an ensemble, the examples collected in the present volume are certainly rich in eroticism, portentousness and visionary allegory.

One circumstance of great relevance to the evolution of French *poèmes en prose*, and of particular relevance to the present project, is that it is much easier to produce rhyming verse in French than in English because of the different ways in which the two languages are organized. Thus, there was a far greater temptation for the greatest writer of English drama, William Shakespeare, gradually to abandon the convention of rhyming in his plays—while retaining it in his poetry—than there was for his French contemporaries. That abandonment, however, did not entirely remove the poetic gloss from his great soliloquies, which anyone in quest of examples of English "poetry in prose" would be tempted to cite as paradigms.

In Medieval France, the compilers of "romances" imitative of Classical epic poems similarly found it convenient sometimes to abandon rhyme and scansion, and many thirteenth- and fourteenth-century romances exist in both verse and prose versions—or, if they did not then, their substance underwent conversion in later centuries as their fundamental narratives were adapted for new audiences. Such moves were, however, always controversial when first made, perennially haunted by the inevitable notion that prose is essentially vulgar and hence less "noble" than verse. We should not forget, however, that in the beginning, the Old French *romanz*—the Latin-derived origin of the term "romance"—meant "vulgar language," and identified works composed in vernacular languages rather than in Classical Latin, knowledge of which distinguished formally-educated people from the "uneducated," and which was employed by the Church in maintaining a centuries-old stranglehold on formal education. In nineteenth-century French drama, not unnaturally, there was still a very marked different in prestige between the Classically-sanctioned and convention-bound genre of tragedy and the vulgar forms of comedy, because rather than in spite of the fact that farces and vaudevilles were far more popular with the bulk of the potential audience; the same prejudice extended into the critical consideration of genres of poetry and prose, helping to make the very idea of *poèmes en prose* seem not merely awkward but almost abominable.

It is not at all surprising, however, that the deliberate invention and profitable exploitation of the oxymoron occurred in France, where French philosophy and literature had long entertained and nurtured "contrarian" tendencies. Jean-Jacques Rousseau famously recorded that he would rather be an "*homme à paradoxes*" than an "*homme* à *préjudés*," and many other eighteenth-century *philosophes* similarly regarded "paradox" as a useful instrument of Enlightenment, performing a vital role in rhetoric. Useful "paradoxical" strategies include sarcasm, *double entendre* and the symbolism of allegory, all providing stern challenge to entrenched prejudice by means of more-or-less subtle attacks.

At the beginning of the Enlightenment in France, under the reign of Louis XIV, many experiments were already being carried out in "translating" poetry into prose, not merely in the recycled substance of romances but in the work of the most renowned fabulist of his era, Jean de La Fontaine, many of whose fables exist in both verse and prose versions, the latter being bound to appeal to any historian as crucial examples of "poems in prose," just as they did to some of the writers who produced "*poèmes en prose*" in the latter half of the century,

Charles Baudelaire was firmly affiliated to the contrarian tradition of the Enlightenment *philosophes*, as a critic and a practitioner, and his contribution to it played a crucial part—albeit not without difficulty and largely posthumously—in carrying the cause forward. Baudelaire's early *poèmes en prose* were accumulated, along with his verses, in *Les Fleurs du Mal* (1857), which became one of the central texts of nineteenth-century French literature, exercising an enormous influence on subsequent literary endeavor in that language. In the volume in question they played an accessory role, supplementing the endeavors that took advantage of scansion and rhyme, but the author immediately moved on to the compilation of a definitive collection of his short prose works, which he intended to call *Le Spleen de Paris*, although he died, in 1867, before completing arrangements for its publication, and it was issued posthumously in 1869.

Some subsequent editions of *Le Spleen de Paris* were retitled *Petits poèmes en prose*. Baudelaire had begun issuing an earlier version of the compilation as "Poèmes en prose" in the pages of the *Revue fantaisiste* in November 1861, although that publication was interrupted when the periodical was shut down, but he had published a further batch as "Petit poèmes en prose" in *L'Artiste* in 1864. The impending appearance of the former set had been advertised in every issue of the *Revue fantaisiste* issued earlier in 1861, and was apparently eagerly awaited, at least by the editor, Catulle Mendès. The fact that the publication could not be completed in its pages could not have come as a complete surprise, however. The first edition of *Les Fleurs du Mal* had been seized by the police and several of the poems suppressed, and Catulle Mendès was imprisoned and fined following the prosecution of the *Revue fantasisite* for publishing the text of his drama *Le Roman d'une nuit*.

Censorship was a fact of life for writers working under the Second Empire, who had been issued a stern warning by Napoléon III when he exiled several leading members of the Romantic Movement from France immediately after seizing power. Most of the exiles took advantage of a proffered amnesty a few years later, although Victor Hugo and Edgar Quinet famously refused to accept it, but the work of those who returned had to be subjected thereafter to careful diplomatic restriction in order to avoid suppression. The serialization of Alexandre Dumas' intended masterpiece, *Isaac Laquedem* (1853) was rudely interrupted, and the novel only exists in truncated form, hardly read and devoid of renown.

Political censorship was by no means a new phenomenon in the 1850s, of course, and French authors had been living with the threat since the tyranny of Louis XIV, when the Sun King's advisors and agents had carefully rationed the supply of royal warrants required for licit publication. They had not merely suppressed individual works but entire genres, including the genre of *contes de fées*, which enjoyed a brief vogue in 1697 before being stamped out, presumably at the behest of the king's court preacher, Jean-Bénigne Bossuet, who found its implicit paganism offensive and did not like his own fervent misogyny being mocked by some of the female writers who had invented and developed the genre. An exception was made, however, for Charles Perrault, who had carefully introduced Christian priests into the tales he recycled for reading to children, and thus was able to be read freely and to become famous, while the writers whose work he appropriated and mangled were effectively consigned to oblivion, sometimes—as in the case of the titan of the genre, the Comtesse de Murat—via long imprisonment without trial.

The first rule of censorship is, of course, that mention of censorship must be censored, so the effects of the refusal of royal warrants intended to annihilate undesirable publications went largely unrecorded by official history. Those effects were, however, a trifle paradoxical, because it was very difficult, in practical terms, to control the spread and usage of printing presses. The attempted suppression of works for which there was a manifest or potential popular demand served as a stimulus to the prolific production in eighteenth-century France of unlicensed books, which could not legally be put on open sale but could circulate as a curious kind of contraband, sometimes selling in enormous quantities in spite of being theoretically illegal to possess. That circulation was aided by deceptive title pages claiming publication in Brussels, London, Geneva or anywhere other than their actual place of publication, Paris, and frequently omitting or disguising the author's name.

The "prehistory" of the *poèmes en prose* advertised by Baudelaire is intricately interwoven with the history of censorship in France. Modern texts attempting to reconstruct that prehistory often select as key examples François Fénelon's prose mock-epic *Les aventures de Télémaque*, written for didactic purposes while Fénelon was the tutor of Louis XIV's grandson, the Duc de Bourgogne, along with various other apologues, some of them cast as *contes de fées*. The liberally-minded author employed his fiction to embody a scathing and only slightly-veiled criticism of autocratic government; by the time that the king was informed of that subtle treason (he did not read himself, of course, having people to do that for him) Fénelon had already been banished from Versailles, presumably at Bossuet's behest, and was confined to his diocese, but when illicitly-printed copies of his works began to be circulated in 1699 it soon became impossible to keep them in check, and by the time that the king's death in 1715 issued in the temporary moral relaxation of the Regency the damage was irreparable and *Télémaque* had become an "underground classic" whose eventual emergence into the daylight of legality had become inevitable.

Another example frequently cited by French historians as an important pre-Baudelairean example of a *poème en prose* is a curious text entitled *Le Temple de Gnide*, published anonymously in 1725, which masqueraded as a translation from the ancient Greek, although it was, in fact, the work of the Baron

de Montesquieu, a courtier who became one of the most notorious—and hence the most suppressed—of the *philosophes* of
the Enlightenment. He was the author of *Considérations sur les
causes de la grandeur des Romains et leur décademce* (1734), which
suggested, indirectly, that the moral decadence of the Bourbon
regime was the repetition of a historical pattern whose development and inevitable conclusion had already been exemplified
by the decline and fall of the Roman Empire. He also wrote
De l'esprit des lois (1748), one of the great classics of political
philosophy, which had a significant effect on the propaganda of
the American Revolution and the formulation of the constitu-
tion of the resultant nation-state. As well as *Le Temple de Gnide*,
Montesquieu had embedded some of his ideas in an anonymous
epistolary novel, *Les Lettres persans* (1721), which included
an apologue detailing the illustrative imaginary history of a
society of "troglodytes." Although his strategies of evasion did
not prevent the attempted suppression of his work, the works
in question were not only widely admired but widely copied,
and many *philosophes* became prolific producers of apologues,
mock-Classical verse and mock-*contes de fées*, which delighted
in subversive irony, paradox and symbolism. Voltaire became
particularly expert in the art, while simultaneously writing verse,
earnest imitation Classical tragedies, and encyclopedias; some of
his *contes philosophiques* could be considered as *poèmes en prose*.

Although the 1789 Revolution eventually put an end to royal
warrants, it did not put an end to political censorship, nor did
it reduce the sensitivity of censors to the various strategies that
were by then being routinely applied to the evasion of their
vigilance, especially the lavish uses of irony, paradox and disguise. Briefly deflected after the turn of the century, censorship
became increasingly fervent again after the Bourbon Restoration
in 1815, although, when Charles X came to the throne in 1824,
the situation was complicated by the fact that the new king
fancied himself as a patron of the arts, and took a sympathetic
interest in the burgeoning Romantic Movement in spite of the
fact that several of its leading members were outspoken radical
Republicans. Periodicals that were allowed to exist because they

declared loudly that their concerns were purely literary and artistic, such as the *Mercure du XIXe siècle*, survived for a while in the late 1820s before being shut down, and established a hypocritical tradition that was echoed throughout the next half-century.

Although the July Revolution of 1830 was welcomed by Romantic writers as the possible advent of a liberation from censorship, the thaw proved temporary, and the secret police that had been inherited by Napoléon I before being handed back to the Bourbons, did not suffer a long interruption to their work. The Revolution of 1848 was supposed to be another watershed, but the rapid advent of Napoléon III—who had long had literary and philosophical ambitions of his own—turned up the heat again, contriving a virtual annihilation of the publication of works considered dubious, without suppressing the fervent desire on the part of many writers and readers to cheat the system by any and all possible means. That was the strange intellectual climate in which Baudelaire developed an interest in ironic *poèmes en prose*, and communicated that interest to many of his contemporaries, with the aid of a party of loyal and ingenious supporters and rivals.

When Baudelaire named his own predecessors, foremost among the exemplars he selected was the provincial poet Louis Bertrand, who preferred to sign himself "Aloysius Bertrand." He had died in 1841, of tuberculosis, in relative obscurity, but a collection of his *poèmes en prose* was published posthumously by his friend David d'Angers as *Gaspard de la Nuit, fantaisies à la manière de Rembrandt et de Callot*, the text of which includes paeans of praise of the great pioneers of Romantic poetry and prose, Victor Hugo and Charles Nodier, supplemented by an appreciative essay by Hugo's friend, the leading critic of the Romantic Movement, Charles Sainte-Beuve. The analogy drawn in the subtitle of the collection between the items it contains and artists' sketches was to appeal to many future writers of *poèmes en prose*, and Baudelaire was best-known before the publication of *Les Fleurs du Mal* as an art critic, commentaries on the annual Salon being one of the most abundant opportunities for publication offered to hard-pressed writers during the Second Empire.

The pairing in the subtitle of Rembrandt and Jacques Callot, the latter being best-known as a caricaturist and exponent of deliberate grotesquerie, was particularly significant in encapsulating the paradoxical potential of *poèmes en prose*, exploited to the full by Bertrand.

The most significant alternative exemplar that might have been chosen by Baudelaire, and was chosen belatedly by Stuart Merrill when he assembled the first collection of French poems in prose in translation, *Pastels in Prose* (1890), was also a provincial poet: the Provençal writer Maurice de Guérin, who also died prematurely, of tuberculosis, in 1839, and was also greatly admired by Charles Sainte-Beuve. Although he is said to have destroyed most of his works before he died, several crucial texts survived for posthumous publication. Guérin was a disciple of the Christian socialist philosopher Hugues de Lamennais, and his attitude to composition was much less playful than Bertrand's; his prose poems have nothing Callotesque about them, but he was a significant pioneer of a different strand of the *poèmes en prose* written in Baudelaire's wake.

Although they never really constituted an organized Movement, the band of disciples and competitors of Baudelaire that formed in the 1860s came to be known as the Parnassians, because one of their key publicity stunts was a series of showcase anthologies, the first of which was published in 1866 by Alphonse Lemerre, entitled *Le Parnasse contemporain*, edited by Catulle Mendès and Louis-Xavier Ricard. Like Mendès, Ricard had previously been the proprietor of a periodical, *La Revue du progrès*, which was ostensibly literary and artistic but was actually determinedly subversive. Unlike the *Revue fantaisiste*, Ricard's periodical did not publish any poems in prose, but it did feature a significant advocacy of what Ricard called *Poésie scientifique*, calling for a renaissance in poetry that would enable it to develop its philosophical concerns much more elaborately, in a thoroughly modern and "realist" fashion. Ricard went on to propagandize the alleged "decadence" of modern art and literature in articles he published in the *Revue des lettres et des arts*, founded in 1867, which briefly became the principle outlet of the Parnassians. The new periodical did a great deal to popularize the notion of *poèmes en prose*, employing that label as a section in its contents pages, reprinting the entirety of *Gaspard de la Nuit*, and publishing numerous new exemplars under that rubric.

The editor of the *Revue des lettres et des arts* was Auguste Villiers de l'Isle Adam, who had inherited his father's delusions of aristocracy along with his fancifully-embellished surname, and became one of the most flamboyant figures in the Parisian literary community before, ironically but perhaps inevitably, dying in the most abject poverty. Before then, however, he had become a paradoxically ironic legend in his lifetime, exercising an influence beyond his published works. Although his own lengthy contributions to the *Revue des letters et des arts* appeared under the rubric of "*histoires moroses*"—a label later amended in the title of his most famous collection to "*contes cruels*"—he probably did more than anyone else to popularize the notion of *poèmes en prose*, in association with Catulle Mendès, and the *poèmes en prose* he featured in the *Revue des lettres et des arts* supplemented the exemplary set published by Baudelaire in the *Revue fantaisiste* in several significant ways.

Villiers advertised his periodical as a celebration of international endeavor, and many of its prose inclusions were advertised as translations, although, following in the footsteps of Montesquieu, many of them were deceptive pastiches. The early issues featured alleged translation from Mandarin by "Judith Walter," alleged translations from German by her then-husband Catulle Mendès, alleged translation from Arabic by "Louis de Lyvron," and a translation from Greek by Charles Leconte de Lisle.

"Judith Walter" and "Louis de Lyvron" both published books of poems in prose with Alphonse Lemerre in 1867, the former in *Le Livre de Jade*, which reprinted a number of items published in the same volume of *L'Artiste* as Baudelaire's "Petits poèmes en prose," and the latter in *Poèmes en prose*, one of several volumes of such work by the author. *Le Livre de Jade* was subsequently reprinted under the author's real name, by which time she had dropped the signature "Judith Mendès" as well as "Judith Walter" and reverted to her maiden name, Judith Gautier. "Judith

Walter's" major contribution to Villiers' revue was a long appreciative essay on Edgar Poe's *Eureka: A Prose Poem* (1848), which Baudelaire had translated and which must have influenced his interest in the notion of poetry in prose, along with such exemplars as "Shadow—a Parable" (1835), "Silence—a Fable" (1838) and the magisterial "The Masque of the Red Death" (1842).

Much of the material in the various Lyvron volumes was revised and recycled for publication after the Franco-Prussian War under the signature A. de L'Estoille, that being the name that the author used in everyday life. In the meantime, "Louis de Lyvron" became the second most prolific and versatile writer of French poems in prose, outstripped only by Catulle Mendès, who was already so prolific that many of his published works were appearing under pseudonyms, including a curious text initially published in the *Revue fantaisiste* as "As You Like It" over the signature "Hippolyte Nazet" and reprinted in the *Revue des letters et des arts* as "La Clef des songes" over the signature "H. Tezan." The first element of the piece, which is represented as two *contes* narrated in the course of a conversation between schoolgirls, was subsequently reprinted in Mendès' collection of such tales, *Les Oiseaux bleus* (1888; tr. as *Bluebirds*), thus confirming its actual authorship. It set a highly significant precedent in fusing prose poetry with quasi-allegorical *contes*, as Poe had done in "The Masque of the Red Death" and Baudelaire did in two of the "petits poèmes en prose" that he published in *L'Artiste*, with the significant variation that one of them, "La Corde" (tr. as "The Rope") was set in contemporary Paris rather than the vague imaginary past in which most *contes* are set.

That kind of fusion was a narrative tactic that Catulle Mendès was not only to repeat himself more than a hundred times over, but of which, in his capacity as literary editor of several periodicals, he was to publish dozens of examples by other writers. Many can be found herein. He made considerable employment of the variation transplanting such exercises from mythical pasts or foreign lands to contemporary Paris, which altered the relationship between the text and its context significantly, but he left it to other writers to carry that alteration, and its significance, to further extremes. "La Corde," in which a rope used by a child to hang himself is preserved by his mother in order that she might sell pieces of it to perverse citizens offered a subtle comment on the supposed moral decademce of the modern city that was to be echoed and amplified by countless damning vignettes closely related to the *contes cruels* whose tradition Villiers de l'Isle Adam liked so much.

It is worth noting that the lists of forthcoming publications given in every issue of the *Revue fantaisiste*, in which Baudelaire's *Poèmes in prose* always had star billing, were followed directly by an advertisement for two "*contes*" by Théodore de Banville, "Le Coeur de cygne" and "L'Amant bossu," which never made it into the pages of the periodical but presumably served as prototypes for a series of short stories that Banville was later to contribute to the satirical newspaper *Gil Blas* in 1880-81, in which he attempted deliberately and methodically to reinvent the long-obsolete genre of *contes de fées* on a new model, which followed the strategy of Mendès' "As You Like It" in substituting Shakespearean "fairies" for the enchantresses borrowed from French Medieval romance two centuries earlier by Baronne d'Aulnoy, the Contesse de Murat and their fellow salon-writers. After writing fifty such tales, collected as *Contes féeriques* (1882; tr. as *Magical Tales*), Banville was instructed by his editors not to do any more, and he stuck scrupulously to his promise to banish *fées* from his work thereafter, although he continued to write occasional surreal prose poems for the slot.

More significantly, where Banville left off in the pages of *Gil Blas*, Catulle Mendès immediately took over, careless of the evident editorial disapproval, although he spaced out his fantastic mini-*contes*, often written in batches, between his mildly satirical erotic vignettes of life in Parisian society: a habit he carried over into several other newspapers for which he subsequently worked in an editorial capacity, most importantly the *Écho de Paris* and *Le Journal*. He consistently defied, to the extent that he could get away with it, the sustained pressure of his various employers to stick to whimsically prosaic accounts of Parisian life. Many of his associates followed his example, albeit far more modestly, preserving a Parnassian influence in what was arguably the least hospitable milieu—except, of course, for the one in which Edgar Poe had been obliged to work.

The Parnassians did not hold quasi-formal seminars in the way that their predecessors in the Romantic *cénacles* hosted by Charles Nodier, Victor Hugo and Théophile Gautier had done, but Gautier's house remained a significant gathering-point for writers in the 1860s, until his protégé-in-chief, Catulle Mendès, spoiled their relationship by marrying the great man's daughter against his will. There were other houses where the Parnassians met, including Xavier de Ricard's mother's house in Batignolles, where he hosted a weekly salon, and the house where the editor of *L'Artiste*, Arsène Houssaye, threw parties that were still being cited nostalgically by Parisian writers thirty years later. *L'Artiste*'s regular contributors included Théophile Gautier and Théodore de Banville, but neither contributed *poèmes en prose* to its pages. Another regular contributor, however, Hector de Callias, published short stories there in which he adopted the affectation of numbering the paragraphs like Biblical "verses," thus giving them a peculiar poetic gloss.

Although Hector de Callias was not a Parnassian—and, indeed, came to loathe them—he had a peculiar indirect influence on the evolution of the Movement. Although he was a comte he was penniless, eking out a precarious living as a journalist, but in November 1864 he married Anne-Marie Gaillard, who was very rich; Houssaye—who judged in his memoirs that both parties in the love-match were *"ruisselants d'insenséisme"* [dripping with insanity]—was one of his witnesses. The marriage did not last long, and the separation was very acrimonious; the Comtesse refused thereafter to use her husband's name, calling herself Nina de Villard, under which name she contributed to the second volume of *Le Parnasse contemporain*; her house then became the venue of the most notorious literary salon in Paris, attended by Paul Verlaine, Catulle Mendès, Théodore de Banville, Auguste Villiers de l'Isle Adam and many younger writers, including Arthur Rimbaud, Jean Richepin, Charles Cros and Germain Nouveau, some of whom assisted her with the writing and performance of her verse drama "Le Moine bleu" (1885 in her posthumous *Feuillets Parisiens*.)

Villiers de l'Isle Adam was the acknowledged star of Nina de Villard's salon for some years, and his performances at her *soirées* helped to inspire Edmond de Goncourt to describe it as a "mental breakdown academy." Like Xavier de Ricard's salon, Nina de Villard's was attended by numerous political radicals, who subsequently became the intellectual hub of the Paris Commune in 1871, and some of the less politically-minded Parnassians preferred to hang out at a bookshop owned by Noël Thibault, nicknamed "Père France," which had long been held in affection by Romantic writers and had been given a warm advertisement in Charles Nodier's ironic study of "Le Bibliomane" (1832). Their gatherings were observed with great fascination by Thibault's young son, Anatole, who contributed alongside Nina de Villard to the second showcase anthology of *Le Parnasse contemporain* under the signature "Anatole France."

Anatole France later recalled having met "Louis de Lyvron" in his father's shop, clad in full military uniform—he was an officer in the spahis at the time—and being suitably impressed; it might have been Noël Thibault who introduced the aspiring poet to Villiers de l'Isle Adam. Lyvron's first publications, however, had been in the *Journal des Demoiselles*, edited at the time by the unexiled but doubtless suspect Samuel-Henri Berthoud, a prolific writer of prose vignettes, who had long been acquainted with Théophile Gautier, and Berthoud might have taken Lyvron to Gautier's house, where he would undoubtedly have met Catulle Mendès. Anatole France's relations with the Parnassians were somewhat spoiled, however, when he began to attend Nina de Villard's salon and became enthusiastically smitten with the hostess, whereupon her lover, Charles Cros, allegedly tried to strangle him.

As to how much the fallout of that incident contributed to Anatole France's subsequent reputation as an anti-social curmudgeon we can only speculate, but Cros became a significant writer of *poèmes en prose*, publishing alongside "Judith Mendès" in the pages of Jules Aicard's periodical *Renaissance Littéraire et artistique*

(1872-1873), which attempted after the political and economic catastrophes of 1870-71 to pick up the baton dropped by the *Revue des arts et lettres*. By then, however, the social context of the Movement had been drastically altered by the abrupt rise and swift fall of the Commune in the wake of the Prussian invasion. Charles Cros narrowly escaped arrest after the army's destruction of the Commune after helping his elder brother, the physician Antoine Cros, to care for the sick and the wounded during the Prussian siege of Paris, because Antoine had influential clients. Nina de Villard, fearing that she might not be so fortunate, fled Paris to Geneva, and remained there for two years. Xavier de Ricard also fled, thus avoiding inevitable arrest and probable execution or transportation, and several other Parnassian poets did the same. Antoine de L'Estoille, the ex-Louis de Lyvron, was recalled to active service when the Prussians invaded but was not reintegrated with the Chasseurs d'Afrique and thus escaped the regiment's massacre at the battle of Sedan, living, if not to fight another day, at least to add the legacy of the war to the longest of his poems in prose, the epic *La Chanson de l'alouette* (1880; tr. as *The Song of the Skylark*).

Charles Cros and Villiers de l'Isle Adam had formed a significant "double act" performing at *soirées* before the catastrophes of 1870-71 for the benefit of Nina de Villard's guests, and although the salon resumed when Nina returned to Paris it was never the same again, and it faded away before her absinthe-assisted death in 1884. By that time Cros was a pillar of Émile Goudeau's literary drinking club, the Hydropathes, and his double act with Villiers was transferred, along with the club, to Rodolphe Salis' cabaret Le Chat Noir. Villiers was by then in dire financial straits, however, and pride inhibited him from sponging off his friends, at least knowingly—several of them paid a restaurateur to send him meals while he was struggling to finish his novel *L'Ève future*, strictly forbidding the waiter to reveal who was paying for them—so Cros replaced him in the double act, before he too fell victim to absinthe, with Alphonse Allais. Both became key contributors to Salis' periodical, *Le Chat Noir*—in which Hector de Callias was also briefly featured. Villiers rarely appeared in the periodical, but his ghostly influence lingered in the Chat Noir, and the tradition of flamboyant performance he had helped to initiate in Nina de Villard's salon was not only carried forward in the cabaret by Cros and Allais but by many of their fellow Hydropathes, who soon attracted the label "decadent." It is unsurprising that the vague "Decadent Movement" formed in the 1880s, in a contrarian spirit of perversity, intricately entangled with the burgeoning Symbolist Movement, became the natural milieu of a new generation of *poèmes en prose*, abundantly sampled herein.

The literary salons of the Third Republic were by no means all as boisterous as Nina de Villard's and the Chat Noir, and the two that became the most celebrated, Edmond de Goncourt's *grenier* and Stéphane Mallarmé's *mardis*, were far more genteel. Mallarmé's salon, in particular, retained the seminar aspect that had first been introduced to the Hôtel de Rambouillet in the golden years of Louis XIV's reign by Mademoiselle de Scudéry and had exercised a very significant influence on the development of French letters, in spite of its members being parodied by Molière as "*précieuses*." Mallarmé, the third most prolific contributor of *poèmes en prose* to the *Revue des lettres et des arts* after Mendès and Lyvron, followed the example of Mademoiselle de Scudéry by running his *mardis* like a modern "writers' workshop," and it became the initial crucible of the Symbolist Movement in the early 1880s, although it did not remain unrivaled for long, as groups formulating alternative creeds of Symbolism formed around Charles Morice and Gustave Kahn. Formally or informally, *poèmes en prose* were on the agenda of all such symposia from the start.

Edmond de Goncourt was already famous before 1880 as a "Naturalist" novelist of a more polite stripe than Émile Zola, and his *grenier* became the crucible of a variant strain of Naturalism, which was often seen—by journalists, at least—as a rival movement to Symbolism, although the perceived opposition of the two was a fantasy, reflecting the fact that Symbolism was primarily a movement in poetry and Naturalism was a tendency in prose fiction, especially the novel. Poetry in prose, inevitably, had greater fundamental affinities with Symbolism than Naturalism, but many of the writers associated with the *grenier* and similar gatherings did dabble in *poèmes en prose* of a sort, more akin to Baudelaire's "La Corde" than to Catulle Mendès' *contes*, because producers of Naturalist short fiction inevitably perfected the artistry of "slice-of-life" narratives in which small-scale incidents become significant, if not strictly symbolic, of entire lives.

Although the editors of mass-market periodicals much preferred to print mock-anecdotal slices of Parisian life rather than the kinds of flights-of-fancy beloved by Catulle Mendès, they could not and did not eliminate "poetic" qualities entirely from the fiction they published, and the writers who produced material for them most prolifically, whether they started out as Symbolists or Naturalists, soon perfected a quasi-poetic artistry for art's sake. Théodore de Banville became a consummate artist of "naturalistic" fiction after being dissuaded from writing about *fées*, and Catulle Mendès had no alternative but to do likewise, although he always seemed uncomfortable in so doing; his "naturalistic" fiction tended far more to the bizarre, the perverse and the frankly paradoxical, than that of many other members of the "stables" of writers he assembled to supply his particular editorial requirements, especially those who were graduates of the Goncourt school—the hard core of which eventually formed the so-called Goncourt Academy, several of whose founder-members, including Joris-Karl Huysmans, are represented in the present showcase.

Huysmans became, arguably, the most celebrated practitioner of *poèmes en prose* after Baudelaire, although the volume with which he followed up his Baudelairean collection of vignettes *Le Drageoir aux épices* (1874), *Croquis parisiens* (1880; expanded 1888; tr. as *Parisian Sketches*) is markedly different, even though its contents overlap, its inclusions resembling short essays rather than poems or *contes*. Huysmans' crucial contribution to the popularization of *poèmes en prose*, however, was not confined to his own exemplars; in his classic Decadent prose text *À rebours* (1884), his hero Jean Des Esseintes, a master of paradox, declares that the *poème en prose* is his favorite literary form, describing it as "the osmazome of literature." Osmazome was a hypothetical essence of meat, which several contemporary organic chemists attempted to produce, exemplars of which were marketed under such trade names as Bovril and Oxo. The idea of poems in prose as literary Oxo cubes has a certain absurdity about it, of which Huysmans might not have approved in later life, when he became dour, "got religion" and started dressing in a monastic habit, but some of his contemporaries, including Alfred Jarry, Guillaume Apollinaire and other forerunners of Callotesque surrealism might well have greeted it with ironic enthusiasm.

By 1884, therefore, with the aid of Des Esseintes' forceful advertisement, *poèmes en prose* constituted a solidly-established and potentially prestigious genre in which writers could choose to work without inhibition, and many did—but not unproblematically. Some of the writers who elected to adopt the Decadent label became intensely and seriously interested in the art of prose poetry, and strove to develop it in conscientious earnest, but some readers and critics could not take them entirely seriously, and if the gray area where *poèmes en prose* overlapped and hybridized with *contes* was problematic, the gray area where poems in prose overlapped and sometimes hybridized with other kinds of prose vignettes, including humorous anecdotes and jokes, was even more so.

There are, of course, comic genres of poetry, which use rhyme and poetic form as devices for generating humor—the most famous in the English language is the limerick, and there are also notorious examples parodying the kind of narrative poetry developed by the American poet Robert W. Service in his "songs of a Sourdough,", notably "The Ballad of Eskimo Nell" and "Casey at the Bat," but precisely because the humor of those traditions was reliant on rhyme and scansion, they did not seem to have any relevance to poems in prose There are, however, elements of humor in Baudelaire's classic *poèmes en prose*, and more obvious ones in Huysmans, and the most prolific publication of short items of prose in the periodicals of the Third Republic was in humorous papers, which enjoyed a spectacular boom in the early 1880s along with other publications in newspaper format.

Those humorous periodicals included *Le Hydropathe*, launched by Émile Goudeau to publicize his club, and, more importantly, the satirical papers *Gil Blas* and *Le Chat Noir*; both hired Parnassian ex-members of Nina de Villard's salon as regular columnists, the former featuring Jean Richepin as well as Banville and Armand Silvestre before they were joined by Mendès. They were inevitably affected—or infected—by the interest in *poèmes en prose*; Salis was assisted in editing his periodical by George Auriol and various "editorial secretaries," who included Villiers de l'Isle Adam's one-time partner in comedy Charles Cros, and Villiers' successor in that double act, Alphonse Allais. *Le Chat Noir* reprinted several of Cros's poems in prose from the *Renaissance littéraire et artistique* and—perhaps more significantly, in view of their conspicuous seriousness—most of Stéphane Mallarmé's from the *Revue des lettres et des arts*. The original poems in prose supplied to *Le Chat Noir* in some profusion by the cabaret's resident piano player, Albert Tinchant, were in much the same vein as Mallarmé's, usually with no humorous element, and when Tinchant died suddenly, his place at the Chat Noir's piano was taken by the Decadent poet Maurice Rollinat and the only female member of the Hydropathes, Marie Krysinska, who sang her own poems alongside Jean Richepin and Edmond Haraucourt. *Gil Blas* was more tentative in its use of prose poetry, but a selection of "petits poèmes en prose" by Armand Silvestre published in 1880, alongside Banville's *contes fantastiques*, was soon followed by further and more pretentious examples by Mendès, Banville and others.

The "Decadent Movement" was, of course, inherently satirical, but its comic element was often underplayed in journalistic commentary, and the comic element of the delight in paradox often manifest in prose poetry similarly attracted less attention than it perhaps deserved—and still does. Outright comedians like Auriol and Allais are not often included in lists of practitioners of prose poetry, and even the lachrymose Tinchant does not usually make such lists, but the spirit of the *Gil Blas* and *Chat Noir* writers was closely akin to the literary strategies developed in more pretentious prose vignettes. Léo Trézenik's articles in the pioneering Symbolist periodical *Lutèce*, partially reprinted in the introduction to the collection *Decadent proses*, made a substantial ironic contribution to the popularization of the term "Decadent," and the humorous component of his "Decadent proses" was echoed in contemporary work by Remy de Gourmont and the co-editor of *Lutéce*, Charles Morice, who are otherwise viewed as the most earnestly serious of writers and critics, in spite of their tendency to witty flamboyance.

Just as there are many commentators on *À rebours* and the Decadent Movement in general who somehow fail to notice that the whole thing was a colossal joke, there are many commentators on the genre of *poèmes en prose* who overlook its comedic aspect—an aspect which has certainly been important within it ever since *Gaspard de la Nuit* and Baudelaire's *poèmes en prose*, and before that in Montesquieu's literary hoaxes. Some writers in the genre, from Maurice de Guérin onwards, have maintained a much more earnest, mystical or even conscientiously tragic expression in their work, but that is surely only to be expected; much as "bittersweet" provides an illuminating and valuable example of a useful oxymoron, so does "tragicomedy." Prose poetry is not entirely a tragicomic genre, but it is understandably hospitable to tragicomedy, and the present sampler would not be truly representative if its spectrum did not stretch all the way from earnest tragedy to blatant farce, passing through all intermediate colors *en route*.

The close association of the genre of poetry in prose with the mercurial idea of "decadence" after 1883 inevitably made its prestige a trifle dubious, and, as the legacy of the Decadent Movement faded away after the turn of the century, *poèmes en prose* went into decline too—a fade-out greatly assisted by Catulle Mendès' withdrawal from editorial service in the newspaper sector as old age took its toll on him. His activity declined considerably in the years before his mysterious death in 1908 (he was struck by a train in a railway tunnel, without anyone being able to determine how he came to be there).

Poèmes en prose survived for a long time after the heyday of their fashionability in the 1890s, and are by no means extinct even now, but after 1900 they came to be seen as a margin-al eccentricity somewhat lacking in form and substance, their most interesting examples usually evaluated as flimsy ultra-short stories rather than as a species of poetry. Poetry itself was in de-cline throughout the twentieth century, of course, and where it continued to thrive—most obviously in popular song—it gradually sacrificed much of its reliance on rhyme and scansion, although not its use of emphatic repetition. It is arguable that popular music in the twenty-first century has become even more prosaic, but it would be difficult to contend that it has done so by becoming more Baudelairean. Where ultra-short fiction still thrives in the commercial marketplace—most obviously in books marketed for young children—it does not necessarily lack sophisticated poetic qualities, but its prestige is inevitably lim-ited by the ostentatious juvenility of its subject-matter and the carefully earnest moralizing typical of fiction produced for par-ents and teachers to inflict on children. "Decadence," however defined, is in conspicuously short supply there.

The narrative of the history of French poetry in prose exem-plified and illustrated in the present volume has to be regard-ed, therefore, as an account of a curious distant past, and of an experiment from which the bulk of the literary world has long moved on—but that does not mean that it ought to be reckoned as a failure no longer worthy of any interest. Perhaps Jean Des Esseintes was wrong to imagine poems in prose as "the osmazome of literature," partly because the idea of "osmazome" is a fantasy, but, just as Oxo cubes are far from being devoid of culinary utility, in terms of enhancing flavor and texture, and fantasy still has a crucial role to play in the nutrition of the intel-lect, Des Esseintes' appreciation of poems in prose was entirely justifiable, and does not disqualify him as a literary gourmet. The present showcase is certainly not devoid of interesting taste sensations, even if some of them might need to be acquired by habituation; nor, in spite of the necessary slenderness of many of the individual items, is it devoid of nutritious food for thought. It is doubtless more than a trifle Decadent. In style as well as substance, but that surely ought to be considered a compliment rather than an insult, at least by Enlightened contrarians.

Although it is, to some extent, a scrupulous exercise in Romantic narrative history, the organization of the present collection is not strictly chronological, especially in its last two sections, much of which run parallel to one another rather than sequentially. There is an element of pure whimsy in its arrangement, just as there is in the selection of its examples, but I see no need to apologize for that, the entire exercise being, inevitably, a celebration of perverse paradoxical whimsy. Although it is a collage with many disparate elements, their accumulation and juxtaposition does illustrate that, as well as Wittgensteinian "family resemblances," they also have multitudinous "blood ties": family connections deriving from the fact that the literary community of Paris was an assembly of intellectual siblings, sometimes as quarrelsome as any other kind of family, but possessed of a deep underlying affection and loyalty. For those incapable of savoring the volume's contents and appreciating the *ensemble* of the collage, I can only feel pity; those who can appreciate the individual works and observe the peculiar artistry of the loosely-knit whole will understand, and will surely enjoy.

—Brian Stableford, June 2021.

POEMS IN PROSE

Part One:
Precursors

MONTESQUIEU
(1689-1755)

Charles-Louis de Secondat, Baron de la Brède et de Montesquieu (1689-1755), who usually signed himself, aristocratically, as "Montesquieu" when it was not a grave diplomatic error to add his signature to documents, was one of the most influential political philosophers of his era, famous, among other things, for having attacked despotism, and thus having to live in fear of the despots under whose rule he lived—the King of France and the Pope—or, more accurately, their pawns and henchmen. His assaults on their hegemony did not prevent many of his works from being banned, but they found audiences anyway, especially outside his homeland, as is proverbially the way with prophets, and he found it convenient to disguise his criticisms of autocracy with allegory and misdirection. *Lettres Persans* (1721) thus attributes its criticisms of contemporary France to the pens of two imaginary "Persian" tourists, and his *Considérations sur les causes de la grandeur des Romans et de leur décadence* (1734) analyses the reasons for the decline and fall of the Roman Empire not as an accident of happenstance but as an instance of a historical law, leaving it largely to his readers to make deductions regarding the present condition of France with regard to the logic of the argument.

The idea that France was in an epoch of decadence became commonplace as well as controversial, and formed an important part of the cultural frame of the development of *poèmes en prose*.

Among sophisticated literary men it eventually engendered a particular interest in the literature of the "Latin decadence" and potential features thereof that might be found in common with the literature of their own time. There is, therefore, a particular propriety in the fact that Montesquieu faked an item of the literature of the Latin decadence in *Le Temple de Gnide* (1725), published anonymously with a title page falsely advertising publication in London. Although written in prose, it masqueraded as a translation of a poetic original, and although its primary subject matter is the operation of the erotic impulse, the fact that its analysis contradicted the ideas of the Catholic Church on that subject, employing the vocabulary of paganism, rendered it vulnerable to political persecution. In so doing, it unwittingly set an example that was to be followed very abundantly in the era when French *poèmes en prose* briefly became a fashionable medium of expression.

The First Canto of *The Temple of Gnide*

Translator's Preface

An Ambassador of France to the Ottoman Gate, known for his liking for letters, had bought several Greek manuscripts and brought them to France. Some of those manuscripts having fallen into my hands, I found the work that I am giving here in translation among them.

Few Greek authors have reached us, either because they have perished in the ruins of libraries or by virtue of the negligence of the families who possessed them.

From time to time we recover a few pieces of those treasures. Works have even been found in the tombs of their authors, and—which is almost the same thing—this one was found among the books of a Greek bishop. Neither the name of the author nor the era in which he lived is known; all that we can say is that it is not anterior to Sappho, since there is mention of her in the work.

As for my translation, it is faithful; I believed that the beauties that were not in my heart were not beauties, and I have often quit a less vivid expression in order to adopt one that expressed its thought better.

I have been encouraged in this translation by the success obtained by that of Tasso.[1] The person who made it has not thought it bad that I am following the same career as him; he has distinguished it in such a manner as to fear nothing even from those who had given it the most competition.

This little romance is a kind of picture for which the painter has chosen the most agreeable subjects. The public has found cheerful ideas therein, a certain magnificence in the descriptions and naivety in the sentiments. It has an original character that has made critics ask what its model was, which becomes great praise when a work is not to be scorned in other respects.

A few scholars have not recognized what they call "art." It is not, they say, in accordance with the rules. But if the work pleases you, you will see that their heart is not in accordance with the rules.

A man who dabbles in translation does not suffer patiently that his author is not esteemed by others as much as he has done, and I confess that those messieurs have put me in a furious wrath, but I beg them to let the young judge a book which, whatever language it was written in, was certainly made for them. I beg others not to trouble them in their decisions. It is only heads well-curled and well-powdered who will know all the merit of *The Temple de Gnide*.

---

1 The Italian poet Torquato Tasso (1544-1585) was the author of the epic poem *Gerusalemme liberata* (1591; tr. into French as *La Jérusalem delivrée* and English as *Jerusalem Delivered*) an imitation of French Medieval romances set during the Crusades. It was greatly admired in nineteenth-century France and was widely used as a textbook in schools, thus becoming familiar to all literary men. The reference must be to the 1724 translation by Jean-Baptiste de Mirabaud, which earned the author election to the Académie française.

With regard to the fair sex, to whom I owe the few happy moments I can count in my life, I wish with all my heart that this work might please them. I still adore it, and if it is no longer the object of my occupations, it is of my regrets.

If grave individuals would like a few works less frivolous from me, I am in a position to satisfy them. For thirty years I have been laboring on a work of twelve pages that should contain everything we know about metaphysics, politics and morality, and everything that great authors have forgotten in the volumes that they have given us on those sciences.

First Canto

Venus prefers the abode of Gnide to that of Paphos or Amathonte. She does not descend from Olympus without visiting the Gnideans. She has so accustomed that fortunate people to the sight of her that they no longer feel the sacred horror that the presence of a god inspires. Sometimes she covers herself with a cloud, and is recognized by the divine odor that emerges from her hair, perfumed by ambrosia.

The city is in the middle of a region on to which the gods have poured their benefits with full hands; one enjoys a perpetual spring there; the earth, fortunately fertile there, foresees all wishes; the flocks pass by there without number; the winds only seem to reign there in order to spread the spirit of flowers everywhere; birds sing there incessantly, you would think that the bushes are harmonious; streams murmur in the meadows; a mild warmth enables everything to bloom; the air is only respired there with sensuality.

Next to the city is the palace of Venus; Vulcan built its foundations personally; he worked for his unfaithful wife when he wanted to forget the cruel insult that he uttered before the gods.

It would be impossible for me to give an idea of that palace; only the Graces could describe the things of which it is made. Gold, azure, rubies and diamonds shine there everywhere; but I am painting its riches, not its beauties.

Its gardens are enchanted; Flora and Pomona take care of them; their nymphs cultivate them. Fruits are reborn there under the hand that cooks them; the flowers succeed the fruits. When Venus walks there, surrounded by her Gnidiennes, you would think that their playful frolics would destroy those delectable gardens, but by means of a secret virtue, everything is repaired in an instant.

Venus loves to see the naïve dances of the daughters of Gnide; her nymphs mingle with them. The goddess takes part in their games; she strips herself of her majesty; sitting in their midst, she sees joy and innocence reigning over their hearts.

One discovers in the distance a vast grassland enameled with flowers; the shepherd comes to pick them with his shepherdess; but the one she finds is always the most beautiful, and he believes that Flora has made it expressly.

The river-god Céphissus irrigates that grassland and makes a thousand detours there. He stops the fugitive shepherdesses; it is necessary that they give the tender kiss that they have promised.[1]

When the nymphs approach the bank they stop, and its fleeing waves find waves that are no longer fleeing. But when one of them bathes Cephissus is more amorous still; his waters turn around her; sometimes he lifts himself up in order better to embrace; he lifts her, he flees, he draws her away. Her timid companions begin to weep, but he sustains her on his waves, and, charged with such a cherished burden, he carries her over the liquid plain; finally, desperate to quit her, he bears her slowly to the bank, and consoles her companions.

Beside the grassland is a myrtle wood, the paths of which make a thousand detours. Lovers come to tell one another their troubles there; Amour, who amuses them, conducts them via paths that are ever more secret.

Not far from there is an ancient and sacred wood where the daylight only enters with difficulty, oaks that seem immortal bear to the skies a head that evades the eyes. One senses a religious fear there; you might think that it was the dwelling of the gods when humans had not yet emerged from the earth.

---

1 In Greek mythology the river-god Cephissus was the father of Narcissus

When one has found the light of day, one climbs a little hill, on which the temple of Venus is situated; the universe has nothing more holy or sacred than that place.

It was in that temple that Venus saw Adonis for the first time; poison ran to the heart of the goddess. "What!" she said. "Shall I love a mortal? Alas, I sense that I adore him. Let no more prayers be addressed to me; there is no longer any god in Gnide but Adonis."

It was to that place that she summoned the Amours when, stung by a reckless challenge, she consulted them. She was in doubt as to whether she should expose herself to the gaze of the Trojan shepherd.[1] She hid her loins beneath her hair; her nymphs perfumed her; she mounted her chariot drawn by swans and arrived in Phrygia. The shepherd was hesitating between Juno and Pallas but he saw her, and his gaze wandered and died. The golden apple fell at the feet of the goddess; he tried to speak, and his disorder decided the issue.

It was into that temple that the young Psyche came with her mother when Amour, who was flying around the gilded paneling, was surprised by one of her gazes. He felt then all the gazes that he made others suffer. "It is thus," he said, "that I wound; I cannot sustain my bow or my arrows." He fell upon Psyche's breast. "Ah," he said, "I am beginning to sense that I am the god of pleasures."

When one enters the temple, one senses a secret charm in the heart, which it is impossible to express; the soul is seized by the delights that the gods only feel themselves when they are in the celestial abode.

All that nature has of the cheerful is combined with all that art can imagine of the noblest, and that which is most worthy of the gods.

A hand, doubtless immortal, has ornamented it everywhere with paintings that seem to respire. One sees the birth of Venus there, the rapture of the gods who see her, her embarrassment at

1 Paris, the son of Priam of Troy, in the story in which he is called upon to judge a beauty contest between three goddesses, and awards the prize to Aphrodite/Venus because she offers him Helen of Troy as a bribe.

finding herself stark naked, and the modesty that is the foremost of the graces.

One sees the amours of Mars and the goddess there. The painter has represented the god on his chariot, proud and even terrible; Renown flies around him; Fear and Death march before his foam-covered chargers; he goes into battle, and thick dust commences to hide him. On another side he is seen lying languidly on a bed of roses; he smiles at Venus; you only recognize him by the few divine features that remain to him. The Pleasures weave garlands, with which they bind the two lovers, their eyes seem confounded; they sigh; and, attentive to one another, they do not look at the Amours who are playing around them.

In a separate apartment the painter has represented the wedding of Venus and Vulcan; the entire celestial court is assembled there. The god appears less somber, but just as pensive, as usual. The goddess gazes at him with a cold expression of common joy; she gives him a hand negligently, which seems to slip away; she retires from him gazes that scarcely carry and turns toward the Graces.

In another painting one sees Juno performing the marriage ceremony. Venus takes the cup in order to swear an eternal fidelity to Vulcan; the gods smile, and Vulcan listens with pleasure.

On the other side one sees the impatient god drawing his divine spouse away; she puts up so much resistance that one might think that she was the daughter of Ceres whom Pluto wished to ravish, if the eye that sees Venus could ever be mistaken.

Further away one sees him lifting her up in order to carry her to the nuptial bed. The gods follow in a crowd; the goddess struggles and tries to escape the arms that are holding her. Her robe flees her knees, the fabric flies away; but Vulcan repairs that beautiful disorder, more attentive to hiding her than ardent to ravish her.

Finally, one sees him coming to lie on the bed that Hymen has prepared; he closes the curtains on her, and believes that he can hold her there forever. The importunate troop retires; he is charmed to see them draw away. The goddesses play among themselves; but the gods seem sad; and the sadness of Mars has something as somber as black jealousy.

Charmed by the magnificence of her temple, the goddess wanted to establish her worship there herself; she has regulated its ceremonies, instituted its festivals, and she is simultaneously the divinity and the priestess.

The worship that is rendered to her by almost the entire world is more a profanation than a religion. She has temples in which all the daughters of a city prostitute themselves in her honor, and make a dowry of the profit of their devotion. She has some where every married woman goes once in her life to give herself to whoever chooses her and throws the money she has received into the sanctuary. There are others to which courtesans of all countries, more honored than matrons, go to carry their offerings; finally, there are some where the men are eunuchs and dress as women to serve in the sanctuary, consecrating to the goddess the sex that they no longer have and the one that they cannot have.

But she has wanted the people of Gnide to have a purer worship, and to render her honors more worthy of her. Here, the sacrifices are sighs and the offerings a tender heart. Each lover addresses his prayers to his mistress, and Venus receives them for her.

Everywhere that beauty is found it is adored, as Venus herself is adored, for beauty is as divine as she is.

Amorous hearts come into that temple; they go to embrace the altars of Fidelity and Constancy.

Those who are crushed by the rigors of a cruel woman come to sigh there; they feel their torments diminishing; they find flattering hope in their hearts.

The goddess, who has promised to make the happiness of true lovers, always measures them by their pains.

Jealousy is a passion that one can have, but about which one must keep quiet. One adores in secret the caprices of one's mistress, as one adores the decrees of the gods, which become more just when one dares to complain about them.

10

Put in the rank of divine favors are fire, the transports of amour, and even fury; for the less one is master of one's heart, the more it belongs to the goddess.

Those who have not given their heart are the profane, who cannot enter the temple; they address their prayers to the goddess from afar, and ask her to deliver them from that liberty, which is only an impotence to form desires.

The goddess inspires young women to modesty; that charming quality gives a new price to all the charms that it hides.

But never, in those fortunate places, does anyone blush at a sincere passion, a naïve sentiment or a tender confession.

The heart always fixes for itself the moment at which it ought to surrender, but it is a profanation to surrender itself without love.

Amour is attentive to the felicity of Gnideans; he chooses the arrows with which he wounds them. When he sees an afflicted mistress overwhelmed by the rigors of a lover, he takes an arrow steeped in the waters of the river of forgetfulness. When he sees two lovers commencing to love one another he fires further arrows at them incessantly. When he sees two whose amour is weakening he enables it suddenly to be reborn or to die, for he always spares the last days of a languishing passion. No one passes to disgust before ceasing to love, but greater sweetnesses cause lesser ones to be forgotten.

Amour has removed from his quiver the cruel arrow with which he wounded Phaedre and Ariadne, which, mingling love and hatred, serves to demonstrate his power as lightning serves to make the empire of Jupiter known.

As the god gives the pleasure of loving, Venus combines it with the joy of pleasing.

Young women enter the sanctuary every day in order to say their prayer to Venus. They express sentiments as naïve as the heart that has engendered them. "Queen of Amathonte," one of them said, "my flame for Tirsis is extinct; I don't ask you to return my amour; only make Ixiphile love me."

Another whispered: "Powerful goddess, give me the strength to hide my love for my shepherd for a while, in order to increase the price of the confession I want to make to him."

"Goddess of Cythera," said a third, "I seek solitude; the games of my companions no longer please me; perhaps I'm in love. Oh, if I love someone, it can only be Daphnis."

On feast days, the girls and boys come to recite hymns in honor of Venus; often they sing her glory in singing their amours.

One young Gnidean, holding his mistress by the hand, sung thus: "Amour, when you saw Psyche, you were doubtless wounded by the same arrows with which you have just wounded my heart; your happiness is not different from mine, for you feel my fires, and I sense your pleasures."

I have seen everything that I describe. I went to Gnide, I saw Thémire[1] there and I loved her; I saw her again and I loved her more. I shall remain in Gnide with her all my life, and I will be the happiest of mortals.

We shall go into the temple, and no lover so faithful will ever have entered it; we shall go into the palace of Venus, and I shall believe that it is the palace of Thémire; I shall go into the grassland and pick flowers that I shall put in her bosom. Perhaps I shall be able to lead her into the boscage where so many paths are confounded, and where she has gone astray . . .

Amour, who inspires me, forbids me to reveal his mysteries.

---

1 The Thémire in the story is a shepherdess, but it might not be a pure coincidence that "Thémire" was a conventional salon nickname disguising Marie-Anne de Bourbon, known as Mademoiselle de Clermont, one of Louis XIV's granddaughters. The name was employed by several painters in symbolic images of "Thémire being crowned by the three Graces," one of which was later used as the basis of a decoration of Sèvres porcelain, samples of which still exist. Montesquieu never went to Louis XV's court at Versailles, but it is not inconceivable that he might have encountered that "Thémire" at a literary salon, some of which were attended, or even hosted, by princesses of the blood. Such salons had been encouraged briefly at Versailles in the 1690s by Mademoiselle de Clermont's aunt, another Marie-Anne de Bourbon, known as the "dowager" Princesse de Conti. Along with Rousseau and Voltaire, Montesquieu was one of the authors associated with the Enlightenment who were guests of another princess of the blood, Louise de Bourbon, Duchesse de Maine, at the Château de Sceaux.

CHARLES NODIER
(1780-1844)

Charles Nodier was the great pioneer of French Romantic prose, whose *cénacle* at the Bibliothèque de l'Arsenal, where he was the librarian from 1824 until his death, was an important crucible of the Romantic Movement. Some time prior to that appointment he had been exiled from Paris for ten years after owning up to the authorship of an anonymous "ode" satirizing Napoléon Bonaparte, then the First Consul. Even before that, however, he had been fascinated with the idea of *proscrits* ("outlaws," so identified by the Revolutionary régime) and they figure large in his early literary works, including a collection of vignettes published while he was in exile, entitled *Les Tristes, ou mélanges tirés des tablettes d'un suicidé* (1806; tr. in the collection *Outlaws and Sorrows*), from which "Sanchette" is taken. Several of that volume's other inclusions also qualify as *poèmes en prose*, as do several chapters of *Stella, ou les proscrits* (1802) and three alleged translations appended to *Smarra, ou les demons de la nuit, conte fantastique* (1821), written while he was running a newspaper in Illyria during the brief interval when it as a province of Napoléon I's Empire. *Smarra* itself can also be regarded as a long prose poem, as can several of Nodier's other *contes*. Nodier received a fulsome dedication in Louis Bertrand's pioneering collection of prose poems, *Gaspard de la Nuit*, and undoubtedly influenced Baudelaire and other Parnassian authors who took up the cause of prose poetry.

Sanchette; or, The Oleander

We were born near to one another.

While still very young, I called him my friend.

I was not as beautiful as him, but I was beautiful.

When he put his arm around me, my voice died on my lips and my heart was squeezed. I felt a frisson that ran all the way to my hair, and I wept with pleasure.

One day, he said to me: "You will be my wife, and I shall be able to kiss your neck without anyone being able to say anything about it. You will no longer reject me by making me afraid of your mother; and when I hear footsteps behind me, I shall not turn round to see whether it is her."

While speaking thus we gave one another intoxicating kisses, and I did not know why I was troubled.

After that he departed for a great voyage, and he brought me an oleander in a box of veined wood. The oleander was in flower.

"You see," he said to me, "these cups of such a soft crimson hue have the freshness and the color of your mouth; they will soon wither, and my heart will wither like them, in the chagrin of your absence. They will be reborn with the first fires of spring, and my heart will also be reborn when your hand comes to press it."

However, your oleander has flowered again, and my hand will not press your heart again.

The cups of your oleander no longer have such a soft crimson hue; they are violet and bruised, because I have watered them with my tears, and my tears burn.

My mouth has lost its color and its freshness; has it not lost your kisses? The flowers of the oleander fade so quickly when they are deprived of the zephyr.

"Sanchette," my mother said to me, "it is necessary to make another choice, since your Emmanuel is dead." My mother said that to me.

Shall I say to my oleander: *It's necessary to take another soil, and to flower in the midst of the mountain snows?*

Listen, Emmanuel, my Emmanuel, it is necessary to die here. At least I shall be near to you; and when I hear the hollow earth resounding a little beneath my feet, I shall say: *Perhaps that's him;* and I will transplant my oleander there.

How can I know where your grave is, and whether anyone has sown flowers there?

They will soon have fallen, the flowers of the oleander; there are only one, two and three now. But there are still a great many leaves, and its leaves are mortal.

14

SAMUEL-HENRI BERTHOUD
(1804-1891)

Samuel-Henri Berthoud signed most of his works "S. Henry Berthoud," because he had been named after his father, who had used his first name for his own published works, although the son also used the pseudonymous signature "Dr. Sam" in newspapers during the difficult years of the Second Empire. Unlike many leading members of the Romantic Movement, Berthoud was not exiled after Louis-Napoléon Bonaparte's 1851 *coup d'état*, but he was obliged to keep a low profile thereafter. He first left his native Cambrai for Paris in the early 1820s, when he became involved with Honoré de Balzac's coterie of aspiring writers, but he was forced by penury to return to Cambrai, where he was living when he published his early books. He was a prolific writer of short stories, many of which were printed in local publications, including some edited by his father, a printer for whom he worked for a while. He developed a strong interest in local folklore and legend, and attempted to collect oral folktales, many of which he adapted into stories, and pastiched in some profusion. "Beauduin Bras-de-fer" is one such pastiche, from *Chroniques et traditions surnaturelles de la Flandre* (1831; expanded 1834), translated with other excerpts from that collection in *The Angel Asrael and Other Legendary Tales* (2017). He returned to Paris in 1834 to work for the Republican publisher Émile de Girardin, and contributed to all of his periodicals, including the popular newspaper *La Presse* and the fashion magazine *La Mode* as well as the *Musée des Familles*, of which he was the accredited editor until he was sacked after causing a scandal by publishing a story asserting that the theory of evolution was true and that humans had evolved from simian ancestors. His subsequent editorial work was usually uncredited, a clandestine activity that sustained him through the Second Empire while he built a considerable reputation as a popularizer of science, especially natural history. He lent covert assistance to several of the Parnassians in enabling them to publish their work before the fall of the Second Empire allowed him to obtain a belated measure of personal success in the 1880s.

Beauduin Bras-de-fer

> There still exist, in Flemish dialect, songs full of originality, which must date back to the remotest epochs. Such, among others, is that of Beauduin Bras-de-Fer.
> —Le Carpentier, *Histoire de Cambrai.*[1]

I

"Flanders to the rescue! Beware the iron hand!" Such was the war-cry of Comte Beauduin Bas-de-Fer.

II

When that cry was heard in the fiercest part of the battle, you could be sure that it would immediately open a wide passage, for death was inevitable for anyone who did not flee before the great sword of Beauduin Bras-de-Fer.

---

1 I have retained Berthoud's spelling of this name, although it is more usually rendered as Baudouin (Baldwin in English). Baudouin I, nicknamed Bras-de-Fer, was Comte de Flandres in the second half of the ninth century, before dying in 879; he leapt to historical prominence when he eloped in 861 with Judith, the daughter of the King of France, Charles the Bold, and widow of both Aethelwulf and Aethelbald, Kings of Wessex, as celebrated in this fake "ballad." Jean Le Carpentier's *Histoire de Cambrai et de Cambrésis* (1664) is one of the principal sources from which Berthoud drew inspiration for his historical fantasies.

III

If the warriors, by night, around a large fire, recounted the prowess of a knight, striking their coats of arms and saying "Our Lady protect him, for no one has a better right to the name of knight," you can be certain that they were talking about Beauduin Bras-de-Fer.

IV

One day, he stood at the entrance of his tent, had the clarion sounded, and started crying himself, and having his heralds repeat it: "Come you all, come hear your lord and master, Comte Beauduin Bras-de-Fer."

V

"Men of war and faithful companions," he said, "Flanders is the most beautiful of comtés."

All the soldiers immediately replied: "And the bravest of comtes is Comte Beauduin Bras-de-Fer."

VI

"My companions," he continued, "who seems to you to be worthy of becoming Comtesse de Flandre and to be put in the bed of your lord and master, Comte Beauduin Bras-de-Fer?"

VII

There was a long murmur among all the men-at-arms, each enquiring of his neighbor and saying: "By the salvation of my soul, there is only one woman worthy of being put in the bed of Beauduin Bras-de-Fer."

VIII

"There is indeed only one!" cried Beauduin. "She is young, she is beautiful, she is fecund; she is so nobly born that one could not ask for better; she wears the bonnet of a queen. Isn't that the one that Comte Beauduin Bras-de-Fer must have?

IX

"The daughter of King Charles of France, the widow of King Edward of England, Madame Judith, whom everyone calls the beautiful widow, is coming back from overseas to go to her father. Four thousand lances escort her; she has eighteen carts full of gold. She will pass by Mons in a little while. Would you like her for your Comtesse, for the wife of Beauduin Bras-de-Fer?"

X

"Yes! Yes! We want that!" That was what the army howled, in a voice like an angry sea. "Yes, yes! We want the beautiful widow, for Comtesse de Flandre, for the wife of Comte Beauduin Bras-de-Fer."

XI

"Then tighten the buckles of your armor, bestride your chargers, and come to conquer a Comtesse for Flanders with the points of your lances, a wife for Beauduin Bras-de-Fer."

XII

"To arms! To arms!"

An hour later, there remained not one man-at-arms of the four thousand English lances.

A knight covered in blood opened the litter of Madame Judith, the beautiful widow, and said to her, courteously: "Noble lady, here comes a husband for you, the Comte de Flandre, Comte Beauduin Bras-de-Fer."

MAURICE DE GUÉRIN
(1810-1839)

Maurice de Guérin was born in Andillac (Tarn) and educated at a seminary in Toulouse before being sent to Paris to the Collège Stanislas, where he befriended Jules-Amédée Barbey d'Aurevilly. After graduating he affiliated himself to a Christian socialist society founded by Hugues de Lanmenais, which was suppressed by the Holy See in 1833. He then moved to Paris, where he composed his two philosophical *poèmes en prose*, "La Bacchante" and "Le Centaure," employing the vocabulary of Classical mythology as a symbolic vehicle for his heretical religious ideas. His poetic labors were interrupted when he fell ill with tuberculosis and eventually returned to Provence; none of his works were published during his lifetime, but those he had not destroyed were issued by his friends after his death, eventually obtaining classic status with the aid of the advocacy of Barbey d'Aurevilly and the chief critic of the Romantic Movement, Charles Sainte-Beuve.

The Bacchante

Behold the mountain deprived of the choirs that travel its summits; the priestesses, the torches and the divine clamors have fallen back into the valleys; the festivities have dissipated, the mysteries have returned to the bosom of the gods. I am the youngest of the bacchantes who have been raised on Mount Citheron. The choirs have not yet transported me to the summits, for the sacred rites set my youth aside and order me to complete the span of time that it is necessary to offer in order to enter into the action of the solemnities. Finally, the Hours, the secret nurses who employ so much duration in rendering us appropriate to the gods, have placed me among the bacchantes, and I have emerged today from the primary mysteries, which have enveloped me.

While I accumulated the years demanded by the rites, I was similar to young fishermen who live on the shore of the sea. They appear for some time at the summit of a rock, their arms extended toward the water and their bodies inclined, like a god ready to dive back in; but their soul is balanced in their mortal bosom and retains their penchant. Finally, they jump, and some are said to return to the surface crowned. Thus I remained for a long time suspended over the mysteries; I abandoned myself there and my head reappeared, crowned and streaming.

Bacchus, eternal youth, profound and omnipresent god, I had the good fortune to recognize your marks in my bosom and assembled all my cares in order to devote them to your divinity. One day I transported myself toward the sunrise, in the time when the god's golden radiance fills fruits with maturity and adds the final virtue to the works of the earth. I reached the hills in order to offer myself to his features and to undo my hair at the first issue of light above the horizon; for it is taught that tresses inundated by matinal flames become more fecund and receive a beauty that equals the tresses of Diana.

My eyes, in opening wide, had surprised the extremities of shadows that were descending again beneath the pole. A few celestial signs, slow to accomplish their decline toward the waves, still marked the almost-abandoned sky, and the silence left by the night occupied the countryside. But although, in the cool valleys of Thessaly, the rivers have the custom of raising a breath similar to the clouds, and which repose on themselves, the virtue of your breath, O Bacchus, was exhaled from the bosom of the earth during darkness, and reigned at the return of the sun over the whole extent of the plains. The constellations that rise palely take on less brightness, while gaining it in the profundity of the night, so that my life only increased in my bosom, in potency or in splendor, as I penetrated into the fields.

When I stopped on the highest of the hills, I tottered like the statue of a god in the arms of the priests who are lifting it up to the sacred base. My bosom, having collected the spirits of the god extended over the plain, conceived thus a disturbance that hastened my steps and agitated my thoughts like waves rendered insensate by the winds. Without a doubt, it was by favor of that aberration that you were precipitated into my bosom, O Bacchus, for the gods surprise the minds of mortals in that fashion, like the sun, which, eager to penetrate the clustered branches full of darkness, opens them up by means of the north wind.

Then Aiello arrived.[1] That bacchante, the daughter of Typhon,[2] the most reckless of all the winds, and of a mother wandering in the mountains of Thrace, had been brought up be the nymphs of those regions, in the depths of caverns, apart from all humans; for the gods confide to rivers that turn their courses toward the greatest deserts or to the nymphs that inhabit the least accessible parts of forests the nurture of children issued from their mingling with the daughters of the elements or mortals.

Aiello descended from Scythia, where she had climbed all the way to the summits of the Monts Riphées,[3] and traveled through Greece, agitating the mysteries everywhere and bearing her clamors over all the mountains. She had reached the age when the gods, like shepherds who divert the streams of meadows, block the currents that irrigate the youth of mortals. Although still possessed by the pride of a life full to the brim, it was necessary to recognize that it was beginning to dry up, and besides, the usage of the mysteries had troubled the order of her beauty, which was

---

1 In Greek mythology Aiello—the name means something like whirlwind or storm-surge—is usually depicted as a harpy whose role is to transport souls to Tartarus, tormenting them *en route*.

2 Typhon is usually represented in Greek mythology as a monster, sometimes described as a many-headed giant serpent, who fought Zeus for the supremacy of the cosmos and was cast into Tartarus after his death. Guérin seems to be adopting an etymology liking the name to the Greek *tuphon* (whirlwind, transposed into English as typhoon), hence the link with his version of Aiello and perhaps to the serpent evoked at the end of the poem.

3 The Monts Riphées were a legendary mountain chain placed by various classical writers in the far north.

presenting considerable marks of pallor. Her tresses, as numerous as those of the night, were still extended over her shoulders, attesting to the force and richness of the gifts she had received from the gods, but, either because it had been exposed too frequently to the turbulence of the hyperborean winds or because she was suffering in her head the travail of some secret destiny, that afflicted hair anticipated the insult of years scarcely commenced.

Her eyes declared from the outset that they had received the empire of vaster countries and the profundity of the sky; they always reigned and moved without haste, extending for preference toward the shores of space where the divine shadows are ranged that receive in their bosom everything that disappears at the horizon. At intervals, however, that great gaze of such long duration became irresolute and fell into a disturbance like that of an eagle whose eyes detect the first indications of night. She also showed inconstancy in the manner of her footfalls. Sometimes she gradually increased the firm and light tread that she adopted along river banks or in forests, like Latona seeking in her long adventure for a refuge in which to give birth to the gods she had conceived.[1] Sometimes, judging by the hesitation of her steps, which were seeking for surety, and her constrained and consternated facial expression, one might have thought that she was walking on the bed of the ocean. When her bosom was persuaded by the night to participate in the universal calm, her voice emerged into the darkness placid and long-sustained, like the song of the Hesperides at the extremity of the seas.

Aiello took me into her amity and educated me with all the care that the gods employ with mortals designated for their favor, and whom they want to raise themselves. Like the young Arcadians who descend with the god Pan into the most secret forests in order to learn from him how to place their fingers on primitive flutes and to collect the moaning of reeds in their minds, I walked with the great bacchante, who directed her steps toward some distant point every day. It was in those deserted

---

1 Latona is the Roman equivalent of the Leto of Greek mythology, the mother of Apollo and Artemis.

places that she made her speeches, I listened to her words take their course as if I were witnessing the hidden source of a river.

"The nymphs who reign in these forests," she said, "take pleasure in exciting perfumes or songs on the edge of the woods so sweet that passers-by break their journeys are tempted to follow them into the most obscure of these retreats. A subtle influence penetrates the mind of the stranger; the aberration that rises within him alters the firmness of his tread, and while he advances, similar to rural demigods who always carry some intoxication in their veins, the nymphs applaud the power of their abode over the minds of mortals.

"But Bacchus makes the intoxication of his exhalation recognizable to everything that breathes, including the unshakable family of the gods. His ever-renewed breath runs over the entire land, nourishes at its extremities the eternal intoxication of the Ocean, and, driven into the divine air, it agitates the stars that circle incessantly around the tenebrous pole. When Saturn mutilated sleeping Uranus in the bosom of the night, the land and the seas received with the shed blood a new fecundity, the first fruits of which to rise up were the nymphs on the land and Aphrodite over the seas. Bacchus, incessantly stopped like a warm vapor in the damp bosom of Cybele, sustains the heat of the old blood that still engenders entire choirs of nymphs in the density of forests and the immortal foam of the waters.

"The rivers have their abode in the profound palaces of the earth, extensive and resounding swellings where those inclined gods preside over the birth of springs and the departure of waves. They reign there, their ears always nourished by the abundance of seethings and their eyes attached to the destiny of their waves. But neither the depth nor the impenetrable estate of their vaults can isolate those divinities from Bacchus, for no access is forbidden to him by destiny. The rivers agitate on their beds and the ancient mud shifts in the bosom of their troubled urns.

"During the reign of one summer I had attached my abode to the summit of the Pangaean mountains. Secret afflictions that I recognized every year, the imminent joys of the earth and the beauty of its countries, engaged me to take to the mountain slopes. Mortals agreeable to the gods, or whom the excess of evils had touched, had been conducted and gathered there by celestial signs: Maia, Cassiopeia, the great Chiron, Cynosure and the sad Hyades have entered into the silent march of the constellations. Guided by the destinies, they climb into the sky and decline with neither deviation nor suspense, and doubtless that pursuit of a march that rises and falls back, and then resumes, instituting a state of good fortune extending to uncertain limits, borrows from the monotony of roads, mingled with a few poppies.

"I wanted a slow march, applied to the slopes of mountains, to engender in me a disposition similar to that of the stars in their courses, my route taking me toward the mountain-tops as they rise up in the steps of the night. But a fruit cannot set aside imminent maturity; every day the soil penetrates it with more urgent gifts, the consuming warmth of which is marked externally by ever-more-advanced colors. Attained likewise and afflicted in my bosom, I was impotent to reject or slow down the life that was suggested to me. Neither belated footsteps, the search beneath the forest for refuges consecrated to those mute divinities, so powerful by virtue of calmness, who put the sharpest dolors to sleep, the long pauses under the breath coming from the west, the sun having set completely, nor the empty shadow of the night, nor dreams, could suspend for a moment the secret pursuits of my mind from whose efforts my mind was suffering,

"I climbed up all the way to the top of the mountains that receive the footsteps of the immortals; for some among them take pleasure in traveling the series of mountains, maintaining their unbreakable march over the undulations of the summits, and others, over the rocks that reign in the distance, consume the hours by plunging into the depression of valleys, welcoming there the approach of night or considering how shadows and dreams engage with mortal minds. Having reached those heights, I obtained the gifts of the night, the calm and slumber that even reduce the agitations stirred up by the gods. But that repose was similar to the repose of birds that love the winds and are incessantly carried in their journeys. When they obey the shadows and lower their flight toward the forests, their feet perch on branches that, piercing the sky, are easily stirred by the breaths that travel the night; for even in sleep they enjoy the effects of the winds and want their plumage to shiver and part to the slightest exhalations emerging from the summit of the woods.

"Thus, in the very bosom of sleep, my mind remained exposed to the breath of Bacchus. That breath observes in spreading forth an eternal measure and communicates with everything that enjoys light; but a small number of mortals, by virtue of a privilege of destiny, are able to inform themselves of its course. It reigns all the way to the extreme summit of Olympus, and even passes through the bosom of those gods covered by the aegis or clad in impenetrable tunics. It resounds in the brass always agitated around Cybele, and conducts the language of the Muses, which draw from their songs the entire history of the generation of the gods in the damp entrails of the earth, in the bosom of the boundless night, or in the Ocean, which has nurtured so many immortals.

"On emerging from sleep I surrendered my steps to the conduct of the Hours. They regulated my course to the degrees of the day, and I went around the mountain, drawn by the sun, like the shadow that accomplishes its revolution at the foot of an oak tree. The steps of a few mortals were stopped by the gods in the vicinity of waters, in the depths of forests or on the slopes of hills. Sudden roots had conducted their feet into the soil, and all the life they contained had extended in branches and deployed in foliage. Some, attached to the banks of dormant waters, retained a sacred calm, and welcomed at the approach of daybreak the swarm of dreams that took shelter in their obscure branches. Others, added to the forest of Jupiter or standing on sterile summits, bore old and savage crowns, which catch all the winds and always stop a few of the stray birds that mortals observe.

"Their destiny is irrevocable, for the divine earth possesses them, and they are submissive to the eternal nurture of her breast; but such as they have been rendered, and in the immobility of their condition, they still retain a few secret movements of their original condition. Whether the seasons decline or rise again, they remain attentive to the sun; of all the moves in the universe they no longer discern anything but him, and it is to him alone that they address the confused prayers as they can still form. A few, such is the force of their amour, can even conduct the movement of their growth to the march of the god and turn the abundance of their branches toward his passage.

"In the road that I entered following the day, I saw my footfalls slow down while my strength was still full, and finally extinguish in complete immobility. Then I became similar to those mortals reduced beneath bark and stopped in the powerful bosom of the earth. Retained at rest, I received the life of the passing gods without marking any movement, my arms turned toward the sun. It was toward the hour of the day when the most powerful brightness rises; everything stopped on the mountain, the profound heart of the forests no longer respired, the fecund flames embraced Cybele and Bacchus inebriated even the roots of islands in the entrails of the Ocean.

"The march of the sun in its decline determined my footfalls toward the westernmost points of the mountain. The god disappeared and, the light that he left having felt the first mixture of darkness, the depths of the valleys and the whole extent of the countryside resumed, albeit slowly, the liberty of their breath. The birds rose up above the woods, searching the sky to see whether the winds had been reestablished, but their wings, still intoxicated, had difficulty furnishing an unsteady flight full of error. A murmur born in the treetops testified to the reawakening of breaths, but the crowns only rendered a light tremor that did not equal the agitation experienced by the branches of cypresses in the hands of Pan when the god withdraws the choirs that he animates during favorable nights; an impetuous measure attaches to his steps and makes him reenter the sleeping woods, staggering. Emerging from the thickness of their retreats, the wild animals came to obtain a keener respiration on the heights; a new flame appeared in their eyes; their terrible voice had fallen into a murmur and their bold step into a languorous amble.

"Meanwhile, shadows filled the depths of the valleys; they were rising toward me, distributing slumber and dreams to everything that breathes; they finally caught up with me and enveloped me, but without penetrating me. I remained firm and alert under the heaviness of the night, while the earth, full of slumber, communicated repose to my limbs and recruited them to the general immobility; my forehead stayed awake without being struck by languor. It was animated by all the gifts distributed by the gods during the day; their charm surrounded it; and the new life that I had collected sent its inflamed spirits thereto.

"Callisto, clad in a savage form because of the jealousy of Juno,[1] wandered for a long time in the deserts, but Jupiter, who had loved her, removed her from the woods in order to associate with her in the stars and conduct their destinies in a repose from which they could no longer depart. She has received her dwelling in the depths of the tenebrous sky that spreads the elements, the gods and mortals in the entrails of Cybele. The sky gathers around her the most ancient of its shades and enables her to respire what it still possesses of the principles of life, combing them with the effects of the indefatigable fire whose emanations animate the universe. Penetrated by an eternal intoxication, Callisto's posture is inclined toward the pole, while the entire order of the constellations passes by, lowering their course toward the Ocean. Likewise, during the night, I remained immobile at the summit of the mountains, my head enveloped by an intoxication that pressed it like the crown of vines and grapes that maintains an unalterable youth at Bacchus' temples."

Thus Aiello instructed me by means of the story of her destiny. Once alerted in order to follow the voice that called to it in the knowledge of the gods, my mind no longer returned me toward the crowd where its original dwelling was; it drew

---

1 In Greek myth Callisto was transformed by Hera—here called Juno in accordance with Guérin's policy of employing Roman nomenclature—into a bear, and was transposed in the heavens into the constellation Ursa Major, employed by navigators as a guide to the north star.

away with its guide toward the less frequented mysteries. Every day the speech of the great bacchante rose up, going before me in the obscurity of the roads. Often, the Muses quit the rapid movement of the choirs in order to commence a slow march in the bosom of the night. Clad in their thickest veils, they opened divine songs beneath the darkness. Aiello's speech drew me toward the gods, advancing in parallel with the voice of the Muses carried in the shadows.

A lair opening over the plains, the peaks reserving the last traces of daylight, and the beds of the most fecund valleys, were the places to which Aiello's choice guided me. The duration of her conversation often penetrated deep into the bosom of the night, and then she retired alone, leaving her discourse suspended in my mind like the nymphs who, having hung their wet garments on an inclined branch, return to the secrecy of their dwellings.

Meanwhile, the mysteries advanced that were finally about to transport me in their course, but their first movements in bacchantes anticipate by a long way the hour of their rising. Each of us, having received within her the signs sent by the god, commenced thereafter to draw away, for mortals attained by the divinities immediately redirect their footsteps, guided by new attractions. Each of us followed the slope to which the inclination of our mind bore us. Similar to the nymphs, daughters of Heaven and Earth, who, as soon as they are born, depart for the openings of springs, various sectors of forests and all the places where Cybele has assembled the marks of her fecundity, those slopes dispersed us into all the regions of the countryside.

We were admitted into the destiny of the gods who are responsible for reigning over the elements. Powerful over rivers, woods and fertile valleys, they rejoice in considering the life that progresses before their eyes. But in the duration of the attentive leisure that they lead, leaning over the waves, their immortal life conforms to their monotonous fall, and their nature engages with the contemplated elements, like a man surprised on a river bank by slumber and dreams whose robe spreads out over the waves. Each bacchante was thus allied with some location signaled by the birth of a natural destiny.

Aiello appeared at the summit of hills and reposed for a long time, her head on the bosom of the Earth; she seemed to be waiting, like Melampus, the son of Amythion, for the serpent marked with a poppy to come to knot itself around her temples.[1]

Hippothea,[2] sitting at the source of springs, was rendered immobile there; her hair, which she had spread out, her arms in abandon and the attachment of her gaze to the flight of the waters, marked her inclination toward their destiny and that her spirit was joining their course.

The march of Plexaure plunged into the most extensive forests.[3] When an oceanide is touched by slumber while she travels the seas, her limbs collapse and find their couch on the waves; she has resigned the conduct of her voyage to their inconstancy. Floating, one might think her from a distance an expired mortal, but she is lying on the wave that carries her away with the lightness of life and her bosom is consumed by a slumber inspired by the Ocean. So the repose of Plexaure appeared in the bed of the forests.

Arrested on the edge of profound descents, Telesto leaned over, extending her arms toward the valleys, similar to Ceres at the summit of Etna when the goddess, leaning over the opening of the crater, lights her pinewood torch in the fire of the volcano.

As for me, who was still ignorant of the god, I ran in disorder through the countryside, carrying in my flight a serpent that could not be recognized by the hand, but by which I felt entirely traveled. Like a ray of sunlight, wrapped around a mortal by the

---

1 According to Herodotus, Melampus, the son of Amythion, was the seer who introduced the worship of Dionysus (Guérin's Bacchus) to Greece. He is mentioned in many other stories by various authors, often featuring snakes, credited by some with teaching him to communicate with animals. The serpent with a poppy on its head appears to be an invention of Guérin's, but the poppy figures extensively in Greek mythology as symbol of divinatory dreams, by virtue of its link to opium.

2 Hippothea [horse-goddess] is a fugitive figure linked in various Greek documents with Neptune; a play by Euripides introduces her into the Athenian foundation-myth.

3 Plexaure or Plexaura is a name attributed in various documents to a nereid or an oceanide. Telesto, or Tlestho, is also the name of an oceanide.

power of the gods, its coils enlaced me with a subtle warmth that irritated my mind and hastened my steps like a spur. I went on, accusing Bacchus and thinking about the waves of the sea where I thought myself constrained, but in very little time the god had exhausted my steps. Inclined toward the fall, I was imploring the earth that gives repose, when the serpent, tightening its coils, attached a long bite to my breast. Pain did not enter into my torn flesh; it was calmness and a kind of languor, as if the serpent had dipped its fang in the cup of Cybele.

A flame rose up in my mind as tranquil as the gleams nourished during the night on a primitive altar erected to the divinities of the mountains. Attentive and in repose, like a nymph of Nysa pressing the infancy of Bacchus in her arms, I occupied the lairs until the hour when, the cry of Aiello having signaled the advent of the mysteries, I rose to my feet in the tracks of that bacchante, who was marching before us like the Night while, her head turned in order to commune with the shadows, she headed toward the occident . . .

LOUIS BERTRAND
(1807-1841)

Louis Bertand, who preferred the signature Aloysius Bertrand, left his definitive collection of prose poems, *Gaspard de la Nuit*, for posthumous publication a year after his death. Intended by his parents for the priesthood, he ran away from the seminary and joined the army. He resumed his education when posted to Dijon as an officer in the gendarmerie in 1816, where he remained for more than twenty years, save for a brief excursion to Paris to meet Victor Hugo and Charles Sainte-Beuve. He published essays and verses in *Le Provincial*, a local newspaper that had previously published the early writings of the Romantic poet Alfred de Musset. In 1831 he became the editor of a Republican periodical. He arranged publication of *Gaspard de la Nuit* in 1839, but it was slow to appear and he died of tuberculosis before it reached print; the 1842 edition, reproduced from a corrupt copy of the manuscript, was riddled with errors. Nevertheless, it was greatly admired by Charles Baudelaire, Théodore de Banville and Stéphane Mallarmé, whose promotion prompted its piece-meal reprinting in the *Revue des lettres et des arts* in 1867 as a key text in the evolution of poetry in prose.

Vignettes from *Gaspard de la Nuit*

My Cottage

> In autumn, the frosts come to repose there,
> attracted by the bright red berries of the sorb-tree or
> bird-catcher
> —R. Mothermé

> Raising her eyes then, the worthy old woman saw
> how the wind was tormenting the trees and
> dissipating the tracks of the crows hopping in the
> snow around the barn.
> —Voss[1]

My cottage would have the foliage of the woods for a parasol in summer and for a garden in autumn, some moss on the window-sill encasing the pearls of the rain, and a few wallflowers growing on the almond tree.

But in winter, what a pleasure it is when morning had shaken its bouquet of frost over my frozen windows, to perceive from afar, on the edge of the forest, a traveler who is moving away, always shrinking, along with his mount, in the snow and the mist.

What a pleasure it is, in the evening, under the mantle of the flamboyant fireplace, perfumed by a handful of juniper, to leaf though chronicles of knights and monks, so marvelously portrayed that the former seem to be jousting and the latter praying.

---

1 The Prussian writer Julius von Voss (1768-1832).

And what a pleasure it is by night, at the dubious and pale hour that precedes daybreak, to hear my cock crow in the poultry-yard and the cock of a farm respond to him feebly, a sentinel perched on the advance-post of the sleeping village.

Oh, if the king were reading us in his Louvre—O my muse unsheltered against the storms of life—the suzerain lord of so many fiefs that he does not know the number of his châteaux would not begrudge us a thatched cottage.

The Viola da Gamba

> In the moonlight,
> My friend Pierrot . . .
> —Popular Song

The choirmaster has no sooner interrogated the bow of the buzzing viol than it responds to him with a burlesque gargle of *lazzis* and *roulades*, as if it had an ingestion of Italian comedy in its stomach.

✳

First, there was the duenna Barbara who was scolding that imbecile Pierrot, the clumsy fool, for having dropped Monsieur Cassandre's wig-box and spread the powder all over the floor.

And Monsieur Cassandre, piteously picking up his wig, and Arlequin, catching the old man with a kick on the behind, and Columbine, wiping away a tear of mad laughter, and Pierrot, extending a floury grin all the way to his ears.

But soon, in the moonlight, Arlequin, whose candle had gone out, begged his friend Pierrot to pull the bolts in order for him to relight it, with the result that the traitor abducted the young woman along with the old man's casket.

e

"To the devil with Job Hans the luthier, who sold me that string!" cried the choirmaster, replacing the dusty viol in its dusty case. The string had broken.

32

Messire Jean

A grave individual whose golden chain
and white stick announced authority.
—Walter Scott

"Messire Jean," the queen said to him, "Go see in the palace courtyard why those two greyhounds are fighting." And he went,

When he got there, the seneschal was scolding the two greyhounds sharply, which were fighting over a ham-bone.

But the dogs, tugging his black breeches and biting his red socks, knocked him over on his buttocks as if he were lame.

"Hola! Hola! Help me!" The halberdiers at the door came running, but the muzzles of the two starvelings had already grabbed the delicacy from the fellow's satchel.

Meanwhile, the queen was fainting with laughter at a window, in her high Malines head-dress, as stiff and as creased as a fan.

"Why were they fighting, Messire?"

"They were fighting, Madame, because one was maintaining against the other that you are the most beautiful, the wisest and the greatest princess in the world."

The Mason

The Master Mason: "Look at these bastions,
these buttresses; one would think they were
constructed for eternity."
—Schiller, *William Tell*

The mason Abraham Knupfer, trowel in hand, is singing on the scaffolding, so high up that, while reading the Gothic verses of the organ, his feet are level with the church with thirty buttresses and the city with thirty churches.

He can see the stone tarasques vomiting water from the slates into the confused abyss of galleries, windows, pendentives, belfries, turrets, roofs and wooden frameworks, which the indented and immobile wing of the tercel patches with a gray dot.

He can see the fortifications cut out in a star, the citadel swollen with pride like a heraldic cockerel in a roundel, the courtyards of palaces where sunlight is drying up the fountains, and the cloisters of monasteries where the shadows are rotating around the pillars.

The imperial troops are lodged in an outlying district. A cavalier is drumming out there. Abraham Knupfer can make out his tricorn hat, his red woolen shoulder-knots, and his cockade, traversed by a cord and knotted with a ribbon.

What he can also see are the soldiers, who, in the park plumed with gigantic branches, on broad emerald lawns, are peppering with musket-fire a wooden bird attaché to the top of a mast.

And in the evening, when the harmonious nave of the cathedral goes to sleep, lying in the crossed arms, he perceives from the ladder, on the horizon, a village set ablaze by men of war, blazing like a comet in the azure.

Evening on the Water

The shores where Venice is the queen of the sea.
—André Chénier[1]

The black gondola glides alongside marble palaces like a bravo running to some nocturnal adventure, with a stiletto and a lantern under his cape.

A cavalier and a lady are talking amorously:

"The oranges so perfumed, and you so indifferent! Ah, signora, you are a statue in a garden!"

---

1 The poet André Chenier (1762-1794) was an important precursor of the Romantic Movement—according to Charles Sainte-Beuve—who fell victim to the Terror three days before it was suspended, having penned a few lines in opposition to the execution of Louis XVI.

"Is this kiss that of a statue, my Giorgio? Why are you sulking?"

"Do you love me, then?"

"There is not a star in the sky that does not know it, and you do not?"

"What is that noise?"

"Nothing; doubtless the splash of the waves rising and falling on one of the steps of the stairways of the Guidecca."

"Help! Help!"

"Oh, Mother of the Savior, someone is drowning!"

"Go away; he's confessed," says a monk who appears on the terrace.

And the black gondola, propelled by oars, glides alongside the marble palaces like a bravo returning from some nocturnal adventure, with a stiletto and a lantern under his cape.

The Five Fingers of the Hand

> An honest family in which there was
> never a bankruptcy and no one was
> ever hanged.
> —*Le Parenté*, Jean de Nivelle.[1]

The thumb is a fat Flemish tavern-keeper, of a mocking and licentious humor, who is smoking at his door under the sign of the double *bière de Mars*.[2]

The index finger is his wife, a virago as dry as a hake, who slaps her maidservant, of whom she is jealous, every morning, and caresses the bottle with which she is in love.

---

1 The nobleman Jean de Nivelle (1422-1477) became notorious after disobeying his father, a liegeman of Louis XI, and fighting for the latter's enemy and rival claimant to the French throne, the Duc de Bourgogne, Charles le Téméraire [Charles the Bold], for which reason he was slandered in popular songs as a traitor and a "dog."

2 The reference is to a traditional seasonal beer also known as "Easter beer".

The middle finger is their son, a companion denuded of the ax, who would be a soldier if he were not a brewer, and a horse if he were not a man.

The ring finger is their daughter, the agile and enticing Zerbine, who sells lace to ladies and does not sell her smiles to cavaliers

And the ear finger is the Benjamin of the family, a weepy brat who is always hanging on to his mother's belt, like a baby suspended from the tooth of an ogress.

The five fingers of the hand are the most wondrous five-petaled wallflower that has ever embroidered the flower-beds of the noble city of Harlem.

Part Two: Parnassians

CHARLES BAUDELAIRE
(1821-1867)

Charles Baudelaire wrote one of the landmark works of French literature in *Les Fleurs du Mal* (1857) and also translated the works of Edgar Poe into French, securing Poe's influence of subsequent French prose. His father died while he was a child and his mother then married an army officer and diplomat, James Aupick, who became Baudelaire's guardian and the custodian of his inheritance—which he refused to relinquish to the poet when he came of age except as a meager monthly allowance, adding what Baudelaire considered to be a dire insult to the injury his stepfather had inflicted by alienating his mother's love. Aupick tried to ship him off to India, allegedly to cure him of his dissolute tendencies, but he returned home without completing the journey, although the experience left him with a rich legacy of tropical imagery. His "dissolution" only grew worse, and his mother failed to pry him from the grip of his wayward mistress Jeanne Duval, whom she condemned as a parasitic "black Venus." Aupick died in 1857, but his removal failed to reconcile Baudelaire with his mother or extract him from a permanent state of debt. He was attracted to Poe's work because he knew about Poe's strained relationship with his own stepfather, and thus considered him a "spiritual brother." *Les Fleurs du Mal* survived a mauling by Napoléon III's censors, which removed several allegedly-obscene poems from the first edition of the collection, but it was not suppressed and swiftly became recognized as a masterpiece. The collection included a number of *poèmes en prose*, and Baudelaire worked for the rest of his life to compile an assembly of such works, *Le Spleen de Paris*, "*spleen*" (an exaggerated form of *ennui*) being a key concept in his work, descriptive of the state of mind associated with the massive chip on his shoulder—which he never shrugged off, or showed any sign of wanting to. He contrived to publish an excerpt from it, translated in full below after the most famous prose-poem from *Les Fleur du Mal*, in Catulle Mendès' doomed *Revue fantaisiste*, and he subsequently contributed to the first volume of *Le Parnasse contemporain*, but he is not routinely included in the list of Parnassians, being widely considered too large a figure to be consigned to any Movement, although he became the figurehead and hero of more than one.

The Double Room

There is a room which resembles a daydream, a truly spiritual room, whose still, stale air is tinted with pink and blue.

Here the soul bathes in idleness, amid the aromas of regret and desire. There is something of the twilight here, in its blueness and its rosiness; it is as though one dreams sensuously during an eclipse.

The furniture extends itself, languidly prostrate. The furniture too seems to be dreaming, as if it existed in a state of permanent sleep, as all things vegetable and mineral do. The fabrics speak a language of silence, as flowers and daylit skies do, and sunsets.

These walls are undefiled by ugly paintings. Relative to the pure dream or the unanalyzed impression, specific and assertive art is blasphemous. Here the light is perfectly sufficient in itself, harmonizing with the delicacy of the shadows.

An infinitesimal hint of fragrance, chosen with exquisite taste, which carries with it a faint vaporous humidity, floats upon the air, lulling the drowsy mind as if it were a hothouse.

Hectic showers of muslin fall across the window and from the canopy of the bed, displayed like cascades of snow. Here upon this bed lies the Goddess, sovereign of dreams. Why is she here? Who brought her? What magical power installed her on this throne of dreaming and delight? What does it matter; she is here! I know who she is.

Those are the eyes which burn bright in the twilight; subtle and terrifying mirrors of the soul whose fearful malice I know so well! They draw, conquer and devour the unwary gaze of any who looks into them. I have made a study of them, those dark stars which command such curiosity and admiration.

What benevolent demon must I thank for thus surrounding me with mystery, silence, peace and perfumes? O bliss! That which we ordinarily call life, even when it can encompass happiness, has nothing to compare with this life beyond life which I have come to understand, and which I savor minute by minute, second by second.

No! There are no more minutes, there are no more seconds! Time is banished; it is Eternity which rules this place: an Eternity of delights!

✳

But a heavy and terrible crash has thundered upon the door, and in nightmarish fashion I feel that I have been struck in the stomach by a pick-axe.

A Specter has rudely intruded upon the feast. It is some bailiff come to taunt me in the name of the law; or some shameless courtesan come to tell a tale of woe and add the trivia of her existence to the sorrows of my own; or perhaps some editor's errand-boy come to demand a manuscript.

The heavenly room, the sovereign Goddess of Dreams—the Sylphide, as she was called by the great René —all their magic is dispelled by the crude hammering of the Specter.

O horror! I remember! I remember! Yes, this tawdry place of infinite tedium is indeed where I live. There are the ridiculous furnishings, dusty and bumped; the hearth devoid of flames and glowing embers; the sad windows where the raindrops have made patterns in the grime; the manuscripts scribbled-over or incomplete; the calendar marked with crayon to show the inauspicious passing of the days.

And that otherworldly perfume which exalted me with heightened sensibility is replaced, alas, by the stale odor of old tobacco, mingled with a sickening dampness. The rankness of desolation lies upon everything here.

In this narrow world, full to the brim with disgust, only one familiar object makes me smile: the vial of laudanum; an old and terrible mistress. Like all mistresses, alas, she gives too freely of her caresses and her treacheries.

Oh yes, Time has resumed control! The sovereignty of that hideous ancient Time is now restored, and with him has come his demonic train of memories and regrets, fits and fears, anguishes and nightmares, angers and neuroses.

I can assure you that every passing second now carries a strong and solemn stress, and that each one, leaping from the clock, says: "I am Life: unbearable, implacable Life!"

There is but a single second in a man's life whose mission is to bring good news—the good news, which strikes such inexplicable terror into everyone.

Yes, Time rules again; he has resumed his brutal tyranny. And he drives me on, as if I were an ox, with his duplicate threat: "Get on with it, churl! Sweat, slave! Live, and be damned!"

Poems in Prose from the *Revue Fantaisiste*

Evening Twilight

Nightfall has always been for me the signal for an interior celebration, and something like the deliverance from an anguish. In solitudes, as in the streets of the capital, the darkening of daylight and the scintillation of stars and lanterns brightens my mind.

However, I had two friends whom twilight made ill. One of them neglected then all the relationships of amity and politeness and maltreated everyone like a savage. I have seen him throw an excellent roast chicken at the head of a waiter.

Evening, the precursor of sensualities, spoiled the most succulent things for him.

The other, as the daylight declined, became more bitter, more somber and more petulant. Indulgent during the day, he was pitiless in the evening; not only for others but also for himself, on whom he exercised his crepuscular mania angrily.

The former died insane, incapable of recognizing his mistress and his son; the latter bears within him the anxiety of a perpetual malaise. Dusk, which illuminates my mind, made night in theirs; and although it is not rare to see the same cause engendering two contrary effects, it always intrigues and astonishes me.

Solitude

The second friend also said to me that solitude was bad for people, and I believe that he cited to me, in support of his thesis, the words of Fathers of the Church. It is true that the spirit of murder and lubricity is marvelously inflamed in solitude. Everyone knows that the Demon frequents arid places.

But that seductive solitude is only dangerous for idle and distracted souls who cannot keep a despotic idea at bay. It was not bad for Robinson Crusoe. It rendered him religious, brave and industrious; it purified him, and taught him how far individual strength could go.

Was it not La Bruyère who said: "The great misfortune of not being alone . . ."? There is, therefore, much in common between solitude and dusk; it is good or bad, criminal or salutary, incendiary or calming, according to the manner in which one employs it, and the manner in which one has employed life.

With regard to pure enjoyment, I believe that the most beautiful fraternal feasts, the most magnificent gatherings of people electrified by a common pleasure, will never provide anything comparable to what a solitary man experiences who has embraced and understood all the sublimity of a landscape at a single glance. That glance has conquered an inalienable private property for him.

Projects

How beautiful you would be in a complicated and sumptuous court costume coming down the marble steps of a palace through the atmosphere of a beautiful evening, in front of great lawns and fountains!

But what is the point of such beautiful décor? Insensate! I forgot that I hate kings and their palaces.

No, it is not in a palace that I would like to possess you and enjoy your whole being. We would not be *at home*. Besides which, those embossed, braided, insolent walls, as dazzling as military uniforms, resemble the soul of the Great King who had no corners for intimacy. Here, there's no *revoir*; on these walls spangled with gold, I don't see the place of a single nail on which to hang your image.

Ah! I know where I would like to love you interminably!

On the edge of the sea, a beautiful wooden cabin enveloped by shade. In the atmosphere, a floating odor of coconut oil, and everywhere, in the house and the garden, a powerful perfume of roses and musk. On the horizon, the tips of masts, which a gradual swell causes to describe slow magical curves in the air. Around us, outside the silent, obscure bedroom full of flowers and mats, decorated with rare furniture in heavy and tenebrous wood—where you are reposing so mildly, so nonchalantly, so well ventilated, smoking tobacco mixed with opium and sugar—and beyond the veranda, the racket of birdsong and the delicate chatter of negresses.

But no! Why that vulgar stage setting? It would cost a lot of money, and money only dances in the pockets of imbeciles who have no understanding of the Beautiful. Pleasure is a few leagues from here; it is two paces away; it is in the first inn one comes to, the hostelry of hazard, so fecund in joys. A big fire, bright faiences on the walls, rude wine and a very large bed with slightly coarse but fresh curtains.

The dream! The dream! Always the accursed dream that kills action and consumes time! Dreams soothe for a moment the devouring beast that agitates within us. It is a poison that soothes it, but which nourishes it.

Where, then, to find a cup deep enough and a poison thick enough to drown the Beast?

The Clock

The Chinese see the hour in the eyes of cats.

One day, a missionary strolling in the suburbs of Nanking perceived that he had forgotten his watch, and asked a small boy what time it was.

The scamp of the Celestial Empire hesitated momentarily; then, changing his mind, he replied: "I'll tell you." A few moments later, he reappeared, holding an exceedingly fat cat in his arms, and looking it, as the saying has it, in the whites of its eyes, he affirmed without hesitation: "It's not quite midday." That was true.

For myself, when I take this extraordinary cat in my arms, which is simultaneously the honor of its race, the pride of my heart and the perfume of my soul, whether it is night or day, in bright light or opaque darkness, I always see the hour distinctly in the depths of its adorable eyes, always the same: a vast, solemn hour as large as space, without division into minutes or seconds—a motionless hour, which is not marked on clocks, and yet as light as a sigh and as rapid as the blink of an eye.

And if some importunate person comes to disturb me while my gaze reposes on that delightful dial, if some dishonest and intolerant Spirit comes to say to me: "What are you looking at so intently? What are you looking for in the eyes of that being? Do you see the hour there, prodigal and idle mortal?" I shall respond without hesitation;

"Yes, I can see the hour; it is Eternity."

Tresses

Let me respire for a long, long time the odor of your hair, plunging my whole face into it like a thirsty man into the water of a spring, and agitating it with my hand like an odorous handkerchief, in order to shake memories into the air.

If you could know all that I see, all that I smell and all that I hear in your tresses! My soul voyages over the perfume as the souls of other men voyage over music.

Your hair contains an entire dream full of sails and masts; its tresses contain great seas whose monsoons bear me toward charming climates, where space is bluer and deeper, where the atmosphere is perfumed by fruits, by foliage and by human skin.

In the ocean of your hair I glimpse a port swarming with melancholy songs, vigorous men of all nations and ships of all forms outlining their arachnean architecture against an immense sky where eternal warmth lounges.

In the caress of your hair I rediscover the languor of long hours spent on a divan in the cabin of a beautiful ship, rocked by the imperceptible swell of the port, between pots of flowers and refreshing water-jugs.

In the ardent hearth of your tresses I respire the odor of tobacco mixed with opium and sugar; in the darkness of your tresses I see the resplendent infinity of the tropical azure; on the soft shores of your tresses I intoxicate myself on the combined odors of tar, musk and coconut oil.

Let me bite the heavy black tresses for a long time. When I nibble your elastic and rebellious hair, it seems to me that I am eating my memories.

Invitation to the Voyage

It is a superb country, a land of Cockayne, it is said, that I dream of visiting with a cherished mistress. A singular country, drowned in the mists of our North, which one could call the Orient of the Occident, the China of Europe, so much is warm and capricious fantasy given free rein there, so much is it patiently and stubbornly illustrated by savant and delicate vegetation.

A true land of Cockayne, where everything is beautiful, rich, tranquil and honest; where luxury takes pleasure in being mirrored in order, where life is fat and sweet to respire; from which disorder, turbulence and the unexpected are excluded; where wellbeing is married to silence; where even the cuisine is poetic, simultaneously fat and stimulating; where everything resembles you, my dear angel.

Oh, if you were the poet, if I were the Darling, loved and protected, always tender, always submissive, but always dreamy and desirous, I would say to you, my poet and my friend: "You know that feverish malady that takes possession of us in cold miseries, that love of unknown countries, that nostalgia of curiosity? It is a country that resembles you, where all is beautiful, rich, tranquil and honest, where fantasy has built and decorated an occidental China, where life is able to respire, where wellbeing is married to silence. It's there that it is necessary to go to live, there that it is necessary to go to die!"

Yes, it is there that it is necessary to go to breathe, to dream and to stretch the hours by means of the multiplicity of sensations. A musician has written an Invitation to the Waltz; who will compose an Invitation to the Voyage, which can be offered to a beloved woman, the sister of election? Yes, it is in that atmosphere that it would be good to live—out there, where the slower hours contain more thoughts, where the clocks chime wellbeing with a more profound and more significant solemnity.

On gleaming panels or gilded leather of a rich darkness, calm and happy paintings live discreetly, like the souls of the artists who created them. Sunsets color the dining room or the drawing room, so richly are filtered by beautiful fabrics and high shaded windows that lend divider into numerous compartments. The items of furniture are vast, curious and bizarre, armed with locks and secrets, like refined souls. The mirrors, the metal fitments, the fabrics, the trimmings and the faience play a mute and mysterious symphony there for the eyes; and from all things, from every corner, from the fissures of drawers and the pleats of fabrics, a singular perfume escapes: a light Oriental perfume that is like the soul of the apartment.

Sunsets that embellish in such a melancholy fashion the bedroom of the beloved woman, the sister of election, when will you sink over my horizon?

A true land of Cockayne, I tell you, where everything is rich, neat and shiny, like a clear conscience, like magnificent kitchen equipment, like splendid silverware, like multicolored jewelry! The treasures of the world flow there, as in the house of a laborious man who has merited the whole world. A singular country, superior to others, as Art is to Nature, where the latter is reformed by dreams, where it is corrected, embellished and reshaped.

Let the alchemists of horticulture search for it, and search for it again, let them recoil incessantly from the limits of their wellbeing! Let prices of sixty and a hundred thousand florins be offered for whoever can resolve their ambitious problems! Personally, I have found my black tulip and my blue dahlia.

Incomparable flower, rediscovered tulip, allegorical dahlia, it is there—is it not?—into that beautiful country, so calm and so thoughtful, that it is necessary to go in order to live and to flourish. Will you not be framed in your analogy, and will you not have your own correspondent for a mirror?

Dreams! Always dreams! And the more delicate the soul is, the further dreams draw away from the possible. Every man bears within him his dose of natural opium, incessantly secreted and renewed, and from birth to death, how many hours filled with positive enjoyment and successful and decisive action can we count? Shall we ever live, shall we ever pass into the picture that my mind has painted, the picture that resembles you?

46

Those treasures, that furniture, that luxury, that order, those perfumes and those miraculous flowers are you. You are also those great rivers and tranquil canals. Those enormous ships that they carry, fully laden with riches, from which the monotonous song of maneuvers rise, are my thoughts, which sleep or fall over your breast. You guide them gently toward the sea that is Infinity, while reflecting the depths of the sky in the limpidity of your beautiful soul—and when, fatigued by the swell and stuffed with the produce of the Orient, they return to their natal port, they are still my enriched thoughts, which are returning from Infinity to you.

Crowds

It is not given to everyone to bathe in the multitude; enjoying crowds is an art, and the only man who can make a tribute of vitality at the expense of the human race is one into whom a fay has breathed in his cradle a taste for disguises and masks, a hatred of the domicile and a passion for voyages.

Multitude and solitude are equal terms, convertible for the poet with an active and fecund brain. Whoever does not know how to populate his solitude does not know either how to be alone in a busy crowd.

The poet enjoys the incomparable privilege of being able, in his fashion, to be himself and someone else. Like errant souls who are in search of a body, he enters whenever he wishes into the personality of another. For him alone, everything is vacant, and if certain places appear to him to be closed it is because, in his view, they are not worth the trouble of being visited.

The solitary and pensive stroller derives a singular intoxication from that universal communion. The man who espouses the crowd easily knows feverish enjoyments, of which the egotist, closed like a casket, and the idler, interned like a mollusk, will be forever deprived. He adopts all the professions, all the joys and all the miseries that circumstances present to him as his own.

What people call amour is very petty, restricted and weak compared to the ineffable orgy, the holy prostitution, of the soul that can give itself entirely, in poetry and charity, to the unexpected that shows itself to the passing stranger.

It is good sometimes to inform the fortunate people of the world, if only to humiliate their stupid pride for a moment, that there are happinesses superior to theirs, vaster and more refined. The founders of colonies, pastors of peoples and missionary priests exiled to the ends of the earth doubtless know something of those mysterious intoxications, and in the bosom of the vast family that their genius has made, they ought to laugh occasionally at those who complain about their precarious fortune and their chaste life.

Widows

Vauvenargues[1] says that in public gardens there are pathways haunted by disappointed ambition, by unfortunate endeavor and broken hearts, by all the tumultuous and closed souls in whom the last sighs of a storm still rumble, and which recoil from the insolent gaze of the joyful and the idle. Those shady retreats are the rendezvous of escapees from life.

It is to those places above all that the poet and the philosopher like to direct their avid conjectures. There is a reliable pasture there; for if there is a place that they disdain to visit, as I insinuated just now, it is, above all, the joy of the rich. That turbulence in the void has nothing that attracts them. On the contrary, they feel irresistibly drawn toward everything that is weak, ruined, saddened and orphaned.

An experienced eye is never mistaken there. In those rigid or dejected features, in those hollow and dull eyes, or brilliant with

1 Luc de Clapiers, Marquis de Vauvenargues (1715-1747) published before his premature death an anonymous collection of stoically-inclined aphorisms, admired by his friends, including Voltaire and the elder Mirabeau, which were belatedly attributed to their author in 1797.

the last flashes of the struggle, in those profound and numerous wrinkles, in those slow and jerky strides, it immediately deciphers the innumerable legends of deceived amour, of mistaken devotion, of unrecompensed efforts, of hunger and cold humbly and silently supported.

Have you ever seen poor widows on solitary benches? Whether they are dressed in mourning or not, it is easy to recognize them. In any case, there is always something lacking in the mourning of the poor, an absence of harmony that renders it more heart-breaking. They are constrained to be miserly in their dolor. The rich wear a full costume in theirs.

Whether the saddest and most desolating widow to behold is one who is dragging a child by the hand with whom she cannot share her reverie or one who is completely alone, I do not know. It happened once that I followed for long hours an afflicted old woman of that species; she was stiff and straight in a worn shawl, wearing a stoical pride throughout her being.

She was evidently condemned by an absolute solitude to the habits of an old bachelor, and the masculine character of her mores added a mysterious piquancy to their austerity. I know in what fashion and in what miserable café she dined. I followed her to the reading room and spied on her for a long time while she searched the gazettes with avid eyes once burned by tears for news of a powerful and personal interest.

Finally, in the afternoon, under a charming autumnal sky, one of those skies from which regrets and memories descend in a host, she sat down to one side in a garden, to listen, far from the crowd, to one of those concerts with which regimental bands gratify the Parisian public.

That was doubtless the petty debauchery of that innocent old woman—or that purified old woman: the well-earned consolation of one of those heavy days devoid of friends, conversation and joy, without a confidant, that God let fall upon her, perhaps for many years, three hundred and sixty-five days a year.

And another:

I can never help casting a glance, if not universally sympathetic, at least curious, over the crowd of pariahs who gather around the enclosure of a public concert. The orchestra hurls songs through the night of celebration, triumph or lust. Robes trail shinily, gazes meet; the idle, fatigued by having done nothing, strut, pretending to be savoring the music indolently. Here, there is nothing but the rich and fortunate, nothing that does not respire and inspire insouciance and the pleasure of letting oneself live—nothing except the rabble leaning on the exterior barrier, catching shreds of the music gratis, at the whim of the wind, and gazing at the sparkling interior furnace.

It is always interesting, that reflection of the joy of the rich in the depths of the eyes of the poor. But that day, among the people dressed in blouses and calico, I perceived an individual whose nobility made a striking contrast with all the surrounding triviality.

It was a tall woman, majestic and so noble in her attitude that I did not remember having seen her like in collections of aristocratic beauties of the past. A perfume of arrogant virtue emanated from her entire person. Her face, sad and thin, was in perfect accordance with the full mourning in which she was dressed. Like the plebeians with whom she was mingled but did not see, she was gazing at the luminous society with profound eyes, and nodding her head gently as she listened.

A singular vision! "Surely," I said to myself, "that poverty, if poverty it is, cannot admit sordid economy; such a noble face responds to me for that. Why, then, does she remain voluntarily in a milieu where she stands out so obviously?"

But in passing close to her curiously, I thought I divined the reason. The tall widow was holding a child by the hand, dressed like her in black; modest as the price of entry was, perhaps that price sufficed to pay for one of the child's needs, or better still, a superfluity, a toy.

And she would go home on foot, meditative and pensive, always alone; for a child is turbulent, egotistical, devoid of mildness and patience, and cannot even serve as a confidant of solitary dolors, like a pure animal, a dog or a cat.

The Old Mountebank

People on holiday were on display, spread out, enjoying themselves everywhere. It was one of those solemnities on which, for a long time, mountebanks, jugglers, showers of animals and ambulant stallholders have relied to repair the bad times of the year.

On those days, it seems that people forget everything, dolor and toil alike; they become similar to children. For the young, it is a day of leave, the horror of school put off for twenty-four hours. For the adult, it is an armistice concluded with the malevolent powers of life, a respite in contention and the universal struggle.

Even the man of the world, the man occupied with intellectual labor, finds it difficult to escape the influence of that popular jubilation. Without wanting to, they absorb their share of that atmosphere of insouciance. For myself, a true Parisian, I never fail to pass in review all the stalls that are paraded in those solemn epochs.

They were engaged, in truth, in a formidable competition. They wailed, bellowed and howled; there was a medley of cries, detonations of brass and explosions of rockets; the red-noses and the Jocrisses convulsed the features of their tanned faces, shriveled by wind, rain and sun; with the aplomb of performers sure of their effect they launched witticisms and jokes of a solid comedy as heavy as Molière's. The Strong Men, proud of the enormity of their limbs, devoid of foreheads and crania, like orangutans, strutted majestically in their leotards, washed the day before for the occasion. The dancers, as beautiful as fays or princesses, leapt and capered under the fire of lanterns that filled their skirts with sparks.

Everything was light, dust, cries, joy, tumult; some were spending money, others earning it, both equally joyful. Children suspended themselves from their mothers' skirts in order to obtain a stick of barley-sugar, or climbed on to their fathers' shoulders in order to get a better view of a conjurer as dazzling as a god. And circulating everywhere, dominating all the perfumes, an odor of frying was like the incense of that festival.

At the extreme end of the row of stalls, as if, ashamed, he had exiled himself from all those splendors, I saw a poor mountebank, stooped, enfeebled and decrepit, a human ruin, leaning against one of the stakes of his hut, a hut more wretched than that of the most brutal savage, the distress of which was illuminated all too clearly by two candle-stubs, melting and smoking.

Everywhere else there was joy, profit and debauchery; everywhere, the certainty of bread for days to come, the frenetic explosion of vitality. Here, there was absolute poverty, poverty clad, to complete the horror, in comical rags, into which necessity, far more than art, had introduced the contrast. The wretch was not laughing; he was not weeping, he was not dancing, he was not gesticulating, he was not shouting and he was not singing any song; neither cheerful not lamentable, he was not begging. He was mute and motionless. He had given up; he had abdicated. His destiny was fulfilled.

But what a profound, unforgettable gaze he was parading over the crowd and the lights, the moving flood of which stopped a few paces away from his repulsive misery! I felt my throat constricted by the terrible hand of hysteria, and it seemed to me that my gaze was obscured by rebellious tears that did not want to fall.

What to do? What was the point of asking the unfortunate what curiosity, what marvel he had to show in the stinking darkness behind his torn curtain? In truth, I dared not, and even though the reason for my timidity might make you laugh, I confess that I feared humiliating him. In the end, I had just resolved to deposit, as I passed by, a little money on one of his planks, hoping that he would divine my intention, when a great flood of people caused by I know not what disturbance dragged me away from him.

As I went home, obsessed by that vision, I tried to analyze my sudden dolor, and I said to myself: "I have just seen the image of the old man of letters who has survived the generation of which he was the brilliant entertainer; of the old poet, devoid of friends, family and children, degraded by poverty and public ingratitude in the stall that forgetful society no longer wants to enter."

STÉPHANE MALLARMÉ
(1842-1898)

Stéphane Mallarmé contributed a series of *poèmes en prose* to the *Revue des arts et des lettres* in 1867 entitled "Pages oubliées" [Forgotten Pages] for reasons that are typically unclear; the first four of them are translated below. At that time, his poetry was heavily influenced by Baudelaire, but it became much more distinctive as time went by. He lived a peripatetic existence for a while, earning a meager living as an English teacher and hack journalist, mostly for fashion magazines, working in various provincial schools before returning to Paris, but his true vocation was the salon he hosted every Tuesday for many years: a writers' workshop in which he worked out the literary theory of a *Grand Oeuvre* that he never completed. The effort he put into its development while procrastinating became the original gospel of the Symbolist Movement; poetry became his religion, or substitute thereof in a godless world, and he became its hierophant. His intense interest in the sonic qualities of his verse and, especially in his later work, in the visual aspects of the typography of printed versions, makes his verse exceedingly difficult to translate, but recommended it very warmly to Jean Des Esseintes in Huysmans' *À rebours*. Extrapolation of Théophile Gautier's classic analysis of Baudelaire's "Decadent style" prompted Remy de Gourmont to consider Mallarmé as *the* Decadent, and thus to declare after his death that Decadence had died with him—a remark subsequently echoed in the context of a different thesis, in Roland Barthes's notion of "the death of the author," which reflected a challenging trend in modern literary theory. The influence that Mallarmé exercised via his *mardis* and their spinoff was enormous, helping to orientate and shape the careers of many of the younger writers of the Symbolist/Decadent Movement, who included several significant writers of *poèmes en prose*.

The Poor Pale Child

Poor pale child, why are you crying your shrill and insolent song at the top of your voice in the street, which is lost among the cats, lords of the rooftops?

For it will not traverse the shutters of the first floor, behind which you are unaware of heavy curtains of incarnadine silk.

However, you sing fatally, with the tenacious assurance of a little man who goes through life alone, not counting on anyone, working for yourself. Have you ever had a father? You do not even have an old woman who will make you forget your hunger by beating you when you come home without a sou.

But you work for yourself. And, standing in the streets, clad in discolored garments cut like a man's, preciously thin and too tall for your age, you sing in order to eat, doggedly, without lowering your malevolent eyes toward the other children playing on the pavement.

And your *complainte* is so loud, so loud that your bare head, which is lifted into the air as your voice rises, seemingly wants to depart from your little shoulders.

Little man, who knows whether it might not go one day, when, after having cried for a long time in the city, you have committed a crime?

For a crime is not very difficult to commit; it is sufficient to have courage in accordance with one's desire, and we who desire . . . Your little face is energetic.

Not one sou descends into the wicker basket that your long hand is holding, hanging hopelessly over your trousers; that will render you wicked, and one day you will commit a crime.

But your head is still lifted up, already wanting to quit you—as if it knows in advance—while you sing a song that is becoming menacing.

It will bid you adieu when you pay for me, and for those who are worth less than me. And you probably came into the world for that purpose, and that is why you are fasting now; we shall see you in the newspapers.

Oh, poor little head!

The Barbary Organ

Since Maria left me to go to another star—oh, which one, Orion, Altair or you, green Venus?—I have always cherished solitude. How many long days I have spent alone with my cat! By "alone" I mean without a material being; my cat is a mystical companion, a spirit. I can therefore say that I have spent long days alone with my cat, and alone with one of the last authors of the Latin decadence; for since the white creature is no more, strangely and singularly, I have loved everything that is summarized by the word "fall." Thus, my favorite season of the year is the last languid days of summer, which immediately precede autumn, and within the day, the hour when I go for a walk is the one in which the sun reposes before vanishing, when its rays are coppery yellow over the gray walls and coppery red on the window-panes. In the same way, the literature from which my mind demands a sad sensuality is the agonizing poetry of the last moments of Rome—as long, however, as it does not respire any of the rejuvenating approach of the Barbarians and does not stammer the infantile Latin of early Christian prose.

So, I was reading one of those dear poems, whose plaques of make-up exercise more charm upon me than the incarnadine of youth, and plunging one hand into the fur of the pure animal, when a Barbary organ sang languidly and melancholically beneath my window.

It was playing in the great avenue of poplars, the leaves of which seemed yellow to me, even in spring, since Maria had passed that way, with church candles, for the last time.

The instrument of sadness *par excellence*! The piano scintillates, the violin opens to the torn soul the light of alleluias, but the Barbary organ, in the dusk of memory, makes me dream desperately.

And yet, it was murmuring a joyously vulgar tune, which put gaiety into the heart of the faubourgs, an old-fashioned, banal tune.

How did it come about that its ritornelle went to my soul and made me weep, like a romantic ballad? I savored it slowly, and I did not throw a sou out of the window for fear of disturbing myself and perceiving that the instrument was not singing on its own.

Oh, the Barbary organ, at five o'clock on an autumn evening, under the yellow poplars, Maria!

The Orphan

An orphan already, a child with sadness anticipating the Poet, I wandered clad in black, eyes lowered from the sky, searching for a family on earth. Once, fairground stalls stopped under trees near a river, whose dead wood broke in the wind. Did I divine a relationship, and that I would later be one of them, loving the life of those comedians and going toward them in order to forget my hideous comrades? Through the planks arrived an ancient wind of choruses, children's voices cursing a tyrant, with shrill tirades, for Thalia[1] lived in the tent and was awaiting the holy hour of Argand lamps. I prowled before the trestles, proud, but more tremulous than the thought of speaking is to a child too young to play with his brethren, one of whom was leaning against the scarlet images of doublets and romantic audacity painted by a master who, perhaps alone at that moment, believed in the Middle Ages. The child—I can still see him, coiffed in a night-cap shaped like Dante's hood—was eating, in the form of a white cheese sandwich, stolen lilies, snow, swansdown, the stars, and all the sacred whiteness of poets; I would have begged him to admit me to his meal if I had not been so timid, but he was sharing it with another who arrived abruptly, leaping: a little acrobat from the neighboring tent, in which feats of strength were about to be shown, a frivolous exercise not refusing the banality of broad daylight. He was stark naked in a washed leotard and pirouetted with a surprising turbulence; it was him who

---

1 Thalia was the muse of comedy and idyllic poetry.

56

spoke to me: "Where are your parents?" "I have none," I said to him. "Oh, you have no father? I have one, myself. If you knew how amusing it is to have a father; one is always laughing . . . even the other evening, when my little brother had been put on the ground, he made more beautiful grimaces when the master launched slaps and kicks at him. My dear," he said, raising his dislocated leg with a glorious facility, "he amuses me greatly, Papa." Then he bit into the younger child's sandwich again, who did not say anything. "And you don't have a Mama either, so you're all alone? Mine eats flax and everyone claps their hands. You don't know that? There it is: parents are funny people who make us laugh," But his parade was about begin and he left after saying that. I went away on my own, thinking that it was very sad that I didn't have parents, like him.

The Pipe

Yesterday I picked up my pipe, dreaming about a long evening of travail, good winter toil. I had thrown away cigarettes, with all the infantile joys of summer, in the past illuminated by the blue foliage of summer, muslins and birds. And I picked up my grave pipe again like a serious man who wants to smoke for a long time without disturbing himself, in order to work better. But I did not expect the nice surprise that that relaxation was preparing for me. I had scarcely expelled the first puff when I forgot the great books I had to write; wonderstruck and moved, I respired last winter, which returned. I had not touched that faithful friend since I had returned to France, and all of London, London as I alone had lived it entirely a year ago, appeared to me: first those dear boulevards that muffle the brain and have an odor of their own when they penetrate the casements. My tobacco smelled like my somber room, with leather furniture powdered by coal-dust, over which my thin black cat wandered; the big fires, and the maid with red arms pouring the coal, and the sound of the coal falling from the metal bucket into the fire-basket in the morning, while the postman solemnly rapped twice, bringing me back to life! I saw once again the sickly trees of the deserted square visible through the window. I also saw the sea, which I had traversed so frequently that winter, shivering on the deck of the steamer, moistened by mist and blackened by smoke—with my poor beloved wandering in traveling costume: a long gray dress the color of the dust of roads, a long gray mantle that clung damply to her cold shoulders, one of those bell-shaped straw hats devoid of a feather and almost devoid of ribbons, which rich ladies throw away when they arrive, ruined by the sea air, and which poor beloveds pick up in order to embellish themselves for several seasons more. Around her neck was wrapped the terrible kerchief that one agitates as one says goodbye forever.

PAUL VERLAINE
(1844-1896)

Paul Verlaine contributed to *Le Parnasse contemporain*, and to almost all of the periodicals that appeared in its wake, especially those espousing the Symbolist cause, but he always seemed something of a maverick. He was an alcoholic who frequently put on a show of repenting and renouncing the demon drink but always relapsed. His career changed fortune and direction several times, most spectacularly in 1872 when he ran away from Paris and his wife with Arthur Rimbaud, first to Brussels and then to London; Rimbaud tried unavailingly to prevent him from being jailed after being wounded by gunshots fired in the course of a drunken quarrel. Verlaine later worked as a teacher in various English schools, and served another term of imprisonment in 1885 before returning to Paris, in poor health but with his legend intact. In his classic collection of literary studies, *Les Poètes maudits* (1884), which can be reckoned one of the key texts of the embryonic Decadent Movement, he analyzed his own works in anagrammatical disguise, attributing them to "Pauvre Lélian." His first published *poème en prose*, "Nevermore," appeared in the *Revue des lettres et des arts*; the other item translated below appeared nearly twenty years later, in the *Revue Independante*, in 1885.

Nevermore

The humble tavern of old is full of the light of the setting sun; the warm glow ignites the windows, dances on the floor tiled with red bricks, sprinkles with bloody stars the oak dresser with brass fittings, and comes all the way to the table where I am dreaming, my hands under my chin, to tint the black beer in the large tankard crimson.

The landlady is still the one that I knew; at most she has a few white hairs in her tawny tresses; she talks to me about her husband, who is a blacksmith, and her children, the eldest of whom will go into the lottery[1] in five years, I have some difficulty understanding her because she expresses herself in patois, and some difficulty in responding, because I am dreaming.

While dreaming, I cast my gaze through the low window at the highway, which leads to the main street of a village whose first habitations are visible. One of them is a little taller than the others, and the radiance coming from the west caresses its roof-tiles with a particular solicitude.

At intervals, a horse passes by, dragging a harrow or a plow guided by a rustic, whistling or swearing, depending on the speed of the rig, or a hunter with light baggage, who regrets the heavy game-bags of six weeks ago. The peasant and the hunter sometimes come in, drink, pay and leave, after smoking a pipe and exchanging some news. For myself, I am dreaming.

---

1 At the time conscription to the army was determined by a lottery of all young men of eligible age—an event whose approach was regarded with horror by peasant families who needed the labor that their sons contributed to their collective endeavour and could not afford to lose them.

And I see myself in that same tavern, younger by only a few months, sitting at the table on which my elbows are resting at present, and drinking there, as today, from a large tankard, black beer that the setting sun has just tinted crimson.

And I think about the Friend, the Sister, who scolded me for being late every evening when I returned, and for whom men clad in black and white, singing in Latin, came in search one winter morning.

And the horrible dejection of unforgettable misfortunes penetrates me, silently, while the night, invading the tavern where I am dreaming, chases me toward the house by the roadside that is a little taller than the other habitations, the joyous and pleasant house of old, where two little girls in somber dresses, cheerful and noisy, came to greet me, who will not remember, and who will be playing *maman*—their favorite recreation—until it is time to go to sleep.

A Clock

In the hotel room in which the Sage was living while awaiting the end of some annoying business affairs, the clock was very particular. Not that it affected some eccentric form or simply more bad taste than all clocks usually exhibit. Even the base was pretty, in white marble with copper corners of a simple and light metalwork.

A subject in bronze electroplating represented Paul under a palm tree, his right hand above his eyes, gazing perpetually toward the sea and the dear vessel that was only bringing Virginie back for shipwreck and death.[1] In sum, considering it purely as a work of horology, it marked the hour exactly and in accord with all the official clocks in the city.

The originality of the clock consisted of a phenomenon that was very simple to explain: a grain of dust to expel from the

---

1 In Bernardin de Saint-Paul's mawkish classic *Paul et Virginie* (1788).

chime or the glass of the globe, and that was all. But he was often dolorously aware of it, and sometimes cruelly. Judge for yourself, and don't laugh too much.

The chime was hoarse, flat and dull; it commenced at seven o'clock and stated, in curt, harsh clicks without any vibration, like a consumptive cough, two o'clock when it was eight and three o'clock when it was nine, and so on, in *striking* contrast with the sincerity of the hands and the tender, cheerful, bright and becoming general appearance of the little item of furniture

Gradually, however, that very contrast came to please him bitterly, severely if you wish. So habituated was he to weighing things—which is nothing, fundamentally, in sum, but leaning on them—and with the aid of a providential gift, he arrived, by virtue of obstinate reflections and accepted suffering, in extracting from that minimal torture, as the strong are able to do with all tortures, an entire philosophy, which it would be ridiculous to summarize in this brief essay, but of which these are the essential lines:

You resemble that clock, you see; you resemble it too much, or not enough.

Too much, because you sing out of tune. Good, you are bad; true, you speak falsely; pure, you are hoarse in conduct. Whereas the hands of your conduct are correct, the chime of your life is absurd, and also disagreeable to everyone and hateful to those who might love you—which would be well done. Not enough, for that Paul, who has the same forename as you, is at least waiting for Virginie under that palm tree and will wait for her forever on that clock. Have you waited for long? Yes, certainly. Will you wait forever? Yes, you say—but I, your conscience, say to you: "Get away!"

Six o'clock; twelve strokes. Seven o'clock, one stroke. Eight o'clock, two strokes.

"Woe!" says the clock. Or: "Patience." It's the same thing. isn't it?

CATULLE MENDÈS
(1841-1909)

Catulle Mendès was the most prolific writer of *poèmes en prose*, and the most enthusiastic promoter of the genre, after setting a crucial precedent by publishing an interrupted set of Baudelaire's under that title in his *Revue fantaisiste* in 1862; in the same periodical he published the first of his many hybrids of poetry in prose with mock-folkloristic *contes*, "As You Like It," signed "Hippolyte Nazet." The item was reprinted in the *Revue des lettres et des arts* in 1868—where it was identified as a *poème en prose* on the contents page—as "La Clef des songes," this time signed "H. Tezan." Mendès went on to write hundreds more times in a similar vein in the 1880s and 1890s for newspapers, initially for *Gil Blas* and then for the literary supplement of the *Petit Parisien*, the *Écho de Paris* and *Le Journal*, among others, often serving as each paper's literary editor and thus able to publish his own work with scant regard for the relative unfashionability of both *contes* and prose poetry, compensating for his idiosyncrasy by interleaving his hybrids with more conventional salacious anecdotes of dubious Parisian mores. He often arranged his hybrid works in series bearing such headings as "Nouveaux Contes de Jadis," "Les Tendres légendes" and "Nouveaux lieds de France."

Many of the authors Mendès recruited to the "stables" whose members contributed a story a week or a fortnight to the newspapers for which he worked joined in the game, and although the great majority of their contributions were framed as orthodox anecdotal tales of Parisian life, many of them featured the kind of fantastic hybridization that Mendès had pioneered, making it impossible to draw a clear distinction between poems in prose and fables, apologues and allegories set in imaginary milieux. He often split his newspaper columns into several vignettes, after the fashion of the items from the 11 December 1889 issue of *L'Écho de Paris*, described therein as "Rondels" which are translated below after "The Key to Dreams," and are followed by another item from the 5 June 1889 issue of the same newspaper.

Translations of many more of Mendès' hybrid tales can be found in the collections *Bluebirds* (2017), *The Little Fays in the Air and Other Tales of Faerie* (2019) and *Don Juan in Paradise and Other Amorous Fantasies* (2019).

The Key to Dreams

A handsome young man in steel armor was riding a white mare; a young woman in a silk bodice saw the handsome young man pass by.

"In truth," she said, "wherever he is coming from and wherever he is going, that cavalier is taking my heart with him."

She made him a signal to stop and said: "I love you."

"I don't love you," replied the young man. And he went on his way.

The young woman ran after him.

"Where have you come from?" she asked. "And where are you going?"

"I've come from the city where my beloved lives, and I'm going to meet my rival, who will arrive this evening."

"What did you say to your beloved when you were with her?"

"I asked her for her heart."

"What will you say to your rival when you encounter him?"

"I shall ask him for his blood."

And the young man wanted to continue his route.

It was morning. The sun opened its eye on the horizon, still furrowed with shadow. The little birds, awakened and chirping in the foliage, were planning pleasure-parties through the spring woods.

"Would you like me to go with you?" asked the young woman.

"No," replied the young man. "The only person by whom I would like to be accompanied is at home presently."

"Only let me climb up on the rump behind you, and I won't ask anything more."

"Men do not have the custom of going into combat with a woman on the rump of their horse."

And the cavalier spurred his beast.

✳

"Bellina," asked Puck, "why are you so desolate?"

"My only amour is going away and I can't follow him."

"Is your lover that handsome young man in steel armor who is riding a white mare?"

"That's him. His eyes are as blue as the sky and his hair as black as the night."

"When I want it, Bellina, the idle tortoise overtakes the clouds, and swift stallions suddenly slow down, to run less rapidly than little children. Follow your only amour, Bellina; where he is going you will arrive at the same time as him."

Bellina started walking, and the pebbles on which she placed her little bare feet said to her: "Thank you, Bellina."

But the malicious Puck had deceived the young woman; she walked all night in vain, and did not catch up with the cavalier whose eyes were as blue as the sky. At midnight, however, she saw a great white phantom pass by on the road.

"Who are you?"

"I was a handsome young man with hair as black as night, and now I am no longer anything. I encountered my rival at a nearby crossroads; we fought and my rival killed me."

"Where are you going?"

"I'm going to the city, to the dwelling where my beloved is asleep."

"Would you like me to go with you?"

"No. Tonight, profiting from my beloved's sleep, I want to bid her adieu in her dreams."

And the phantom vanished.

✳

"Why are you weeping?" asked Puck, stupidly.

"Alas, my only amour is dead, and I'm still alive."

"Is the specter that has just passed along the road the phantom of your lover?"

"That's him. His rival has torn out his hair as black as night, and his eyes as blue as the sky have wept with regret for having quit his beloved."

"I know the herbs that revive and I know the herbs that cause death. Find the body of your lover and I'll give him a herb that revives."

"O Puck, you deceive when it's a matter of doing good, but you tell the truth when it's a matter of doing harm. Give me a herb that causes death."

Puck gave her four leaves of a plant that is called Simonne in memory of an amorous story.[1] Bellina bore the leaves to her lips and died without suffering.

Bellina's soul rose up toward the sky; she saw a soul that was descending toward Hell. By the light of a star she recognized the soul of the handsome young man.

"Where are you going, soul of my only love?"

"Alas, alas, I talked abut love to my beloved in her dreams, and my posthumous kisses brushed her forehead. I'm damned and I'm going to Hell."

"Would you like me to go with you? I'll console you in your torments, I'll lift you up in your weakness, I'll love you in eternity! My amour will be the source of calm and resignation extended over the lips of your dolor. Would you like me to go with you?"

"No, only the memory of my beloved will accompany me."

And the soul of the handsome young man was engulfed in darkness, while the soul of the young woman rose up toward the light.

✳

"My dear," said Ninon to Ninette, "doubtless this means that within a week you'll marry your friend Étienne, who has eyes as blue as the sky and hair as black as the night!"

✳

As it was very hot, Madelette decided to go bathe in the sea. She approached the shore and considered the deep and tumultuous water for a long time. But Madelette was the daughter of a siren

---

1 Possibly Victor Magnin's *Simonne* (1832).

and the fury of the waves was pleasant for her. She undressed, hung her clothes on a willow and went down to the sea along the fine sand. For a long time she rocked herself on the waves, swimming easily, delighted with the freshness that penetrated her. When she had enjoyed herself thoroughly in that way, she went back up to the beach. A cunning zephyr had carried away her clothes on its wing, like a thief, and Madelette searched for them in vain. A great anger seized her when she heard the wind among the branches, happy to see her so beautiful and naked, laughing and applauding the success of its ruse, but anger solves nothing. The bather was forced to return to her abode without a dress; and I can assure you that she was deeply ashamed.

Fortunately, on her way she found an old tree with broad smooth leaves.

"Take one of my branches," said the merciful tree, "and strip it of leaves."

Madelette chose the bushiest branch; but it did no good to apply the leaves to her skin; they fell to the ground, in spite of their keen desire to remain attached to that beautiful snowy body.

Madelette, greatly chagrined, went on her way. At a bend in the path she saw a hawthorn, which divined her embarrassment.

"My sister," said the spring bush, "break off some of my thorns and you can use them as needles to sew your green dress."

Madelette's fingers took possession of the pointed darts, and she tried to pin them in her flesh in order to fix the flighty foliage; but at the first attempt a tear of pink blood sprang forth under the thorn and Madelette uttered a cry of alarm.

However, the Virgin Mary, not liking young women to go naked through the fields in that fashion, let her choose a few pieces of thread from her celestial distaff. Madelette sat down on the edge of the ditch and, in less time than it takes to pull the petals off a hollyhock, with the charming artistry that only women have, she had made a dress that sparkled like a rose-chafer's corselet. A nutshell served her as a thimble, hawthorn thorns are good needles, and the Virgin's thread stitched a cloth of foliage delightfully.

66

Madelette went on her way, very happy and proud of her beautiful costume.

"Uh oh!" said a faint, hissing voice that emerged from beneath a clump of forget-me-nots, "the silly girl is going to Titania's ball without a necklace."

"Handsome green lizard," said Madelette, "would you like to serve as my necklace?"

"Gladly," replied the lizard.

Madelette went to look for it under the flowers, put it on her shoulder, and the cold and shiny reptile wrapped itself around the young woman's neck of its own accord.

"What, Madelette," said the glow-worms, "you don't have pearls or rubies in your ears?"

"That's true," said Madelette, and she suspended a living amethyst from each of her delicate ears.

Thus adorned, Madelette went to Titania's ball.

Little fays were dancing in the shade of great trees. And Madelette was so pretty with her singular costume that the king of the Gnomes fell in love with her. He invited her to dance.

"Refuse," said the lizard, moved by jealousy and lifting his head toward the child's ear.

Madelete took no notice of what the lizard said.

"Darling," sighed the king during the languorous waltz, "if you want, I'll wait for you down there and I'll marry you."

"I'd like that, milord," the girl replied.

"Don't go there," said the lizard, when the waltz ended.

Madelette pretended not to have heard, and, perceiving that the king of the Gnomes had disappeared, she got up in order to go down there, where he was waiting for her.

"Beware," said the lizard; and, opening its little green mouth, it stuck out its menacing dart.

Madelette felt her living necklace tighten, but, entirely given to the joy of marrying the king of the Gnomes, she did not understand that warning.

"Milord," she said to the king when she had rejoined him, "speak to me amorously and I'll give you my little finger to kiss."

At that moment, a shrill hiss was heard; Madelette went pale, and suddenly, with a brief muffled cry, she collapsed on the ground, strangled, dead! The lizard, which strongly resembled a viper, slipped away through the grass, and the king of the Gnomes had to return to the ball in search of another wife.

✳

"My dear," said Ninette to Ninon, "this one means that your wedding dress will be the most beautiful in the world, and that your husband will give you a necklace of topazes, and ruby earrings!"

✳

And that is how, under the tall trees of the convent where they had made their novitiate of amour, the two little girls, Ninon and Ninette, interpreted their whimsies, to the profit of their dreams.

For Her and Them

I
The Perfume Less Sweet

In approaching my mouth to the adorable mouth, the pink threshold of the only paradise that my pilgrimage sometimes desires, I could not defend myself from a sad surprise because of the perfume that emanated that day from the dear half-closed lips.

Sweet and exquisite as it was, the odor of fresh breath that I sensed coming to meet my breath was not as sweet as usual as I approached my mouth to the adorable mouth, the pink threshold of the only paradise that my pilgrim sometimes desires.

By what cruel miracle were you less delectably aromal, crimson calyx of young flesh? I was astonished and anxious; but I smiled, having seen that my darling, playfully, had put a rose between her teeth, and it was a veritable flower that I had respired as I approached my mouth to the adorable mouth.

II
The Lying Snow

Why should I not go along the pale path to ask that snow—which, in its whiteness, resembles daisies, wild daisies, loyal and veridical diviners of amour—by shredding it flake by flake, what it augurs of the eternal kiss that my darling swore to me?

Certainly, being so pure, that snow—which, in its whiteness, resembles daisies, wild daisies, loyal and veridical diviners of amour—would not want to deceive, on a point of that importance, the poet who so often makes it know the glory of beautiful metaphors.

But no, I have not gone along the pale path and I have not interrogated the snow. For, in its visible candor, it is also like your breast, darling, your breast which had abused me so many times with its lying beats; and doubtless it would have lied, like your sighs and your delights, that snow, which, in its whiteness, resembles daisies.

III
The Chemise of the Wayfaring Tree

A diaphanous and light veil in which two roundnesses are transparent, a chemise is quivering on the flowering wayfaring tree beside the path! And I am surprised, for ordinarily, it is the wings of turtle-doves, and not the chemises of young women, that settle on bushes.

I am mistaken; it isn't fabric that is trembling there; but why is that wisp of morning mist imitating, unmistakably, a diaphanous and light veil in which two roundnesses are transparent, a chemise, on the flowering wayfaring tree beside the path?

The wayfaring tree responds to me: "Once when you wanted to undress her in solitude, I saw your mistress retain the supreme modesty of a little pale mystery; and since my snowballs resemble her beautiful timid breasts, it is befitting for me, like her, to have a chemise, of almost-batiste mist, a diaphanous and light veil in which two roundnesses are transparent!"

IV
The Little Corpse

Dead at fifteen! Suzon was fifteen years old, and she is dead. She has been put into a very small coffin, hardly any larger than a cradle. A gravestone has been ordered from the marble-cutter with the inscription: *Here lies Suzon.*

I had come back from far away—oh, so far!—to ask her for a kiss she had promised me once, as a little girl. But someone said to me on the way: "What? You don't know! Dead at fifteen! Suzon was fifteen yeas old, and she is dead."

I cried: "I can't believe it! There are so many old people in the region who are still alive. It's not in spring that lilies wither." They replied: "She has been put into a very small coffin, hardly any larger than a cradle."

In the cemetery, I looked for her grave. I couldn't find it at first among so many others. "Can you tell me where Suzette has been buried, Monsieur?" "No, Monsieur; all that I know is that a gravestone was ordered from the marble-cutter with an inscription."

But at the foot of a birch tree, I saw a little pink rose that was partly open. Oh, how pretty it was and how good it smelled! "Surely," I said to myself, "it's here that Suzon lies."

Dead at fifteen.

V
The Good Excuse

It's me who wanted her not to wear a corset any longer,[1] because the whalebone, in spite of the plush and the silk, bruised her delicate flesh. I never believed that because of that, she would allow herself to be embraced by others, alas, than me, eight or ten times a day, morning or evening, no matter!

---

1 In her autobiography, Judith Gautier reported, ruefully, that her father had only ever given her two pieces of advice, both of which she had ignored, to her cost: always wear a corset; and don't marry Catulle Mendès.

I was annoyed, I quarreled with her; she replied: "Nothing is more painful to my modesty, I assure you, than those frequent embraces. But there it is, I'm obliged to do it; It's necessary not . . ." (It's me who wanted her not to wear a corset any longer, because the whalebone, in spite of the plush and the silk, bruised her delicate flesh.)

". . . It's necessary not to order me to quit the continuous embrace wherever the upper body feels compressed; I'm so accustomed to it that, no longer having it, I need to replace it as often as I can." What could I reply to that? Evidently, she was not wrong, the poor darling. It's me who wanted her not to wear a corset any longer.

The Embarrassment of God the Father after Creating the Sun and the Moon

One night in June, beautiful with azure and stars, when they had kissed one another on the lips for three happy hours—and believe that, far from being clad in samite and furs, he had had no other garment during the time of that long kiss than his lover's caresses, nor she any but her lover's accolade—they thought that they would experience some pleasure in considering the stars, as luminous and vacillating as golden dragonflies caught in a blue lake. Ladies and demoiselles, if, before obliging you to supreme sighs, a lover takes it into his head to lead you to the window in order to enable you to admire the constellation, it is your right to experience, with regard to that strange servant, all the disdain of which you are capable; but what is hardly appropriate, when the moments offer themselves to a sweeter employment, is not at all inappropriate after moments that have been employed as well as possible; and contemplating the celestial gleams is another fashion of rendering homage, ladies and demoiselles, to your eyes.

Thus, on that June night, Azalaïs de Roquemartine—than whom there was no one more beautiful between the Rhône and the Adour—had not refused to lean on the window sill of the turret in order to gaze at the clear azure in the company of her lover, Giraud de Salignac, who, as well as being a nobleman, was a very good composer of tensons and sirventes.

In a voice to which the nightingale of the nearby wood listened with a jealous pleasure, she said: "How pretty they are to look at! Couldn't one believe that marvelous flowers of flame and diamond were opening and palpitating in the delectable heavens? For myself, I can't believe that a few clerics are well-indoctrinated who imagine, and try to make us believe, that the stars are worlds similar to the obscure earth on which we exist."

Giraud de Salignac would have had his ten fingers cut off rather than contradict Dame Azalaïs—and, truly, who would dare not to agree with the opinion of a beautiful mouth? Not without a fine appearance of emphasis, he cried:

"Rose, clarity, perfume, delight—it's you that I mean, my love—you have spoken with a great deal of sense. No, those lights aren't kneaded from our mud, somber rocks and tenebrous waves, and since it's in them rather than anything else created that beauty and soft clarity reside, it's necessary that the stars were made out of you, my lady, or a reflection of you!"

Azalaïs de Roquemartine, accustomed as she was to the excessive gallantries of her servant, could not help judging, this time, that he was going a little beyond plausibility in his desire to praise.

However, he continued: "May the mandolin break between my fingers if I can't prove what I say with good arguments!"

With the air of someone sure of his facts, he said: "When our Lord God had created light on the first day, and the heavens on the second, when, to distract himself in his labor, he immediately made his thunder crash, and on the third he had assembled the waters in a single place, at the beginning of the fourth day he made the sun and the moon, and he was very content with having made them, for the magnificence of middays must have been superb over the florid earth and the seas white with foam, and the moon must have been tender and plaintive in the melancholy nights. However, it seemed to him that the moon was insufficient for the perfect enchantment of evenings; something was lacking in the nocturnal sky with that sole icy splendor; it was necessary to imagine and produce another marvel; and our Lord God meditated, rather perplexed. Now, at that moment, my love, you were strolling through the new creation, full of surprise and joy."

At that statement, Azalaïs de Roquemarine burst out laughing, as was quite natural, for what means was there of imagining that she had been born in the time when Eve had not yet smiled among the as-yet-unopened roses of the future Eden?

"Well," Giraud de Salignac continued, "were you not, on that fourth day of the world, the woman that you are today for the ecstasy of my eyes and the delights of my heart? But since, as no one is unaware, all beautiful women were angels in heaven before charming us on earth, you were in the most exquisite divine abode of the seraphim. And as I said, you were strolling, full of a happy surprise, among the prodigies of the recent creation, admiring the great verdant trees, as yet devoid of birds, and the blooming bushes. But what pleased you most of all was the sea, the lakes and the streams.

"As it was not very warm down here, because the light, being very young, did not have much strength as yet, the water was solidified into ice everywhere, with the consequence that it was as if there were countless large and small mirrors everywhere. Already coquettish, you took an infinite pleasure in looking at yourself in the water, and the water was no less content than you were; and the reflection of your eyes, more luminous than the sun, of your forehead, which resembled the first snow, of your radiant hair, and of all your grace—for angels are only clad in diaphanous cloud—was so precious to it that it was careful, when you had gone, not to let it escape; it kept it in its entirety in the solidity of its mirrors; your image was scattered, innumerably, in the universal water.

"Meanwhile, still perplexed, the Lord God was still thinking about the fashion in which he ought to complete the nocturnal beauty of the heavens. He had racked his brain without finding anything that appeared to be worth the trouble of creating it, to such an extent that he finally became irritated at having, by the fourth day, such an uninventive mind, and, seizing the lightning in a gesture of chagrin, he launched it into space. Now, you can guess what happened: throughout the firmament, all the way to the furthest extremes of pace, billions of exquisite gleams suddenly scintillated. The stars had been created, because the thunder, in splintering, and shattering all the water hardened into ice, had scattered your luminous image throughout the sky!"

When she had pardoned the extravagant praise of that tale with a kiss, she said: "Well, I'd like to believe you; all those stars, since it pleases you to think so, are the debris of my angelic reflection. But I'll wager that, even by applying yourself as best you can, you aren't capable of recognizing in any one of these stars some particular part of me."

"Oh, how wrong you are to wager!" he replied. "Those two celestial scintillations up there, so far away, a little golden and a little blue, are your eyes, my love! In the pale snow of the Milky Way I rediscover the whiteness of your shoulders and your flowery cleavage. That cluster of almost red radiance is the ardent redness of your hair. Here, in the direction of Orion, is not that little dot of pink flame the tip of your little finger? Mars is shining like the nail of your big toe. That dainty little white cameo veiled by a cloud, which one might think a diaphanous fabric, is precisely your dainty navel, my lady! And, deeper in the mysteries of the unknown, in the fleeting delights of infinity, that gilded, burning and living star, like a foam of flame, that star opening like a strange blonde flower with a russet pistil is . . ."

"Aiee!" said Azakaïs de Roquemartine. "Stop there, if you please, for your astrology can only be disquieting for an honest, slightly prudish person like me; and you have so little respect for the stars that you might be capable eventually of wanting to take them in your hand."

LOUIS DE LYVRON
(1835-1894)

"Louis de Lyvron" was a pseudonym employed by Antoine-Louis Duclaux, Comte de L'Estoille, who called himself Antoine de L'Estoille in everyday life and used the signature "A. de L'Estoille" in the second phase of his career. He first began writing while he was an officer in the spahis stationed in Algeria, and excerpts from a journal of that service were printed in *Le Journal des Desmoiselles* in 1862-63, where they were followed by a handful of *contes* and articles before the appearance as a book of the prose-poem *Les Runes d'Attila* (1866). In the *Revue des lettres et des arts*, he published collages of fragmentary memoirs and prose-poems as "Fusains" [charcoal sketches] as well as prose-poems imitative of Arab songs. Lyvron became an avid composer of *poèmes en prose,* some of them long, often presented in a dramatic format that was later employed frequently by Catulle Mendés in newspaper pieces, which he often labeled "pantomimes."

L'Estoille began to work in the 1860s on an epic poem of French mythical history as reconstituted by such fanciful Romantic historians as Henri Martin—two parts of which were printed in *Poèmes en prose* (1868), one of four volumes issued by Alphonse Lemerre, the publisher of *Le Parnasse contemporain* (all tr. in *The Miller of Carnac and Other Works*). L'Éstoille had resigned from the army after a brief posting to Italy, but he was recalled to service in 1870 when the Prussians invaded; he did not take part in the ill-fated charge of the Chasseurs d'Afrique at the battle of Sedan, but he was traumatized by the defeat, and when he returned to his epic poem thereafter it was in a very different frame of mind and under a new signature. It was eventually published in three volumes as *Le Chanson de l'alouette* (1880; tr. as *The Song of the Skylark*), and was followed by two further volumes of hybrid prose poems and *contes*, many of them revised versions of items originally published under the Lyvron pseudonym, including *Les Runes d'Attila* and "Le Poène d'un fou" (1867). The following translation of the former is made from the final version, retitled "Attila: A Danish Tale" and published in *Contes du Nord* (1892), but the translation of the other was made from the original, in the *Revue des lettres et des arts*. In spite of the overlaps, commentators at the time do not seem to have realized that "Louis de Lyvron" and "A. de L'Estoille" were the same person.

Attila

The wind weeps in the leather sail, the blonde young woman smiles at the hollow waves and the pilot, standing at the front of the boat, says:

"You are the white reindeer of my green prairie, Elf of the tempest; whip the dormant waves with your wings, my boat is a salmon playing in the foam; whip the dormant waves with your wings, my boat is a falcon fishing in the foam."

The waves howl, the boat groans; the stiffened pilot listens and, with her head on the shoulder of the man of the North, the blonde young woman says:

"The Elf of the tempest loves the song of the brave; sing, my blue elk, until the promised kiss, until the night of amour; I am like the teal that smoothes its feathers in the first days of April, like the snow awaiting the spring."

"I know many songs! While watching my oxen I have searched for them in the spots of the reeds, under the tongue of the reindeer and in the mouth of the squirrel; but my ear is full of the clash of words . . .

"Thrush with green plumage, make your nest in my helmet; squirrel of the woods; make your nest in my shield; crow, perch on my ash-wood bow; until the snows of winter I want to sing runes to my bride.

"I know many songs! I have found them along the roads, on the heads of swallows, on the shoulders of geese, on the bark of beeches; but my ear is full of the rumble of waves . . .

76

"Snowdrop with the golden heart, blue periwinkle, pale violet, scatter your seeds, your little seeds, in my fir-wood boat, in my new sail; until the dews of spring, I want to sing runes to my bride.

"I know many songs! I have sung while arrows flew like seagulls; I have sung while cups filled up beneath open veins; today, I shall sing better, my ear is full of the sound of a kiss.

"Rocked by the swell in my floating net, go to sleep smiling, undines with blue-green eyes; I shall sing to my bride a song of love, a song of war: the runes of Attila, the king of horsemen."

I

At sunset, the old world slumbers in its ruins. At dawn, in their maple-wood chariots, the awaited awake, hungry. Over the land, Attila weighs.

In the flat valley cut by a road as broad as a sea and as straight as a spear, under ragged willows, in the confines of two worlds, the great river is silvery.

Dew spangles the plain; on the road, crows are croaking; two elks are drinking from the river . . . But a dark cloud appears, and the dew freezes, and the crows fly away.

Under the cloud of russet wings race twenty thousand horsemen; wolves gallop behind. In front, the chief with the shaven hair mounts a white stallion. The two elks flee . . .

The stallion cleaves the waves; the horsemen stop; the chief releases the reins, raises his arms and cries:

"Old river, Attila salutes you!"

A gust of wind passes through the willows, the dew falls as frost, in the steppe the echo rumbles:

"Attila! Attila . . . !"

"Greetings, Brother!" cries the king. "I am the river with crimson waves."

"Greetings, Brother!" the Volga responds.

Attila crosses the river. He has blackened the marble, he wants to redden the snow; but before then, he wants to dream where he played as a child, while his mother milked the mares with curly manes in the reeds.

Before attacking the Purs,[1] the unvanquished sons of the Aesir, the man driven by the Unknown comes to ask the voice of the desert, engendered by the wind in a clump of aspens, for his route . . .

He dreamed alone until sunset, until moonrise . . .[2] When night fell, he laid his wolf-skin lined with crimson on the russet grass, and went to sleep bare-headed.

The horsemen waited on the soil of Europe, but the vultures and the wolves had accompanied the king on to the soil of Asia, for the vultures and the wolves followed Attila, not the horsemen.

Alone, his head bare, Attila sleeps, but he is well guarded; the gray backs form a steely circle around him; the tawny wings make a rounded tent above his head.

As he fell asleep, he sighed—the voice of the desert not having replied to him, the future loomed up before him like a black shield—but now he smiles; he dreams that he is playing with the foals . . .

He awakes; he sees the white teeth, he hears the yellow beaks, and he sighs: "Amour! I do not have amour, which is necessary to all those who desire, to all those who found."

However, in his maple-wood palace he had priestesses and courtesans, dancers with starry foreheads, singers with rosy lips, and virgins trembling like an ear of wheat.

But in his maple-wood palace he did not have amour. That is why he sighs while the dawn with full udders gaily strews the grass of the plain with its necklace of pearls.

She runs, laughing, but she perceives, on the russet grass, the reaper of forests, the bloodier of rivers, is horrified, and flees. Then a dull murmur rises from the corrupted grass.

Attila hears the voice of the grass, and he is afraid. He is so fearful that he crosses the river without looking back; the blades

1 *Purs* is L'Estoille's translation of an enigmatic term in runic script whose first letter only resembles a P, and which probably means "giant"
2 L'Estoille routinely switches between the present and past tenses in his works, in a fashion that sometimes seems arbitrary; he is not the only French writer of the period to do so, and numerous other examples can be found in the present volume.

of grass were asking one another how they would cause the death of the man who crushed them.

They were asking one another that, but, none of them finding a means, the heather began to weep, while the sun, irritated by still finding darkness, bounded into the starry sky.

"Why has the dawn not waited longer for me?" said the most handsome of the great Aesir, who watches from the city of gold over the hills where the beech has grown. "Is she too afraid of the king of horsemen?"

And the blond young man, leaning over the ardent manes of his horses with winged hooves, says to the tearful heather: "Before your flowers fade, I shall cause the death of the king of horsemen."

The sun said that, but the sun is not the master; into the dark abyss the Aesir will fall one day; only the Old One will remain over his devastated work; the Old One alone is the master.

On his throne of ice, the Old One, the father of the world, hears everything, and his voice growls: "The hand of a man cannot kill, and the hand of a god must not kill Attila the reaper!"

He hears the voice, the Aes with the golden lips, and anger swells his heart; the red sword-bearer hears the voice, and his brow furrows. The weeping heather also hears the voice.

It says: "The promises of the gods shine like the frost, but melt likewise."

"Before your flowers fade, he will die," replies the blond charmer, the sweet singer of runes.

In the meantime, Attila thought: "I am the master's scythe; where his grain is about to sprout, I cut the brambles; where his grain is about to ripen, I cut the tares; the scythe will never be blunted.

"I shall do my day's work, but at the hour of noonday the reaper may repose momentarily in the shade. O Thou whom I meekly obey, make a clear spring well up beneath my feet.

"The flame has burned my lips; I am thirsty, Master! The blood is burning on my hands; make a clear spring well up before me; in the hour of noonday make a woman love me."

The sun hears; his mares are already razing with their brazen hooves the green hill where the Northern dew comes every morning to dream under the birches while gazing at the sea . . .

The eyes of Hildewige are beautiful; they are neither blue nor dark, they are as brown as rushes; but the eyes of a virgin ought to gaze at the spindle and not at the clouds.

The great Aes said: "The hand of a man cannot kill him, the hand of a god must not kill him, but the eyes of a woman slay like a serpent's tongue, like the tip of a sword.

"You have blackened the marble, but you shall not redden the snow, man with the shaven hair; those who have loved me do not forget me, their kisses are no longer for sale, and you shall love the Northern rose."

On the white moss at the foot of the sorb-tree, her chin in her hand, the virgin who is dreaming instead of spinning, said while watching the hawk soar over the blue gulf: "Oh, if I only had wings!

"If my soul had wings, like the hawk, I would glide over the bottomless gulf." Slowly, she passes her hand over her forehead; slowly, she passes her fingers through her hair.

She bounds to her feet, her lip disdainful, her breasts swollen; her foot trampling the moss she says: "Oh, if I had wings like the hawk, I would fly to where the swords are blunted!"

Confused, she lowers her eyes; a man is smiling at her. She has not seen a swan fall from the cloudless sky; she has not seen him change into a soldier, the great Aes with the curly hair.

"If I had wings," said the blond warrior, "I would break them on the green hill; your eyes are more brilliant than the fire of swords, your gaze is sweeter than the mist of the gulf . . ."

And Attila went back to his horsemen, where the heavy carts, buckling under the booty, arranged in circles, awaited him. In the breath of the wolves, under the wings of the vultures, he is dreaming of the clear spring . . .

When the night, shaking her veil, sowed stars over the crimson of the evening, the blond warrior was still smiling at the intoxicated virgin, and the man with the shaven hair went to sleep in order to dream . . .

"Under the birches of the hill, what does the hawk say to the dove, my beloved? You would like me to speak like a god, and the feet of the hare to efface my amorous runes in the snow . . ."

The stars shining, the palpitating virgin has descended the hill of birches; the blond young man resumes the form of a swan and he flies toward the tent where Attila is falling asleep.

"King of horsemen," he says to him, "on a Northern eglantine bush, a rose is blooming; if you want to pluck her, follow me to where the raspberry-bushes are growing, where the sorb-berries are reddening.

"Her arms are whiter than my wings, follow me, her cheeks are softer than my neck; if you want to love her, follow me to where the raspberry-bushes are growing, where the plum-trees are in flower . . ."

Attila followed the swan. For a week, two weeks, nearly three weeks, he marched every night, stopping when the swan was lost in the whiteness of the morning.

For two weeks, nearly three, he went. His horsemen fell behind him, the vultures letting their wings hang down, the breathless wolves drooling; the swan flew so rapidly!

Shining like an emerald, the green isle finally appeared; but the spotted stallion did not want to enter the unfurling waves. "I am also the king of the vultures and the wolves!" Attila cries.

"Vultures that I have sated with flesh, wolves that I have intoxicated with blood, bring me to the green isle where the raspberries are growing."

"Our feet are tremulous!"

"Our wings are limp!"

"From my sword a river flows that summer does not drink," cries the reaper with tired hands. "Foamy sea, part thy pale waves; I am the divine river that washes mud in blood."

A wave casts its foam over Attila's forehead.

"We're thirsty!" howl the wolves.

"We're hungry!" cry the vultures.

The wolves approach, menacingly, the vultures fly lower . . .

But the great Aes has crossed the ivory threshold; he has released the golden reins, and now, a rapid salmon is gliding through the waves. Then he makes a boat out of seaweed and changes into an old man.

White teeth shine, yellow beaks click, the sea laughs. Attila nods his shaven head, the boat appears in the sunset, with its divine pilot.

The boat glided over the waves; it was neither large nor small; its sail was blue, its mast bent like a red, and the old man said to the king of horsemen:

"King, I have set up for you in my new boat this mast as think as a mountain pine; for you I have hoisted this sail like a juniper of the hills; come to where you want to go . . ."

"Thrush with green plumage, make your nest in my helmet; squirrel of the woods, make your nest n my shield; crow, perch on my oaken spear; until the snows of winter, I want to sing runes to my beloved!"

II

The old man says to the king: "I have set up for you in my new boat this mast as think as a mountain pine; for you I have hoisted this sail like a juniper of the hills.

"Come into my red boat, into my oaken boat, into my new boat; mount my dragon with broad wings, and I will take you where the Northern rose blooms."

Attila sits down on the fir-wood bench and the boat steered northwards. The wolves swim in its wake and the vultures whipped the blue sail with their sharp wings.

The coastline shrinks, the waves swelled. "Fly, fly, red boat," said the old man, "dance on the waves like a light bubble, glide like a lily in the midst of the waves."

The wind roars, lightning flashes, waves rise up; saliva drips from gaping mouths; feathers fall from crumpled wings; Attila sings, nodding his shaven head:

"When the harvest is complete I shall wash my red hands in the river of fresh water, and my soul will go to a palace of clouds. Attila will always be king!"

The waves rear up; their green arms grip the flanks of the wolves, their white tongues lick the wings of the vultures, and Attila sings, nodding his shaven head:

"Row, row, old man, Attila will always be king!" The old man takes the oars, and the boat lands on the green isle where the raspberry bushes grow, the green isle of the pale sea.

Attila leaps on to the sand . . . he can no longer see the boat. The boat, however, was moored to the shore, but it was not the hands of women that had woven its blue sail.

The swan was no longer there to indicate the route. He was not in the red boat, he was already on the hill, in the birch-wood, where the Northern virgin waited for him every evening.

He is more beautiful than the rainbow when Hildewige perceives him. She sees him in a moonbeam, and stops, trembling, like a hind that hears the baying of the dogs.

Hildewige's eyes are neither blue nor dark; they are brighter than an iridescent bubble, browner than the rushes of the marsh, shinier than the leaves of water-lentils.

"Like the serpent's tongue, like the tip of a sword, the eyes of a virgin slay, and I am lying down like a wounded hind at your feet," said the great Aes, changed into a warrior.

"Like the flowery peat, like the sparkling dune, the oaths of warriors attract; but his cold the water is beneath the sand! How black the mud is beneath the flowers!"

"Under the glacier iridescent with the fires of the setting sun, dwarves have forges a bed of copper with silver feet; Elves have woven a soft cushion of white linen for you."

"For a bed, Master, you shall have my heart, for cushions my blonde tresses. In the iridescent grotto, my beloved, you shall have my lips for a cup and my amour for a breastplate . . ."

Sweeter than honey, the sonorous runes glide from the lips of the great Aes, and the cheeks of the Northern rose redden like the petals of the eglantine under the kisses of the sun . . .

"Sing, my master, my sweet master, what the blond charmer, the handsome warrior, said to his beloved; I want to see whether you can speak better than a great Aes."

"The words of the god! On the foreheads of old men, on the door of the temple, on the hill of tombs, I have read them . . . but my ear is full of the noise of swords . . ."

On the cold sand of the pale gulf, in his wolf-skin, the king awaits sleep. His gaze follows the rising moon, a falling star; his soul follows his dream.

And his dream says: "Where the raspberry-bushes grow, the virgin is a seamew, the mother a bee, the father an elk. There, the wheat has no chaff, the temple has no nettles."

"From dawn to sunset, I have passed like a river," replied the king of horsemen; "in the fertile mud, the future can germinate. To the white land of runes, I am going to repose.

"On these sonorous beaches, on these green hills, my people will camp . . . and the bloody river will no longer be anything but a lake, entirely limpid and blue, and the great killer of men will be happy . . ."

When Attila awakes, he sees on the sand a pear-wood sleigh harnessed to two black horses, the manes of which are braided with wool.

A golden cuckoo opens its wings at the tip of the helm; two golden cuckoos are flapping their wings over the circles of the collars; silver bells are tinkling on the breasts of the horses.

Attila mounts the sleigh. He cracks the whip garnished with pearls, shakes the reins of gold and silver, and the sleigh glides rapidly over the nacreous snow.

The vultures had smoothed their wings, the wolves were marching like cavaliers, a hundred before and a hundred behind, a hundred to the left and a hundred to the right of the pear-wood sleigh.

The host of the green isle was on the threshold of the painted house; he heard the sound of the sleigh and he looked in the direction of the sea. On seeing the vultures and the wolves he cried:

"A god is coming to repose in my painted house, under my oaken beams, on my polished bench, before my red fire!"

Attila stopped his sleigh and said to him. "Have you a virgin for me, a bride, a swallow to sleep beside me?"

"I have a virgin, a bride, a swallow to sleep beside you," replied the host.

Hildewige appeared then on the road of the hill. Her hair was undone, her eyes were moist; she was thinking about the blond young man, the handsome warrior.

"Virgin, for two weeks, nearly three, I have been marching in order to find you. Come to sleep in my tent; I am Attila, the king of horsemen."

"There is no virgin here who wants to become your wife, no swallow here who wants to sleep beside you," the Northern virgin replies, putting up her hair.

"Host of the green isle, I am Attila; give me your daughter, and I will give you ten boats full of silver and two boats full of gold."

The host replies to the king of horsemen:

"I give you my daughter, my swallow, to sleep beside you. Hildewige, comb your hair, put on your bracelets; you are the bride of the king of the vultures and the wolves."

"We are not sold for silver, we do not give ourselves for red gold to passing heroes," replies the Northern rose, frowning.

"Attila, I give her to you," says the host . . .

An elk was slain for the king, an ox for the guests, a hundred sheep for the vultures, a hundred sheep for the wolves, and the marriage was made.

At the end of the meal, the aged mother, the venerable hostess, took Hildewige behind the hedge, near to the door of the cowshed where the oxen were ruminating, and said to her in a whisper:

"Let your ear be as fine as that of a mouse, let your feet be as light as those of a hare, let your heart be as tender as the crown of a young plum tree."

"Oh, my mother, you who have nourished me, why have you sold me? I do not love the king of the wolves; I love a warrior that I saw last night on the hill of birches."

"Oh, my daughter, my golden apple, my flowery staff, let the sorb-trees of your husband's orchard be sacred to you. Oh, my daughter, let their fruits be more sacred still . . . ."

But the cups were empty, and the sleigh was harnessed! Hildewige combed her hair, weeping; she put on her bracelets, weeping; she bid the painted house adieu.

She already has one foot in Attila's sleigh and she says adieu again to the trees of the orchard; but the sleigh pulls away and at sunset, it stops near the red boat.

Hildewige sits down at the bow, Attila sits down at the stern, the old man takes the oars, the wolves enter into the dark water and the vultures fly into the gray sky . . .

In front of the palace of maple-wood, where they are stationed every evening, the riders sitting on the heads of aurochs say sadly: "Under the threshold the grass has paled; already, ivy is attaching itself to the walls."

In the round hall of the maple-wood palace, on the crimson cushions, the women leaning sadly on their elbows say sadly: "The hall is already full; which of us will make way for the master's chosen one . . . ?"

It was not the hands of women that had woven the blue sail; it inflates, the mast bends and the boat dances on the waves like a light bubble on an iridescent cascade.

Hildewige sings, letting her white hand dangle in the green water, she sings letting her blonde hair float free, she sings in the old language of the runes.

Attila does not understand what she is singing, but the vultures and the wolves understand it, and the fish too, and the daughters of the sea who rear up on the waves.

She says: "When he calls to me this evening under the silver birches, only the echo will respond . . ."

Attila smiles; he does not understand the language of the runes.

The wolves weep as they swim. The vultures weep as they fly, the daughters of the sea weep and the fish say to one another: "The Northern rose will wither."

The old man sings, while dipping the oars: "When one sows blood, swords grow! When on sown swords, blood grows! Perhaps . . . often!"

The boat touches the sand. "Attila!" cry the horsemen. The king leaps into the foam, but when he turns round, the boat has disappeared, and a short sword is shining in Hildewige's hand . . .

"Snowdrop with the golden heart, blue periwinkle, pale violet, scatter your seeds, your little seeds, in my fir-wood boat, in my new sail; until the dews of spring, I want to sing runes to my bride."

III

The king leaps into the foam, but when he turns round, the boat has disappeared, and a short sword is shining in Hildewige's hand. "Attila!" cry the horsemen.

"She has a sword for a distaff, your bride, hurrah, hurrah! Her veil will have red pearls, hurrah, hurrah! For the morning gift will deck her tent with the heads of kings."

The horsemen launched their arrows at the clouds; their feet muffled, the wild wolves howled; the vultures circled like dry leaves; Attila smiled.

And the Northern virgin, her cheek pale, her eyes lowered, folded her two pale hands over the agate hilt. "Hurrah for the bride!" cry the horsemen.

A dappled stallion has been saddled for the king, as light as oat straw, as sleek as the stem of a sweet-pea. Hildewige sits down on the silky rump.

The Northern rose holds the naked sword in her hand.

"What is that sword?" asks Attila. "Did the old man give it to you?"

"Perhaps. Who knows?"

Attila spurs his horse and murmurs: "Fly, white stallion. Fly to the maple-wood palace, to the hall of the golden shields; I know how to speak to women as well as horsemen."

In the evening, a tent of felt was erected for the virgin. Before the lowered flap, Attila plants his spear, and he lies down next to his horse, bare-headed, his arms folded.

He dreamed of the time when the young women forgot their full pitchers in the spring, in order to watch the indefatigable horseman circling, and while dreaming, he smiled . . .

"Has he slipped into the tent of felt, the sweet charmer, the handsome warrior?" At the bronze table of the palace of the great Aesir, in his marked place among the Strong and the Sage, he is seated.

He speaks, and everyone falls silent. "Why, Father of Men," he says, "do you allow the son of a deformed dwarf to turn like a mill-wheel over the crushed world?"

"Is it wheat or chaff," replies the Father, "that the wheel is crushing? Who knows? Who knows? The Old Man alone is the master; tomorrow is his secret.

"For as long as the sun shines in the sky of the Aesir, the ash-tree will flourish on the green hills of the Northern isles; the raspberry-bushes will not be trampled by the feet of Attila . . ."

Attila marches for two weeks, nearly three, and he arrives at the maple-wood palace, the palace with the polished beams. All his warriors are waiting for him, all his women are waiting for him.

When they saw Hildewige, the warriors uttered a cry of joy; she was beautiful. When they saw Hildewige, the women uttered a cry of dolor; she was the most beautiful.

The wolves, fatigued, lay down before the door; the vultures, fatigued, perched on the top of the roof; and the women, pale with jealousy, set the table for the feast . . .

Attila had all his men sit down. He had a silver plate and a golden cup set before each of them; he had one of his women stationed behind each of them, in festival garments.

Then he sat down, with his bride, on the wooden bench with the twisted feet. Hildewige places her naked sword on the bench, and in the battle hall the feast commences.

It is a fine feast; the cups are overflowing, the table buckling, the women moisten their lips in the cups, the men plunge their swords into the tables, and a hundred bards sing.

Then, at the door of the hall, a stranger appears, a shield over his shoulder. He says: "The coward only comes when invited, but the brave man knocks and enters the palace of kings.

"The brave man sits down at the table; his invitation is engraved on the blade of his sword." He is handsome, the stranger; dazzling flowers shine on his shield.

Attila invites him to sit down on the bench with the twisted feet and he says: "The unknown guest must be received like a god; Queen of the World, fill the stranger's cup."

Hildewige smiles.

The cups, filled a hundred times, have been emptied a hundred times; the king says: "Take the golden cups, and also take the women, but bend the knee before the Queen of the World."

Everyone has bent the knee, but the blond young man has said, as he bent his knee: "Amour has wings like white birds . . ."

Hildewige smiles.

She is still smiling when the king carries her away in the hall where the golden shields are flamboyant. She is still smiling when the king places her on the bed of bearskins with ruby claws.

The men cried: "She has a sword for a distaff, hurrah, hurrah! We are the ones who will put flax in her distaff, hurrah, hurrah!" Wine was foaming in the cups like blood.

The king places Hildewige on the bearskin bed, and then he kneels down and opens his mouth to speak . . .

But he does not have time to speak; she plunges her sword into his heart.

Attila cries: "Men of the Orient, lacerate your cheeks, a woman has killed me."

She says: "My oaths have roots like the iris; they yield fruits like the pear-tree."

Hildewige is pale but her eyes are dry. Attila said: "Weep, gray wolves! Weep, tawny vultures! A woman has killed me!"

Blood flows from the breast of the king over Hildegarde's robe.

The blood flows and the king says: "Let me sit down next to you. Will you sustain my head? Don't withdraw the sword, don't take back your kiss."

Attila smiled.

The Northern rose gazes at the man who is smiling with a sword in his heart; she gazes at the man who speaks of amour with a sword in his heart, and her eyes widen, astonished.

The king sang softly: "I have a palace of clouds for my bride; I have washed my red hands . . . Weep, gray wolves; weep, tawny vultures; weep, men of the Orient!"

The shields groan, the wolves howl, the vultures flap their wings, and a loud voice cries: "Weep not, heather, I have kept my oath."

The shields groan, the wolves howl, the vultures flap their wings, and in a ray of sunlight the unknown guest of the feast appears, the warrior of the green hill.

As soon as Hildewige sees him, she applies her lips to the blue lips of Attila. "I am coming to join you, king of swords," she says, "I shall pour you hydromel in the palace of the brave."

Then, pale, her hand raised, she says to the great Aes: "When your enemies pursue you, let your horse fall! Let the arrow that you launch turn back upon you and avenge Attila!"

She draws out the sword . . .

Attila falls; the wolves flee; the vultures fly away; the shields break . . .

She draws out the sword, strikes herself, and falls upon the heart she has struck.

Then, on his iceberg, the Old One says: "The hand of a man cannot kill, the hand of a god must not kill, and a woman has not killed Attila the reaper.

"But when the sheaf is tied, in the hour of noon, the reaper may repose for a moment in the shade; he may moisten his lips in the cool spring . . ."

A lightning bolt has ripped through the maple roof; a mare with black wings and a fiery mane launches forth into the fall where the shields are flamboyant; Hildewige smiles and Attila gets up.

"The Old One alone is the master!" sighs the radiant Aes, frowning.

"Tomorrow is his secret," replies the man who is still the king of horsemen.

"Why have you not taken the form of a swan? I recognize you, owner of the boat with the blue sail. You have not lied; the arms of my bride are whiter than the foam.

"You have not lied; from the eglantine-bush of the green isle I have plucked the rose of amour; now take me to the celestial spring, where I must wash my red hands.

"From dawn to sunset I have passed like a river; in the fertile mud, the future may germinate; handsome swan, carry me to the blue land of the runes . . . Attila! Attila!"

Beneath the muscular thigh of the king of horsemen, the mare bucks; quivering, she extends her bloody wings. Lightning flashes in the fiery sky; the mare launches forth.

The virgin leans her hand on the king's shoulder, her loose blonde hair caresses his brown cheek. The mare bounds; on her ebony rump the bare feet of the virgin shine like seamews.

"Attila! The Romans!" cry the horsemen. "Attila, get up! An iron circle is closing around us, wake up!"

Trembling, they raise the lowered curtain, the curtain of the hall of golden shields.

But in the round hall, through the torn roof, a ray of light slides . . . On the sandy floor, a red patch is fuming; on the empty bed, a sword shines . . .

"Attila!" cry the horsemen.

Like a swallow in the paling sky the mare describes great circles as she rises.

"Beloved," says the virgin, "your children are calling you; the iron circle is closing in."

"The straw is dry, the sheaf is tied," replies the reaper, "tomorrow we shall take up our heavy scythes. The hour of rest is sounding; come with me to the pathless plains!"

Like a black whirlwind, the squadrons take flight; the heavy cartwheels turn; the great bulls shake the clouds with their horns; the surprised army rises toward the stars . . .

And ever since, Attila's army, like a river of milk, has been shining between the stars; in order to descend again to cut the brambles, it is waiting for the hour to chime . . .

❋

In the leather sail the North wind is weeping. "Until the promised kiss, until the night of amour, sing, my master, my sweet master."

"I know many more songs, but my ear is full of the sound of swords . . ."

The Madman's Poem

When I was rich, I deflected a river and I directed it, through a thousand conduits, into the arid plain where the sun was burning the merchants. The plain became a garden; but when I passed, a poor man, before the merchants sitting in the shade, they shouted: "Look at the madman!"

"Madmen uproot trees, but they do not irrigate them," my soul murmured in my ear, and I became a camel-driver.

When I saw the road encumbered with cadavers I said to the chiefs of the caravans: "Let us search for a virgin route, bordered by clear springs." They let me search on my own, and when I came back with my mouth dry, they said: "Look at the madman!"

"Madmen lose themselves on beaten tracks, but they do not trace new ones," my soul murmured in my ear, and I fell in love with the Sultan's daughter.

✳

The Sultan's daughter is more beautiful than the moon; I made a poem for her as profound as the night.

When my poems are similar to a rose-bush, I shall perfume my mouth and I shall sit down before the one I love on an embroidered carpet. To my right and my left I shall light cassolettes, and I shall recite my verses slowly, marking the measure.

The Sultan's daughter is whiter than jasmine; a smile sings in the corner of her lip, but her soft eyes love to see the blood of those who talk to her about love fuming.

✳

My poem is similar to a honeycomb, and I am sitting on freshly-cut flowers.

I shall sing softly, swaying my head. If the Sultan's daughter does not give me her hand to kiss when I have sung a thousand lines, and if she does not give me her lips to kiss when I have sung ten thousand, I shall say to her: "I am mad!" and I will no longer love her.

Light of my eyes, put a cushion under your elbow, light your nargileh, take your little feet out of your green slippers, and listen to the poem that I have made for you while gazing at the moon.

Listen to my poem; you are the Sultan's daughter, but it is the son of Amour.

Houris of a woman's heart, put a cushion under your elbow in order to be able to sleep if the weight of your eyelashes makes your eyelids fall.

Listen:

✳

Further away than Gizeh, further away than Memphis, further away than Thebes, going up the Nile, I lay down one evening in a round valley that resembles an amethyst cup half full of sand.

All day I had traveled upriver, seeking a ford, and all day I had said to myself: "Why does the Nile, when it floods, not make grass grow on this plain?"

✳

Half of my soul, the feet swell up quickly when one asks why at every step.

Sing, warbler, without ever asking why you sing, and your days will go by like a stream in a faience channel.

✳

I lay down and I saw great sphinxes crouching on the crest of the mountain the color of amethyst.

"Why, I said to myself, "are the great sphinxes crouching around this plain, as shiny as the bowl of an ewer?"

✳

Sister of blonde ears of wheat, let my verses caress the tip of the wing of your soul as it takes flight.

Close your azure eyes, blonde sister of ears of wheat, and my verses, flapping their wings, will sway your soul as the evening wind sways fields of barley.

✳

While I was gazing at the sphinxes, the simoom drank my water-skins.

The Nile was close by, but the crowds drink from the Nile and I only like new cups, myself. I lay down on the sand and, as the vultures were soaring over my head, I recited beautiful verses to them: "When you alight in order to eat my eyes, your wings dangling over my forehead, still warm, you will see in my eyes the portrait of my beloved; her sweet face is engraved on my pupils in streaks of fire. Since I have contemplated that star fallen from the sky I am like a man blind for having gazed intently at the sun, who sees the star that blinded him in the darkness."

I have only sung a hundred lines, and you have given me your hand to kiss. Have you, then, seen that my heart is a cool oasis in which the flower of amour blooms brightly? Have you seen that my heart is a deep sea in which the boat of our amour will never capsize?

You have given me your fingers, more transparent than cloudless shadow; you have given me your fingernails, brighter than a drop of blood on a golden stirrup; you have given me your wrist, more delicate than an ivory flute, and I have only made a hundred lines as yet.

Sweet incense of my soul, my verses will be ardent coals, and your heart will be changed into an embalmed cloud.

Oh, my poem is no longer marching like a hare that takes ten steps and looks around; it is running like a white camel that traverses the desert without stopping.

Listen, beloved:

Lying down on the plain, I gazed at the cloud floating before the moon.

That cloud descended, and when it touched the earth, three almahs emerged from it. The thinnest had a cup, the most beautiful had a flute, and the palest was naked to the waist.

The thinnest said to me: "Drink, and you will never be thirsty."

I replied to the almah: "My amour is a cool spring from which I drink long draughts."

The vultures looked at me askance.

94

The palest of the almahs said to me then: "Come into my arms and you will see Heaven."

I replied: "My amour is a garden in which the tree with golden fruits grows."

The vultures stretched out their bald necks.

Then the most beautiful of the almahs played the flute. The sphinxes crouching on the summit of the mountain stood up, the almahs disappeared and the blue cloud rose up again toward the moon.

Then I saw two palm trees and, under the palm trees, a woman with dark eyes who resembled you.

❈

Messaouda, what I saw last night is strange.

What I saw last night has made me an infidel; I believe, now, what old men teach beneath the cedars of Lebanon.

They say, those old men, that the life of the soul is a ladder that resembles a crescent, the middle of which is in darkness, and the two points in the light. They say that at each death the soul, when it is young, descends one rung and that it climbs one when it is old.

If what the old men say is true, we have lived before, and I shall rediscover, on your lips, the perfume that intoxicated me in the valley of the Nile.

❈

I have rediscovered, on your lips, the sweet perfume. What the old men say is true!

Listen, Messaouda, to the story of our last amour.

❈

The sphinxes, descended from the mountain, bathed in the waters of the Nile. I forgot that people called me a madman and I said to the woman with the dark eyes: "My heart had found what it was waiting for."

❈

Alight, nightingale, on that pomegranate bush, whose bleeding eyes are gazing at the sister of my soul. Squeeze in your little feet a branch whose bark is still smooth, retract your pretty gray head into the feathers of your neck and sing your most beautiful song of love.

You alone can repeat what I heard in my dream, under the palm trees of the Nile. You alone can repeat what the virgin with the perfumed lips sighed in my ear.

Listen, Messaouda, to the nightingale's song.

✳

No, my Messaouda, no, I shall not tell you, in a word, the end of our story. It is necessary now, if one wants to be called a poet, to say very little in a great many words.

Once a poet was similar to a palm tree which grows straight toward the sky; now he resembles a cep that crawls along walls in order to climb two meters.

When I sing for you, my verses will flow like the waves of the Nile; my verses will be composed of images and not of words, of perfumes and not of letters. Today, I sing for the crowd; I want your name to be written in letters of gold on the doors of the Kaaba.

✳

When the sphinxes had sung the wedding song, the virgin who resembles you took me into a palace where men of stone were dreaming, their hands on their knees.

I know the route that leads to the palace of Amour, daughter of the Sultan; would you like to follow me, as you have followed me before. When I pass by, the crowd shouts: "Look at the madman!" But will you repeat the cries of the crowd?

Yes, I am a madman; I have sown my ideas in the furrows of others. Yes, I am a madman; I have emptied my heart in order that the sun can shine therein, in order that the desert wind can spread its wings there.

Let the crowd speak; the spirit of God dwells in empty heads.

✳

The crowd is malevolent. Hide yourself, white asphodel, under the leaves of the laurel; when the madman has finished his poem, the cavalier will make his spurs ring, and instead of laughing, the crowd will tremble.

Apple of the tree with golden fruits, hide yourself in a calyx like a drop of dew; tomorrow you will shine like a pearl on the hilt of my flittas, and the heads that do not incline will roll in the dust.

You do not want to hide like an expectant lover; you want, like a proud wife, to stand upright on the threshold; come with me to the kadi.

Come, you shall be the shadow of my body, and I shall put your heart into my empty head.

In my empty head your heart will find a garden where streams are chirping, and a sandy path bordered by clear springs.

Come to the kadi's house, blonde sister of the roses; he will read the two verses and you will attach with my name the pleats of your veil, and your veil will be retained by a solid pin.

"Look at the madman! Look at the madman!

They cried "Look at the madman! And they named a blind kadi. When I conducted to that man the star fallen from the sky, when I said to him: "She wants to be my wife," he replied to me: "You are alone and you have in your hand a handful of sand . . ."

※

Come, my Messaouda, into the round valley where the waves of the Nile no longer make the grass grow, since the flame of our amour has changed the sand there into rubies.

Come into the palace where we have loved one another before, when the old plane tree was still a seed. Come, the great sphinxes are waiting for us on the steps of the terrace,

HENRI CAZALIS
(1840-1909)

Henri Cazalis was a physician, and a correspondent of Stéphane Mallarmé, under whose influence he dabbled in Symbolist poetry. His early work, generally gloomy in tone, was collected in *Vita tristis, Reevries fantastiques, Romances sans musique* (1867) and *Melancholia* (1868). Several of his poems were set to music; one of them formed the basis of Camille

Saint-Saëns' famous *Danse macabre* (1874). The following prose poems appeared in the *Revue des lettres et des arts* in a collection of brief "pensées."

Pensées

Poor people are scorned, maltreated and manhandled, and if one cries, he is a coward, and when one laughs, a laborer, and when one drinks, a drunkard.

And yet, if one knew all that the people do for us!

To army they give children in order that we should have glory. Death takes their sons and we take their daughters, and their pretty daughters save the honor of ours.

Poor people, in truth, if one knew all that they give!

They give the milk of their women in order that we should be strong; all day long, under the hot sun, they curb their heads like livestock, in order that we should have bread. Having grown old, they give their exhausted bodies to the hospital, and, of course, we toil thereupon in order to learn to save others.

Poor people are scorned, maltreated and manhandled, and if one cries, he is a coward, and when one laughs, a laborer, and when one drinks, a drunkard.

❈

It was in a square where the moon was shining; an old man in rags was showing the stars for a few sous, and then, in a grain of wheat, an entire world of infusoria. Like queens, one could see the stars moving, and, like laborers, the beasts in a grain of wheat eating one another. And from the infinitely small to the infinitely large, as one goes there by turns, one is astonished by those two abysms, between which one finds oneself, frightened by those two silences, between which the ear perceives the sounds of the streets and the cry of the old man in rags, whom those infinities enable to earn his sous.

Thus, for the poet, the spectacle of things enables him to earn, so painfully, a few thoughts and a few dreams.

CHARLES LECONTE DE LISLE
(1818-1894)

Charles Leconte de Lisle was one of the heroes of the Parnassian Movement. Unrepentantly scholarly, his work is deliberately antiquarian and exotic in its themes and its lush style. His *Poèmes antiques* (1852) and *Poèmes barbares* (1862) became important models for later Symbolist poets as well as the Parnassians. Napoléon III admired his work and showered him with decorations and rewards in spite of his being a fervent Republican. He was elected to the Académie to fill Victor Hugo's seat, although he could not occupy it for long. A collection of his early prose fiction was published posthumously as *Contes en prose* (1910) but there is a relatively clear distinction in his work between his prose works and his narrative poems, and the sample offered below, from the pages of the *Revue des lettres et des arts*, was represented there as an extract from an unpublished translation of Hesiod's *Theogony*, although it is definitely free enough as an innovative adaptation to qualify as an example of French poetry in prose.

The Combat of the Kronides and the Titans

On that day they engaged in rude battle—all of them, whoever they were, males and females, the Titan Gods and the Gods born of Kronos, and those whom Zeus had rendered to the light from the depths of subterranean Erebus, violent and robust. Possessed of infinite forces; for a hundred arms stiffened their shoulders, and each of them had fifty heads that rose from the back above their vigorous limbs; and against the Titans, in that disastrous war, they carried enormous rocks in their solid hands.

And on the other side, ardently, the Titans affirmed their phalanges; and the vigor of arms and courage burst forth on either part.

The immense sea resonated horribly, and the earth roared mightily, and the broad Ouranos groaned, all shaken, and the great Olympus trembled on its base as the Gods collided; and a vast resonance penetrated black Tartarus, a sonorous noise of feet, the tumult of the battle and the violence of blows.

They launched lamentable darts against one another, and their confused clamor rose all the way to starry Ouranos, while they exhorted one another and clashed with one another, with loud cries.

Then Zeus ceased to contain his strength, and his soul immediately filled with wrath, and he deployed all his vigor, while he precipitated himself, flamboyant, from Ouranos and Olympus. And thunderbolts, with thunder and lightning, flew rapidly from his robust hand, rolling sacred fire into the distance. And in all parts, the fecund earth roared, flamboyant, and the great forests crackled in the fire, and the entire Earth burned, and the waves of Okeanos and the immense Pontos caught fire, and hot vapor enveloped the terrestrial Titans. The flames rose high into the divine air, and the eyes of the bravest were dazzled by the radiant splendor of the thunderbolts and the lightning.

The immense conflagration invaded Khaos, and it seemed that one saw with one's eyes and heard with one's ears the over-turning of those times when, of old, the Earth and the broad Ouranos rose up in collision, when, in a limitless resonance, one was broken by the other, which rushed upwards; such was the horrible noise of the combat of the Gods!

And all the raging winds lifted up whirlwinds of dust in the midst of the thunder, lightning and ardent thunderbolts, those darts of great Zeus; and they threw their noise and their clamors through the two parties. And an immense fracas enveloped the frightful combat, and the vigor of arms was deployed on both sides. But the victory was in the balance.

Until then, rushing upon one another, all of them had fought bravely in the terrible battle; but then, in the first ranks, engaging in a violent struggle, Kottos, Briareos and Gyges, insatiable in combat, launched three hundred rocks from their robust hands, one after another, and they sheltered with their darts the Titan Gods, and into the depths of the broad Earth they precipitated them, charged with bonds, having tamed those courageous adversaries with their hands.

And they plunged them under the Earth, as far as the Earth is distant from Ouranos; for the distance is the same between the Earth and black Tartarus.

After falling for nine nights and nine days, a bronze anvil fallen from Ouranos arrived on the tenth day on Earth; and, falling for nine nights and nine days, a bronze anvil fallen from the Earth arrived on the tenth day in Tartarus. A cage of bronze surrounds it, and the night spreads three walls of shadow around the opening; and above are the roots of the Earth and the sterile sea. And there, the Titan Gods are hidden under the black fog, by the order of Zeus, who amasses clouds in that noxious place at the extremities of the immense Earth.

And that place has no exit. Poseidon has made bronze gates for it, and a wall surrounds it on all sides; and there, Gyges, Kottos and Briareos live, sure prisoners of tempestuous Zeus. And there, from the somber Earth and black Tartarus, from the sterile sea and from starry Ouranos, the sources and the limits are ranged, frightful, noxious and detested by the Gods themselves.

It is an enormous gulf, and in an entire year the depths of it cannot be reached by a man who passes through the gates, but he will be borne here and there by an impetuous, frightful tempest. And that monstrous gulf is horrible for the immortal Gods themselves. And there, in black Night, the horrible abode stands, entirely covered by somber clouds.

Standing at the entrance, the son of Iapetos[1] sustains the broad Ouranos with his head and his indefatigable hands, full of vigor. And Nyx and Hemera go all around, calling to one another and passing the large bronze threshold by turns, And, in fact, one enters and the other emerges, and the place never encloses

---

1 Atlas.

both; but always, existing out of that place, one moves over the Earth; and the other goes back in, while waiting for the hour of departure to arrive. Hemera carries the piercing light to mortal humans; and the dangerous Nyx comes in her turn, enveloped by a black cloud and carrying in her arms Hypnos, brother of Thanatos. For that is where the children of the obscure Nyx, the terrible Gods Hypnos and Thanatos, dwell. And the brilliant Helios never illuminates them with his rays, whether he is climbing Ouranos or descending therefrom.

One strolls tranquilly over the Earth and on the broad back of the sea, mild to humans; but the heart of the other is made of bronze and the soul in her breast is bronze, and she does not release the first she seizes among humans, and is detested by the immortal Gods themselves.

In the utmost depths are the sonorous dwellings of the subterranean God, the powerful Aides and the terrible Persephoneia. A ferocious, frightful Dog guards its gates, and in his evil cunning he strikes those who enter with his tail and ears; but he does not let them leave again, and, full of vigilance, he devours all those who try to cross back over the threshold of the powerful Aides and the terrible Persephoneia.

And there also lives the Goddess frightful to the Immortals, the horrible Styx, elder daughter of Okeankos of the prompt ebb-tide. Far from the Gods she lives in illustrious dwellings, covered with enormous rocks, the enclosure of which is sustained, all the way to Ouranos, by silver columns.

Sometimes, the daughter of Thaumas, light-footed Iris, flies as a messenger over the vast back of the sea, when a quarrel or dissent rises up among the Gods. If some inhabitant of the Olympian dwellings has lied, Zeus then sends Iris to fetch in a golden ewer the famous icy Water that falls from a sheer high rock, for the great oath of the Gods.

And in the bosom of the spacious Earth, the Water of the sacred River becomes, in flowing through the black night, an arm of Okeanos; and the tenth part of it is reserved. The other nine, around the Earth and the broad back of the sea, fall back into the sea in silver turbulence; but the one that flows from the rock is the great chastisement of the Gods. And if, in making libations, a God perjures himself among the Immortals who inhabit the summit of snowy Olympus, he lies breathless for an entire year, savoring neither Ambrosia nor Nectar; he lies breathless and mute on his bed, and a frightful numbness envelops him.

※

And thus the Gods consecrate to the Oath of the incorruptible Water of Styx, the ancient Water that traverses the arid place where the sources and the limits are of the Earth, black Tartarus, the sterile sea and starry Ouranos, frightful and detested by the Gods themselves. And there are the splendid gates of the threshold of bronze, immutable, having emerged spontaneously, on profound bases. And before that threshold, far from all the Gods, the Titans live, beyond Khaos covered in fog.

AUGUSTA HOLMÈS
(1847-1903)

Augusta Holmès was born in Paris to an Irish father; she added a grave accent to her surname as an affectation. The Romantic poet Alfred de Vigny was her godfather. She devoted herself to musical composition after studying under Cesar Franck but thought it politic to publish her early works under the male pseudonym Hermann Zenta, and sometimes added an intermediate Z. to her own signature. She often wrote scripts for her own musical compositions and wrote musical accompaniments for other poets, including "Louis de Lyvron." She set up home with Catulle Mendès after he separated from Judith Gautier, and bore him five children although they never married. She was commissioned to write a "triumphal ode" for the centenary of the 1789 Revolution. "La Harpe de l'océan" was published in the *Revue des lettres et des arts* in 1867, one of the first items published in the periodical to be identified in the contents as a *"poème en prose."*

The Harp of the Ocean

I

The sea is bellowing.

Like an amorous woman it enlaces the reefs with its green arms. Breathlessly, it kisses the summit of the rock where the seagulls nest; it embraces the tower where the crows nest.

Far away, on the horizon, between the waves and the gray sky, a streak of fire dies away.

The sea growls.

The thunder roars in the plain of the skies, and lightning flashes make the crests of the waves iridescent.

※

Can you not hear, amid the confused voices of the Ocean, the voice of a bard? Can you not hear the chords of a harp?

That harp is the harp of Erin; that bard is the bard of stormy nights.

II

"When the leaden crown of the foreigner had not blackened the beautiful forehead of Ireland, when the foreign plows had not torn her flanks, when the foreigner's sons had not dishonored her daughters, in the time when there were still soldiers and poets in the green isle, I sang in the tower that the waves are embracing. While leading the oxen to the pasture, driving marauding birds away from the wheat and picking up dry branches for the winter fire, I dreamed.

"On the velveted meadows, where the heels of the fays traced dark green circles, on the yellow stones, where the woman with the crooked fingers weeps when a chief is going to die, on the sand of the shore, the bark of the oaks, the foam of the waves and the roseate mists of the sunset, I read the history of the world."

III

One day, he wanted to sing what only a poet can read. He took a harp and went from village to village, and from palace to palace, telling the young women what the undines tell sleeping fishermen, the warriors what swords imagine as they plunge into a heart, and the woodcutters what old trees weep when the ax strikes them.

One evening, Fionn of the hairy hand was celebrating his marriage with the beautiful Aileen, daughter of Diarmid the Dark.

Beggars were crowding the threshold. Servants with iron bracelets and long hair were distributing the debris of the wedding feast. Torches were flamboyant in the banqueting hall and their ruddy light illuminated the eyes of the beggars.

The bard lifted his harp and the crowd parted. In those days, singers found a frank welcome and open hands everywhere. He stopped on the threshold of the hall.

The table is immense. Roe deer, sheep and oxen are fuming before the guests, who were drinking red wine from silver horns. Under an awning of foliage, Fionn of the hairy hand is presiding. Gold circles shine on his bare arms. One of his hands, covered with red hair, is weighing heavily on the table; with the other he sustains the frail waist of Aileen. He laughs as he gazes at her.

He laughed because he did not know how to smile, and his bride was beautiful.

With her black hair and his green tunic, Aileen of the soft eyes resembles a fay of the fields. The guests drink to her health with savage cries that shake the oak beams and make the flames of the torches quiver.

The day before, Fionn had massacred Diarmid, burned his palace, slaughtered his livestock and carried off his daughter.

Aileen is laughing as she fills her husband's cup.

"Children," says Fionn, when the bard comes in, "here is the man who is going to sing my wealth and your battles. Make room for him. Be welcome, you whose heart is sonorous; may my land be mild to your feet."

The clamors cease. The bard looks at Aileen, takes up his harp and sings.

"On a northern rock the giant with long arms had built his palace. He smiles when the clink of swords rises from the valley.

"Weep, great oak trees; the bear has taken the lamb and thorns have torn its wool."

Aileen whispers into her husband's ear.

"In a blue lake the queen of the waters has built her palace. She has the down of swans for a carpet and the nacreous waves rock her slumber.

"Weep, fir trees; the vulture has taken the dove and the wind has chilled its feathers."

Aileen raises her eyes and listens.

"On the foam of the seas, on the redness of the dawn, on the evening mists, I have built my palace. The sky ignites its stars to illuminate my feasts, and mine will be the carpet that my beloved's feet will tread.

"Weep, birch trees; the falcon has taken a speckled partridge and its blood is reddening the heather."

The bard stops singing.

Leaning on his harp, he is still looking at Aileen.

The king frowns; the husband is pensive; the guests wonder what they have just heard.

✳

Fionn detaches one of his bracelets, and says as he gives it to the bard: "Go in peace. You have not sung of gold or of battles; your voice is too soft to resonate in our halls. Go in peace, and keep that ring in memory of us. Drink, friends; wine warms the heart better than songs."

The bard threw the ring on the ground and went out. The guests resumed drinking.

✳

The words become cries, the cries become insults. Faïlge the Wolf throws a horn full of wine at the head of Milcho Dinast. Fionn, heavy with drunkenness, goes to separate the combatants; a blow of an ax fells him.

※

The chief was carried away and the feast resumed its course. Aileen had disappeared.

IV

In quitting the palace the bard wanted to return to the tower, but the black hair of the bride hid the route from him. He sensed the threads woven by the sublime spider emerging from his heart, which attach predestined existences together and break souls when they break. He clutched his harp to his breast and lay down under an oak.

The stars gazed at him through the branches.

The leaves fell noisily. A woman kneels down; two arms surround the bard's neck; a stifled voice says to him: "You have sung amour, you must know how to love. Take me away; I want to go with you."

"Oh! You are the beat of my heart! Aileen, Aileen, I love you! Come; I shall be greater than kings."

V

Black clouds were accumulating. Curbed by the wind, the trees seemed to be extending their arms to ask for help. A dull murmur rose from the sea. The bard took his beloved away.

He stopped at the door of the round tower, on a rock beaten by the waves.

"This is my dwelling," he said. "Here the spirit of dreams often visited me. On that bed of ferns, I slept better than chiefs in their multicolored mantles. Here people worshiped omnipotent fire; I worship it too; you have brought it in a crease in your robe.

※

"I will love you so much, my fay, that dolors felt and joys promised will vanish like mist before the sun.

"I will love you so much, my queen, my beloved, that you will become the soul of Erin.

"Everywhere that your feet set down, the sacred trefoil will grow. Everywhere that your gaze rests, swords will germinate. To every appeal of your voice, people will respond with enthusiastic songs, and I, your slave, your faithful dog, will set my heart beneath your feet in order to make you taller, and the wings of my soul will bear you to immortality."

Aileen recoiled. She threw her long hair back and, astonished, looking at the sea, the cliff and the somber tower, she said: "Where, then, is the palace you promised me? Where are your servants? I'm returning to Fionn of the hairy hand. I want to be queen."

A clap of thunder shook the rock.

The bard knelt down and kissed the hem of Aileeen's robe. Large tears ran from his eyes. He got up, took his harp and tore out its strings. Then, approaching the young woman he said: "You shall be mine, and for all eternity."

He seized her, and precipitated himself with her from the top of the cliff.

✳

Since then, many centuries have passed, and the heart of Erin has bled. To make royal purple dye, the blood of peoples is required. But when the sea, the vast sea, roars and groans, when the seagulls cry as they cleave through the mist, when the thunder roars in the plain of the sky, on stormy nights, the bard still sings beneath the waves.

His harp is made of the coral of profound grottoes, and its strings are Aileen's hair.

Then, if the waves bring from distant shores a salute to Ireland, joy swells the bard's heart and he sings of love and liberty.

ARTHUR RIMBAUD
(1854-1891)

Arthur Rimbaud, the estranged son of a career soldier, ran away from home during the turmoil of the Franco-Prussian War and was arrested and imprisoned for vagrancy; he was soon released but ran away again in 1871 in order to pursue a literary career, with the encouragement of Paul Verlaine, with whom he had a turbulent and scandalous relationship for two years, which ended when Verlaine was imprisoned after wounding Rimbaud in a druken quarrel. After their separation Rimbaud wrote *Un Saison en enfer* (self-published in 1873), and then returned to London in company with the poet Germain Nouveau, where he wrote the prose-poems eventually published in 1886 as *Illuminations*. He then wandered extensively, enlisting in the Dutch Colonial Army in order to obtain a passage to the Far East, but deserting thereafter and living on the run for some time before settling in Aden, eventually making a living as a merchant. He returned to France in 1891, incapacitated by illness, and his leg was amputated in a hospital in Marseille before his death in November. In the meantime, Verlaine had featured him in *Poètes maudits*, assuming incorrectly that he was dead, and had arranged for belated publication of *Illuminations* (from which the samples below are taken), which rapidly rehabilitated his reputation; his explorations of "the alchemy of the word" identified him as an important precursor of symbolism, and later of surrealism. His subsequent influence has been enormous.

After the Deluge

As soon as the idea of the Deluge had subsided a hare stopped in the sainfoin and the moving flower-heads and said its prayer to the rainbow through a spider-web.

Oh, the precious stones that hid, the flowers that were already staring!

Stalls were set up in the dirty main street and boats were pulled down to the edge of the sea, which was layered as in old engravings.

Blood flowered in Bluebeard's house, in abattoirs and in circuses, where the seal of God whitened the windows. Blood and milk flowed.

Beavers built. Cups of black coffee fumed in the bars.

In the big greenhouse, still streaming, children in mourning gazed at the marvelous images.

A door slammed, and in the square of the hamlet the child waved his arms, understood by the weathervanes and cocks on steeples everywhere, under the sudden rainstorm.

Madame *** installed a piano in the Alps. Mass and first communions were celebrated at the hundred thousand altars of the cathedral.

Caravans departed, and the Hôtel Splendide was built in the icy chaos of the polar darkness.

After that, the Moon heard jackals mewling in deserts of thyme, and eclogues in clogs were grunted in the orchard. Then, in the violet forest in bud, Eucharis told me that it was spring.

Well up, pond; flow over the bridge, foam, and pass over the wood; rise and roll, thunder and lightning, black cloth and organ-music; rise, waters and sorrows, and renew the downpours.

For since they have dissipated—oh, the precious stones in hiding and the open flowers!—life is tedious, as the Queen, the Sorceress who lights her furnace in an earthenware pot, will never consent to tell us what she knows, which we do not.

Mystique

On the slope of the bank the angels spin their woolen robes in the vegetation of steel and emerald.

Nearby, flames leap up to the crest of the mound. To the left, the earth of the ridge is trampled by all the homicides and all the battles, and all the disastrous noises thread their curve. Behind the ridge to the right is the line of orients, of progress.

110

Meanwhile, the band at the top of the tableau is formed by the swirling and bounding rumor of conch-shells and human nights.

The flowery mildness of stars, of the sky, and the rest, descends the slope of the bank, like a basket, facing us, and makes the abyss down there florid and blue.

Antique

Gracious son of Pan! Around your forehead crowned with florets and barriers, your eyes move, precious balls. Patches of brown lees, your cheeks are hollow. Your teeth gleam. Your breast resembles a cithare, jingles circulate in your blond arms. Your heart beats in the abdomen where the double sex is dormant. Roam by night, moving that thigh gently, that second thigh, and that left leg.

Lives

I

Oh, the enormous avenues of the holy land, the terraces of the temple! What has become of the Brahmin who explained the Proverbs to me? Of that time, out there, I can still see even the old women. I remember hours of silver and sunlight on the rivers, my companion's hand on my shoulder, and our caresses standing before the peppery plains. A flock of scarlet pigeons thunders around my thoughts. Exiled here, I have had a stage on which to perform the dramatic masterpieces of all literatures. I can indicate extraordinary riches to you. I observe the history of the treasures you have found. I see the consequences! My wisdom is as disdained as chaos. What is my void compared with the stupor that awaits you?

111

II

I am an inventor far more meritorious than all those who have preceded me; a musician of sorts, who has found something like the key to amour. At present, a gentleman of a meager land with a sober sky, I am trying to stir the memory of a mendicant childhood, the apprenticeship or the arrival in clogs, the polemics, the five or six widowhoods, and a few marriages in which my strong head prevented me from moving to the rhythm of comrades. I don't regret my old share of divine gaiety; the sober air of this bitter land actively aliments my atrocious skepticism. But as that skepticism cannot be put to work henceforth, and as, in addition. I am devoted to a new trouble, I expect to become a very malevolent madman.

III

In a loft where I was imprisoned at twelve I got to know the world; I illustrated the human comedy. In a wine-cellar, I learned history. At some nocturnal celebration in a northern city I encountered all the women of the ancient painters. I was taught the classical sciences in an old passage in Paris. In a magnificent dwelling circled by the entire Orient I accomplished my immense work and spent my illustrious retirement. I stirred my blood. My duty was rewarded. It's not even necessary to think about that any longer. I am really in the afterlife, and have no commissions.

City

I am an ephemeral and not overly discontented citizen of a metropolis believed to be modern, because all known taste has been eluded in the furnishings and exteriors of houses as well as in the plan of the city. Here you cannot find the traces of any monument to superstition. Morality and language are reduced to their simplest expression, in sum. These millions of people who have no need to know one another, so similarly are they led by their education, work and old age, that the course of life must be several times shorter than a foolish statistic finds for the peoples of the Continent. So, from my window I can see new specters rolling through the thick eternal smoke of coal fires—the shade of our woods, our summer nights!—new Furies before my cottage, which is my homeland and my entire heart, since everything here resembles it: Death without tears, our active daughter and maidservant, desperate Amour and pretty Crime whimpering in the mud of the street.

Conte

A prince was vexed by only ever having devoted himself to the perfection of vulgar generosities. He foresaw astonishing evolutions of amour, and suspected his wives of being capable of more than complaisance enhanced by the sky and luxury. He wanted to see the truth, the moment of desire and essential satisfactions. Whether or not that was an aberration of piety, he wanted it. At least he possessed a large enough human power.

All the women he had known were murdered. What a ravage of the garden of beauty! Under the saber, they blessed him. He did not order any new ones, but the women reappeared.

He killed all those who followed him after hunts or libations, but they all followed him.

He amused himself slaughtering rare beasts. He set fire to palaces. He attacked people and hacked them to pieces. But the crowd, golden roofs and beautiful beasts still existed.

Can one ecstasize in destruction, rejuvenate oneself by mean of cruelty? The people did not murmur. No one offered competition to his views.

One evening he was galloping proudly. A Spirit appeared, of an ineffable, even inadmissible, beauty. Its physiognomy and bearing radiated the promise of a multiple and complex amour, an indescribable, even insupportable, wellbeing! The Prince and the Spirit were probably annihilated by essential health. How could they not die of it? Together, then, they would die.

But the Prince died in his palace, at an ordinary age. The Prince was the Spirit. The Spirit was the Prince. Savant music falls short of our desire.

THÉODORE DE BANVILLE
(1823-1891)

Théodore de Banville, the son of a naval captain, devoted himself to a career in letters as soon as he left school, and swiftly became a leading Romantic poet. Settling permanently in Paris after being sent to a *lycée* there from his birthplace—Moulins, in the Auvergnat department of Allier—he endured periods in which it was very difficult to publish his poetry, but he worked extensively for the theater and as a critic before eventually becoming a columnist for *Gil Blas* in 1880, where he routinely substituted short stories for his journalistic commentaries. An extremely disciplined writer, he adapted himself without difficulty to a regime of producing a story every week, eventually moving with Catulle Mendès and Armand Silvestre to the pages of the *Écho de Paris*. In a major study of his work, Barbey d'Aurevilly condemned his move into commercial prose as a disaster, artistically speaking, but Banville took that hackwork as seriously as he took everything else, and cultivated a consummate expertise that provided important models for Mendès and other ex-Parnassians who followed the same route. His employers dissuaded him from writing more *contes* after an experimental series collected as *Contes féeriques* (1882; tr. as *Magical Tales*), which included tales apparently first planned in 1861 and intended for the *Revue fantaisiste*, many of which have elements of prose poetry, but he contrived for a while thereafter to publish the more obvious *poèmes en prose* collected in *La Lanterne magique* (1883; tr. as *Magic Lantern*), from which the samples translated below are taken.

114

The Good God

Under the portico whose stones are ecstatic light, burned by amour, and whose slightest atom, if it could flee, would blind the mad flock of the Suns, the good God, clad as an emperor, seated on his throne, sees and contemplates Infinities. Beneath his feet the quivering ether unfurls, enhanced by imperceptible sparkling dots, which are the Universe. Nearby are the terrible Angels, who are excited because they can hear laments, sobs and gasps reaching all the way to them.

"Oh, Listen, Lord," says Ananiel. "Those are innumerable worlds dying of old age, frozen or icy. Look at their cadavers, stiffening and dangling their inert tresses desperately."

But scarcely has he spoken than thousands of new worlds are born, awake, grow and flee like joyful children, carried away in the ardent music of the universal Rhythm.

"My servant," the good God says to the angel, "why are you afflicted by that which can renew and repair inexhaustible Life? But tell me, what is that plaintive cry that I hear, like a faint murmur?"

"Lord," says Zadakiel, speaking in his turn, "it is coming from the humble planet, forever blessed, where the divine blood was shed. It's a little child in Moulins (Allier) who wants to have a Polichinelle."

"But look, Lord," says Raziel, "on that same earth a ferocious conqueror has devastated realms, destroyed cities and tinted rivers red with blood. He has murdered many people personally, whom he had fed to his lions, and he has crushed cohorts under the feet of his elephants. He leaves behind him disemboweled women with blanched lips, pyramids made of severed heads, field where grass will never grow again, skeletons of burned hamlets and bare roads where there is no longer anything but black ash."

At those words the Angels lower their heads sadly. But as the thought of God has pity on their sadness, and as Time does not exist for them, when they raise their eyes again they see the temples rebuilt, the cities thriving, the gardens in flower, the fields full of ripe wheat, and next to tranquil rivers, mothers giving the breast to their new-born children while the midday sun kisses the foreheads of reapers.

"Messenger," says the good God, "you can see that the evils and disasters are cured, and that no dolor will have cried in vain. But go quickly to inspire good thoughts in the mother of the poor ingenuous creature who was lamenting just now. I really want that little child in Moulins to have his Polichinelle."

Monsieur le Soleil

In the midst of the dazzle of his radiant furnace Monsieur le Soleil is getting ready to climb into his topaz chariot, the door of which is already open, and whose orange horses, always rearing up, are projecting showers of light and pearls from their nostrils. He is clad as a Roman general, in a yellow breastplate with embossed ornaments, a belt with a broad knot, flamboyant lambrequins with fringes, at the top of which shines a figurine of Hercules, an épée, a cutlass and lion-skin shoes with thick soles, which allow the toes of his bare feet to stick out.

High above his floating wig of flame a ruby laurel is posed, from which long ribbons of pink braid hang down, and his golden face, cut above the lip by a tiny straight moustache, as if drawn with a pen, is framed by a cravat of fiery lace.

A few paces away, in another carriage, the vague profile of an old lady can be seen. Around Monsieur le Soleil the princely and ducal Stars are crowding, and to one side, an old courtier, white hot and writing on his knees, is taking notes. However, the Victorious, the Lightning-Bearer, has seen some of the rutilant lords repressing a rapid smile; he wants to know the reason for that, and he interrogates them.

"I order you to speak frankly," he says to one of them. "What is being said about me in the gazettes?"

"Sire," murmurs the incandescent seigneur, "I dare not. Respect . . ."

"I have said: 'I want.'"

"Well, Sire, chagrined minds think that, by dint of having illuminated them too brightly, your blinding light renders objects vulgar and paltry, showing their infirmity and ugliness, and that Night, with her tender blue softness, gives things a more penetrating and more intimate charm."

"Good!" says Monsieur le Soleil, setting foot on the step of the carriage, "those are simple romantic ideas, to which the legislature of Parnassus will do justice. And all that would not have happened if Monsieur Racine's excellent theatrical work had continued to be performed regularly."

With those words the carriage door closes again. The princely and ducal Stars mount horses, and soon, all the carriages and cavaliers take flight in furious light, and the cortege is no more than flame and conflagration, except for the large thigh-boots of the coachmen, which appear entirely black in the triumphant glory of the universal blaze.

Madame la Lune

Pale and plump, and showing her charming features, quite similar to those of the divine Théophile Gautier, Madame la Lune, half set in an arc in an ebony boat ornamented with plates of tin, lead and yellow brass, and incrustations of nacre and silver, with a very high poop and prow, is sailing on the Lac du Bourget, surrounded by the last lunar poets, chimerical grandchildren of the *bousingots*[1] and the Jeune-Frances. As extraordinary as if they had been strolling on the boulevard costumed as Arlequins, those pale lyricists are rigorously clad in the fashion of 1830, and there are even two or three who are wearing boots with tassels and cloaks in which the wind is engulfed.

---

1 The literal meaning of *bousingot* referred to a kind of hat worn by sailors, although it became a slang term for a tavern, especially a riotous one, and was applied contemptuously by Royalists during the reign of Louis-Philippe to refer to young Republican trouble-makers.

They are meditating in fatal poses, and a few ladies of the same epoch appear among them, with mutton-chop sleeves and Medieval headbands, as thin as willows, striving to manifest a little presence but evidently relegated, by the very nature of things, to the floating penumbra of dreams.

By contrast, their celestial Mistress, who has not remained a stranger either to modernity or the Impressionist Movement, is dressed in the Japanese style, in order to flatter recent ideas; her intelligence is a little behind the times but her coquetry is not. Her hair lifted up in front, she is coiffed in a tiara in which brass, pewter, lead, pearls, silver and opals gleam, the languid fires of which are mingled in the most various and the most ingenious combinations, and from which her long jet black hair is escaping, dusted with mica and blue powder. Behind the tiara, from which two large pendants in white jet and pale gold hang down, a long veil of blue gauze descends, with designs forming long and complicated meanders in steel-blue pearls.

Lying on a large dog-skin rug, Madame la Lune wears several satin robes one atop another, the most intimate of which is pearl gray, while the others become increasingly bright, until the outer one, which is blue-white, tightened by a broad pigeon-throat belt, and ornamented by pale metal plaques. Around her neck shines a necklace made with the eyes of owls, and she is shod in little curved-back white leather shoes with silver soles, decorated with yellow leather crescents.

"Ah, Messieurs and dear poets," she says, in a sleepy voice, "the amiable lake, with its feudal castle on a rock and its convent of monks lacks nothing! It's there that Lamartine sang of Elvire. How thin and aerial she must have been to have inspired such melancholy lines, like the moaning of the wind in the plaintive iron strings of an Aeolian harp!"

"Madame," says an Oswald slightly smitten with realism, "it's necessary not to exaggerate. It's reliably said that Elvire was a laundress . . ."

"Oh!" sighs the lady with the silver brow, with a little moue. "Don't take away my illusions!"

And immediately, to show that it is perfectly indifferent to her, she laughs, uncovering her little teeth of brilliant opal; she wafts herself with her fan of cygnet feathers, and the reflection of her celestial Pierrot face casts thousands and thousands of silver spangles over the gently-agitated waves, which fringe them with delicate and capricious embroideries.

JUDITH GAUTIER
(1845-1917)

Judith Gautier was the daughter of Théophile Gautier and Ernesta Grisi; the latter was the sister of the ballet dancer Carlotta Grisi, with whom Gautier was infatuated. Judith was educated in a pension, but was seduced by Catulle Mendès, her father's protégé, while on vacation. She married him, against her father's wishes, and for several years signed herself Judith Mendès, under which name she published several *poèmes en prose* in 1872-3 in Jules Aicard's *Renaissance litteraire et artistique* (from which the samples below are taken). As "Judith Walter" she had earlier published *The Book of Jade* (1867), a volume of prose poems based on antique Chinese sources, and she retained a strong interest in Orientalism, displayed in several volumes of poetry and short stories.

L'île De Chiloë[1]

There, since the beginning of the world, it rains. Slowly, a warm rain descends with a monotonous rattle.

The gentle waves of the Pacific Ocean unfurl silently; their azure pales under the mist near the soft shores of the melancholy and lukewarm island.

---

1 This island, the largest in an archipelago off the west coast of Chile, is nowadays rendered Chiloé in French. In the mid-nineteenth century, when Pacific islands had the reputation among Romantic Frenchmen of being "tropical paradises," Chiloë was employed as a base of operation for French whaling expeditions, thus presenting would-be realists with a template for spoiled paradises.

119

A great opal in the white sky, such is the star that illuminates Chiloë, through the falling rain.

No sand, nothing is solid beneath that immemorial deluge; the ground is a marsh, the tallest tree the torn-out arm of a child.

Nothing is definite, no precise form; a warm mist rises from the ground and envelops the strange forest.

At a distance one can only see a blue fog, and the vague forms of trees that seem to be a more intense fog.

At close range, arborescent ferns such as grew on the young crust of the world, launch forth like rockets and widen the spray of their nebulous foliage.

One can also distinguish lianas streaming with rain, which descend from a high branch, dangling long green tresses, and then go to attach themselves in the mist to a branch one cannot see.

When it rains, no bird interrupts its flight for the thin threads of the tranquil downpour; no gazelle, in its passage, discharges the branches heavy with water.

Only a few reptiles move through the long grass and, under the broad shiny leaves extended over pools of water, the carapace of a crustacean, a strange being of ancient times, which nature disdains and no longer remakes.

I don't know why I would like to weep on this island—to weep without a cause, for I have no chagrin—in the midst of the perpetual rain that would mingle its droplets with my tears on my cheeks.

I would like to weep for as long as the rain falls on that melancholy island, for as long as it will rain on the foggy island of Chiloë, surrounded by the Pacific Ocean

Forgetfulness

A burning desire gnaws at me night and day, from dawn to dusk.

Is it a desire for vengeance? For glory? For amour?

I don't know, but I desire it furiously, with anguish.

In vain I search in all the joys of life, in all the hatreds, in all the follies.

Are the words lost, then, that would express my desire? Does its object no longer exist?

Perhaps I have brought it back from an anterior life, and have forgotten its cause.

But the unsatisfied desire has remained cruel and blind for me.

Suicide

A boat on the sea, without a sail or oars. It is abandoned. The placid sea rolls and pitches it gently,

It is like an abandoned cradle. The somnolent waves are rocking it gently.

The day is dawning faintly in the misty sky; the sea is deserted and tranquil.

Who, then, can be asleep in that boat rocked by the swell? The seagulls passing by can see.

They are not asleep. Their open eyes are shiny. Like the waves that reflect the sunlight, their eyes reflect the confession of an irremediable amour.

The sea, a mute accomplice, slowly filters into that soft cradle like blood leaking from a wound, and it sinks gradually, heavy and silent.

Then it disappears. A circle stripes the surface of the water; it broadens, running from wave to wave.

It runs toward the open sea, and toward the shore, where it comes to die softy, near a stake from which the chain of a boat hangs down.

Punishment

How did we come to be in that boat launched hither and yon by the violent waves, you at the prow and me silent at the stern.

Disheveled and flagellated by the brutal wind, I contemplated you with a joyous stupor, paying no heed either to the danger or the glaucous chill that penetrated me and made my teeth chatter.

You, grave and placid, were gazing into the distance.

A sinister man was holding the oars and separating me from you. He sniggered as he looked at me.

Where were you taking me, then? Was this the last voyage of my soul? Were you the judge? Was that man Charon, or simply a sailor darkened and tanned by the sea wind?

Your eyes turned toward me and looked at me without anger, as they looked at all things, and your voice vibrated and caused me to tremble more than the icy cold of the tempest.

"You will be punished," you said to me, and the wind took the words from your lips and threw them to the waves, which were agitating like furies; and the sniggering boatman repeated: "You will be punished."

But I smiled, forgetting my crimes; I had wanted to navigate thus, endlessly, in the tempest.

But a furious wave launched itself over me and carried me out of the boat. The waves pushed me from one to another as if none of them wanted to swallow me.

They threw me on to a shore that I did not know, and I searched the sea with my eyes for the boat in which you were, but I could no longer see it.

Then my heart swelled with sighs, and, running along the strand, I held out my arms to your vanished image.

The wind hissed in my ears: "You will be punished." My conscience seemed as heavy to me as an over-full satchel.

And it seemed to me that all the dolors of those who loved me in vain were weighing upon me. Phantoms appeared around me, which watched me suffer.

Give me your hands, sad shades, and let us moan together. Listen: I can no longer see his eyes, sapphires in which the sky is mirrored, nor his mouth, nor his grim forehead.

Look, I have been knocked down; the point of his spear is pricking my throat, his divine foot is crushing my heart. Alas, I am in love with the Archangel Michael!

The Seagull

Oh, the tranquil Ocean! Perfect beauty! Space!

The bitter freshness of the marine breeze passes over the forehead with a memory. O clamor of the sea, vibrant in the ear with its voice!

What a charming accord: the sea and its harmonious beauty.

The swell comes and goes, returns and strives toward the shore. The wave of reverie rolls and beats incessantly an indecisive desire, a fragile skiff soon submerged.

What placid horizons under the silent sky! O anguish of a shipwreck in the middle of the calm sea!

The water is transparent under the sun, the waves calm, clamoring very quietly. Oh, her sweet nonchalant head abandoning itself to the waves; her beautiful insouciant eyes that absorb all of the sea and the sky!

How dull and monotonous that bare sheet is, O memory of eyes as pure as the transparent water!

How morose and cold those eyes are, O nostalgia of the limpid sea!

A bird passes over the waves. Oh, to caress the virgin plumage of the seagull that flees over the sea!

Here is the wild bird, captive in the hands. Oh, the desire that flies away like the seagull over the sea!

AUGUSTE VILLIERS DE L'ISLE ADAM
(1838-1890)

Auguste Villiers de l'Isle Adam, represented himself as a Comte on the basis of abstruse genealogical research, an endeavor he inherited from his eccentric father. His aspiring parents were convinced while he was still a child that he was a genius—a conviction that he never abandoned—and he began to compose poems and music at an early age. The family was supported financially by his father's sister until she died in 1871, leaving Auguste with expensive tastes but no money. He asked for the hand of Théophile Gautier's younger daughter, Estelle, but his suit was rejected, in part because Gautier had been soured by Judith's marriage to Catulle Mendès, who was closely associated with Villiers in the late 1860s, when both were fervent Wagnerians; Mendès probably assisted Villiers in the editorship of the *Revue des lettres et des arts*. Villiers' literary work was as quirky and mercurial as he was. Several of his many "*contes cruels*" the first collection of which appeared under that title in 1883, qualify, wholly or in part, as *poèmes en prose*, including the sample translated below, as do pages in his novels *Isis* (1862) and *L'Ève future* (1886), his pretentious novella *Akedysseril* (1886) and his archetypal Symbolist play *Axël* (1890), but his principal contribution to the evolution of the genre was the ardent promotion he gifted to it in the *Revue des lettres et des arts*.

Introduction to *Akedysseril*

> Everything is constituted only by its emptiness.
> —Hindu Books.

The holy city appeared, violet in the depths of a golden haze. It was an evening of olden times; the dying of the star Surya,[1] the phoenix of the world, drew a myriad gems from the domes of Benares.

On the occidental heights, vast forests of palmyra palms were extending the gilded blueness of their shadows over the valleys of Habad towards their opposed shadows alternating with the flames of dusk: mystic palaces separated by widespread rose-bushes, whose blooms undulate by the thousand in the

---

1 The Sun.

stifling breeze. In their gardens, fountains flowed whose jets fell back in droplets of fire-colored snow.

At the center of the Secrole district, the colossal colonnades of the temple of Eternal Vishnu towered over the city. Its portals, lavishly inlaid with gold, reflected the clarity of the sky. Separated from the surrounding edifices, the hundred-and-ninety-six sanctuaries of the Devas extended the marbled whiteness of their steps downwards to be washed by the sparkling waters of the Ganges, while the sections of sky chiseled out by their crenellations extended upwards as far as the purple vapor of slow passing clouds.

The radiant water slept beneath the sacred quays; distance suspended veils, shimmering with light, over the magnificence of the river, and the immense riverside city stretched out in oriental disorder, its avenues terraced, its white-domed houses innumerable. Its monuments, from the quarters of Parsees to the pyramidion of Shiva's lingam, the ardent Wissikhor, seemed to be set afire by the azure blaze.

In the more profound distances the circular mouth of the well, the interminable military barracks, the bazaars of the market zone and the towers of citadels built in the reign of Wisvamithra sank into opal tints so pure that stars already twinkled therein. And overhanging the horizon, as if they were creatures of the sky laying siege to the earth, the immeasurable figures of divine beings were sculpted on the rocky crests of the mountains of the Habad, widening their knees in the immensity: summits cut in the form of gods. The greater number of these silhouettes lifted up into the abyss, at the extremity of their vertiginous arms, lotuses of stone—and the immobility of those presences disquieted space and set life afright.

At the decline of this particular day, however, a rumor of glory and celebration astonished the accustomed silence of nightfall in Benares. The multitude filled the streets, the public places, the avenues, the highways and the sandy slopes of both riverbanks, with a grave gladness—for the old men of the holy towers were coming out to strike their gongs with their bronze mallets, whereupon it suddenly seemed that the thunder had commenced to sing. This signal, which resounded at sublime hours, announced the return of Akedysseril: the young conqueror of the two kings of Agra; the svelte pearl-tinted, dazzling-eyed widow—in sum, the sovereign—who, while wearing her mourning-dress of woven gold, had made herself famous in the assault of Elephanta by feats of heroism that had inflamed the courage of thousands around her.

The Lovers of Toledo

> Would it have been just, then,
> if God had condemned man to Good Fortune?
> (One of the responses of Roman theology to an objection
> to the doctrine of Original Sin.)

An eastern dawn reddened the granite sculptures on the facade of the Inquisition in Toledo—and, between them, the *Dog-carrying-a-flaming-torch-in-its-mouth*: the arms of the Holy Office.

Two stout figures shadowed the bronze portal. Within the threshold, four sets of stone steps surged upwards from the bowels of the palace—a tangle of calculated precipices, with subtle variations in the ascending and descending flights. Some of these spirals unwound into the council chambers, the cells of the inquisitors, the secret chapel, the hundred and sixty-two dungeons, the orchard and the servants' dormitory, others into long, cold and interminable corridors which led to the refectories, the library and various private retreats.

In one of these chambers, richly furnished with Cordovan wall-hangings, plants and paintings sliced to excise the nudities of former days, stood a skinny old man of giant stature clad in a white cassock with a red cross. There was a long black cloak upon his shoulders, a black biretta on his head and an iron rosary at his waist. He stood, as the dawn light streamed through the windows, with his sandaled feet at the center of the

126

rosette of a Byzantine carpet, his hands clasped and his vast eyes staring. He seemed to be at least eighty years old. Pale, scarred by self-flagellation, doubtless still bloodied beneath the invisible hair-shirt that he never took off, he was studying an alcove where an opulent and soft bed was set, draped and festooned with garlands of flowers. That man was Tomas de Torquemada.

All around him, in the immense palace, a frightful silence fell from the vaults: a silence formed by a thousand sonorous breaths of the air, which never ceased to chill the stones.

Suddenly, the Grand Inquisitor of Spain pulled the cord of a bell whose ringing was inaudible. A monstrous block of granite, along with its wall-hanging, turned sideways. Three servants appeared, their hoods lowered, leaping from a narrow staircase hollowed out of the night—and the block closed again. It was over in two seconds—a lightning flash! But those two seconds had been sufficient for a red gleam, refracted from some subterranean hall, to illuminate the room, and for a terrible, confused squall of cries—so harrowing, so sharp and so frightful that one could neither distinguish nor guess the age or the sex of the howling voices—to pass through the chink of that door like a distant whiff of the inferno.

Then the gloomy silence and the cold draughts resumed, while angled shafts of sunlight fell upon the flagstones in the deserted corridors, disturbed at rare intervals by the clicking of an inquisitor's sandals.

Torquemada uttered a few words in a low voice.

One of the servants went out, returning a few moments later to usher in before him two handsome adolescents, hardly more than children: a young man and a young woman, perhaps sixteen or eighteen years of age. The distinction of their faces and their bearing testified to the nobility of their race, and their clothes—of the noblest elegance, sumptuous but discreet—indicated the elevated rank of their families. One might have thought that Romeo and Juliet, the lovebirds of Verona, had been transported to Toledo! They both looked at the aged holy man with smiles of astonished innocence, blushing slightly to find themselves already together.

"Dear and gentle infants," said Tomas de Torquemada, placing his hands upon them, "you have loved one another for close to a year—which is a long time at your age—with a love so chaste and so profound that, tremulous in one another's presence and lowering your eyes in church, you have not dared to speak to one another. That is why, knowing your secret, I have brought you here this morning, to unite you in marriage—which has been done. Your wise and powerful families have been notified that you are espoused, and that the palace which awaits you has been prepared for the celebration of your marriage. You shall soon be there, where you will live in a manner appropriate to your rank—doubtless surrounded, in due course, by lovely children, the flower of Christianity.

"Ah, you do well to love one another, to choose according to your young hearts! I too understand love: its effusions; its tears; its anxieties; its celestial tremors! It is with love that my own heart burns, for love is the law of life and the seal of sanctity. So, therefore, I have taken it upon myself to unite you in marriage, in order that the very essence of love—which is nothing but the good Lord—is not troubled, in you, by excessive desires of the flesh, or too long delayed by that lust which can, alas, inflame the senses of newlyweds in their legitimate possession of one another. Your prayers might become distracted! The fixity of your thoughts might obscure your natal purity! You are two angels who, in order to recollect that element in your love which is *real*, are already thirsty to appease, to blunt and to exhaust its delights.

"So be it! You are here in the Chamber of Fortune. You shall only pass your first conjugal hours here; then—blessing me, I hope, for having thus given you to one another, which is to say, to God—you shall return, I assure you, to everyday human life, at the rank to which God has assigned you."

At a gesture from the Grand Inquisitor, the servants rapidly undressed the charming couple, who—slightly dazed and enraptured—put up no resistance. Having placed them face to face, like juvenile statues, the servants quickly enveloped them in large bands of perfumed leather, which they gently tightened to press one against the other. The subdued couple were then transported, securely bound together heart-to-heart and lips-to-lips, to the nuptial couch and extended upon it, in an embrace subtly immobilized by their bonds. An instant later they were left alone, to their intense delight—which was not long delayed in overcoming their anxiety. Then they tasted such great and ardent delights that they whispered to one another, between distracted kisses: "Oh, if this could last forever!"

But nothing down here is eternal—and their gentle embrace, alas, *only lasted forty-eight hours.*

Then the servants came in, throwing the windows wide open to the pure air of the gardens. The two lovers' bonds were released and they were removed to neighboring cells. Baths, of which they were sorely in need, revived them. Once they were dressed again—while they shivered, livid, mute, grave and wild-eyed—Torquemada reappeared. The austere old man, giving them a supreme accolade, whispered in their ears: "My children, now that you have been provided with lasting proof of your good fortune, I give you up to life and to your love—for I believe that your prayers to the good Lord will be less distracted henceforth than they were in the past."

An escort conducted them to their palace, where a feast awaited them. They were expected, rumors of their joy had been broadcast.

During the marriage-feast, however, all the noble guests remarked—not without astonishment—a sort of stiffness between the two spouses, who spoke to one another briefly, with averted gazes and cold smiles.

They lived, almost separately, in their personal apartments and died without issue—because, to put it bluntly, they never embraced one another again, for fear . . . *for fear that it was not repeatable.*

EMMANUEL DES ESSARTS
(1839-1909)

Emmanuel des Essarts was the son of Alfred des Essarts, a notable Romantic poet and novelist. He completed his education at the École Normal supérieeure and had a successful academic career, which culminated in teaching literature at Dijon and in his birth-place, Clermont-Ferrand. He published two volumes of verse in the early 1860s and contributed pseudonymously to *La Revue fantaisiste* before being featured in *Le Parnasse contemporain*, and *L'Artiste*, but almost all of his later work was non-fiction. The item translated below was published in the *Renaissance littéraire et artistique* in 1872.

The Eternity of Don Juan

Sleep is a strange painter. In the savant variety of dreams it organizes the purest lines, disposes the riches colors, sometimes more Venetian than Veronese, more Correggian than Correggio. Oh, the landscapes that live on these nocturnal décors!

Once, among those artificial magnificences, in the midst of a natural enchantment in which perfumes and saps were seen flowing, I recognized Don Juan in mourning-dress at the foot of a gigantic myrtle, in chains. Under that funereal costume he still retained the air of a god, but a fallen god, for one no longer sensed in him anything but a theatrical pride and an ironic showmanship. He was vanquished, because, for the first time, a heart could be heard beating in his breast, and a tear was surprised on his eyelashes. Around the condemned man a crazy wind was frolicking; above his head alternated, in honor of Cypris, the sighs of wood-pigeons and doves; at his feet insects similar to flowers exchanged their ephemeral life in a flame; in front of him, two by two, but in hundreds and thousands, lovers passed, all bearing on their foreheads the terrestrial glory of fidelity, devotion and sacrifice, forever enlaced in a divine embrace, affianced eternally! And everywhere, the ineffable word "always" vibrated in that music of souls. And everyone loved in that Amathonte of my dream. Only Don Juan was unloved!

ANATOLE FRANCE
(1844-1924)

Anatole France was the pseudonym of Jacques-Anatole Thibault, the son of a well-known bookseller nicknamed "Père France," in whose shop the Parnassians held gatherings, as a result of which the bibliophilic Anatole became a contributor to the second volume in the *Parnasse contemporain* series in 1869. After Victor Hugo's death he was widely recognized as the greatest living writer in France; he was awarded hr Nobel Prize for Literature in 1921, after which his entire works were placed on the Index Liborum Prohibitorum by the Church, which he regarded as a further distinction, richly earned by his classic exercises in literary Satanism, *Thaïs* (1890), "L'Humaine tragédie" (1895 in *Le Puits de Sainte Claire*) and *La Révolte des anges* (1914; tr, as *The Revolt of the Angels*). His work is very various, but always rich in elegant irony; his antiquarian fantasies, in particular, are rich in poetic ornamentation; some of them—including the item below, reprinted in *L'Étui de nacre* (1892; tr. as *Mother-of-Pearl*)—show the influence of Catulle Mendès, who recruited him to the stable of writers he assembled for *L'Écho de Paris*, in which France stayed after most of the stable had migrated to *Le Journal* in 1895.

Amycus and Célestin

Prostrate on the threshold of his grotto, the hermit Célestin was spending his Easter vigil in prayer, on the angelic night when the shuddering demons were precipitated into the abyss. And while the shadows covered the earth, at the hour when the exterminating angel had soared over Egypt, Célestin shivered, gripped by anguish and anxiety. In the distance, in the forest, he could hear the mewling of wild cats and the fluty voices of toads; plunged in the impure darkness, he doubted that the glorious mystery could be accomplished. But when he saw the day break, delight entered his soul with the dawn; he knew that Christ was resuscitated and he cried:

"Jesus has emerged from the tomb! Love has vanquished death, Alleluia! He is rising up radiant from the foot of the hill, Alleluia! Creation is remade and repaired. The shadow and evil are dissipated; grace and light are spreading over the world, Alleluia!"

A lark that had woken up in the wheat responded to him in song.

And the hermit Célestin emerged from his grotto in order to go to the nearby chapel and solemnize the holy day of Easter.

As he was going through the forest he saw a beautiful beech tree in the middle of a clearing, the swollen buds of which were already allowing little tender green leaves to escape. Garlands of ivy and hanks of wool were suspended from the branches, which hung down all the way to the ground. Votive tablets attached to the gnarled trunk spoke of youth and amour, and here and there, clay effigies of Eros, his wings open and his tunic flying, swayed in the branches. At that sight, the hermit Célestin's white eyebrows frowned.

"That is the tree of the fays," he said to himself, "and the young women of the region have charged it with offerings, in accordance with ancient custom. My life is spent struggling against the fays, and no one can imagine the trouble those little folk give me. They don't resist me overtly. Every year, at harvest time, I exorcize the tree in accordance with the rites, and I sing them the Gospel of Saint John.

"One can't do any better; the holy water and the Gospel of Saint John put them to flight, and no more mention of those ladies is heard all winter, but they come back in the spring and recommence every year.

"They are subtle; it only requires a hawthorn bush to shelter a whole swarm. And they cast spells on the young men and the young women.

"Since I have grown old, my sight has deteriorated and I can scarcely perceive them any more. They make fun of me, thumbing their noses at me and laughing at my beard. But when I was twenty I saw them in the clearings, dancing rounds in flower hats in the moonlight. Lord God, who made the sky and the dew, be praised in your works! But why have you made pagan trees and magical springs? Why have you put under the hazel tree the mandrake that sings? Those natural things induce youth to sin and cause fatigues without number to anchorites like me, who have undertaken to sanctify creatures. If only the Gospel of Saint John were still sufficient to expel demons! But it is not sufficient, and I no longer know what to do."

"And as the good hermit drew away, sighing, the tree, which was enchanted, said to him in a fresh rustle: "Célestin, Célestin, my buds are eggs, true Easter eggs! Aleluia! Alleluia!"

Célestin plunged into the wood without turning his head. He was advancing with difficulty along a narrow path, in the midst of thorns that tore his robe, when a young boy bounding from a bush barred his way. He was half-clad in an animal skin, and was a faun rather than a boy; his gaze was piercing, his nose snub, his face laughing. His curly hair hid two little horns on his stubborn head; his lips uncovered sharp white teeth; blond hair descended from his chin in two points. A golden down shone on his breast. He was agile and svelte; his cloven feet were dissimulated in the grass.

Célestin, who possessed all the knowledge that meditation gives, saw immediately what he was dealing with and he raised his arm in order to describe the sign of the cross; but the faun, seizing his hand, prevented him from completing that powerful gesture.

"Good hermit," he said to him, "don't exorcize me. For me as for you, today is a feast day. It would not be charitable to sadden me at Easter. If you wish, we can walk together, and you'll see that I'm not wicked.

Fortunately, Célestin was well versed in the sacred sciences. He remembered appropriately that Saint Jerome had had satyrs and centaurs for traveling companions in the desert, who had confessed the truth.

He said to the faun: "Faun, be a hymn of God. Say: *he is resuscitated.*"

"He is resuscitated," replied the faun, "and you see me full of joy."

The path had broadened, and they were walking side by side. The hermit was pensive and thought: *He isn't a demon since he's confessed the truth. I did well not to sadden him. The example of the great Saint Jerome has not been wasted on me.*

Turning to his companion, he asked him: "What is your name?"

"My name is Amycus," the faun replied. "I live in these woods, where I was born. I came to you, Father, because you have a rather benevolent air under the long white beard. It seems to me that hermits are fauns overwhelmed by the years. When I'm old, I will be like you."

"He is resuscitated," said the hermit.

"He is resuscitated," said Amycus.

And, conversing thus, they climbed the hill where a chapel stood, consecrated to the true God. It was small and primitive in structure; Célestin had built it with his own hands with the debris of a temple of Venus. Inside, the Lord's table was deformed and bare.

"Let us kneel down," said the hermit, "and sing Alleluia, for he is resuscitated. And you, obscure creature, remain on your knees while I offer the sacrifice."

But the faun, drawing nearer to the hermit, caressed his beard and said: "Good old man, you are more knowledgeable than me, and you see the invisible; but I know the woods and the springs better than you do. I have brought the good foliage and flowers. I know the banks where the water-cress opens its lilac corymbs, the meadows where the cowslip flowers in yellow clusters. I divine by its odor the mistletoe of the wild apple tree. Already, a flowery snow is crowning the blackthorn bushes. Wait for me, old man."

134

In three caprine bounds he was in the wood, and when he came back, Célestin thought he was seeing a walking hawthorn bush. Amycus disappeared beneath his perfumed harvest. He suspended garlands of flowers from the rustic altar; he covered it with violets and sad, gravely: "These flowers to the god who gave them birth!"

And while Célestin celebrated the sacrifice of the mass, the capriped, bowing his horned head all the way to the ground, adored the sun and said: "The earth is a great egg, which you fecundate, sun, sacred sun!"

From that day on, Célestin and Amycus lived together. In spite of all his efforts, the hermit never succeeded in enabling the half-human to understand the ineffable mysteries, but, by virtue of the cares of Amycus, the chapel of the true God was always ornamented with garlands, and more florid than the tree of the fays, so the holy priest said: "The faun is a hymn of God."

That is why he gave him holy baptism.

On the hill where Célestin had constructed the narrow chapel that Amycus ornamented with flowers from the mountains, woods and streams, a church stands today, the nave of which dates back to the eleventh century and the porch of which was re-edified under Henri II in the style of the Renaissance. It is a place of pilgrimage, and the faithful venerate there the blessed memory of Saints Amic and Célestin.

Part Three:
The Third Republic

JORIS-KARL HUYSMANS
(1848-1907)

Joris-Karl Huysmans was the form of his name employed for his published works by Charles-Georges Huysmans; while working as a civil servant, he produced a number of seemingly paradoxical quasi-autobiographical works that contrasted sharply in certain respects with his own life, although he altered his behavior and attitudes in the wake of each one in order to bring his life more into line with their conclusions. Although he began his career as a Naturalist writer in the analytical mode of Edmond and Jules de Goncourt, his *À rebours* (1884) is a long character-study of a bizarre aristocratic aesthete, Jean Des Esseintes, who adopts an extreme contrarian stance in all matters. The novel is a comedy that mocks the attitudes and actions of its "hero," but which seemed very serious to many readers—and eventually, even to its author. At the end of the novel, Des Esseintes, after experimenting with taking his nourishment via the wrong end of the gut, by enema (a circumstance disguised in bowdlerized early translations of the novel) he decides to reinvest in religious faith, precisely because it is incredible and absurd—which is exactly what Huysmans elected to do himself, following a path mapped out in a series of novels begun with *Là-Bas* (1891), which popularized the notion that Satanism was thriving secretly and dangerously in contemporary Paris. The theme was suggested to him by his brief affair with Berthe Courrière, an eccentric poseur with connections in the darker sector of the Occult Revival—then in full swing—who subsequently had a more intense affair with

Huysmans' close friend Remy de Gourmont, on whose work she also had a brief but intense effect.

Previously, in the prose poems and short essays collected in *La dragéoir des épices* (1875)—from which the samples below are taken—Huysmans had combined the strong influence of Baudelaire with an ironic dose of Naturalism to produce a new hybrid, and he added a determinedly perverse poetic element to the subsequent quasi-journalistic essays he collected in *Croquis parisiens* (1890; tr. as *Parisian Sketches*), the most notorious of which is "La Bièvre," in which the eponymous industrially-polluted river is presented as a symbol of the degradation of the provincial girls recruited to work in the factories tainting its waters. Frequently reprinted in pamphlets with one or two other "character-studies" of run-down and polluted outlying districts of Paris, the perverse romanticism of "La Bièvre" had a powerful influence on another of Huysmans' once-close friends, Jean Lorrain, and on Lorrain's principal disciple, Delphi Fabrice, thus helping to formulate an entire subgenre of raptly scathing studies of the physical and spiritual pollution of the most deprived and depraved areas of Paris. That dovetailed very neatly with the ambient advancement of the Decadent Movement, for which *À rebours* became a kind of Holy Writ, with particular relevance to the evolution of prose-poetry because of Des Esseintes' great liking for the oxymoronic genre and his characterization of it as the "osmazome" of literature. That was written at least half in jest, but even the author surely did not know how much proverbial truth might be present, intended or unintended, in the jest. Because of that, Huysmans' influence on the prose poetry written after the recovery from the Franco-Prussian War—which seemed to many people to mark the beginning of a new era, removing one of the chief *raisons-d'être* of the Parnassian Movement—far outweighed the exemplary value of his own specimen texts.

Japanese Rococo

You whose eyes are black, tresses black and flesh blonde, listen to me, my flighty she-wolf!

I love your eccentric eyes, the eyes that are tucked up over the temples; I love your mouth as red as a sorb-berry, your rounded yellow cheeks; I love your twisted feet, your stiff throat, your long lanceolate fingernails, as brilliant as mother-of-pearl.

I love, dainty she-wolf, your enervating nonchalance, your languid smile, your indolent attitude, your prim gestures.

I love, seductive she-wolf, the mewling of your voice; I love its hoarse and ululating tones, but above all I love, to die for, your nose, your little nose, which escapes from the waves of your hair like a yellow rose blossoming in black foliage.

Ritornelle

Her deceased man had beaten her, given her three children and died soaked in absinthe.

Since that time she has wallowed in the mud, pushing a cart, shouting at the top of her voice. So it goes! So it goes!

She is ineffably ugly. She is a monster who bobs a red, grimacing head on the neck of a wrestler, holed by bloodshot eyes, humped by a nose whose wide wings, tobacco-bunkers, are covered with little violet spots.

They have good appetites, the three children; it's for them that she wallows in the mud, pushing the cart, shouting at the top of her voice. So it goes! So it goes!

Her neighbor has just died.

Her deceased man had beaten her, given her three children and died soaked in absinthe.

The monster has not hesitated to take them in.

They have good appetites, the six children! To work! To work! Without respite, unrelentingly, she wallows in the mud, pushing the cart, shouting at the top of her voice. So it goes! So it goes!

Declaration of Love

I sense, dully, an unspeakable rage in my soul when I think about you, Ninon. If a girl whose mother has said: "You're young, you're beautiful, you're a virgin, that's saleable," delivers herself to a rich libertine and falls, step by step, into the most degrading excesses, I excuse her, as I excuse a girl who gives herself by virtue of amour to a man who, after making her pregnant, abandons her like the coward he is, and that girl then displays herself before the first man who comes along in order to nourish her child; but if a well-brought up girl who can earn her living honestly, deliberately rolls in every kind of mud and filth, I hate her and I despise her.

Do you hear, infamous slut? I hate you, I despise you . . . and I love you.

The Kipper

Your robe, O herring, is the palette of sunsets, has the patina of old brass, the burnished gold of Cordovan leather, the sandal-wood and saffron tinges of autumn foliage.

Your head, O herring, is as flamboyant as a golden helmet, and one might think that your eyes were black nails planted in brass rings!

All the sad and bleak hues, and all the radiant and cheerful hues, deaden and illuminate your scaly robe by turns.

Alongside the bitumens and Judean earths of Cassel, and the burnt umbers and greens of Scheele, Van Dyck browns and Florentine bronzes, glints of rust and dead leaves, resplendent with all their brightness, are greenish golds and yellow ambers, orpiments and ochers of rum, the chromes and oranges of cheap brandy.

O shiny and dull kipper, when I contemplate your coat of mail, I think of Rembrandt's paintings; I remember his superb heads, his sunlit freshness, his sparkling jewels on black velvet; I remember his beams of light in darkness, his trails of gold powder in the shadow, his explosions of sunlight beneath black arches!

CHARLES CROS
(1842-1888)

Charles Cros divided his time between his poetic endeavors and technological explorations in the recording of sound, telegraphy and color photography. He teamed up before the Franco-Prussian War with Auguste Villiers de l'Isle Adam for performances staged at soirées hosted by his mistress, Nina de Villard, and afterwards with the humorist Alphonse Allais in similar performances in the Chat Noir, where he finished committing slow suicide by absinthe. During the siege of Paris he and his younger brother assisted their elder brother, the physician Antoine Cros, to care for the sick and wounded, and only narrowly avoided arrest and deportation as a Communard. His ventures in devising mono-logues for delivery in Nina de Villard's salon, the most famous of which was "Le Herang saur" [The Kipper], were taken up and greatly extrapolated by the actor Ernest Coquelin and other performers on various Parisian stages. A lecture on the possi-bility of interplanetary communication delivered in Camille Flammarion's salon had a considerable influence on the devel-opment of the *roman scientifique*, his suggested method being featured in several novels. His early prose poems, including those translated below, were first published in the *Renaissance littéraire et artistique* in 1873, when Ernest Blémont had succeeded Jean Aicard as its editor, and most were reprinted a decade later in *Le Chat Noir*.

The Distractress

The bedroom is full of perfumes. On the low table, in baskets, there is reseda, jasmine and all sorts of little red, yellow and blue flowers

Emigrant blondes from lands of long dusks, from the land of dreams, visions disembark in my fantasy. They run and shout there, pressing one another so much that I would like to bring them out.

I take sheets of very white and very smooth paper, and quills the color of amber, which glide over the paper with the cries of swallows. I want to give the disquieting visions the shelter of rhythm and rhyme.

But then, on the white and smooth paper over which my pen was crying like a swallow over a lake, reseda and jasmine flowers fell, and other little red, yellow and blue flowers.

It was *Her*, unseen, shaking the bouquets in the baskets on the low table.

But visions were still agitating and wanted to set out again. Then, forgetting that *She* was there, beautiful and blonde, I blew away the little flowers strewn on the paper and resumed running after the visions, which, in their traveling cloaks, have treacherous wings.

I went to imprison one—a savage girl with green eyes—in a narrow strophe, when *She* came to lean her elbows on the low table beside me, so that her irritating breasts were caressing the smooth paper.

The last line of the strophe remained to be soldered. It was thus that *She* prevented me from doing it, and the vision and the green gaze fled, only leaving in the open strophe her traveling cloak and a little nacre from her wings.

Oh, the distractress! I was about to give her the kiss she was expecting, when shifting visions, dear emigrants with distant odors, re-formed their dances in my fantasy.

So, I forgot again that *She* was there, white and naked. I wanted to close the narrow strophe with the last line, an indestructible chain of ideal steel, nielloed with stellar gold, encrusted with the splendors of sunsets crystallized in my memory.

And with my hand I moved aside the breasts swollen by irritating desires, which were masking the place of the last line on the smooth paper. My pen resumed its flight, crying like a swallow skimming the surface of a tranquil lake, before a storm.

But then she stretched herself, beautiful, white and naked, over the low table, below the baskets, hiding the entire sheet of smooth paper under her beautiful languid body.

Then the visions all flew far away, no longer to return.

My eyes, my lips and my hands were lost in the aromatic brushwood of her nape, in the obstinate embrace of her arms, on her breasts swollen with desire.

And I could no longer see that beautiful languid body, warm, white and smooth, on to which resedas and jasmines fell from agitated baskets, and other little red, yellow and blue flowers.

The Piece of Furniture

I needed to have a rapid eye, a fine ear and a very keen attention,

To discover the mystery of the item of furniture, to penetrate behind the perspectives of the marquetry, to reach the imaginary world through the little mirrors.

But I finally glimpsed the clandestine fête, I heard the minuscule minuets, I surprised the complicated intrigues that were being woven inside the case.

The doors open, one sees a kind of drawing room for insects; one notices the white, brown and black tiling in exaggerated perspective.

A mirror in the middle, a mirror to the right, a mirror to the left, like the doors in symmetrical comedies. In truth, those mirrors are doors open to the imaginary.

But there is an evidently-unaccustomed solitude, an inexplicable neatness, in that empty drawing room, a luxury without reason in an interior where only darkness reigns.

One is duped by that; one says to oneself: "It's an item of furniture, and that's all"; one thinks that there is nothing behind the mirrors except the reflection of what is presented to them.

Insinuations that come from somewhere else, lies whispered to our reason by a deliberate politics, an ignorance in which we hold certain interests that I cannot define.

However, I can no longer exercise prudence; I don't care what might happen, I don't care about fantastic rancors.

When the cupboard is shut, when importunate heads are blockaded by sleep or filled by external sounds, when human thought weighs upon some positive object,

Then strange scenes unfold in the drawing-room of the piece of furniture; a number of individuals of unusual dimension and appearance emerge from the little mirrors; certain groups, illuminated by strange gleams, agitate there in its exaggerated perspectives,

Advancing from the depths of the marquetry, from behind the simulated colonnades, from artificial corridors accommodated in the backs of the doors,

In outdated costumes, with fluttering steps, for a festival of an extraterrestrial almanac:

Elegant men of an epoch of dream, young women seeking an establishment in that society of reflections, and finally, aged parents, corpulent diplomats and acned dowagers.

On the wall of polished wood, suspended who knows how, girandoles light up. In the middle of the room, hanging from a non-existent ceiling, a resplendent chandelier is overloaded with stout pink candles, as long as the horns of snails. On unexpected fireplaces, fires blaze like glow-worms.

Who has put those armchairs there, as deep as nutshells, arranged in a circle, those tables laid with immaterial refreshments or microscopic wagers, those sumptuous curtains as heavy as spider-webs?

But the ball commences. The orchestra, which one would think composed of cockchafers, throws out fizzing notes and imperceptible whistles. The young people hold hands and make reverences to one another.

Perhaps some kisses of fictitious amour are exchanged surreptitiously, casual smiles hidden behind fly-wing fans, and faded flowers in corsages requested and given with signs of reciprocal indifference.

How long will all that last? What conversations are held in those parties? Where does that insubstantial society go after the soirée?

No one knows.

Since the lights go out if one opens the item of furniture, the guests—fops, coquettes and aged relatives—disappear pell-mell, with no concern for their dignity, into the mirrors, corridors and colonnades; the armchairs, tables and curtains evaporate,

And the drawing room remains empty, silent and neat;

So everyone says: "it's an item of marqurety furniture and that's all," without suspecting that as soon as the gaze is turned away,

Sly little faces risk emerging from the symmetrical mirrors, from behind the incrusted columns and from the depths of the artificial shadows.

And it requires a particularly expert, scrupulous and rapid eye to surprise them as they draw way into those exaggerated perspectives, when they take refuge in the imaginary depths of the little mirrors, at the moment when they go back into the unreal hidey-holes of the polished wood.

Madrigal
Translated from the surface of one of Lady Hamilton's fans

Time, the implacable alchemist, will drain the warm perfume of sandalwood.

But these words, written on your fan, will subsist, and you will still find therein the immaterial perfume of memory.

Then the picture of your splendid youth will unfurl in your memory. You will be dazzled and delighted, as we are dazzled and delighted when your coppery hair unfurls over your shoulders.

Afterwards, time, momentarily tamed, will resume its devouring work and your flesh, a palpable dawn, will be suddenly carried away by the wrath of fate or of mankind, or slowly desiccated by the wind of old age, finally to dissolve in the brown earth.

That fan too, sold, bought, sold again, soiled in drawers, broken by children, a disdained item of bric-à-brac, will perhaps end up in a bright fire, or, a wreck of the gutter, it will descend streams in order to be scattered, rotten, in the immense sea.

In the meantime, retain the pride of your flesh the color of dawn, let your hair blaze indolently, play with the perverse omnipotence of your transparent eyes.

For you are the present link of the perpetual chain of beauty, and what has once been will shine forever in the absolute; because the symphony of your life requires a severe and grandiose final chord.

In any case, these words, which speak of you, transmitted from memory to memory, will incessantly revive the sovereign hand that held this fan, and the flesh that it has caressed with its perfumed flapping.

The Song of the Aryan Road

On our horses we carry away the beautiful daughters of our tribe.

We drive the flocks before us. The ewes nurse the lambs on the run. The calves pursue the cows whose idle march the slaves hasten with the prod.

We sometimes dismount in order to change gait, and the beautiful young women march proudly, parting the low branches of the forests with their white arms.

They are beautiful, the daughters of our tribe, with their bodies in which gold and silver jewelry clinks when they place their white feet on the moss and the dry leaves.

We are the strongest of men, we are white and we are going to live in beautiful unknown lands.

We come from a snowy land that has left us fresh memories, but not plaintive songs.[1]

We shall fill the unknown lands with fresh songs learned in our homeland or found on our route by those of our tribe who listen by night to the sound of rivers and the frissons of woods.

We are the strongest of men, we are white and we will subjugate the red, yellow or black dwarfs who are in the unknown lands. They will labor the earth and sow it for us, in order that we can listen in the wind to the sound of rivers and the frissons of woods. They will clean our cowsheds and grease our carts, in order that our daughters can keep their hands soft and their fingers white.

We drive our flocks before us. Never kill the fecund ewes or sheep, for they give us their milk and their wool.

Never kill the fecund cows, nor the bulls, not the oxen; for the cow gives us her milk, which rejoices the women, guardians of the tents, and the pink children who chase away melancholy.

From milk comes the piquant white cheese, good with beer and wine.

The bulls are beautiful in their amorous and jealous combats.

In addition, bulls and oxen pull our carts, mingling their profound bellowing with the sound of rivers and the frissons of woods, while the slaves hasten their idle gait with prods.

The flesh of sheep and oxen is insipid. It is only necessary to eat it if excessively rare wild animals escape our arrows and our spears.

What better meals are there than those of the evening? The wild boars with black flesh and partridges perfumed with juniper roast before cheerful fires.

---

1 In a mythical history gradually pieced together by French Romantic historians and proto-anthropologists, the ultimate ancestors of Western Europeans were supposedly "Aryans" who had originated in the Pamir Mountains in what is now Tajikistan and had migrated westwards in search of greener pastures. Such ideas were widely accepted and influential in the Parisian literary community, elaborately developed on such works as Camille Mauclair's *L'Orient vierge* (1897; tr. as *The Virgin Orient*), long before Nazi Germany stamped the myth with the indelible seal of political incorrectness—by which the present prose-poem is inevitably and justly cursed.

It is the return from the hunt. We find the beautiful young women joyful. They have spun fine chemises for themselves with the frail flax with blue flowers, and warm tunics for us with the wool of the bleating flocks.

Beer is foaming in the pots, and we sing, after eating, the songs of the cool native land or the trailing songs of the road.

They are beautiful, the daughters of our race. They come from lands of snowy mountains. Each of us is glad that each of them delivers her body, as white as the snowy mountains of the land of cheerful memories!

The man does wrong, therefore, who goes behind the tents on evenings full of visions, after the wild boar is eaten and the foamy beer drunk, behind the tents where the pink children are asleep, to unite himself with red, yellow or black slaves.

He does wrong because children of mixed race are born from that, which make bad servants of our children and rebellious chiefs among the slaves who clean the cowsheds.

Let the slaves unite with one another, therefore, and remember that the white girls, the daughters of our race, are beautiful and sing us the true fresh songs of the native land or the trailing songs of the road.

This song will be sung on the road, to the sound of rivers, of agitated woods, of the bellowing of beasts pulling carts, when we hear the gold and silver jewelry clinking in the meadows on the white breasts of beautiful young women, and the monotonous bells around the necks of the horses.

CHALES DE SIVRY
(1848-1900)

Charles de Sivry was primarily known as a musician and composer of operettas; his half-sister was the wife that Paul Verlaine deserted when he ran away with Arthur Rimbaud. Verlaine introduced him into the Parisian literary community before the Prussian invasion. He was appointed as the official archivist of the Commune, and was imprisoned when the Commune was suppressed. Verlaine entrusted him with the manuscript of Rimbaud's *Illuminations*, which helped to inspire him to produce his own *poèmes en prose*, most of which—including the sample translated below—were published in the *Revue artistique et littéraire* in the late 1870s, along with a number of short stories belatedly collected in *Les Mauvais sous et autres contes fantastiques* (2014). He associated with Charles Cros and his brothers at the Chat Noir, and collaborated with Antoine Cros on a Freemasonic "spectacle" that illustrated his peripheral involvement with the Occult Revival.

The Spinner
Song in prose

The spinning-wheel hums and whistles, the heart of the old clock beats slowly in its oak box, and, as it is not yet midnight, the old woman with the joyful wrinkles lets the spindle run between her agile fingers, while Berthe looks at her reflection in a polished pewter lid.

"Eh! What are you spinning there, good woman?" says the great voice of the nocturnal wind.

"I'm spinning a wedding chemise for Berthe, a wedding chemise in pure linen."

"Eh! What are you thinking there, blonde girl?" says the rattle of the leaded window-panes that are shaking with the noise of the little bell of the mass.

"I'm thinking that I'll be fully adorned when *he* comes to take me away at midnight, when my mother has gone to bed."

The spinning-wheel hums and whistles; the old clock coughs, as if to draw breath before chiming midnight.

"Berthe . . . Berthe . . . it's time to go to sleep . . . Berthe, where are you, then . . . ?"

"I saw her passing by, carried away by a rider on a black horse," replies the great voice of the nocturnal wind.

"Berthe . . . Berthe, my daughter!" And the old woman gets up and takes the pewter lid in which Berthe was mirroring herself—but even her reflection has gone.

The spinning-wheel is humming and whistling. It is the third time, since Berthe's departure, that the old clock is chiming its sinister midnight. The old woman with the saddened wrinkles makes the spindle run between her agile fingers, while Berthe, lying on the oak dresser, seems to be sleeping dreamlessly in a white dress.

"Eh! What are you spinning there, good woman?" says the great voice of the nocturnal wind.

"I'm spinning a shroud for Berthe, a shroud of pure linen."

"Eh! What is your soul thinking, dead woman?" say the little leaded panes, rattling.

"I'm thinking that the seigneur Enguerrand de Vauvenargues will be punished by the stars for having seduced me and abandoned me in the corner of the woods, which caused me to die of shame and made the spinner weep."

ROBERT CAZE
(1853-1886)

Robert Caze was a friend of the Goncourt brothers, Joris-Karl Huysmans and Paul Verlaine, and very highly regarded as a poet and prose writer; he founded a periodical, *La Jeunesse*, with Jean Richepin. He was a Communard, along with another friend, Paschal Grousset (later to be well-known as the writer of popular fiction André Laurie), who obtained him an appointment in the Commune's hastily-constituted Ministry of Foreign Affairs. He fled thereafter to Switzerland—although born in Paris he was a Swiss National—but he took advantage of an amnesty to return to Paris in 1880, where he contributed prolifically to several *Revues*. An unfortunate tendency to quarrel over reviews embroiled him in duels, first with Paul Bonnetain, who wounded him in 1883, and later with Charles Vignier, who had published an account of his refusal to fight Félicien Champsaur in the *Revue moderniste*. Vignier wounded Caze fatally, apparently by accident, and frequently referred to himself thereafter as "the killer of my friend Robert Caze." The item translated below was published in the *Renaissance littéraire et artistique* in 1873.

Far, Far Away

"Why, why are you weeping? Am I not by your side, child? What are your desires, daughter of slow amours and powerful lusts?"

"What I want, O love of my life, is to leave; to go far, far away, and even further. The blue mountains and the white snows are not worth, believe me, the crazy sun of our creole savannahs. It's there that one can roll naked in the long grass, in the cool of the evening; where supple bodies can slither, voluptuously enlaced, like dear reptiles in the bushy prairies. There, that's why I want to go far, far away and even further!

"My brown body is all ablaze. It wants to be impregnated by warm breaths. Oh, I'm in haste to quit heavy and ridiculous garments in order to put on light and ample fabrics that fall quickly in moments of fever. You see, it's necessary to liberate charming forms. I'm proud of my bust. There, that's why I want to go far, far away and even further!

"Pale child of snowy lands, your amours are melancholy, like the sky of your homeland. Come, I will make your sinews creak in mad embraces. You will acquire our powerful fire . . . There, that's why I want to go far, far away and even further!

"If it were necessary for me to die here, my body would fasten your meager earth, and my sap would be seen, in summer, spreading with difficulty in a few etiolated flowers scattered on my tomb. It's in the midst of savannahs, or in the most profound virgin forest that I want to repose. The giant trees of new lands would cover my cadaver with their shade. There, at least, I would return to Life all that I have received from her. I would be a good creature. There, that's why I want to go far, far away and even further!"

JULES-AMÉDÉE BARBEY D'AUREVILLY
(1808-1889)

Jules-Amédee Barbey-d'Aurevilly was an ultra-Romantic critic who began publishing poetry in the 1820s and fiction in the 1830s. He elaborated his personal philosophy of "Dandyism," first described in the *avant garde* character-study *La Bague d'Annibal* (1842; tr. as Hannibal's Ring) in the classic essay *Du Dandysme et de George Brummel* (1845)—which had a powerful influence on Charles Baudelaire and later on Jean Lorrain. He only achieved a substantial success with his own literary works under the Third Republic, when he published a classic collection of short stories, *Les Diaboliques* (1874; tr. as *The She-Devils*), which is closely affiliated to the tradition of *contes cruels* then being sophisticated by Auguste Villiers de l'Isle Adam. His criticism, which included a significant analysis of *À Rebours*, was feared as well as respected, and the legend that he became in his lifetime was spectacularly problematic and perverse. The typically-eccentric and typically-extravagant sample of his prose-poetry translated below was one of his last works to be published, in the *Revue indépendante* in 1886.

Chameleon Eyes

I

It was one of those nights such as you and I once spent, you out there in the four oak-clad feet of your solitary cell, like a coffin, and me in an even sadder place. For the room that I inhabit is my heart. She whom we both detest, but who loves us and haunts our bedside, Insomnia, came to sit down beside me and started looking at me, with her eyes so wide, so bleak and so pale—those eyes so immeasurably open, which, by an implacable magnetism, dilated the eyes that were looking at them and prevented them from closing!

II

And that night, those open eyes seemed larger and paler than mine in the depths of the darkness. How did they stand out, for they were not brilliant? They were not shining, and yet they were there, appearing in the obscurity like the blue gaze of a statue that suddenly makes us shiver at the corner of path through a wood, at dusk.

III

And they were so desperate, those pale eyes, so desperate and so fixed, there was something in the immanence of their fixity so devoured, so consumed, and yet so unconsumable, that one sensed that, in spite of their wan color of dust, they were burning more forcefully inside, in a secret agony, that it was truly astonishing that Albrecht Durer had not put such a gaze in the face of Atlas, overwhelmed by his terrible Melancholy!

IV

And in order not to see them, those insupportable eyes that opened mine by force, as a shelling knife opens oysters, I relit my extinct lamp. A golden droplet filtered along the somber wood paneling, and, falling like a tear into my quivering mirror in the depths of its ebony frame, attached its faint spark to the tips of the clenched knees of the black bronze crucifix, but it did not chase away the vision of the open eyes, so madly wide and so cruelly fixed, but of which no radiance could any longer revive the ash!

V

Dead stars, but still visible, they remained, as tenacious as a bad dream, in the gilded light as well as in the darkness. And I could not see anything but them! I forgot to what head they belonged, for they were so large that only they appeared. And I said to myself: "Strange sight! Is she nothing but an open gaze from head to foot, Insomnia?" The Night passed. The Hours fled, those immortal cowards who always flee, but in quitting us, like Parthians, unleash one arrow more into our hearts, which are already completely full! The exhausted lamp went out, and in the black curtain of obscurity that fell along the walls, the pale eyes of the nocturnal Monster continued to magnify their two immense orbs until morning, when they disappeared, as if their eyelids, still magnified, had folded up like living shutters, one in the cupboard with bleak sculpted roses, the other in the violet scabious of the carpet.

VI

And, obverted from that eternal obsession, I thought of the pallor that had only been vanquished by the sparkling features of Daylight, and I said to myself that a little beyond that sepulchral nuance there was no more color—that those eyes, a little paler, would disappear! I told myself that I would not see them again, that I could close mine and engulf myself beneath my eyelids!

VII

For they could change. You have not always had that phantom pallor, O indefatigable eyes of Insomnia! You have not always been gaping, stupefied, immobile. You have sometimes lowered an eyelid. You have had the brightness and movement of life. I have seen you, not long ago, dotting my nights, with your light, more beautiful, more scintillating and more nuanced than stars that are no longer dormant in our heads and which are the eyes of horizons. O pale eyes, you had the nuances of rainbows and the dawn then, when you brought me in the jet of night the emerald of green hope, the tender jealousies, of the azure and the ruby rain of amour in flames! All the eyes of women that I had loved, reflections of memories, velveted by the past, divinized by the impossibility of caresses, passed through the ardent mirrors of your chameleon eyes, O insomnia, and we even rediscovered their tears therein!

VIII

But you are no longer there, O chameleon eyes! The reflection of eyes that one loved has vanished again before our soul. Insomnia resembles Life. Our nights resemble our days. Is there now for us, in deprived and extinct existence, a single color, even sad but still soft, from which you can, O chameleon eyes, draw echoes for the gaze of the soul and repeat to us—vaguely, alas! Chameleon eyes of the Insomnia of our youth, you are now like the other inanimate eyes that we contemplate in life, the long evening of the day so long in finishing!

IX

Undoubtedly, it is necessarily thus, and I know it. Is it not destiny? But then, O chameleon eyes, why not close ours when you have ceased to shine in our sad nights? Why not put us to sleep in the slumber that has no dreams—not even the dream of dreaming, the dream of vanished reflections? Why, in sum, do you come every night, O Insomnia, like the specter of drowned Ophelia, bearing in your tangled hair the wisps of straw of the bed on which we lay awake in anguish, to sit down at our feet and look at us, O Magnetizer of Madness, and kill us slowly with your pale eyes, which used to be Chameleon Eyes?

J.-H. ROSNY
(1856-1940)

"J.-H. Rosny" was the pseudonym of Joseph-Henri Boëx, a member of a coterie of young writers who developed their ideas in the context of Edmond de Goncourt's salon, the *grenier*, and eventually became the core of the Académie Goncourt—by which time Joseph Boëx had decided to share his pseudonym with his younger brother Séraphin-Justin, so they occupied two seats in the "Academy," and their fierce quarrels became the bane of its meetings, continuing long after they had divided the pseudonym again, signing themselves thereafter as J.-H. Rosny *aîné* and J.-H. Rosny *jeune*. In 1887, Rosny was one of the signatories, along with Paul Bonnetain, Lucien Descaves, Paul Magueritte and Gustave Guiches, of the *Manifeste des cinq*, which attacked Goncourt's rival Émile Zola and stirred up a great controversy. Both Rosnys eventually became prolific writers of newspaper fiction, and the elder became a notable pioneer of prehistoric fantasy and a species of *roman scientifique*, which his friend and fellow newspaper-writer Maurice Renard dubbed "scientific marvel fiction." The elder brother's work always retained a strong streak of visionary mysticism, first developed in an assembly of vignettes published in the *Revue indépendante* before being reprinted as *La Légende sceptique* (1888; tr. as "The Skeptical Legend" in *The Navigators of Space and Other Stories*, the first of seven volumes of the elder Rosny's works in translation issued by Black Coat Press); they included the sequence of experimental prose-poems translated below. titled "Psaumes" in the periodical but relabeled "Rêves obscurs" in the collage.

Psalms

I

O Sediment of Great Rivers, which the centuries refine, go back to your Point of Departure, when the Frost and Chemistry, and the impacts of the Storm and the efforts of the Lichen mortified

156

the old mountain contemporary with the Secondary Ocean, whence emerged the Beasts of Fable: Pterodactyls with scaly wings, Iguanodons standing in the mire of marshes, lifting their jaws to the tops of tall trees.

Sediment, there was an era when the bare mountain, glacial and arid, seemed an offspring of Eternity, immobile for Eternity—but on the day when the primal snows melted, when the waters and glaciers hollowed out the veins of the rock, Sediment, you began to descend in heavy blocks. Wedged into fissures, the torrent tormented you, and you had scarcely progressed a hundred cubits in a century when the marvelous Gothic spires of the summits began to sketch themselves, slender Steeples alternating with cavernous Pyramids. Sediment, you descended then in round pebbles, and became the fine dust of sand, and, finally, you fertilized the plains and ran all the way to the immeasurable depths . . .

O rivulets and great rivers, symbols of the red fluid that carries the Sediment in our arteries and will fertilize the valleys of the Flesh and the ravines of the Encephalum, go back to your Point of Departure, when the Frost and Chemistry, and the impacts of the Storm and the efforts of the Lichen mortified the old mountain contemporary with the Cretaceous Ocean!

II

Marsupials, in the Jurassic matrix, when the atmosphere still weighed so heavily and you appeared, timid and exceedingly humble among the dominant beasts . . .

The Reptiles had warmer arteries then, and those which advanced on to the promontories, and those which soared on their membranous wings, were the icings of a half-deaf and taciturn Creation. Crouched between the plantules,[1] the pressure of ox-

---

1 Strictly speaking, the French word *plantule*, and its English equivalent, refer to a plant embryo, but Rosny subsequently couples the term with "animalcule" in a fashion that makes it clear that he is using it to refer to primitive plants, and I have taken the liberty of importing his improvised second meaning into English.

ygen would only have had to remain constant, Marsupials, and you would have remained timid and exceedingly humble debris of the animal register. The King of Creation, clad in scales, with the three-chambered heart, would doubtless have been some Reptile-Human, immensely tall and oviparous.

Ah, if the rocks had not drunk the atmosphere; if, in the lighter fluid, the blood of Saurians had not chilled their vanished wings and the colossi of their class had not died in the stagnating marshes, what would their world have become, and what subtleties, what variations of the pattern, what organic auxiliaries and corollaries, what languages and what labors, what weavings of forms would have been born of the Reptile-Human, with the three-chambered heart? What attitudes would he have imposed on matter, what metamorphoses on the terrestrial surface?

Oh, Marsupials, if you had not known the gentler pressure, your loins would never have elaborated our Ancestors, Dinotherium, Hipparion and Machaerodus, and the day would never have come when the Anthropoid emerged mysteriously from the bosom of the tall trees! Marsupials, in the Jurassic matrix, when the atmosphere still weighed so heavily and you appeared, timid and exceedingly humble, among the dominant beasts!

III

Do not imagine, Plum-Weevils, Vine-Beetles and you, Grain-Weevils, that the poem of your battle against Humankind does not move my soul. While your legions rise up in the mysteries of cereals and foliage, opposing the power of numbers and fecundity to the weapons of your ponderous adversary, I think of the subtleties of your series in organic algebra and my soul has never desired your annihilation more.

Grasshoppers, Crickets and Locusts, avid and rapidly-multiplying races, when the stridulations of your love rise up, my heart enters into the tumult and trembles with mercy. Oh, when the Dragonfly and the Mayfly rise up from the banks of ponds, or clouds of Midges drift in the arborescent summits, or hordes of Gnats couple in their millions on warm evenings, or armored Ground-Beetles emerge at the corners of paths, fraternity torments me, purifies and enchains me in the gulfs of Life, in the menstrual flow where animal colonies flourished, Isidae, Gorgonians, Madrepores,[1] in the primitive time when the waves grew cold, where the lace of mother-cells floated in pale clouds and the troubled Energies confused Animalcules and Plantules.

Oh, my nerves soon remember those abysms of Genesis, my flesh whispers mysterious debuts, and everything in my higher self, in my sensitive fibres complicated by millions of years, comes back and narrates their effort to construct me: Hydras, Nostocs and Thallophytes, Colonial Polyps, Tubeworms and Saurians crouching in the terrestrial marshes.

Then, Plum-Weevils, Vine-Beetles and you, Grain-Weevils, and you, Locusts Grasshoppers, Dragonflies on the banks of ponds, Gnats buzzing on warm evenings, resplendent warrior Ground-Beetles, I see you sketched in my bones and in my veins. Offspring of the same origins, formed by the same harmonious anastomoses, and the poem of your battle moves more intensely and more suavely, while your legions rise up in the mystery of cereals and foliage, opposing the power of numbers and fecundity to the weapons of your ponderous adversary!

IV

Great Dynamo rotating to the chaos of the wave, captivator of Forces whose subtle power runs along nerves of metal . . .

Great Dynamo, here comes Life through space, along your frail conductors, and far from torrents, on the edges of Cities, the Wheels of the future are turning in silence and clarity, the Labors of the future whispering without exhausting the Artisan

---

1 These are all species of coral, although the names contain mythological echoes of which Rosny was doubtless conscious. I have generally followed a policy of using common names for the various creatures named in the prose-poem rather than Latin ones—although there is a much greater overlap between the two systems of nomenclature in French, because it is a Latin-derived language (which makes it much easier to distinguish different kinds of weevil, coral, and so on)—but I had no alternative but to retain Isidae.

and without rusting his face. The horrible respiration of industrial monsters has vanished into Legend.

Great Dynamo, your Hymn is euphonic over Metropolitan pallor; a natural Atmosphere strays over the walls, and if it is not yet bliss, here at least is purity; overly harsh famines abolished humankind is elevated in the vital hierarchy, a creature of brain and blood exonerated from muscular weariness.

The fevers of the Ocean and the wrath of the Abyss are your captives, Dynamo, and nourish you as much as the rays of the summer sun. From your rotating heart, slender veins extend through roofs and underground; and your supple force obeys the whim of accumulators, reducible to infinity, the slave of the humblest.

Great Dynamo rotating to the impacts of the wave, captivator of forces, whose subtle power runs along nerves of metal!

V

Long after the death of the Sun, on the Earth roaming the cosmic darkness, a light greyness quivered, the nebulosity of an infinitesimal gleam. A timid vermilion floated, suspended from a vault, scattered in unreal powder, and then became gray-green. Then it extended a beam of light, a thread of stellar Spider-silk, exceedingly long, and on that filament perched some kind of Apparition with wings: wings of primrose-yellow and nemophila-blue, which opened, trembled and closed again over centuries . . .

But as the wings paled, a metamorphosis occurred, into leaves of living paper, which persisted in opening, vibrating and closing, laying down through Infinity a library of delicate books. And they were the works of Humankind, extinct for billions of years; they were the vibration on the diaphanous Spider-Silk of thoughts inscribed in the bowels of the Star by the metamorphoses of the Brains, which vanished into some nebula in genesis, and which began to nourish young Creations . . .

Then, in further centuries, punctuated by a soft comet appearing in vaults of ink, the greening of Space paled tenderly, in a symphony of lilac sown with snowdrops and beams of light, and the works of humankind faded away. Then, in the death-throes of nuances, a frightful multitude of white worms began to climb slowly up the mountains, the most distant microscopic, twisted by the summits, the nearest vast, like pale boa constrictors: exceedingly soft boas, horribly blind, with neither pupils nor orbits.

Then came the Frost again, eternally, and the eternal darkness, the Firmament on high was strewn with the immutability of crystal stars, the fading away of all forms in the Immensity of Chaos, in the Immensity of Silence.

VI

There will be born, in the soul of the human elite, the horror that awakes in rare exquisite brains, the idea *that the chain of Being has been broken*. A prescience, instinctive today, reasoned tomorrow, will reveal how important it is that the ontological symphony conserves all its notes, and the peril stemming from an extermination of Genre, Species and Race. The terror is doubtless prophetic that thrills in profoundly naturalistic individuals at the thought of an animality reduced to a minimum of types. It is the invasion of sterility: the certainty that the most adorable of our acquaintances, the gropings of the Eternal Artist, the genius of the infinitely delicate and the infinitely complex, the great poem of animal strophes, are threatened with absence.

In order that the elephant or the giraffe might perish before their time, or the great Arabic Lion, or the fascinating Beasts inhabiting the plateaux and the forests, the Axis Deer, the Bison or the poor crepuscular long-eared bat, or the colossi of the Ocean and any shade-loving plantule it is necessary, without very long hesitation, that there should be religious attempts at preservation.

So, for the beasts useless as nourishment or in the service of humankind, Edens will be built. Calculated for all the inhabitants of the Earth, furnished with jungles or savannahs, brushwood or high forests, marshes, ponds, streams and heathlands, the poetic Beast and Plant, conserved *solely* for the sake of Art and Science, will live there in relative liberty and not in the horrible cloisters of our Sewers of Acclimation.[1]

Thus, in spite of the abominable struggle for existence, the beauty of creation and the sentiment of ontological grandeur will never be lost to humankind; and uniquely created, on this principle, out of respect for the venerable Mother, perhaps, over the centuries, the Gardens of Eden, the Arks of the Industrial Deluge, will eventually become saviors from cataclysms, or at least such precious indicators of the very progress of Humankind that our disinterest will be rewarded a hundred times over.

VII

Subtle sensuality of humid weather, beatitudes of the Hydrophile, when the cracked lips of the glebe have drunk the Storm, when the pure wells open in the shredding of the clouds the blanched tiny creatures strew the Earth, the sweet flower of renewal opens, and the clothes of the Hydrophile acquire a marine viscosity, an ineffable freshness strays over his pupils, bringing a tremor to the brackish lichen of its beard, and dips its soft leather shoes in the mire. Implacable, the blue Ether sets about drinking the moisture of the clay, and the Hydrophile gradually dries out, dries out and dies . . .

Subtle melancholy of arid weather, terror of the cracked lips awaiting the Storm, when the frightful firmament is denuded of clouds with palpitating edges! Will the moment return when the tiny creatures strew the Earth, when the Hydrophile dips its soft leather shoes in the mire?

VIII

The Spark! She has seized in her feeble grip the frail tip of a blade of grass. She launches forth, animating herself, overtaking

---

1 The original purpose of modern botanical and zoological gardens—as opposed to mere menageries—was to investigate the practicalities of transplantation of crops and domestic animals for the purposes of colonization; several such projects were labelled *Jardins d'Acclimation* in France. *Cloaques d'Acclimation* is, therefore, Rosny's unsympathetic characterization of zoos.

the fearful gallop of hinds, surpassing the bounds of panthers in distress, the hectic wing-beats of wood-pigeons. She hummed at first like an insect buzzing above the branches, but her voice has amplified into a tempest, swelling the horizons, drowning out the breathless clamor of lions, elephants and zebras. She has seized everything in her enormous claws, she agitates the ashen purple of its tresses, devours ancient forests, crosses eternal rivers, fleeing with the wind, insatiable and destructive—she is the Creator!

She speaks, in her thunderous voice, in the sonorous bosom of the globe, she flows there, bearing away the fuliginous sulfurs, striking in resounding dust-clouds against the heavy walls, pupil of a hearth of thunderbolts, projecting prodigious lavas into the air, creating a growling fête at the summit of a mountain.

Gentler, a friend of life, she filters subtly through avid pores, penetrates particles, swells roots, incenses flowers. Luring in the pulp of fruits, guiding the pistil toward the stamen, ardent to complete the amorous pollens, dilating the hearts and circulating the red rivers, she is the delicate enchantment inexhaustible and merciful!

IX

"Soul of things, whisper of the Expanse, when, on nights like this, the old hieratics constructed their adorable lies, did they glimpse Dynamos, Transmutation, Atoms and Luminous Oscillation? For me, the shadows remain, and god subsists in Force, and the disturbance of this darkness, the tremor of infancy, the aspiration of ecstasy in the dull contact of shadows, the Darkness in the depths of sensitivity!"

"Is the answer written in the margins of the Abyss rather than in a few atoms? If Egypt makes Astronomical Science sacred, if the herdsman becomes a priest, is an understanding of the delicate prescience of Genesis preferable to the hypnotism of Enormity on simple brains? Are not the laws that radiate through Space contained in a corpuscle floating on a tide, O wailing of the Infant-Human, verse of the young Word inscribed in Bibles?"

"Are the harmonies seeking to weave the Beautiful, as the radiance of stars is weaving worlds from the feeble light of empty space? Missal of the Petal, canticle of the amorous Beast, tremor of the Root, is your initial esthetic power surpassed, your feeble beacon flickering on the cliff?"

"Does uncertainty alone exist? Every day, though, adds a further affirmation to affirmations acquired. The incalculable horizon of probabilities shrinks before certainty, a wholly charming clarity dissipates the ancient shadows. No, not doubt but science. Whoever seeks may find. *I seek.*"

"Is it necessary to marvel at mystery and not distress oneself with analyses: the brutalization of things, the annihilation of social joys, opposing the serenity of a Dream? Is it necessary to animalize oneself to the sensualities that muffle renunciations, mineralize oneself in causeless scorn, and *wait?*"

"Ophiuchus, and you, Corona, and you, Capella, are you not the oil-drop on the Slide?[1] And must I still, in the abysm of Space, demand the fundamental Principle? Simply to continue, without tiring, always condemned to imperfection, always aspiring to perfection, moving forward, erring, losing myself continually . . . but persevering, no matter how tremulous the beacon is! The road has no end! It is necessary to refuse to sit down, in dark despair, because, for each stage covered, a tremor of joy follows, in spite of the fact that infinity still extends ahead! *I seek.*"

X

Your gropings, Planet, the sickly appearance of your Phenomena, the chaotic Destructions, the Negligences, the Ferocities, the Waste, the Injustice and the Inconsequence, bring forth, in indolent eras, the idea of some pupil of the Infinite, an Individual involved in nebular genesis to whom a parent or educator has given the problem of our corner of Space to resolve. Bent over our Universe, he slowly works upon it, and from the depths of

---

1 The reference is to a microscope slide, on which preparations for examination were often contained in the late nineteenth century within a drop of oil.

his brain, the Theme has emerged, which he will vary according to inspirational phases. As the Duration and Logic of his actions are proportional to his power and longevity, however, as a Precession of Equinoxes is for him a drop in the timetable of billions of centuries, we promulgate *laws* in accordance with one page of his studies, the page that covers our igneous period (a sort of sketch and vague exordium) and our ontological period (a sort of narration by the sidereal Schoolboy, in which he attempts to move, hesitatingly, toward Order).

In spite of the vertiginous transcendence of such an Individual, however, in spite of the complication of his methods and their exhausting harmonies, we have already discovered the lacunae that make impossible for us the conception of a merciful or omnipotent God, which allow us to glimpse that the incommensurable brain leaning over us is merely *relative*. And by virtue of that, belief in Rules, in the reality of all Ideality as well as all Experience, flows away—and the end of Logic, the vanishment of all our laws, will be some caprice of the Individual in posing the problem differently, to the extent that neither Chemistry, nor Physics, nor the courses of the Planets will any longer correspond to our poor formulas!

CHARLES VIGNIER
(1863-1934)

Charles Vignier was one of the writers who attended Stéphane Mallarmé's *mardis*; he also befriended Paul Verlaine before contributing to the Symbolist periodicals *Lutèce* and *La Vogue*, as well as *La Revue indépendante*, from which the items below, published there in 1885, are taken. His first volume of poetry was published in 1886, the year in which he wounded Robert Caze fatally in an unfortunate duel; it was followed by *Album de vers et de prose* (1888). He subsequently became an expert on Oriental art, working for the leading auction house in Paris, and his literary work became sparse thereafter.

Morituri

I

The well-waxed floor-tiles and the furniture are gleaming; a cat is purring before the fire, and the tall antique clock, in its worm-eaten case, is talking nonsense, indefatigably and imperturbably. On her chair, spreading her plump forms at the corners, a nurse with cow-like eyes is somnolently rocking the child she is feeding in her arms, while an aged grandmother is wandering around doing housework with awkward gestures.

II

After a yawn, the cat has stretched itself; the nurse has opened her eyes indolently; and the old woman draws nearer, coming and going, circling the group, as if regretting sitting down. With her soft hands crossed, the thumbs never cease twiddling. The child has stopped suckling.

III

Under the heavy, unconscious gaze of the grandmother, the child turns away from the breast, a drop of milk still on his lips. The grandmother is now considering him obstinately, impatient at not being able to penetrate the azure mirror of those eyes, opened yesterday.

IV

And while the child interests himself in the tourney of the thumbs, the old woman shakes her heads and murmurs: "Blond and very pale children whose eyes are immense and so blue, whom the angels enable to see paradise and hear the music of the good God, don't live long."

166

Undines' Chorus

Come, good friend who is languishing over there, far away from us; we have such pleasant things to tell you. Come, we know songs to make you weep, to make you dream, to make you sleep. Come, friend; for us the wind modulates its profoundest laments, for us the sea growls more savagely and the moon has bluer regrets.

Come, we will crown your forehead with white flowers, green flowers, red flowers and black flowers, if you wish, according to the color and the hour of your dream.

Come, our kisses are reliable for closing wounds.

The Mage's Daughter

"Chimera, are all cups drained, all flowers respired, all kisses flown away? Is there no longer anything to satisfy our desires than to die, desiring in vain?"

"Come."

❋

"What is that castle?"

"Here, since time immemorial, an old king of realms that have disappeared has been hiding his daughter, whom he venerates, and for whom he has been able to find philters of eternal beauty and eternal youth."

❋

"Old mage, to obtain your daughter, what is it necessary to do?"

For all response, laughter, and then these words:

"When the ditches of my castle are filled with fine gold, I shall tell you."

❋

"Old mage, to obtain your daughter, what is it necessary to do?"

"When the doors of my castle, overloaded with diamonds, have collapsed, I shall tell you."

❉

"Old mage, to obtain your daughter, what is it necessary to do?"

"When you have flown with the wings of a swan to the summit of that tower, which confines the sun, you shall see her."

❉

"Princess, I am here!"

"Let us depart, handsome prince; I have been waiting for you for a long time."

And they fled, while the old mage howled, pursuing them at a distance, sowing the wind with fragments of his long beard, which he tore out desperately.

❉

"You have said that my voice is sweeter than a chorus of citoles and praised my eyes as profound as the sea; is not each of my hairs a virtue, and do my kisses not always dispense their soporific charms?"

"Die!"

❉

The pale princess has been asleep for many years, and will sleep for many more years, forever!

The prince and the old mage, living nearby, interrogate her half-closed eyes incessantly. But they will never know what mysterious attraction fixes them there, in granite poses.

MARIE KRYSINSKA
(1857-1908)

Marie Krysinska left her native Poland in her teens to study music at the Paris *Conservatoire,* and threw herself into the Bohemian lifestyle of the French capital. She was the only woman allowed to join Emile Goudeau's Hydropathes, and when the club relocated to the Chat Noir cabaret she was allowed, a trifle grudgingly, to recite her poetry, sing and play the piano between the acts put on by the likes of Maurice Rollinat, Jean Richepin and Edmomd Haraucourt. Her first poetry collection was *Rythmes pittoresques* (1890), which reprinted the first of the items below, and was followed by her first collection of stories, *L'Amour chemine* (1892; tr. with other material in *The Path of Love*). When Gustave Kahn claimed to have invented "free verse" (i.e. verse free of rhymes) she pointed out that she had already published work of that kind, promoting a controversy that sometimes became fierce, her opponents claiming that her alleged examples of free verse were really just poems in prose—under which rubric some of them had, indeed, been published. She published many more prose poems when the pioneering feminist newspaper *La Fronde* began in 1898 to feature an item of fiction on its front page, in imitation of *Le Journal*, where she set examples that influenced the other writers who supplied the slot, including "Jacques Fréhel," May Armand Blanc, and, somewhat later, Renée Vivien.

Ballade

I

In the perfume of violets, rose and acacias—they encountered one another one morning.

Next to her slightly-open bodice slept roses less sweet than her breasts—and her eyes, which resembled two black violets embalmed like spring.

Rapid are the hours of amour.

One evening, under the stars, she said to him: "I am yours forever."

And the stars betrothed them—the mocking and cold stars.

In the perfume of violets, roses and acacias.

Rapid are the hours of amour.

One day he left, as the little acacia flowers were snowing—
Putting great white patches on the desolate grass, like shrouds
Where butterflies came to die.

II

Are there, then, perfumes that kill?
  Once only he breathed the tenebrous flower of her hair,
  Once only.
  And he forgot the blonde child he had encountered one
morning,
  In the perfume of violets, roses and acacias.

  O the unreal nights, the marvelous nights!
  The intoxicating mortal caresses,
  The kisses that have the taste of the Dream.
  And the languors sweeter than sensuality.
  O the unreal nights, the marvelous nights!

  An attenuated musk haunted her alcove.
  Are there, then, perfumes that kill?

  She said: I will only love you—the traitress.
  And her unforgettable body had the movements of a beauti-
ful tame animal,
  Of a beautiful and dangerous animal—tamed.

  One day he found her lips mute and sulky.
  Oh, but still with that same taste of the Dream—mortally
intoxicating.
  Lips as cruel and mute as perfumed roses, which attract but
do not return kisses.

  It is in vain that he weeps more than on the day when his
mother was laid in the tomb.

The eyes of the beloved have a gaze colder than the marble of mausolea.

And her lips, her lips so dear, remain as mute as roses.

Are there, then, perfumes that kill?

The beautiful and dangerous animal he thought tamed, had eaten his heart in play.

Then he cursed the azure of the sky and the scintillating stars.

He cursed the immutable light of the moon, the song of birds,

And the foliage that whispers mysteriously and perfidiously when appeasing night approaches.

III

But the human heart is forgetful and infidel,

And cursing is very sad when the season of young calices is reborn,

And breezes as tender as kisses.

He remembers the blonde child who said to him one evening under the stars: "I am yours forever."

And he came back.

But she had gone to sleep in the cemetery,

In the perfume of violets, roses and acacias.

Windows

Along the boulevards and along the streets they star the houses;

In the gray hour of the morning, folding their shutter-wings, they shelter the exquisite and muffled idleness of the darkness of chilly Dream.

But the sun enables them to blossom like flowers, with their white, red or roseate curtains,
    Along the boulevards and along the streets

※

And while the pane mirrors like dormant water, what disquieting charm and what mute confidences between the pleats of the white, red or roseate curtains!
    The arabesques of guipures sing of happy existences,
    The joyous fires in the hearth,
    The rare flowers with perfumes conveyors of forgetfulness,
    The hospitable armchairs in which voluptuous dreams slumber and—in the splendor of frames—the evocations of dreamlands.

※

But how they weep, the lamentable tattered muslin curtains;
    What plaints and what anguish in the scrap of dirty percale that resembles a shroud;
    And how tragic are windows devoid of curtains,
    Windows as empty as blind eyes,
    Where, stuck on the broken pane, pieces of paper plaster over livid scars.
    Sometimes, however, it is radiant, the poor window, on the edge of the roof
    When, to hide its sad nudity, the sky has painted it all in blue;
    With its pot of paltry geraniums, the poor window on the edge of the roof then resembles a fragment of the azure in which flowers are growing;
    Along the boulevards and along the streets, they star the houses.

※

And when the sun sets on its blazing pyre, splashing the horizon with gold and blood,
    They are resplendent, like armor
    Until the distressing hour when, in the meditation of all objects, obscurity falls, like black snow, in flakes.

※

Then all the reflections are extinguished; all the colors are confounded and effaced;

Only the windows of churches, illuminated by some solitary lamp, radiate softly, mysterious and symbolic.

✷

But it will soon wake up, noctambulatory Paris;

It will open its millions of gas-jet eyes,

And in the turbulent and frenetic evening atmosphere, the windows revive

Along the boulevards and along the streets.

✷

The lamp suspends its familiar globe, a mild sun that enables the intimate hours to blossom;

The candles of chandeliers reflect their joyful clusters in mirrors, like marvelous fruits,

And over the window, which is opal, one sees fugitive shadows glide, to the rhythm of music vaguer than breaths;

Nearby, the windows of houses under construction open like yawns of perpetual ennui;

Under the eaves, the poor candle shivers,

The gas-jet injects its riotous light into the entresols of restaurants, showing the end of a red banquette with gilded nails.

✷

And lamps, candlesticks, candelabra and gas-jets confound their disparate notes in a symphony of radiance,

In which the radiant cantilena of blessed hours mingles with the howling voice of false gaieties,

In which the sounds of celebrations and the sounds of kisses mingle with the gasps of solitary agonies and the clamors of lugubrious debauchery.

Then the silent and cold hour comes to extinguish lights and sounds.

Only the regular tread of a *sergent de ville* goes back and forth on the sonorous sidewalk under the windows, which fall asleep like weary eyes

Along the boulevards and along the streets.

A Romance in the Moon

He was a poet tormented by a strange disease;

He lived without desires, without ambitions, without jealousy and without joy;

Ignorant of tears sweeter than honey and mortal kisses;

For one evening, full of ecstasy and serenity, he had perceived in the Moon the woman he loved with a unique amour;

He had perceived the luminous fiancée who appealed to him with a blue smile.

Destinies had cursed that dreamer. And it was with the disgust of a sick man that he struggled for the exceedingly stale bread and the exceedingly adulterated wine every day.

But when evening came, he forgot the struggle and his long nauseas; and, leaning on his window sill, he sang songs full of amour and superhuman clarity to the luminous fiancée who appealed to him with a blue smile.

The daughters of the Earth dazzled him in vain with the white lightning of their amorous breasts;

In vain they prowled around him with their eyes full of promises;

He remained faithful to the fiancée he had perceived in the Moon, who appealed to him with a blue smile.

He lived thus for many years, awaiting the hour of the eternal hymen;

Then, one evening, full of ecstasy and serenity, he died, the poet tormented by that strange disease.

And his soul flew away, singing a hymn of joy, up there, to the dreamed land, into the arms of the beloved who had appeared to him for such a long time with a blue smile.

And in an alcove made of radiance, intoxicated by amour, he embraced forever his luminous fiancée;

And they loved one another for a long time, a very long time,

With an amour as limpid as the ether, devoid of anxieties, devoid of anguish, devoid of jealousy and devoid of tears.

But one evening, the poet leaned on his window sill as before, and gazed at the Earth . . . with regret.

Russian Legend

The prince, the young prince as handsome as a king, is mortally wounded.

While he was hunting in the depths of the woods—O the distracted hunter, distracted by the unique haunting of golden tresses, the heavy golden tresses of the princess, his wife—he was attacked by a malevolent wild boar that wounded him with its sharp fangs.

✳

And now, here he is, as pale as a sprig of jasmine, lying on the bloody brocades of the bed.

Of the fortunate bed where, a few weeks before, he had received the virginal spouse, his princess with the golden hair.

Around the bed, three weeping women are standing: the mother, the sister and the wife.

✳

"Let us run," says the mother, "let us run quickly to the magician who lives wild in the depths of the woods.

"He alone can compose a balm that will cure my handsome prince, as handsome as a king."

✳

When they had reached the depths of the woods, the magician said to them:

"I can cure the young prince; I can give you a balm that will cure the young prince, but in order to pay me for that incomparable balm, it is necessary to give me: you, the mother, your entire right arm; you, the sister, the white hand with the ring on the finger; and you, the wife, the heavy golden tress."

Now they are there, the three weeping women around the dead body.

The mother is weeping, sustaining the head of her beloved prince, felled like a fir tree in the woods.

The sister is weeping at the feet of the prince as handsome as a king.

And the wife is weeping next to his heart.

Next to the dead heart that palpitated with such tender amour for her golden tresses.

✳

And at the place where the mother was weeping there emerged a beautiful river with immortal waves, which still flows today.

Where the sister was weeping there was a lively spring.

But where the wife was weeping there was a little pool, which the first sunlight dried up.

Amorous Siesta

The summer afternoon pours a milky light through the rural muslin curtains, and the foliage of the garden mingles glaucous reflections with it, as in a submarine palace.

Nelly and Jacques, abandoned limply in the hollow of a divan, are doubtless savoring an unforgettable moment, sweeter than the excitement of embraces: a weary inebriation made of fulgurant intoxications.

Their hands have found one another without searching, and they both sense their hearts living precisely in the other loving heart.

Two successful human specimens:

She, tall and slim, but not thin, with soft chestnut hair, her face refined by an interesting neurosis, supple and fresh of complexion: he, blond in the eyes and the hair, with energetic features, with a flavorsome mouth.

The chirping of birds comes from the garden.

Syringas in vases exhale an innocent and perverse perfume, as complex as the sensuality of a kiss stolen by surprise.

What are they thinking while their embrace is mute?

Overwhelmed by an excess of bliss, they surely feel sorry for the rest of humankind, who waste a brief existence in vain agitations, for want of knowing this unique wealth: mutual tenderness?

Or perhaps, sensing themselves so happy, they fear the revenge of Fatality?

It might be that beneath the benediction of a superhuman felicity, their hearts—already brushed by chilling social life and its skepticism—are returning to the candor of primary beliefs and confident in the protection of Heaven and the fragile treasure of their amour?

Well, no.

She is thinking, with a signal bitterness about her dearest childhood friend, who has stolen her husband.

He is haunted by the vision of his only child, dead of the despair of the mother, who collapsed at the moment when she discovered the treason.

The chirping of birds comes from the garden . . .

The summer afternoon pours a milky light through the rural muslin curtains . . .

GEORGE AURIOL
(1863-1938)

"George Auriol" was the adopted name of Jean-Georges Huyot, nowadays remembered for the font of type named after him; he was an important pioneer of Art Nouveau and an associate of the *avant garde* composer Erik Satie, but he was best-known in his own day as the guiding spirit of Rodolphe Salis' periodical *Le Chat Noir*, where he published numerous brief items of humorous fiction—including the samples translated below, from the 25 September 1883 and the 22 March 1884 issues—often with an ironic poetic element. His works frequently appeared in tandem with those of Alphonse Allais.

The Spider

In the morning half-light that envelops the trinkets on the shelves, the statuettes, the paintings and the furniture with a gauze, and covers the fantastically-framed mirrors with a fog, the exquisite cantatrice Rosa Bambini, pale in her large Venetian bed, her head partly submerged by the undulating blonde waves of her hair, savors sensually the perfumed warmth that escapes from it, and idly lets her bare arms, folded over her breasts, rise, fall and rise again at the behest of her gentle respiration.

With naïve eyes she watches a large black spider that, suspended from its invisible thread, slowly allows itself to fall from the baldaquin, outlining its hideous silhouette against the pink plush curtains.

From one moment to the next, with little jerks, the frightful beast descends a few millimeters, sometimes turning on itself like a stone allowed to vacillate at the end of a string. Finally, it reaches the white surah coverlet, on the snow of which its deformed body designs an enormous inky stain.

For a second, it gets its bearings and then, standing up on its hairy legs, it heads for Rosa, darting its ferocious eyes at her. Meanwhile, its head, like the flight of a bat, vibrates and quivers the stanzas of macabre poets; and one by one, all the terrifying stores of Edgar Poe accumulate in the grand salon of her memory. The spider is still walking, attracted by the dazzling flesh, made even more irresistible by a golden down. And very slowly, it arrives on the lace that is touching the elbow of the nonchalant beauty. She does not move or shudder, but suddenly, a tender, caressant song escapes from her lips, so tenuous and so sweet that one might believe that one were hearing the faint echo of an aubade of cherubim.

Immediately, the spider turns round, and rapidly returns to its point of departure; then, with the aid of its minuscule ladder, it slowly climbs back up to its lair; it has already made half its aerial journey when Rosa, who has not stopped singing, abruptly seizes a match from her night-table and lights it; then, with a bound, without paying any heed to the flying lace, or her hair, which scatters, or her breasts, which escape from an excessively transparent linen prison, she burns the monster pitilessly, which expires with a lugubrious crackle.

Having expelled the ember fallen in to the coverlet with a flick of her finger, she lies down again and concludes her melody, her superb bare arms folded over her bosom, still rising and descending at the whim of her soft and rhythmic respiration.

The Ballad of Wasted Time

"Hasten, child, to rosy joys! Leave behind your Aunt Money-Box and the Be-Careful Tower. It's necessary to quit the lovely paradise of Insouciance and draw away from the cheerful banks of the River Naivety. Here come the Legendary Times! Cut your blond curls and run to learn vice with the Epitome. Hasten scamp, hasten! This is the time to weed algebra and clear the forest of rhetoric. Go, ephebes with new moustaches, make the journey without turning your head and without watching the clouds go by. Don't touch the forbidden fruit along the way, and march sagely all the way to the land of Canaan, where you'll find the beef stew promised by the Scriptures. Then you can get married. As for you, old men, force your tremulous legs, stop circling the tomb and go straight to Death. The time one spends in armchairs is wasted time, and *wasted time is never recovered!*"

Thus speaks, in his infinite wisdom, the god Common Sense, who has gone mad by dint of being sensible. But the Folly that follows him everywhere sings in her clear voice: "Let your souls frolic as they wish, O mortals! Be babies still at twenty if it seems good to you. Allow yourselves to be cradled by your whim and don't make your mind a beast of burden overladen with excessively heavy ideas. Have no law, no rule, and don't know how to read when you wander, in order not to know what the signposts say that lie in ambush at street-corners. Play truant and roll in the grass without thinking about the infamous distribution of prizes, and pay your court to all the butterflies and all the fays, for *wasted time is never recovered!*

"Idle in the sunshine and get drunk on the spring. Let yourself glide gently down the stream in Madame Sloth's boat and don't worry about the creepers that bar your passage. Watch the tourneys of the damsel-flies in the reeds, eat the forbidden fruits and make love. Don't think about anything and dream in the moonlight. Let the beautiful weeds grown in the frightful fields of algebra. It isn't into the forests of rhetoric that you should take your darling. So sing under the hawthorn bushes and prefer the mulberries that blacken the lips to beef stew, enemy of flavor and the unexpected. Walk on the grass in spite of fences and pick all the roses. Let the old men still be ours. Let's allow ourselves to be intoxicated by the breath of incense-burners and idleness, and let's profit from existence like sultans, for *wasted time is never recovered!*"

Princes and princesses, I shall always laugh, love and drink without caring about the days that are going by, the hours that are crumbling and the dust of the minutes that the wind carries away. I shall never have the nostalgia of the future, and since you have cast me into Eternity, I shall stroll there smelling the flowers, dancing rounds and caressing women, and I shall throw all my years out of the window until the day when I am effaced from life, for *wasted time is never recovered!*

ALBERT TINCHANT
(1862-1892)

Albert Tinchant was educated in his native Le Havre, where one of his teachers was the writer Jules Lemaître. When he moved to Paris with a view to continuing his education there he obtained employment instead at the Chat Noir cabaret, where he became the resident pianist and one of the "secretaries" assisting George Auriol with the production of *Le Chat Noir*, to which he contributed a great deal of verse and numerous often-lachrymose *poèmes en prose*—including the sample translated below, from the 4 July 1885 issue—until he fell out with Rodolphe Salis in 1889. His serious musical endeavors were carried out in association with Erik Satie, and included an operetta based on Albert Robida's future war stories, *La Nuit du temps* (1889). A heavy drinker, absinthe probably made a significant contribution to his premature death.

Empty Heart

I have seen the young women passing, brunettes, blondes or redheads, wearing lilies, lilies-of-the-valley or tea-roses in their bosom. In their presence, desires awoke in my flesh, numbed by the pain of poor dead idylls. None of them have fixed me with their cruelly troubling and tender gazes. I have refused to understand the caresses of their smiles, although I would have been able to love them, on my knees, so tenderly, with all the delicacy of a sick heart and the exquisite sensibility of those who have suffered a great deal.

Brunettes, blondes or redheads, wearing lilies, lilies-of-the-valley or tea-roses in their bosom, through the world they go, forgetting between their arms the lovers that exist down here, unworthy of adorations so naïve and so penetrating, whose souls remain sunlit by them even beyond the tomb. Fops, ruffians and sexagenarians have shredded the flowers of their corsage and soiled the youth of their kisses in the alcove. And, gone astray, dragged relentlessly in the mud toward old age and solitude, they have departed, no longer having even the memory of a sincere embrace to soothe the heartbreak of the past.

Silently I watched the flowers of their corsages being shredded and the youth of their kisses being soiled. Sometimes the bitter rancor gripped me of having, disdainful of offered sensualities, respecting the chastities that the first person to come along would profane. And I approached the sinners, but they fled me, the beauties hungry for joy divining the tears beneath my feigned gaiety, and in the melancholy of my dreams the bitterness of mourning lived, which belied the words of love on the amorous lips.

❋

Wounded by the abandonment of the Beloved, in the sadness of being alone after the golden hours of a romance *à deux*, heartbroken and defenseless, I experienced a need for solicitude and consolation that might have delivered me for life to the caprices of a temporary mistress. And in the dread that, by cherishing her too profoundly, marriage would be nothing for us but a long martyrdom, I let the heavy lid of a coffin fall forever upon my heart, which the frail hands of women tried to lift in order to throw the flower of their youth and the perfumes of their spring into it.

ALPHONSE ALLAIS
(1854-1905)

Alphonse Allais, a native of Honfleur, became the most famous humorist in Paris. He exhibited art-work in the Salon des arts incohérents and produced *avant garde* musical compositions, including a silent funeral march. He published work in *Le Hydropathe*, the periodical associated with Émile Goudeau's club in 1879, where he was featured in one of the profiles of its members, in which attention was called to his unfruitful technological ventures in collaboration with Charles Cros. He developed his literary reputation considerably writing for George Auriol's *Le Chat Noir* in the early 1880s, before going on to write regularly for other newspapers, including *Le Courrier français*—where the sample translated below appeared in the 1 Seprtember 1885 issue—and especially *Le Journal*. His complete works, including those originally reprinted in twelve volumes between 1887 and

1902, were reprinted in two mammoth omnibuses (1989-90) by Robert Laffont in his Bouquins series, which helped to maintain his fame into the twenty-first century.

God

To Doctor Antoine Cros.

It is getting late.

The party is coming to an end.

The cheerful companions are red-faced, noisy and amorous.

The lovely young women, unbuttoned, are abandoning themselves. Their eyes, gently half-closed, and their parted lips, allow humid treasures of crimson and nacre to be perceived.

Cups never full and never empty!

Songs flutter, rhythmed by the clink of glasses and pearly cascades of female laughter.

Then, the antique clock in the dining room interrupts its monotonous tick-tock and hums, grating outrageously, as it always does when it prepares to chime the hour.

It is midnight.

The twelve strokes fall, slow, grave and solemn, with the air of reproach particular to old patrimonial clocks. They seem to be telling you that they have sounded many others for your disappeared ancestors and that they will sound many others for your grandchildren when you are no longer here.

Without being aware of it, the companions have muted their tumult, and the lovely young women are no longer laughing.

But Alberic, the craziest of the band, has raised his glass and says, with a comic gravity:

"It's midnight, Mesieurs: the time to deny the existence of God."

Knock knock!

Someone is knocking at the door.

"Who's there?" No one is expected and the domestics have been given leave to retire.

Knock knock!

The door opens and they perceive the long silver beard of an old man of tall stature, clad in a long white robe.

"Who are you, old man?"

And the old man replies, with great simplicity:

"I'm God."

At that declaration, all the young people experience a certain embarrassment; but Alberic, who definitely has too much sang-froid, said:

"That won't prevent you, I hope, from clinking glasses with us."

In his infinite bounty, God accepted the young man's offer, and everyone soon relaxed.

They started to drink and sing again.

The morning was making the stars pale when they thought of separating.

Before taking his leave of the guests, God agreed, with the best grace in the world, that he did not exist.

GABRIEL MOUREY
(1865-1942)

Gabriel Mourey published his first collection of poems, *Voix eparses* (1883), in his native Marseille while still a teenager, and founded a short-lived revue, *Mireille,* the following year. He published a translation of the complete poems of Edgar Poe in 1889, and went on to translate Algernon Swinburne. He was a regular at Mallarmé's *mardis,* and built a solid career as a journalist, especially as an art critic, promoting the English pre-Raphaelites and the Arts and Crafts Movement. *Automne*, a play he wrote with Paul Adam in 1893, was banned by the censor, but his musical collaborations with Claude Debussy were more fortunate, even though many of those they planned never came to fruition. His correspondence with his friend Jean Lorrain, in which the two slandered their contemporaries outrageously, was published after the latter's death in 1906. The two poems in prose translated below were first published in the *Revue moderniste* in 1884.

The Song of the Stars

In the profound calm of clear nights, when the innumerable stars slowly let the gentle caress of their radiance fall upon the earth, like a dew of flames, this is what the stars say up there, the beautiful, divine stars dotted like diamonds in the blue tresses of the sky:

"Come to us, you who weep, you who make your dreams of the future too large and too sublime, all of you who are suffering.

"Come to us, for we are the consolatrices.

"Come, we will cradle you in waves of light in order to relight within you the extinct glimmers of hope.

"Come; we will sing you soporific songs that will silence in your hearts the voice of death and the funereal knell of disappointed amour . . .

"Come, we will take you in our arms for caressant embraces, like your blonde but excessively vulgar lovers.

"We will carry you, sad and weary, into the gardens of the heavens, and you will rediscover there, in blissful repose, your joy and your strength . . ."

✳

And you would think that you were hearing a siren song escaping from the waves of infinity.

✳

"Come, you will pick the marvelous flowers that grow in the gardens of the heavens, the rare—oh, sublime!—flowers with divine and penetrating perfumes . . .

"Come, come to us . . .

"Tell us, is it not true that all the flowers born on earth soon curb their accursed heads under the implacable storm of destiny?

185

"Is it not true that all the caresses down there are mendacious and brief?

"Is it not true, beloved poets, that all amours end and all dreams die?

"Do you not know that your heart will bleed eternally and your lyre will soon be broken, for nothing endures, everything passes and flies away?

"Then why not come to us?

"Do you fear that our promises are deceptive?

"No, for you love us like mistresses; for your hearts always sail toward our radiant beaches, for your desires reach upwards toward our beauty, for your hopes rise toward our superbly luminous bodies in an instiable need to love us . . .

"Come, come, and we will be yours forever."

And you would think you were hearing the song of crazed courtesans rising from terrestrial dwellings into the immensity of the skies.

And you would like to depart for the celestial gardens at that very instant, because you understand that there will no longer be time tomorrow, because the song of the stars resonates again in the calm air . . . Then, gradually, the echoes die away, and silence falls as soon as the desire had entered your soul. Up above, the stars are going out amid the immense horizons, and only the wings of our dreams and our foolish thoughts are soaring, leaving in the bosom of infinity a vague gleam that is slowly effaced, like a meteor, under the cold and murderous caress of destiny.

Crucifixion

On the eternal Golgotha where the three crosses loom up—the three divine and accursed crosses—in the bloody dawn that is surging from the horizon, the angels of Amour and Death are soaring. One has white wings, all white, whose plumes are

Desires, Dreams, Illusions and Confessions: all the things that trouble the soul and enable it to hope. The other has black wings, indented like those of bats, his garments somber and his gaze profoundly luminous, which plunges into the abyss.

On the eternal Golgotha, the sinister crosses loom up, barring the cloud with their black arms. And the hour of torture has come, the hour of the great martyrdom of love, the crucifixion of the heart, the body and the mind. One climbs the holy mountain and one is gripped by a sudden terror before the atrocity of those tortures. Oh, the torture of the heart above all . . . and those long streams of blood that are flowing therefrom, bathing the soil with red stains; and the soil drinks them avidly, like an expiatory beverage. But the torture will never end.

Then a great cry is heard: "I'm thirsty . . ."

Then the beloved woman appears. And instead of weeping before her work and repenting, instead if taking you down from the cross and giving you her caresses to drink, instead of taking you in her arms and warming you with her embrace, as before, she comes to shower you with her irony and her smile. But she will be forgiven, because she does not understand our dolors, because she does not know what she is doing. And that smile, which is no longer even pity, one loves in spite of everything, because a woman's smile is a divine thing.

However, a single word from her would have saved you. A single one of her words with have given you back hope and faith, and you would have set forth again with confidence on the road of the future; the mind would have lost the depression into which suffering had cast it, and life would have returned to this fatigued body, bringing strength and courage.

Doubtless one would have retained nevertheless an incurable wound in the soul . . . but you would have been so glad to forgive that woman, if a single word from her had opened in your heart the sublime wellspring of mercy and pardon, that you would have loved her for a long time yet, as before, with a love full of abnegation and sacrifice.

But her impassivity scares you; she is standing there, at the foot of the cross, no sign of dolor on her face, nor in her eyes, a single glance from which could have cured you. That woman, however, one ought to curse, and one would like to, for it is her who has nailed you to this ignoble cross; but you cannot, and you would rather love her forever, even if you die of it.

A crown of thorns is lacerating your forehead, gripping you more tightly every day; it is woven with the accursed branches of the tree of Despair. And you feel at times on your lips, like bites, the old kisses of the idol . . . And in the calm of nights, when the caressant light of the stars bathes the sky with a long shudder of kisses, and in the sweet agony of things, amid the harmonious prayer of evenings, and in the splendor of dawns, and in the sinister cataclysms of storms, the two angels of Amour and Death soar above the eternal Golgotha, until the day when, as it is written in the book of fatality, they will mingle in a first and last embrace . . . and that will be the hour of your annihilation in infinity, out there, far from the noise of the clamors of the world.

ɷɷ ɷɷ ɷɷ ɷɷ ɷɷ ɷɷ ɷɷ ɷɷ ɷɷ ɷɷ ɷɷ ɷɷ ɷɷ ɷɷ ɷɷ ɷɷ ɷɷ ɷɷ ɷɷ

Part Four:
Decadent Proses

ɷɷ ɷɷ ɷɷ ɷɷ ɷɷ ɷɷ ɷɷ ɷɷ ɷɷ ɷɷ ɷɷ ɷɷ ɷɷ ɷɷ ɷɷ ɷɷ ɷɷ ɷɷ ɷɷ

LÉO TRÉZENIK
(1855-1902)

"Leo Trézenik" was the pseudonym of Léon Épinette. He abandoned studies in medicine at the Université de Caen to move
to Paris with his family, where he involved himself in literary
"Bohemia," eventually becoming a leading member of the
Hydropathes. He collaborated with Charles Morice on a student
newspaper before they took over *La Nouvelle rive gauche* and
changed its title in 1883 to *Lutèce*, the first of several explicitly
Symbolist publications. He commented extensively in its pages
on a literary hoax perpetrated by Henri Beauclair and Gabriel
Vicaire, *Les Déliquescence—poèmes decadents d'Adoré Floupette*,
and went to some trouble to track the recent revival of the term
"decadent," redeployed as an insult by disapproving journalists
but then embraced ironically by certain writers in the same
perverse spirit that had led Baudelaire to cherish the term after
Desiré Nisard had adopted it in attacks on Victor Hugo in the
early 1830s. Trézenik's novel *Le Confession d'un fou* (1890; tr.
as *The Confession of a Madman*) and such verse collections as
Les Fromages: vers symboliques (1895) exhibit a similar spirit of
cheerful perversity while speaking seriously in jest.

Trézenik invented an imaginary literary Movement of his
own, the "Hirsutes," and he titled a collection of his vignettes
Decadent proses (1886), introducing it as an adventure in
"Floupetterie." The improvised term "*proses*" never caught on as
an alternative to the solidly entrenched "*poèmes en prose*," but it
was adopted by Remy de Gourmont in the significant collection

189

Proses moroses (1894). The calculated prosaicism of Trézenik's vignettes was not new, being reminiscent of Huysmans' *Croquis parisiennes* and many of the inclusions in *Gaspard de la Nuit*, but the complication of the terminology was not inapt. While such earnest Symbolist periodicals as *La Vogue* and the *Revue Blanche* took a "purist" approach to the celebration of earnest *poèmes en prose*, the periodical that published brief prose pieces in the greatest profusion in the 1880s, *Le Chat Noir*, used that term very sparingly. Its routine humorous inclusions are similar in spirit to Trézenik's "proses"—which are not unpoetic, however paradoxical that might seem. Those "proses," samples of which are translated below, also have an obvious kinship with newspaper pieces by Théodore de Banville and Catulle Mendès as well as earlier items by Huysmans, so their "literary genealogy" can easily be traced directly back to Baudelaire. They might be reckoned to be among the black sheep of the family, but they surely belong to the same species.

The Good God

One morning, God, who had been somnolent for billions and billions of years in damnable idleness, woke up with a very natural question on his lips:

"Where am I?"

"But I'm nowhere, since nothing but me exists.

"I exist without being anywhere; I exist in nothing; I'm nowhere, and yet I AM.

"Bizarre!

"But if that's an odd situation, on the one hand, it's intolerable on the other. And more than one sinister joker won't fail to abuse my position by declaring *urbi et orbi*—there isn't yet any *urbi* or any *orbi*, but it makes no difference—that I have no domicile, that I'm in a state of vagabondage. Perhaps they'll go as far as claiming that I can't exist in those conditions.

"It's definitely necessary for me to have a 'home,' as the English say—but no anachronisms!"

So, HE created the World—from nothing, naturally, since nothing existed. HE simply said: "Let the World be," and the World was.

Funnily enough, that hadn't cost him any fatigue, since he had only had to wish to do it. However, that wish took seven days—seven periods, if you prefer, it's necessary to satisfy everyone—to execute, during which God sat on a cloud blissfully being amazed by his work, the curvature of which he found astonishing; on the seventh HE rested

So, there was the world created, with its infinite multitude of heavenly bodies rolling in the immensity; but all of that—stars and nebulae, planets and moons—was only done, the gracious Fénelon informs us, by making use of Jabloskoff[1] during the night on the earth, that grain of sand lost in a corner of the ether, because, by day, God had installed a special luminary, which he called the sun.

One morning, when HE was wandering in his immense domicile in order to judge the excellent distribution of the rooms, the Creator arrived by chance on the abovementioned grain of sand, which he found quite deserted; and in order to populate it, and at the same time to make a puppet with which to distract himself, he created Man.

As he was in a generous mood, he gave him a magnificent orchard, which he planted with all sorts of fruit trees, but as he was also in a playful mood he placed a superb apple tree in the very center, saying to the Man:

"You know, I forbid you to eat the fruits of this tree; you would know everything, good and evil, as well as I do, and that would irritate me."

The Man, still naïve—he was so new—did not think of making the remark that it would have been simpler not to put the tree there with the others, the number of which was already sufficient.

---

1 The reference is to the "Yablochkov candle," a type of electric arc lamp invented in 1876, first demonstrated in the Avenue de l'Opéra during the Paris Exhibition of that year.

It is true to say, in order to excuse the Man, that God already knew what would happen, since the future had no secrets from him. The proof is that, in order to help him to disobey, God gave him a companion, a Woman.

Having done that. God reasoned as follows:

"So, there's man created; I've ordered him not to eat an apple from the famous tree, but I know very well that he's going to eat one, precisely because I've forbidden him to do it. Naturally, I'll punish him for his disobedience, and for that I'll expel him with his woman from the garden I gave him, and what's more, I'll punish all his descendants, who aren't guilty of the fault of the first humans; I'll punish them because I'm JUST.

"On the other hand, as I'm GOOD, I'll save them. I'll send them my son, who will be born of a virgin by . . . the operation of the Holy Spirit, and who will die in order to redeem them from a sin they won't have committed: that just individual, dying for the guilty who aren't, seems to me to be a sufficient reparation."

The Serpent, who happened to be passing, hissed: "But it would be much simpler not to constrain the Man to disobey, in order to avoid the trouble of punishing him in his descendants, who will never understand what they have to do with it."

God replied to it:

"Logic hasn't been invented yet; you're in advance of the centuries to come, my lad, and humans will take a long time to see that I've been making fun of them."

Egotisms

Her head is framed in the yellow lace of the white pillow, where her hair, uncurled for a long time, was tangled in disorder: in lace less yellow than her complexion, her former lily-white complexion, where all the wax seems to have run from the candles that will burn tomorrow to either side of the cadaver.

Through the mist of hair uncurled for a long time, her eyes, aureoled by the bistre of phthisis, dart a dark gaze at her lover—disinterested by that death, which is dragging on—whose egotistical amour has been gradually worn away by the angles of that thinness.

The strange fixity of her dark gaze, which is blazing in her dilated pupils, troubles the lover, who is prowling around the room, vaguely decked out in a mask of sympathy, to the extent of embarrassment.

With the clear sight of people who are about to die, she senses that the man has only ever loved the flesh in her, in her who had given him everything: heart, soul and body. And before that discovery of the final hour, a cry escapes her throat:

"The other . . . the one with whom you will replace me when I'm no more . . . do you know her?"

He protests, without conviction:

"Can you believe that, my darling? You will be my only amour."

"You're lying," she roars, between her teeth, which are already clicking with the spasms of her death-throes.

And after a silence that he dares not interrupt, she says, in an excited voice, whipped by commencing delirium:

"But I shall come back from out there; I shall come back during moonless nights to haunt your alcove and blow fear into the midst of your caresses. My stubborn Shade will strive to enervate the quiet lassitudes and sweet annihilations of the aftermaths of your amour . . ."

"I beg you, my adored," he hazards, "not to excite yourself so . . ."

"I don't want . . ." she bursts forth, "I don't want . . . no, I don't want you . . . to love another woman after me."

And as, leaning over her, he kissed her on the forehead in order to calm her excitement, a red flash striped the green sky of her iris; and with a supreme effort, drawing her lover's head toward her with her knotted arms, she bit him hard on the neck, and, with a clash of teeth whose force was multiplied a hundred-fold by fever, she sliced through his carotid.

And while that banal lover, to whom she had given every-thing and whom she had adored until death, was dying; while a jet of blood sprang from the artery, turning the white pillow crimson on which her hair, uncurled for a long time, was tangled in disorder, she expired blissfully.

Child's Play

In the crushing torpor of a somnolent evening, at the high window wide open over the park, where the leafy plane-trees are agitating the languid fan of their branches gently, with the soft rhythm of a caress, two children are leaning on their elbows, their gazes lost in a dreamy boredom, staring without seeing at the great rubescent sun setting in the distance, its last oblique rays drilling through the thick tangle of leafy boughs and powdering the flavescent hair of the two children with gold dust.

"Make me butterflies," the little sister begs, suddenly, already disinterested in the illusion of dolls.

And as the brother does not reply, and, his eyes staring, he refuses to extract himself from his vague reverie, the mysterious and troubling reverie of children that transports them to distant lands forgotten, alas, by those who have lived too long, she persists, with a pretty blue imploring gaze:

"I'll catch the flies for you."

And with her slender and diaphanous hand, where the azure network of veins runs beneath the transparency of delicate skin, she catches a fly that is confidently cleaning itself on the sunlit edge of the high window.

By condescension, more to rid himself of an insistence who obstinacy he foresees, the brother briskly decapitates the fly with an expert fingernail into a piece of paper, folded in two, which his sister presents to him. Then, slipping the whole between the pages of a stout missal florid with naïve illuminations, he leans on the cover momentarily with both hands.

In the missal there is a little moist click.

And when they reopen it and unstick the two leaves of blank paper, the two children utter cries of admiration.

The head of the little fly had burst under the pressure; the gray splashes of the brain, the pink spurts of blood from the abruptly severed arteries, and the dots of the thousand scattered eyes of the fly traced a fantastic silhouette in the center of the sheet, with colors harmoniously melted and curiously jagged contours displayed on the sides and bizarrely elongated in the middle, the design of which evidently evoked, in the infantile imagination, the image of a multicolored and fantastic butterfly.

And the little sister, enthused, clapped her hands and cried, in her shrill little girlish voice:

"Again! Again!"

CHARLES MORICE
(1860-1919)

Charles Morice joined forces with Léo Trézenik to convert *La Nouvelle rive gauche* to *Lutèce*, and he became the Symbolist periodical's theoretician, setting out to explain what that term implied with reference to a literary Movement, and why it was important. He arranged the publication in *Lutèce* of Paul Verlaine's *Les Poètes maudits*, helping it to become a central exemplary document of the Decadent Movement. Morice's prospectus for Symbolism differed slightly from the one devised by Stéphane Mallarmé, as did the formal Symbolist Manifesto published by Jean Moréas and the alternative version promoted by Gustave Kahn. His personal life was troubled and he underwent several significant changes of attitude and philosophy, aborting several employments and embryonic careers, and his literary output, apart from his critical essays, was sparse, only amounting in sum to one novel—a sardonic account of the Second Coming—and the collection *Quincaille* (1914; partially tr. in *Babels, Balloons and Innocent Eyes*), from which the samples below are taken.

Listen, Listen, See if it's Raining

In a noble and powerful attitude, leaning on his elbow amid cushions, his forehead in his hand, illuminated by the flickering light of a candle, with a book before his eyes—eyes often distracted, which go astray pursuing visions in the curtains, on the walls and in the dark corners of the vast, sad room—is a Young Man. Whether he is one of those whose hour will not sound, or whether the days to come will be his days, know that he does not care, know, oh, be sure, that glory alone tempts him of knowing what all this signifies, all this that is life and death, memory without appearance and the past, hope without certainty and the future, the mystery of calices, the problem of eyes and the reasoning of the moon.

Now he turns away from the walls, from the dark corners, from the curtains; it is toward the window that he dreams, wide-open to the redoubtable darkness. Beyond, the nightmare of nocturnal confessions tortures everything that is, and everything that is an endless plaint rises, a plaint rises with the incense of slumbers, rises, borne by Hatred and Amour, rises toward the disdainful clouds, and, in passing, bursts in the tranquil and vast, tranquil and sad, room in which, both orientated toward the same Questions, meditating on the anxiety of life, are the Young Man with the passionate pale face and Goethe, in a portrait, the sole luxury in the sad room, a proposed Ideal of conscious serenity.

A plaint rises, and you see: the host of the living, collapsed, weary, with their burden of lies and confessions, trampling underfoot the dream of things; you see: the host of the living, the man with the two great bitter creases that the disappointment of laughter leaves on his dolorous mouth, the woman with infinite eyes because immense desire and immense despair cannot fill them, and the child who is already weeping in the woman's arms; you see: the host of the living, the host of unfortunates identical from age to age. Go on! Hesitate no longer between their plaint and your book, choose both, listen while reading. Their plaint and your book are two echoes, and there is only one voice—distant, oh, distant! Do you say that the errors of the writer, whoever he is, or his tyrannical authority, and the very prestige of his genius, dazzle you, and that you lose yourself in the detours of a language forced crosswise to the Sense of Right? What does it matter, since the Words know, since they are abundant in supernatural suggestions, since they remain

196

in spite of our departures and since they are sincere in spite of our duplicities? Go on! What is said is utterly indifferent if you can hear, IF YOU MUST HEAR. And how do you know—the merit of being!—that you are not the man who was elected since time immemorial to hear the unheard response? Do you know? Who can say?

Listen, then, my brother: the meaning of all this is in all this; but the words have a significance beyond their noise, even beyond silence. Listen and see when the lips move without speaking, when the eyes have darted their last glance. It is the divine smoke that rises from the broken heart, it is the burning rose of hearts washed with tears, it is the cry—oh, listen avidly—it is the cry of the sick in the night.

Interior Testimony

I

The gentle line of the plains undulates in the distance of eyes and attenuates in the neat darkness, beyond the empire that the Moon holds, and no path is indicated across the labored terrains where I go, wearied by the journey, already long, and wearied further by the difficult march over the slippery ground, which seems to flee beneath my steps. But however far I go, without the certainty of attaining it, toward a goal capable of luring me, I go valiantly, proud of going.

II

For days and days I have been marching thus, and the gentle ironic line of the plains has not ceased undulating to infinity. The Moon and the Sun have risen by turns and set in the sky of this landscape that astonishes my courage or my candor, and I sense clearly that I am going along an endless road. But I have measured my eternity against its own; they are equal.

III

Something like a habitual intoxication has gripped me, although it appears that I am not alone. An invisible multitude surrounds me: my Dead. I converse familiarly with them; I will say more, I argue; for we are not in accord, and gladly, if you find us a judge—very gladly—I will ask him to arbitrate between them and me. Nevertheless, even if it makes me seem litigious, I would consent even more to reckon with them—if only I could!

IV

They say that I am wrong to follow this route after them, for they have followed it in vain, and that I will not see the end of it any more than they did. They say that to the left and right, on the banks of cool springs, on the slopes of florid hills, in the hollows of soft valleys, in the depths of clumps of hawthorn, delights are in preparation, banquets set up, women without veils recumbent, and children singing, without understanding them, odes in which Amour is celebrated. They say . . . and the gentle line of the plains undulates in the distance of the eyes.

V

"O my elders, my Dead, my very dear, all these benefits, all these benefits with which you solicit me, more than any other I have savored them, more than other I have bathed all my senses in the sweet horrors of all sensualities. But one morning, the morning of a feast day, the young Roman Sextius, his head still crowned with festival roses, saw passing, borne by four holy women, in her open coffin, the Christian woman Sextia, who had just died for having confessed her faith . . ."

VI

They interrupted me with loud cries, in which I perceived: "Some for the sake of melancholy devotions like yours, others for the sake of ambitious hopes, and others because they were Scholars, and others because they were Poets, all your dead—as disobedient as tearful—have wasted their lives running after chimeras. Oh, you will hear them forbid you, their heir, to imitate their folly and their misfortune, you, the last stake of revenge against Destiny . . . !" They spoke—and the gentle ironic line of the plains has not finished undulating to infinity.

VII

"My very venerated Dead, since the young Roman Sextius has seen the beautiful face of the defunct Sextia, the Christian woman, the liquor of Cyprus has lost its savor for him and the vital colors on the most beautiful faces irritate him and sicken his heart. The taste of Life has become insipid for him since he has suspected the taste of Death . . ." (Then the multitude that surrounds me makes a terrible gesture of silent anathema.)

VIII

"O my Dead! The living eyes of the skeptic Sextius adored the splendor of the faith that he saw radiant in a flash of features forever asleep and rigid. What he felt he could not say, and questions only awakened from his dream, to the peril of his questioners. But it is not the contagion of belief that he desires, nor the contagion of dying. It is the impossible that he is attempting, it is to see through closed eyes, it is to believe by means of a heart that is no longer beating . . ."

IX

For, young as he is, the Roman Sextius has lived too much to be able to believe and to be able to die. However, since Death and Faith have loomed up on his route, he remains uniquely avid for the spectacle that magnifies humanity to the extent of God—and all day, every day, he follows in dream the Appian Way where he once encountered the cortege of the defunct Sextia, and those who see him pass by talk among themselves in low voices.

X

With words bathed in tears, my dear and very compassionate dead sympathize with my wretched mania, and, in order to console them, I say to them: "O my elders, my Dead, my very dear, the dream of the Roman Sextius is not my dream, but like him, before he encountered the dead Sextia, I have drunk from the cup of follies to which your wisdom invites me, and like him, I have now lost my taste for Bacchus and Venus. No pale virgin has, however, arisen in my passage and I have not seen the cold eyes of the stone Sphinx that guards your tombs weeping. But, innocent or guilty, I want a spectacle that merits my contemplating it; it is toward that spectacle that I have set my route, and it is before it that I shall stop. O my masters, it is your fault, in sum, if I am immortally unsatisfied; why have you not realized that which would crown and seal my pride in being human? I am sad and disgusted with the forms in which you have, with predilection, reflected your finite forms—and I am going, I am going, I am going still, toward the ultimate Out There, toward which the gentle, ironic line of the plains draws me."

And I am the One of Your Souls . . .

And I am the one of your souls, of your most baleful souls, of the desperate days of abandonment, which went away, having cast over everything that you were an angry gaze, over the hours that will never return, the hours that became knells, which sounded so much of life, and over the hour that vibrates, ringing false, it is said, an unreal appearance, and over the hours that might perhaps sound in the future, greatly discounted—which went away to a bleak land of which legends had informed it, where there is, in a landscape that three exceedingly old birches impregnate with solitude, an ancient well with edges worn away by generations: it is the Well of Maledictions; and whoever dies a bad and sad death, his name will have been pronounced in the resounding night of the millennial well, as is attested, for the quivering horror of the living by numerous examples that tradition reports. And I am the one of your souls, the most baleful of all, which, on a day of abandonment, leaned over the worn rim of the Well of Maledictions in order to drop your name into its resonant darkness.

I Know Them . . .

I know many who have made their decision about things and cleverly extracted a profit from everything—I know many of them. They enjoy life such as it is, without remorse and without disgust.

I know some who retain forever in their eyes the virginal horror of the first gaze—I only know a few of them. Their entire life is just one long echo of their first tears. Far from seeking to return the blows they receive, those resigned individuals, they don't even bandage their wounds.

I know several in whom the fear has turned to anger: bellicose souls, spirits in revolt, hearts adulterated by vengeance. If they write, they write proclamations and challenges, the smoke of combat. They neither accept nor grant mercy. They do not dedicate their pity to anyone. They do not implore forgiveness of anyone. They die without a whimper. I know them . . .

I know one who neither wept nor became irritated, disdainfully. I know one who absented himself from that; but he collected stones and rare flowers in his soul in order to build and decorate the temple, the interior temple that everyone would admire one day—when the frail walls of flesh that presently hide it from the world have fallen—the symphonic temple in which plaints and blasphemies will be resolved into amorous harmonies; for no one will weep any longer then and no one will become irritated any longer. I know one who let people believe that he was in revolt, even though he was resigned, wearing his life like a cloak. I know one who knows the secret of Future Joy.

REMY DE GOURMONT
(1858-1915)

Remy de Gourmont was one of the most prolific writers of Symbolist prose, especially *poènes en prose*, and he became the Movement's leading historian and commentator. After studying law at the Université de Caen he moved to Paris, intent on devoting his life to *"livres et amour"* and formed a close friendship with Joris-Karl Huysman, the warmth of which waned after he "inherited" Huysmans' turbulent mistress Berthe Courrière. He also formed a close friendship with Alfred Vallette, helping him to found the most successful of the Symbolist periodicals of the *fin-de-siècle*, the *Mercure de France*, and another with Alfred Jarry, with whom he co-edited an eccentric spinoff from the *Mercure* dedicated to Symbolist art, *L'Ymagier*. He obtained a post at the Bibliothèque Nationale, but was sacked because he promoted unfashionable political views. He was badly stricken by the autoimmune disease lupus, which disfigured his face so badly that he became a recluse, hardly ever leaving his room and receiving visitors sitting stubbornly in shadow, but continuing to work relentlessly and publishing numerous books, including several collections of short prose pieces, including *Proses moroses* (1894; tr. as *Morose vignettes*), *Histoires magiques* (tr. as "Studies in Fascination"), *D'un pays lointain* (1898; tr. as *From a Faraway Land*) and *Couleurs* (1908), in which it is exceedingly difficult to distinguish *poèmes en prose* from *contes*. The last of his several novels, *Un Nuit au Luxembourg* (1906; tr. as *A Night in the Luxemburg*), is a long poem in prose. His association with the *Mercure* allowed him to publish much of his work himself, and such is its eccentricity and esotericism that it would probably have been difficult to find sympathetic editors elsewhere until he had gathered sufficient renown. One of the undoubted Titans of Symbolism, he was nevertheless a writer *sui generis*, especially with regard to his poems in prose and his *contes*.

Litanies of the Rose

Hypocritical flower,
  Flower of silence.

Rose color of copper, more fraudulent than our joys, rose color of copper, embalm us in your lies, hypocritical flower, flower of silence.

Rose with a face painted like a whore, rose with a prostituted heart, rose with a painted face, put on a semblance of being pitiful, hypocritical flower, flower of silence.

Rose with a puerile face, virgin of future treasons, rose with a puerile face, innocent and red, open the snare of your bright eyes, hypocritical flower, flower of silence.

Rose with black eyes, mirror of your void, rose with black eyes, make us believe in the mystery, hypocritical flower, flower of silence.

Rose the color of pure gold, casket of the ideal, rose the color of pure gold, give us the key to your abdomen, hypocritical flower, flower of silence.

Rose the color of silver, censer of our dreams, rose the color of silver, take our heart and make it smoke, hypocritical flower, flower of silence.

Rose with a crimson face, anger of disdained women, rose with a crimson face, tell us the secret of your pride, hypocritical flower, flower of silence.

Rose with a yellow ivory face, lover of yourself, rose with a yellow ivory face, tell us the secret of your virginal nights, hypocritical flower, flower of silence.

Rose with bloody lips, eater of flesh, rose with bloody lips, what shall we do with it? Drink it, hypocritical flower, flower of silence.

Rose the color of sulfur, inferno of vain desires, rose the color of sulfur, light the pyre where you hover, soul and flame, hypocritical flower, flower of silence.

Rose the color of peach, velvety fruit of make-up, sly rose, rose the color of peach, poison our teeth, hypocritical flower, flower of silence.

Rose the color of flesh, goddess of good will, rose the color of flesh, make us kiss the sadness of your cool and insipid skin, hypocritical flower, flower of silence.

Winy rose, flower of inn-arbors and cellars, winy rose, mad alcohols caper in your breath; murmur to us the horror of amour, hypocritical flower, flower of silence.

Violet rose, modesty of perverse girls, violet rose, your eyes are larger than the rest, hypocritical flower, flower of silence.

Pink rose, virgin with an overflowing heart, pink rose, muslin robe, open your false angelic wings, hypocritical flower, flower of silence.

Rose in silk paper, adorable simulacrum of increate graces, rose in silk paper, are you not the true rose, hypocritical flower, flower of silence.

Rose the color of dawn, the color of time, the color of nothing, smile of the Sphinx, rose the color of dawn, we love you because you lie, hypocritical flower, flower of silence.

Rose hortensia, banal delight of distinguished souls, neo-Christian rose, rose hortensia, you give us a distaste for Jesus, hypocritical flower, flower of silence.

Pink rose of China, so mild and faded, miraculous amour of flowering women, pink rose of China, your thorns are muffled and your claws withdrawn, O velvet paw, hypocritical flower, flower of silence.

Blonde rose, light mantle of chrome over frail shoulders, blonde rose, female stronger than males, hypocritical flower, flower of silence.

Orange-colored rose, fabulous Venetian, patrician, dogaress, orange-colored rose, maw of a tiger asleep under the lampas of your foliage, hypocritical flower, flower of silence.

Apricot rose, your warm amour has little fire, apricot rose, and your heart is like a bowl in which charlottes are simmering, hypocritical flower, flower of silence.

Rose in the form of a cup, red vase into which the teeth bite when the mouth comes to drink there, rose in the form of a cup, our bites make you smile and our kisses make you weep, hypocritical flower, flower of silence.

Rose all white, innocent and the color of milk, rose all white, so much candor frightens us, hypocritical flower, flower of silence.

Rose the color of straw, yellow diamond amid the crudities of the prism, rose the color of straw, you have been seen, heart to heart behind a fan, respiring the perfume of beards, hypocritical flower, flower of silence.

Rose the color of wheat, heavy sheaf at the loose belt, rose the color of wheat, you would like to be molded and you would like to be kneaded, hypocritical flower, flower of silence.

Lilac rose, dubious heart, lilac rose, a flood has rusted you, but you will only sell your oxidized flesh more dearly, hypocritical flower, flower of silence.

Crimson rose, color of sumptuous autumn sunsets, crimson rose, you lie down and you hold yourself out, an imperial offering, to prepuberal covetousness, hypocritical flower, flower of silence.

Rose marbled with pink and red, melting and mature, marbled rose, you still show willingly the underside of your petals in the strictest intimacy, hypocritical flower, flower of silence.

Rose the color of bronze, pastry coked by the sun, rose the color of bronze, the hardest javelins are blunted on your skin, hypocritical flower, flower of silence.

Rose the color of fire, special crucible for refractory flesh, rose the color of fire, providence of alliances in childhood, hypocritical flower, flower of silence.

Incarnadine rose, stupid and full of health, incarnadine rose, you slake our thirst and you lure us with a very red and very benign wine, hypocritical flower, flower of silence.

Rose in glazed velvet, pink and yellow dignity and presidential grace, rose in glazed velvet, corsage of neo-princesses, doublet of the worthy Tartuffe, hypocritical flower, flower of silence.

Rose in cherry satin, exquisite munificence of triumphant lips, rose in cherry satin, your illuminated mouth has placed on our flesh the crimson seal of its mirage, hypocritical flower, flower of silence.

Rose with a virginal heart, louche and pink adolescence that has not yet spoken, rose with a virginal heart, you have nothing to say to us, hypocritical flower, flower of silence.

Redcurrant rose, shame and blush of ridiculous sins, redcurrant rose, your dress has been crumpled too often, hypocritical flower, flower of silence.

Rose the color of dusk, half-dead of ennui, crepuscular smoke, rose the color of dusk, you are dying of amour while kissing your idle hands, hypocritical flower, flower of silence.

Blue rose, iridine rose, monster the color of the Chimera's eyes, blue rose, raise your eyelids a little; are you afraid that someone might look you in the eyes, Chimera, hypocritical flower, flower of silence?

Green rose, rose the color of the sea, navel of sirens, green rose, undulating and fabulous gem, you are no longer water as soon as a finger has touched you, hypocritical flower, flower of silence.

Carbuncle rose, rose flowering in the black brow of a dragon, carbuncle rose, you are nothing more than a belt buckle, hypocritical flower, flower of silence.

Rose the color of vermilion, enamored shepherdess lying down in the furrows, rose the color of vermilion, the shepherd sniffs you but the goat has browsed you, hypocritical flower, flower of silence.

Rose of tombs, freshness emanated from carrion, rose of tombs, all dainty and pink, adorable perfume of fine putrescence, you put on a semblance of life, hypocritical flower, flower of silence.

Brown rose, the color of dull mahogany, brown rose, permitted pleasures, wisdom, prudence and foresight, you look at us with mischievous eyes, hypocritical flower, flower of silence.

Poppy-red rose, ribbon of model little girls, poppy-red rose, glory of little dolls, are you simple or sly, plaything of little brothers, hypocritical flower, flower of silence?

Red and black rose, insolent and secret rose, red and black rose, your insolence and your redness pale amid the compromises that virtue invents, hypocritical flower, flower of silence.

Climbing rose, creeper that winds around the oleanders in gardens of Academe, and which also flourishes in the Elysian Fields, climbing rose, you no longer have any perfume or beauty, witless ephebe, hypocritical flower, flower of silence.

Poppy rose, flower of the laboratory, torpor of charlatan philters, roseate rose of the helmets of false mages, poppy rose, the hands of some fools tremble over your ruff, hypocritical flower, flower of silence.

Slate rose, grayness of vaporous virtues, you climb and you flower around solitary old benches, evening rose, hypocritical flower, flower of silence.

Peony rose, modest vanity of lush gardens, peony rose, the wind only tucked up your leaves by chance, and you were discontented, hypocritical flower, flower of silence.

Snowy rose, the color of snow and swansdown, snowy rose, you know that the snow is fragile and you only open your swan's feathers emblematically, hypocritical flower, flower of silence.

Hyaline rose, the color of clear springs gushing in the grass, hyaline rose, Hylas died for having loved your eyes, hypocritical flower, flower of silence.

Topaz rose, princess of abolished legends, topaz rose, your fortress is a monthly hotel, your keep marks the hour and your white hands make equivocal gestures, hypocritical flower, flower of silence.

Ruby rose, Indian princess in a palanquin, ruby rose, sister of Akedysseril, degenerate sister, your blood is no longer the flower of your skin, hypocritical flower, flower of silence.

Amaranth rose, princess of the Fronde and queen of the *Précieuses*, amaranth rose, lover of beautiful verses, amorous impromptus are legible in the curtains of your alcove, hypocritical flower, flower of silence.

Opal rose, sultana somnolent in the odor of the harem, opal rose, languor of constant caresses, your heart knows the profound peace of satisfied vices, hypocritical flower, flower of silence.

Amethyst rose, morning star, Episcopal tenderness, amethyst rose, you sleep on devoted and padded breasts, gem offered to Marie, sacristine gem, hypocritical flower, flower of silence.

Cardinal rose, rose the color of the blood of the Roman Church, cardinal rose, you make the wide eyes of the dainty dream, and more than one pins you to the knot of your garter, hypocritical flower, flower of silence.

Papal rose, rose watered by the hands that bless the world, papal rose, your heart of gold is brass, and the tears that pearl in your vain corolla are the tears of Christ, hypocritical flower, flower of silence.

Hypocritical flower.

Flower of silence.

News of the Unfortunate Isles

To Jules Renard

It was a mild country, sad and green, as if recuperating from an ancient misfortune, a vast plain, afflicted and resigned. I took a path confined between two thorny hedges devoid of flowers, with lamentable thorns that seemed to be weeping over the cruelty of their destination, and after having marched for two hours in the prison of the lamentable thorns I was stopped by a barrier erected like an absurd stockade between me and infinity.

The brutally-squared logs intersected, delimiting narrow chinks of light; I looked through and I saw:

A mild garden, sad and green, where there were sad, tender and green salad vegetables, fresh and dappled, nothing but lettuces, and amid that tender pasturage, a troop of naked women. I was not mistaken about that for an instant; the descriptions of voyagers were precise; I had never seen women before, but I was seeing them now.

The spectacle interested me.

Woman appeared to me then as a rather graceful animal, which I classified immediately between the kangaroo and the opossum, but she differed from those species by virtue of a few very characteristic details. Thus, like the horse, women have a mane, black, bay or chestnut, which descends over the eyes in front and trails all the way to the ground; their hair is sparse, thick in certain places, brighter or darker than the mane; they have no tail; in order to scratch themselves they raise the front paw, unlike the majority of animals, which raise the hind paw; their udders are pectoral, whereas in the majority of mammals they are inguinal.

They wander hither and yon, grazing the tender green lettuce, one leaf here and one leaf there, with an anxious and searching air, sometimes sniffing for minutes a vegetable that I would have found very satisfactory, but which they disdained for another, similar or even less appetizing.

In spite of their anxious appearance, it seemed to me that they bent over the ground with pleasure, content to justify their material appetites, because for more than an hour, while I was examining them, not one of them raised her head even once; the salad vegetable, the good lettuce, was their entire passion.

Never, in truth, had any animals interested me to that degree; I would have liked to see them a closer range and touch them; I whistled, I called out, I imagined the sweetest modulations; as in the zoological gardens I passed my hand through the bars, making appealing signs, pretending to be holding good things in my hands, but the herd was unmoved.

I was impatient and I became angry; I threw stones at the beautiful beasts, but my aim was poor, I did not hit a single rump, and the herd was unmoved.

However, I wanted one of those beasts!

The thorny hedge, the lamentable hedge, in sorrow at its destination, surrounded the garden with an ineluctable defense, but the barrier was not insurmountable. I mounted the assault of my desire; I succeeded, and the ruse of falling on all fours allowed me to approach unperceived a small chestnut separate from the bulk of the herd. She was seized and thrown over my shoulders; I found myself, after a feverish climb, on the other side of the barrier, without a very clear consciousness of that strange abduction being affirmed in my mind; and, troubled and frightened, not having got my breath back, nor looking behind me, I fled, glad of my burden, the good stolen beast—who moaned a little, but allowed herself to be taken with a singularly mild inertia.

What happened at home, in the little house that I had organized near the shore, while waiting for the ship with white sails that was to take me to the Unfortunate Isles?

Alas, I cannot say.

But as soon as I had deposited the woman in my enclosure, as soon as I had stroked her, as soon as I had kissed her agreeable mane playfully, as soon as, taking her head between my hands, I had gazed into her green eyes—eyes truly the color of fresh, tender green lettuce—yes, at that moment, as soon the green eyes of the beautiful beast, her eyes drowned in such an ingenuously animal mist, her eyes as profound as the idea of eternal spring, her resigned eyes full of an imperious charity, as soon as her eyes, eyes such as I had never seen before, were impregnated with their fluids—I became intoxicated, and perhaps mad,

What was happening?

Nothing that I can describe, since I was drunk, and perhaps mad.

But from that moment on, the beast, standing up on two paws, became very similar to what I was, dominated me and tamed me.

And it is now me who grazes the salads, the fresh, tender green lettuce.

And I know now that no ship with white sails will come to take me away from the prison that I have made for myself, to the Unfortunate Isles.

Hell

To Louis Dumur[1]

In his humble cell, traversed by strange gleams that did not come from either the nascent dawn or the moribund lamp, the illustrious Heretic was writing

At the head of his monitory epistle he had placed the undeniable aphorism, the basis of all truly se-rious morality:

THERE IS A HELL

Now, in red-hot flasks, he distilled the filthy sulfurs, stirred pea soups in the devil's cauldrons, cooked the bitumen sauces, doled out the rations of boiling oil, steeped in resin for the anniversary illuminations the blonde hair of beloveds and the beards of lovers; he enlarged vast ponds of alcohol where fanatics were floating like slices of lemon in a punch, topped with green flames; he sprinkled with molten lead skulls resistant to the eternal Word, and the devoured flesh was magically regenerated in order to sizzle again under the immortal rain of fire; here, a terrible grinder made mincemeat of ly-ing hands; there a rasp of superhuman mechanism scraped the sterile flesh of foolish virgins from their groaning bones; and hearts fell under the infernal millstone as multitudinously as grains of wheat.

The illustrious Heretic did not forget the souls furbished with the greatest care by the forks of fear, the arrows of remorse, the necklaces of anguish, the hammers of terror, the chains of shame and the pincers of desolation.

Then he passed on to ordeals.

He invoked sinister damned souls, lamentable cadavers during forth and saying, with eyes full of an infinite error: "I am in Hell!" Ratbod, the king of the Friesians,[2] emerged thus

---

1 Louis Dumur (1860-1933) was a Swiss writer closely associated with the *Mercure de France* in the 1890s; he eventually enjoyed considerable success as a novelist.
2 Translating *Frisons* as "Friesians" loses the double meaning implicit in the

from the depths of the abyss and came to shake his red-hot shackles before his surprised officers. In the same way, Comte Orloff,[1] quitting Gehenna momentarily, manifested, thanks to his unusual presence in slippers and a dressing-gown, the truth of the Hell denied by an incredulous general. And others—many others—rejected momentarily by the gulf, marked on the living, on furniture and on tapestries, the carbonized traces of their fiery fingers, or, with a veritably demonic joviality, amused themselves, like the famous damned soul of whom the Venerable Peter, Abbot of Cluny,[2] speaks, returning to sprinkle innocent creatures with a liquid more corrosive than nitric acid, crying out in a voice not devoid of a certain iro-ny: "This is the cold water with which one refreshes oneself in Hell."

✳

Clouds covered the sky, and the humble cell was traversed by gleams that did not come from either the veiled sun or the dead lamp.

The illustrious Heretic had inclined his meditative head over the table; he raised it suddenly and, seized by a dolorous snigger, he proffered these few syllables:

"And I too will go to Hell."

. . . And hearts fell under the infernal millstone as multitudi-nously as grains of wheat.

---

fact that the trivial noun *frisons* refers to small curls, especially wood-shavings. The king of the Friesians named Redbad, Radbod or Ratbod, who died in 717 A.D. was notorious as the last ruler to resist the Christianiza-tion of his people imposed by the Franks; the choice made of the spelling of his name captures a double meaning retained in English. Legend has it that Ratbod almost consented to being bap-tized, but eventually refused, saying that he would rather spend eternity in Hell with his ancestors than in Heaven with his enemies.

1 Grigory Orlov (1734-1783), a favorite of Catherine the Great, who led the coup that installed her as empress. An anecdote reported by Monseigneur Louis-Gaston de Ségur in *L'Enfer—S'il y en a un . . .* (1876) related that he made a pact with a "General V." that whichever of them died first would return to inform the other as to the nature of the afterlife, a pact honored by General V. af-ter his death in battle, who appeared to his friend in order to say: "There is a Hell and I am in it!"

2 The theologian and Islamist known as Pierre le Vénérable was abbot of Cluny in the early twelfth century.

The City of the Sphinxes

There was a marvelous city that rose up in the middle of a great desert, so vast that it enclosed in its walls meadows full of livestock, fields of crops, forests, orchards, springs and an amorous lake where the young women went to bathe in the nude on the third day of the new moon.

No one had ever entered the marvelous city, and no one had ever left it.

It extended in the middle of the great desert, proud of being unique, in being the world, in being life, in being the joy fallen from the heavens amid the infinite sadness of the sands.

Its inhabitants, mild, simple and voluptuous, were ignorant of the forms of a precise religion and the tyranny of a strict government, like the divine Indians whom Benjamin of Tudela visited, who knew no other magistracy than good will.[1] However, the sight of the marvels that burst forth on their horizon had enabled them to conceive the possibility of future delights, the probable prolongation beyond death of the enjoyments of their humanity.

For a long distance around the walls there was nothing but sand, stones or little white rocks like old bones, but out there, near the circle, on very clear days, it was possible to distinguish miraculous forests, all shades of blue, a high white tower capped with gold, and, toward the sunset, a roseate palace with a thousand windows of light; flocks of angels flew above the treetops, and their wings inscribed flashes of lightning in the pure air.

Those marvels consoled the inhabitants of the unique city at the hour of their death. They imagined a migration of souls toward the blue forests, toward the white tower capped with

---

1 Rabbi Benjamin of Tudela (1130-1173) travelled extensively in Europe, north Africa and western Asia and published graphic descriptions of what he found there; although he did not get as far as India he did gather information in the near East as to what might be found there and in China.

gold and the palace with a thousand windows of light; they saw themselves, angelic and immortally joyful, their wings striping the pure air with lightning flashes; and the voluptuousness of soaring above the treetops seemed so sweet to them that some died voluntarily, because of the desire for such a metamorphosis.

Fortunate as the people were, the idea of a happiness that drowns in darkness was insupportable to them; they aspired to absolute pleasure, and did not want to comprehend the rights of death, the infelicity of life that induces humans to desire to dissolve like a grain of salt in the ocean of oblivion; so they believed in the perpetuity of their innocent souls, not by virtue of dogma or doctrine, but as one believes in the veracity of a charming tale and the caresses of an illusion.

No one in that land cared any longer about the truth; they admitted the axiom: *The truth is what I believe*. And they permitted others to have their own truth, as one has a pet dog or caged birds. There was a legend regarding the Truth, which represented it as a kind of bogey-man, who stupefied children and the impudent with a single glance; some people, doubtless by divination, depicted it as a hateful and ferocious monster that grabbed human beings by one leg and made use of them as clubs to crush other humans.

(Those simple folk, on the day when they wanted gods, would doubtless have adopted as a patron candid Liberty, a woman with large indulgent eyes, a creature of love and grace, with a proud gesture.)

No one in that land, therefore, had ever had the idea of going to see whether the distant marvels of the horizon were true marvels, edifications worthy of faith, authentic trees and real angels; no one had ever attempted to cross the threshold watched by the two sphinxes.

Beasts of bronze, but oracular, alive when it pleased them to be, frightful works of a preadamite magic, two sphinxes guarded the city's only gate, the gate through which it was forbidden to go out. They smiled in their brazen sleep, the two guardian beasts established there by Istakar, the founder of the city; and, as mediators, they seemed only to have chosen the immobility of death out of disdain for the action of life. Sometimes, words emerged from their immutable lips: there were poems or tales so ancient that they were scarcely comprehensible any longer; but, collected and written down, they served as talismans and formulae of amour. Sphinx and sphinge,[1] at the moment of nobility, adolescents came to visit the beasts of bronze and kiss them on the mouth; the young women kissed the mouth of the beast whose face was triangulated by a pointed beard, and males kissed the mouth of the beast that had female breasts.

One day, an adolescent, already as strong as a man and more learned than an old man, after having kissed the mouth of the sphinge, touched with his lips the nipples of the bronze breasts and said: "Sphinge, reply to me."

The sphinge responded: "Child, how have you found the secret of Istakar?"

"I've found it, since you're replying to me."

"Come back tomorrow," said the sphinge. "It's the day when the people amuse themselves at the game of the sacred bath, the day when, for the first time, the young women blossomed during the year to the amorous life show themselves naked on the shores of the lake. Instead of following the people, come here, and I'll do as you wish, since you know the secret of Istakar."

The next day, as soon as the adolescent had arrived, a little door opened slowly in the wall, while the sphinge, in a lamentable voice, pronounced the single word: "Go."

Then the adolescent entered into the exterior world. He walked for a long time, his eyes raised toward the distant blue forests, the white towers capped with gold, the windows of light, and the radiant flight of angels—so long that night fell upon the desert, and he went to sleep.

Three times night fell upon the desert, and three times the adolescent went to sleep with his head on a stone.

On the fourth day, in the morning, as he extended his imploring and weary arms toward the marvels of the horizon, still

---

1 A *sphinge*, or *sphynge* is a female sphinx; English does not differentiate the sexes of the species, but French does, and as it is important to do so in the context of the present story I have followed the French practice.

as distant and still as beautiful, an eagle swooped down and alighted on the stone where he was asleep.

"Eagle," said the adolescent, "have pity on me; pick me up and carry me out there, to the summit of the ivory tower."

The eagle took hold of the adolescent.

"Adolescent, lie down on my back, between my two wings, and I'll carry you to the ivory tower."

The eagle flew away, like Geryon,[1] and the adolescent lay down between its two wings, exalted by amour, his gaze stubbornly fixed on the white tower capped with gold, still distant and still beautiful.

The eagle flew for a long time, so long that they arrived in the land where the days are years and the years are centuries, and still the tower stood on the horizon, amid the flight of angels, above the blue forest and the palace with windows of light.

Every century, the adolescent asked with the anxiety of desire: "Eagle, will we arrive soon?"

But the eagle, without replying, flapped its wings violently, and they passed over the land where the flowers are suns and the women attach stars to their ears, and still the ivory tower was resplendent in the distance, still pure and still beautiful.

"Eagle, will we arrive soon?" asked the adolescent, in a sad and hoarse voice. "Eagle, my hands have become yellow and my hair has turned entirely white. Eagle, will we arrive soon?"

"We have arrived, old man," replied the eagle, alighting on the stone on which the adolescent had laid his head on the third night of his journey. "Here is the tower, here is the forest, here is the palace, here are the angels, such as you saw them when I took you between my two wings; we have gone around the world without attaining your desire, and now you're old, you're going to die, but at least you're going to die at home."

The eagle disappeared, having shaken off its burden; and, having fallen rudely on the stones, the old man went to sleep and dreamed.

---

1 The reference is not to the Geryon of Greek myth but to the Geryon of Dante's *Inferno*, the winged monster that carries Dante and Virgil on its back to the circle of Fraud.

The first thing he did when he awoke was to search with his fatigued eyes for the divine marvels for which he had nourished amour for so long, but the horizon was bare, only forming a black circle. He was not surprised, for his dream had prepared him finally to know and comprehend the truth; saddened by a lost light, he rejoiced in knowing that the horizon was a black circle, and, scorning the primitive illusions of humans, marching without repose, he only took two days to reach the gate guarded by the sphinxes.

It was open.

He went in and said: "O sphinx, friend of my youth, here I am. I've come back from such a long voyage that my hands are all yellow and my hair is completely white—but I know the truth. There is no blue forest out there, nor a white tower capped with gold, nor a palace with windows of light, not a radiant flock of archangels; I have traveled the world and the worlds, lying on an eagle's back, and now I know; I know that the world is ringed by a black circle made of darkness, and that the marvel of the horizons is only the futile flower of eternal Illusion. I know, and I shall kill Illusion. I know, and I shall tell the truth. People, this is the truth . . ."

But the sphinge, at the sign made to her by the bronze male, stood up sadly, and crushed beneath her claw, like a compassionate lioness, the monster who had traversed the worlds between Geryon's wings.

PIERRE LOUŸS
(1870-1925)

Pierre Louÿs was the form of his name adopted by Pierre-Félix Louis. His novel *Aphrodite, moeurs antiques* (1896) became the best-selling novel of the *fin-de-siècle* in France and prompted a boom in the production of eroticized accounts of "ancient mores," many of them stylistically flamboyant and closely affiliated to the more extravagant forms of *poèmes en prose*. Louÿs had previously published a collection of prose poems, *Les Chansons de Bilitis* (1894), which did not sell as rapidly but was eventually established as the most famous such collection; the samples below are taken from it. With Marcel Schwob, Louÿs had also helped Oscar Wilde produce the French version of his play *Salomé* in 1891, which the Irishman hoped to stage in Paris because he knew that he could not get it past the English censor. His first publications, in the short-lived revue *La Conque* in 1891, had been a set of erotic verses. *Les Chansons de Bilitis* were set firmly in the tradition of Montesquieu's *Temple de Gnide*, falsely represented as a translation from ancient Greek of poems authored by a contemporary of Sappho, whose name is rendered therein as Psappha, as Renée Vivien was later to do; the imposture was distinctly half-hearted. A later collection, *Le Crépuscule des nymphes* (1925) consists of long *poèmes en prose* recycling erotic Greek myths.

Some Songs of Bilitis

Psappha

I rub my eyes . . . it is already daylight, I think. Ah! who is beside me? . . . a woman? . . . By the Paphia,[1] I had forgotten . . . O Charites, how ashamed I am.

Into what country have I come, and what is this isle in which love is understood thus? If I were so utterly weary I would believe it to be some dream . . . Is it possible that this is Psappha?

She's asleep . . . She is certainly beautiful, although her hair is cut like that of an athlete. But that strange face, that virile breast and those narrow hips . . .

I want to go before she wakes. Alas, I am on the side of the wall. It would be necessary for me to step over her. I'm afraid of brushing her hip and that she might catch me in passing.

---

1 The reference is to the sanctuary of Aphrodite Paphia in ancient Paphos, on Cyprus, where the goddess was allegedly born from the sea.

The Dance of Glottis and Kyse

Two little girls have taken me to their home, and as soon as the door was closed they lit the wick of the lamp and wanted to dance for me.

Their cheeks had no make-up, as brown as their little bellies. They linked their arms and spoke at the same time, in an agony of gaiety.

Sitting on a mattress borne on two raised trestles, Glottis sang in a high-pitched voice and beat time with her sonorous little hands.

Kyse danced jerkily, then stopped, breathless with laughter, and, taking her sister by the breasts, bit her shoulder and tipped her over like a playful goat.

Advice

Then Syllikhmas came in, and, seeing us so familiar, she sat down on the bench. She took Glottis on one knee and Lyse on the other, and she said:

"Come here, child," but I remained at a distance. "Are you afraid of us? Come closer! these children love you. They will teach you what you do not know: the honey of a woman's caresses.

"Men are violent and lazy. Doubtless you know that. Hate them. They have flat chests, rough skin, short-cropped hair and hairy arms. But women are entirely beautiful.

"Only women know how to love; stay with us, Bilitis, stay. And if you have an ardent soul, you will see your beauty, as if in a mirror, on the bodies of your lovers."

Uncertainty

Glottis or Kyse, I do not know which to espouse. As they are dissimilar, one would not console me for the other and I'm afraid of choosing poorly.

Each of them has one of my hands, and also one of my breasts. But to which should I give my mouth? to which should I give my heart and all that cannot be shared?

It is shameful for all three to remain like this in the same house. There is talk about it in Mytilene. Yesterday, outside the temple of Ares, did not a woman passing by say to me: "Slut!"?

It's Glottis that I prefer, but I can't repudiate Kyse. What would become of her all alone? Should I leave them together as they were and take another lover?

The Encounter

I have found a kind of treasure in a field under a myrtle bush, enveloped from the throat to the feet in a yellow peplum embroidered with blue.

"I have no lover," she said to me, "for the nearest town is forty stadia from here. I live alone with my mother, who is a widow and always sad. If you wish, I'll go with you.

"I'll go with you all the way to your house, even if it's on the other side of the island, and I'll live with you until you send me away. Your hand is tender, your eyes are blue.

"Let's go. I won't take anything with me except the little naked Astarte that is suspended from my necklace. We'll put her next to yours and we'll give them roses in recompense every night."

The Little Terracotta Astarte

The little guardian Astarte that protects Massidika was modeled in Camiros by a very skillful potter. She is as long as a thumb and made of fine yellow clay.

Her tresses fall and round out over her narrow shoulders. Her eyes are slit horizontally and her mouth is very small; for she is the Very Beautiful.

With her right hand she is pointing to her delta, which is riddled with little holes on the underbelly and along the groin; for she is the Very Amorous.

220

With her left arm she is sustaining her heavy round breasts. Between her wide hips a pregnant belly swells; for she is the Mother of All Things.

Desire

She entered, and passionately, her eyes half-closed, she united her lips with mine and our tongues met. Never in my life had there been a kiss like that one.

She was standing against me, totally amorous and consenting. One of my knees gradually rose between her warm thighs, which yielded as for a lover.

My hand, crawling over her tunic, sought to divine the fugitive body, which alternately yielded, undulating, and stiffened, rearing up, with quiverings of the skin.

With her delirious eyes she indicated the bed, but we did not have the right to love before the wedding ceremony, and we separated abruptly.

MARCEL SCHWOB
(1867-1905)

Marcel Schwob was a journalist on the staff of the *Écho de Paris* before Catulle Mendès was hired as its literary editor, and might have been instrumental in his hiring. At any rate, he joined Mendès' stable of writers supplying the paper with short fiction, and became its star, supplying an innovative and wide-ranging series of stories that provided important models for his colleagues, in spite of their author's resolutely esoteric antiquarian interests, from which he often drew his own inspiration. In addition to *contes* shaped expressly to fit the slot allocated in the paper to short fiction he occasionally imitated Mendès by dividing it up to accommodate groups of shorter prose poems, usually headed *Mimes*, under which title they were eventually collected in a slim volume in 1893. Perpetually ill, although his illness could not be specifically diagnosed or successfully treated—even by the famous surgeon Samuel Pozzi, who also treated Robert de Montesquiou and Jean Lorrain as well as equipping Sarah Bernhardt with a wooden leg—Schwob had great difficulty working for much of the latter part of his life, but persisted stubbornly, presumably having discovered the important truth that obsession is the only viable opposition that can be mounted temporarily against fatal despair. With Pierre Louÿs, Adolphe Retté and Stuart Merrill—all intensely interested in the art of *poèmes en prose*—he helped Oscar Wilde prepare *Salomé* for production in Paris, and was presumably not without influence on Wilde's prose poems and *contes*. The samples translated below appeared in the 9 February 1892 issue of the *Écho* before being reprinted in *Mimes*.

The Mirror, the Needle and the Poppy

The mirror speaks:

"I have been fashioned in silver by a skilful worker; at first I was as hollow as his hand, and my other face was similar to a globe of dull glass, but then I received the concavity appropriate to render images. Finally, Athene blew wisdom into me. I am not unaware of what the young woman who holds me desires, and I respond to her in advance that she is pretty. However, she gets up in the night and lights her bronze lamp. She directs the golden feather of flame toward me, and her heart wishes for a face other than her own. I show her her white face, her shapely cheeks, the swollen nascence of her breasts and her eyes full of curiosity. She almost touches me with her trembling lips, but the gold that burns only illuminates her face and all the rest is obscure in me."

The golden needle speaks:

"As I was traversing ingloriously a byssus thread, having been stolen from a Tyrian's house by a black slave, I was seized by a perfumed courtesan. She placed me in her hair and I pricked the imprudent woman's fingers. Aphrodite has instructed me and sharpened my point with lust. I have finally arrived in the coiffure of this young woman, and have made her tresses quiver. She bonds under me like a crazy filly, and does not see the cause of her pain. During the four parts of the night I agitate the ideas in her head and her heart obeys. The unquiet flame of the lamp makes shadows dance, which bend their winged arms. Then she perceives rapid tumultuous visions and falls upon her mirror. But it only shows her her face, tormented by desire."

The head of the poppy speaks:

"I was born in subterranean fields, among plants whose colors are unknown. I know all the nuances of obscurity; I have seen the luminous flowers of darkness. Persephone has held me in her lap and I have fallen asleep there.

When Aphrodite's needle wounds the young woman with curiosity I show her the forms that wander in the eternal night. They are handsome young men adorned with graces that no longer exist. Aphrodite is able to give desires, and Athene shows mortals the inanity of their dreams, but Persephone holds the mysterious keys to the two gates of horn and ivory. Through the former gate she sends by night the shadows that haunt humans; Aphrodite takes possession of them, and Athene kills them. But through the second gate the Good Goddess receives those who are weary of Aphrodite and Athene.

Hermes Psychagogos

Whether the dead are enclosed in sculpted stone sarcophagi, or contained in the bellies of metallic or earthenware urns, or stood erect, gilded and painted blue, devoid of brains and viscera, enveloped in linen bandages, I gather them in a troop and I guide their steps with my conductive wand.

We advance along a rapid path that humans cannot see. Courtesans press against virgins, murderers against philosophers, mothers against those who refuse to give birth, and priests against perjurers; for they repent of their crimes, whether they have imagined them in their heads or carried them out with their hands. And having not been free on earth, because they were bound by laws and customs, or their own memory, they dread isolation and they sustain one another. A woman who lay naked among men in flagstoned chambers consoles a young woman who died before her wedding and who dreamed imperiously about amour. A man who killed on the roads, his face soiled by ash and soot, places his hand on the forehead of a thinker who wanted to regenerate the world and preached death. A lady who loved her children and suffered because of them hides her head in the bosom of a hetaera who was voluntarily sterile. A man clad in a long robe who persuaded himself to believe in his God and constrained himself to genuflections weeps on the shoulder of a cynic who broke all the oaths of flesh and spirit before the eyes of citizens. Thus they help one another along their route, marching under the yoke of memory.

Then they come to the bank of the Lethe, where I place them along the silently flowing water. Some plunge their heads into it, which contain evil thoughts, others dip their hands into it, which committed evil actions. When they get up again, the water of the Lethe has extinguished their memory. Immediately, they separate, and all of them smile for themselves, believing themselves to be free.

The Three Bottles

The tyrant Polycrates commanded that three sealed bottles be brought to him containing three delicious wines of different species. A diligent slave took a bottle of black stone, a bottle of yellow gold and a bottle of limpid glass, but the forgetful cup-bearer poured the same wine of Samos into all three bottles.

Polycrates considered the bottle of black stone and frowned, He broke the gypsum seal and sniffed the wine. "The bottle," he said, "is of vulgar matter, and the odor of what it contains is not engaging for me."

He lifted the bottle of yellow gold and admired it. "This wine," he said, is certainly inferior to its beautiful container, rich in vermilion clusters and luminous grapes."

Seizing the third bottle of limpid glass, however, he held it up against the sunlight. The bloody wine scintillated. Polycrates broke the seal, emptied the wine into his cup and drank it in a single draught. "This," he said, with a sigh, is the best wine I have tasted." Then, in placing his cup on the table, he bumped the bottle, which fell into dust.

GUSTAVE KAHN
(1859-1936)

Gustave Kahn was the co-founder with Jean Moréas of the short-lived periodical *Le Symboliste*, in the pages of which he strove to distinguish the Symbolist Movement from the Decadent Movement, which had recently acquired a propagandist voice of its own in Anatole Baju's *Le Décadent*. He also founded *La Vogue*, and contributed to other Symbolist periodicals, including the *Revue Blanche* and the *Mercure de France*. He claimed to be the inventor of *vers libre*, although the claim was disputed by Marie Krysinska and had been bandied about previously, notably in the pages of *L'Artiste*. Under the umbrella of the Symbolist Movement he published several volumes of poetry, the novel *Le Roi fou* (1896; tr. as *The Mad King*) and the collage of prose pieces *Le Conte de l'or et du silence* (1898; tr. as *The Tale of Gold and Silence*), but his later collections of prose fiction drifted away from Symbolism, putting more emphasis on other ideologies dear to his heart, particularly Socialism and Zionism. Although his free verse is understandably difficult to distinguish from *poèmes en prose*, the distinction was obviously clear in his own mind; some of the samples below are improvised by reconnection of the prose passages that link the sections of his first and most successful collection, *Palais nomades* (1887). Because one of the sections of that text is titled "Interludes" I have improvised the title "Transitions" for the connective text. The earlier piece appeared in *Tout-Paris*, the successor to *L'Hydropathe*, in 1880.

The Smoker

She was red, he called her Gertrude; she was long and thin, worth two sous. She launched fleecy blue smoke that spread out over the ceiling and then accumulated around him. She was his heaven, shining like a star, or a match, from time to time; and then he drank beer. On the bottom of the glass he had painted a forget-me-not, for he was a painter. He was also, under the suzerainty of the hammer, a chorist at the Opéra-Comique. What a gaiety there was when he brandished a decorated standard and smoked an imaginary pipe; they were theatrical solemnities for Gertrude. Then, his voice having broken, he earned twenty sous a day uttering inarticulate sounds outside a bazaar; but he could smoke. Sometimes he sold a miniature filled with an opulent bourgeois smoking his pipe in front of beer. One day he married a tobacconist. He grew jealous seeing her sell pipes and tobacco to just anyone, so he sold her amours—infamy!

One evening, his wife had gone to the theater. In the haunted bedroom, shadows obscured the furniture. The tobacco-jar was drowned in the confusion of the mantelpiece; the pipe-rack became vague. He suspended a bit of string from a nail and lit Gertrude. Click! She had broken; he was dead.

At Père-Lachaise, in a lost pathway, surrounded by yellow flowers, there is a tomb. The flowers remain immutable, faded, a wreath of jet. But every Sunday his chaste spouse deposits a pipe and a packet of tobacco there.

In *L'Officiel* one read: *Yesterday, in a corner of Père-Lachaise, light smoke rose up. Thanks to the devotion of the employees, we have no disaster to deplore.*

Transitions

I

The evocative sorcery of hazard creates similitudes.

Memory vibrates feathered with dolor; visions flow identically in light and darkness. The appeasement of squares and plazas evoke the fuse of streets. The sufferings of memory exacerbate the similitudes.

Present desire murmurs toward the past, toward distance; chimeras unfurl their wings in taverns; and the basis of the harmonic development of ambulant hazard is the effaced smiles and chimes of another cycle; the similar awakens similar entities differently and only seeks.

And without seeking the exit from the labyrinth, where the poor soul somnambulates, relive the perpetual rebirths, the perpetual awakenings of appetencies, the deceptive renascences.

II

Fugitive are times of loving, impertinent the jumps of the young maidservant whom you ennoble with the gaze.

The long ennui of slavery and the muted struggles of weakness. Her poor irony, bad and devoid of smiles; a little pity for the eternal captive, consecrated to poorly-chosen falls.

After the crisis and the calm, in the momentous silence, listen to its voice, the voice of your past, in all serenity.

III

The brief accord beneath the bright branches is unmade by slow sadness.

The sporadic lassitude that distant hours bury in the mind adapts a wintry mantle to insufficiently new flesh.

Nothing survives the brief moment, the accord evaporates in regrets, the act dissolves and then resolves, nothing lives again or flowers again.

Soon, toward the distant buried hours, the minutes return, reentering the necessary lassitudes.

IV

And since everything is similar, all the suns of the years, all the suffering of the days, listen to the soul of legend float and sound.

The old dream moved in a loving atmosphere. To the distant dolor, facile pardons, listen in the smiling times to your dead brethren.

Look into the garden of legend, and the profound eyes rapidly glimpsed, ships eternally wandering, and the song that is heard on all routes. Look at the variegations of the passers-by, and so many similar hearts under so many similar robes.

V

To the instant of luminous life, to the error sought and cherished, crossroads of the voices of life, everything leads indefatigably.

Regrets that wish for some relief. So beautiful is everything lost, so regretted everything exiled, so desired everything expelled, in the evil hours of isolation.

Flee toward the past and cite the veracity of the illusory, the weak prowesses, and always and everywhere the recent past rises up, troubles and devastates.

What first instant threw us, debilitated, at the feet of clay; what ineluctable future orders dolor and silence to be separated?

Everywhere and always the recent past, the minute that perpetuates terrifying solitude.

VI

In that poor being, when repose descends.

Is it necessary to wait for his loins to be demolished, his eyes to be dull, and his mantle in rags, his hands pensive with a few scattered regrets of which he is ignorant?

Clinging to ephemeral clear gazes, haunted by disgust, seated on the banal verge, sickened by the ulcer of memory, will he see the heavy barges of dreams dragging themselves along indefinitely?

Weary of the glass and the cup, of the landscape and the human, inclining his forehead, shivering, into memories of hands, calming hands, so small and bulging with sinews, gaping at words that are lacking and no longer able to understand, a wordless Job, debris of his debris; will that be the repose of the poor, perhaps wretched, being henceforth?

In the unconsoled hovel adorned by no festival, the anterior masks are gathering dust in the corners, and ennui stripes with gray the futile tomes of lovers of old, turning in the void.

Of the suspected Babylon of the never-born fatherland only count the brutal forces: the curtain of a preparatory forgetfulness of the dead, fallen into the opacity of silence, and nothing but a memory of the Moloch of adolescences.

The Phantasmagoria of the unelucidated times of infancy, the passing memory of disappointment, the furnaces of the fires of old, and the blackness around and before the eyes: is that all, then, save for the brutal undertow of some unknown ebb-tide?

JEAN MORÉAS
(1856-1910)

Jean Moréas was the name employed in France by the poet and critic originally named Ioannis Papadiamantopoulos after his grandfather, a hero of the Greek War of Independence. Educated in Paris, he studied law there in 1875 and associated himself with the Hydropathes as well as with Stéphane Mallarmé. He embraced the philosophy of Symbolism and penned the Symbolist Manifesto that was published in the literary supplement of *Le Figaro* in 1886, trying, like Gustave Kahn, to defend the Movement from the accusation of "decadence" leveled against it by hostile journalists. He collaborated with Paul Adam on two volumes of prose but his contributions were not overtly

Symbolist, unlike some of his contributions to newspapers—including the *Écho de Paris*, from which the sample below, published in the 30 January 1891 issue—is taken. He soon drifted away from the Movement and looked more to the influence of Classical sources, associating himself with a short-lived École Romane.

Narcissus

Narcissus might have been sixteen years old. He is pleasant in face and body, for Nature had put all her understanding into his portrait. In his laughing and simple eyes the God of amours had seated a soft gaze that surprised everyone. His forehead and his chin shone more brightly than crystal or ice. And as for his mouth, Venus had touched it so gently that a woman who had once felt it was captivated by it permanently. His hair was curly and his complexion colored without artifice; it was the same in the evening as well as the morning, and did not stir, however hot or rainy it was.

Narcissus wandered in the woods and along the streams, and his pleasure was throwing his spears at stags and hinds. Of love he knew nothing, and did not care; he fled and hated Ladies of high status.

One day, by chance, Narcissus, mounted on a tawny mule, passed beneath the tower in which the daughter of the king of the city was working on a golden embroidery in her window. Echo was the damsel's name, and her beauty flourished above all beauties. She saw the beast that was going past, making the air quiver, and she saw the rider, slender in the flanks and broad in the chest, his feet straight in silver stirrups.

Echo watches the rider, and nothing he does is able to displease her.

Echo palpates her breast with her hand, searching for an external wound, but it is inside her body.

O Amour, how great your lordship is; you fear neither kings nor queens, you defeat the most sage.

Echo is sometimes cold and sometimes hot; she shivers all over, trembles and starts.

Night is falling and the day ending. The virgin is weary of thinking. She lies down, but turns over and over, unable to sleep.

"Alas," she said, "I can neither sleep nor repose, needing to turn over and over. I'm in pain and hard-worked. What's the matter with me?" She summons her nurse.

"Nurse," she said, "my bed is too hard, the feathers are not shifting."

"At your service, Madame," said the nurse

"Nurse," she said, "my bed is too high."

"At your service, Madame," said the nurse.

"Nurse," she said, "my bed is too flat."

"At your service, Madame," said the nurse.

"Nurse," she said, "the feet are too low."

"At your service, Madame," said the nurse.

"Nurse," she said, "the bed-head is too high."

"At your service, Madame," said the nurse.

"Nurse," she said, "the bed-head is too low."

"At your service, Madame," said the nurse.

"Oh, Nurse, what's the matter with me? I can't lie comfortably on my left side; now I'm on my right side," she said.

"Madame," said the nurse, "have you not been looking out of the window for too long?"

"Oh, nurse, nurse. I'm thinking about the man I saw passing by yesterday."

"Marvelous is amour!" said the nurse.

"It's the thing that does me most harm, when I remember his beauty."

"Amour deceives, betrays and lies," said the nurse. "Amour causes anguish."

"Nurse, he's very handsome, but he isn't bountiful."

"Perhaps he's a felon and full of anger," said the nurse.

"Nurse, such a handsome man can't be wicked!"

"Certainly not," said the nurse.

"By my faith, he's as good as he is handsome," she said.

"By my faith, I think so," said the nurse.

"Nurse, I want him to know that he pleases me in every way."

"Marvelous is amour!" said the nurse.

"Alas, alas! Grievous concern!"

She weeps from then on, lies down, then sits up, then chastises herself, and then comforts herself. As the morning light appears, Echo drags herself to the window. In the distance she sees the young man coming. She watches him, and merriment seizes her as soon as she can see him at close range; but when she sees him draw away, her heart fails.

"Ha ha," she said, "are you mad, Echo, and frantic? Don't you know that you're the King's daughter?"

"Ha ha," she said, "What message is my whole heart giving to him!"

"Ha ha," she said. "I'll go wait for him on the road."

✳

In the wood, Echo is sitting under a bush, naked except for a chemise, and decked in a mantle.

Narcissus comes along; he perceives the virgin, looks at her and believes her to be a goddess or fay. He descends from his horse and bows. He asks her who she is and where she is going.

"Sire," she said, "I am plaintive; I am fleeing all wealth, and set little price on my life. Handsome sire, I tell you this: I desire you above all things. And know that I am the daughter of your lord, the King. Handsome sire, grant me your amour, render my health, take away my dolor. For we are nearly of an age, and similar in beauty."

Narcissus hears her, smiles, looks at her and says:

"My God, young women, you're foolish and aberrant; it's a bad cause you're undertaking, and you're very bold; you must go away, daughter of the King. No amour whatsoever can belong to us, for we're still too young."

Echo throws back her mantle; her flesh is white beneath the chemise. Her hands, which she holds out, sighing, are whiter than spun linen. Narcissus sees the young woman's eyes, which are looking at him tenderly, weeping. But he has no pity.

232

Oh, hard heart devoid of mercy. There is not under Heaven any rich baron, prince, comte, emperor, admiral or king so highly placed that he would not have wept likewise.

"Ha ha," said Princess Echo, "if he were ugly, would that weigh upon me? It weighs upon me because he's so handsome. He has spoken to me nastily. I don't know what in me can displease him! Am I not noble enough, and beautiful? I have beautiful hands and beautiful feet. But he is vile and discourteous."

"Ha ha," said Princess Echo, "What if he were going to repent, if he were going to make amends? But I believe that he doesn't care.

"Ha ha," said Princess Echo. "Who am I? Who is my father? The King? Who is my mother? Don't you know? The Queen. No, no, I'm an orphan, I have no friends and no parents."

Then, as she was going through the wood, in great mourning and distress, she saw a man coming straight toward her, neither young nor white-haired, who was well-dressed in green samite.

"Damsel," said the man, "who are you, and why are you going forth in such great mourning and lamentation?"

"Alas, alas!" she said, "I'm the king's daughter, but I'm only a plaintive person, who puts little price on her life. Amour has gripped me, Venus has betrayed me."

"How?" said the man,

"The young man I'm mourning," she said, "surpasses in beauty Adonis and Tristan, the one who drank the beverage. But his heart is felonious and merciless. Narcissus is his name. Oh, who can enable me to take vengeance on him, by enabling him to know what lovesickness is?"

"Damsel," said the man, "I will enable you to take vengeance on him. Put your trust in me. My name is Bel-acueil, and I am something of a miracle-worker and necromancer."

❊

Narcissus had perceived a stag and had followed it all day.

An anguishing heat is spearing him, for the sun is very high, and Narcissus is in quest of a spring from which to drink. Eventually, he found a spring that was clear and sweet, well-garnished with thick grass. He sees deep water, always renewed, running over gravel. But when he tries to slake his thirst, he is warmed by another thirst.

When he bends down to drink, he sees his shadow in the spring. He thinks that it is looking at him; he believes it to be the fay of the waters. He cannot turn his eyes away; the more he looks at her, the more she pleases him.

Then he prays, sighs and weeps:

"What should I call you? Are you a summoned nymph, a fay or a goddess? Ah, whoever you are, come out of the spring and show me your whole body. Why are you proud in my regard? I am scarcely less beautiful than you; many a time I have been requisitioned by amour. Alas, can she hear what I am saying? No, no. Ha ha! She's responding to me; I can see her lips moving. But I can't hear her."

He does not know what he can see; the water is lying to him.

"When I smile at her, she smiles at me; if I touch my hair she does the same, Alas, alas, if she loved me she would emerge from the spring."

Then he prays, sighs and weeps. His tears disturb the spring; he cannot see therein what he desires.

"Alas, alas!" he said. "What has become of her? Where has she gone?"

Now, while he wept and became very mournful he saw a man coming toward him, neither young nor white-haired, well-dressed in green samite.

"Young man," he said, "why are you crying like that and why are you discomfited?"

"Alas, alas," said Narcissus, "there is a beautiful Lady in this spring . . ."

"How?" said the man,

"Alas, alas," said Narcissus, "she is a fay or a goddess. What has become of her?"

"Young man," said the man, "I believe that Amour has dazed you."

"Alas, alas!" said Narcissus.

"Young man," said the man, "what foolishness to put desire thus into a vain shadow and hate a beautiful princess!"

"Alas, alas," said Narcissus, "although I saw her, the water lied to me."

"Young man," said the man, "Come here." Taking him by the hand, he led him under branches where songbirds were passing back and forth. Echo, the beautiful virgin, was there.

"Damsel," said the man, "behold this felonious heart, which wants to make amends and render you loyal service."

From now on, Princess Echo has Narcissus where she wants him; she kisses his eyes and face; she swoons. And Narcissus clings to her very gently.

ADOLPHE RETTÉ
(1863-1930)

Adolphe Retté embarked on a military career in 1881 and served in the army until 1887 before deciding to devote himself to literature. He married a cousin the following year, but the marriage was unhappy and did not last long; the couple had separated before his wife died in 1890. Retté's ultra-Symbolist work *Thulé de brumes* (1891; tr. as *Misty Thule*), written in the aftermath of that personal catastrophe between October 1889 and January 1891, is a collage of *poèmes en prose*, from which the samples reproduced below are taken. It is heavily influenced by hallucinations he experienced during a period of heavy drinking, and is to some extent an eccentric reflective analysis of his state of mind. Although he continued writing for the rest of his life, and never abandoned Symbolism entirely, he never wrote anything similar again; he became an ardent Anarchist in the mid-1890s and much of his subsequent work was propagandistic, until 1906, when he experienced another conversion, or relapse, to Catholicism, and the final phase of his career was devoted to doctrinaire work. *Thulé de brumes* remained a classic work, almost *sui generis*, in spite of its affinities with the work of Stéphane Mallarmé and Remy de Gourmont.

The Little Goddess

Oh, the slightly mad countryside where you passed by, my little black and rosy dream—and your laughter, in scintillating sheaves of false notes, amused my ear.

You know our garden of dahlias, primroses and hollyhocks; and the networks of grass and narrow paths; and you, like an Atalanta, with your ringlets of dark hair in the wind?

And then, your laughter again behind the garish trellis of the arbor exuberant with convolvulus and nasturtiums.

At other times, your eyes—that night of unknowing stars—drank the dusk swept with gold and blood around the agonizing sun—red. And you marveled because—like me—you love red; not a certain red, but all reds, whether it be the dusk, or the violent fabrics that your fingernails scratch voluptuously, or, in winter, the berries as bright as the lips of a bacchante—oh, are they not your strong lips?—amid the somber green of the holly.

Do you remember the great silence, as soon as night fell, until cock-crow? Scarcely, in the distance, the whisper of running water, and the undulating murmur of the slumbering forest; the smoky evening, blue over the mauve meadows chilled by lunar silver: and the crystal cymbals of toads quivering here and there. When you were fearful you huddled against me—you, delicate thin bird—like one who does not dare, you gazed furtively into the shadow. One might almost have been able to imagine that you were dreaming!

All that, all that, is quite dead; dead too the passionate lyre, all of whose strings we caused to vibrate. Since then, we have known winter and malevolent village gossip and ennui, like a marsh in which one gets bogged down, each on one side. Since then, we rendered one another very unhappy. You held your resentment against me so politely that I can't help forgiving *you* for the harm that I did to you.

Hélène

Hélène, these phrases are not intended to prevail upon you as a madrigal; it is even passably indifferent to me whether you listen to them; they please me—that is enough.

Do you know, beauty almost equal to a portrait, that as soon as our first encounter, the syllables of your name evoked for me a very white sweetness, a happy slumber on the slow flakes of a calm snow, which would fall for hours and hours, while the little bells of a sleigh tinkled in the far distance . . . Yes, that whiteness, when I close my eyes, breathes the syllables of your name, thus, amid the opiate smoke of Oriental tobacco. And I feel so tranquil.

Afterwards, my head supported on your harmonious breasts, I scrutinize the oddly quasi-Chinese corners of your slightly hooded eyes—and I am then, entirely, the mandarin who philosophizes for himself while waiting for you in a garden planted with unique jonquils, around the great porcelain tower—out there.

Let me search for some soul hiding behind the dark green silk screen on which golden swans are sailing, and which leaves transparent, in its weave, a certain treacherous ember: your eyes. It's singular, my gaze palpates them but I can't penetrate therein. I don't know whether I'm mistaken, but one might think that they were lined with *emptiness*. Tell me, my love, do you, perchance have no soul?

Let us reserve the question, and let me respire the odor of your hair. Oh, what a flower-bed of frail artificial geraniums rises up, which I love for their self-regarding air and their rosy, brazenly modest hue, faintly stained by a suspicion of blood at the birth of every petal—whence disengages now the memory of a rare perfume whose name I have forgotten . . .

I believe, Madame, that you have nibbled my earlobe. I have not, moreover, done you any harm, since you're smiling—oh, but that smile . . . !

By that means, we are reposing on gilded sand in the utmost depths of the vermilion sea; the shadow of steamships furrowing the sea descends from above in a dust of ruby sparks, to caress our two heads crowned with delicate seaweed; huge corals rise stiffly on all sides, where many an undine-polyp lies in ambush, thumbing its nose at us.

A warm rutilant sea, your smile; one can easily think of nothing therein!

You're falling asleep? Come into my arms. Very sage, happy to delight in the rainbow reflections that the tremulous flame of the night-light slides over your satiny epidermis, I become torpid in an April twilight—stifled yellows, young blues, dying mauves—lilacs in flower scintillate in a light rain that is falling almost soundlessly, in accordance with some frictional rhythm: a slightly sharp wind pinches my nerves agreeably—and as I fall asleep too, amid the wind, the musical rain, and the lilacs, and the April twilight, the white syllables of your name waltz for me alone—Hélène!

GASTON DANVILLE
(1870-1933)

"Gaston Danville" was the pseudonym of Armand Blocq. He was the brother of the psychologist Paul Blocq, and he declared that in his writings he was trying to develop a new kind of Naturalism based on contemporary psychological theories, especially those of Théodule Ribot. He was, however, one of the authors who supplied the *Mercure de France* with much of its prose poetry during its first few years of existence, alongside Remy de Gourmont, Jules Renard and Saint-Pol-Roux. Danville's contributions were published under the heading *Contes d'au-delà*, and were collected under that title in 1893. The later items exhibit a marked transition from *poèmes en prose* to short stories, but in all of them, and in his novels, the "beyond" featured therein is not the afterlife but the unconscious mind. The first few items in the series (translated below) had been published in the *Revue indépendante* in May 1890 while it was an explicitly Symbolist periodical; the later ones are translated in *The Anatomy of Love and Murder* (2013).

Contes d'Au-delà

Avant-Propos

A large room with curtains of black gauze laminated with silver, where a crimson awning floats with reflections of flowing blood.

Heavy copper lamps with precious sculptures are swinging slowly, spreading a wan moonlight.

And an insipid odor of myrrh and cinnamon rises in little blue spirals from curiously-wrought thurifers.

How had I come to this lugubrious place? I can't tell. There are memories here of a distant life, almost unknown to me, semi-effaced impressions, unfurling before my consciousness, which notes them in passing.

An ebony cathedra stood in the center, under a gleaming dome of whitened bones, where a being is seated of indecisive and changing form, like drifting clouds,

which grew enormously, or was almost annihilated in a confused mass of somber quivering veils.

Finally, it took on an almost human form.

In his right hand an adamantine scepter shone; he extended it toward the wall, which opened . . .

I
The Valley of Hearts

Ah! What I saw then passed like a dream, a frightful, monstrous, unreal dream,

A cold sweat inundated my revulsed face; the marrow in my bones was congealed by fear, and my trembling knees tottered.

No!

No, no human being could remain impasive before such an apparition.

Beyond the gaping opening a bleak landscape stagnated,

of rocks, enormous rocks, which no vegetation stained, not even leprous lichen or gray moss, were accumulated in two high mountains,

between them, a valley,

and in the valley, hearts, horrible hearts, thousands, myriads of hearts, lying in a red swarm.

They were still beating, and that sound reverberated to infinity, augmented at each echo, becoming terrifying in its rhythmic monotony.

They were all alive, bloody, hideous, and the swell of that frightful sea undulated, sometimes shaken by abrupt spasms similar to frissons of agony.

Among them, some were bounding furiously, with stumps of arteries agitating around them like sectioned snakes or worms.

Some, immobile, allowed a black liquid to escape languidly from their open flanks, which oozed out in semi-coagulated drops.

Others, bruised, were displayed like flaccid and bleeding pouches, marbled with violet tints.

Then a breath of wind passed through the valley, carrying away the lamentations and the acrid vapor that floated there.

And from the summit of the rocks where they slept, invisibly, great vultures with livid bare necks launched forth, pinions extended. Describing circles, broad at first and then diminishing, they descended, gliding with hoarse cries of joy,

over the hearts,

palpitating.

With their sharp claws and their curved beaks they rummaged as they pleased in the rubescent mass, rendered inert by dolor.

They gorged themselves, flapping their immense wings, sometimes burying their heads and necks entirely in the yielding flesh.

Finally sated, they rose up in heavy flight, dripping blood, their feathers splashed, happy.

And disappeared . . .

II
Unknown Harmonies

A lukewarm mist of ecstasy came to perfume the sad room.

And the choir of the blessed sang,

softly,

with delicacies so tenuous that the sound appeared to dissolve in space, and only a scarcely-perceptible emanation arrived at his soul.

It sang of plains in winter, uniform in their mute whiteness, extending into the distance, covered in an even mantle of snow, where a few clumps of trees appeared, fleshless, in the thinness of their skeletons, laid bare, having shaken off that soft and cold burden, forming little brown patches on the dazzling carpet.

It sang of cold dusks in which pale suns shone with a feeble glare, like large golden nails fixed in the azure wave of the firmament.

Trills, with a shrill modulation, simulated flocks of little birds passing rapidly through the dormant air uttering brief cries.

Sometimes, too, a bass note rose up; thus, a crow, heavy in its grave flight, gathers speed, in order to describe black circles on the white sky.

Arpeggios descended by a tone.

The star is now very distant on the rim of the effaced hills. Clouds form, seemingly veiling the fall of the king. His disk diminishes gradually. Finally, he disappears.

The choir falls silent.

Then resumes.

From the icy void, uncertain and confused phrases emerge, the stammering of a soul awakening, unclear aspirations toward ill-defined ideals, the first scarcely-perceptible lineaments of a strange melody, which is affirmed by the plaints of oboes and viols.

The veiled cortege files past in primary concepts, initial sensations that are gradually augmented, and hasten.

The cadence becomes more precise with the arrival of more vivid impressions.

And the choir relates the mysterious labors of the unconscious, where the unknown of psychic life is elaborated, and bizarre chains of abrupt associations; the ever-renewed combat of ideas, sisters and enemies, the stronger killing the weaker, to which, being poor, it is not given to cross the threshold of consciousness and penetrate the intimacy of the self.

Afterwards, it sang the Mind launching forth to conquer the True, departing armed with good will and defended by protective illusions; which, in its arduous course through accumulated doctrines and obstinate convictions and holy prejudices, fatigues its initial ardor and strews the protective illusions along the road, arriving near the goal sickened and desperate to attain it, renouncing the continuation of its course.

But after the last tremors of sad notes, the alleluias of the soul rise up, believing that it can see, in a crazy and sublime hallucination, the glory of the Beautiful.

And admirations thunder in triumphant symphonies; and enthusiasms rage on the keyboard of contented passions blossoms, the organ of satisfied desires, in the glorification of shred amours.

To fall back into the B flat of skepticism and disdain, which accompany all satiation and the plenitude of senses that have swooned too frequently.

And after having traveled thus the eternal and ever-similar cycle of human life, and the scale of its vain agitation, returns to the Void, the only Truth.

III
The Crystal Cup

Darkness reigns.

Unfathomable.

Profound: a sea of ink that surrounds everything, completely.

Nothing pierces it; nothing is perceptible.

Night, mother of secrets, veil of misdeeds, is extended like a mourning crepe.

But now, in the distance, far away, lamentations and sobs are heard, as faint as the indistinct whimpers of the new-born. Like an incoming tide, which leads roaring waves to assault high cliffs, precipitate to break and then return. Hoarse plaints suddenly howl, diminishing thereafter, dissolving into a dolorous murmur, to be reborn in a terrifying crescendo.

A half-light, wan at first, dissipates the obscurity by gradual degrees. It is now a rosy mist of dawn or dusk.

The sounds draw closer.

Finally, an interminable farandole of bodies passes by, bent in horrible vibrant contractions, infinite to the point of atrocity, with anguished faces, bulging bloodshot eyes and tight lips, letting out long cries of pain, thousands of agonies, united in a chain that seems endless.

The silhouettes become more precise, the forms more emphatic, in a luminous crimson atmosphere with metallic reflections.

Pale apparitions of virgins with floating hair and moist eyes, whose curvaceous bodies are convulsed, tortured. Brief visions of old men, whose senility grimaces frightfully, moaning.

O hideous and plaintive saraband!

Suddenly, immense in its harmonious and simple gracility, a cup made of pure crystal is outlined,

which sparkles, radiant and iridescent.

Everything else disappears.

The clamors are extinguished, and nothing is heard any longer.

Then, the immensity that it fills, alone, glitters like an enormous diamond.

That is because warm tears fall from all parts, in serried droplets, through air that has become calm. They fall like a chaplet of gems, with limpid radiance.

They fall densely, like a rainstorm, over the dry countryside.

They fall perpetually.

And they fall everywhere.

And the cup collects them, streaming, preciously.

Then they arrive more sparsely. It was time; the cup was full.

All they filled it to the rim, so diaphanous that they were invisible.

Full to the point of not admitting any more, no matter how small. Filled exactly with bitter dew.

But now, through space, minuscule and almost imperceptible, the warm tear of a child falls.

And from the overflowing cup, it is a cascade of pearls of marvelous orient that falls. Countless treasure, their milky transparency scintillates and springs from the broken cup . . .

. . . Distant fanfares ring out gloriously, marrying their clear notes with the fall of tears,

becoming pearls.

JULES RENARD
(1864-1910)

Jules Renard was one of four writers who developed *poèmes en prose* in the early issues of the *Mercure de France*, alongside Remy de Gourmont, Saint-Pol-Roux and Gaston Danville. Like Danville he considered himself to be a Naturalist, but of a markedly different stripe, being a graduate of Edmond de Goncourt's *grenier*. He was a pillar of the "Goncourt Academy," and wrote an informative memoir of its early days in his journal, which he kept from 1887 until his death; it was posthumously published, along with the prose poems translated below, in his *Oeuvres* (1925). Many of Renard's early poems in prose take the form of ambivalent glimpses of childhood, as experienced by a small boy nicknamed *Poil de carotte* [the equivalent of the Anglo-American Carrot-Top]. (The red-haired Renard was the youngest of four children.) He also published many studies of nature, having developed a strong affinity for the region in Nièvre where he spent most of his childhood while his father was working as a railway engineer.

The Lock of Hair

To Henry Gauthier-Villars (Willy)

My good friend, who likes scene-setting, said to me, with a sly look, as red as a schoolgirl on the point of playing a practical joke: "Will you be passing a letter-box when you go out?"

"Yes, dear Madame."

"Will you take charge of this letter?"

"Of course, dear Madame."

I was glad to perceive that the letter my good friend confided to me had no address. It was not sealed. I had the delicacy to understand that it was a little mystery. I opened the envelope and made out at the bottom, crushed and rolled up like a caterpillar, a lock of hair intended for me.

Ha!

I go home and, oddly, I don't experience any kind of pleasure; truly, women have bizarre manias. What shall I do with that lock of hair? It's there, in front of me. I daren't touch it. In the end, I empty the envelope on to the table. The lock is freshly cut, brand new, still vegetating, and, as my good friend had not thought that she ought to knot it into a favor, the hair scatters over my open Baudelaire. I recall the books hired out in reading rooms, over which a hundred readers have scratched their heads and picked their noses. I pass a bad quarter of an hour of insensibility. It's possible that my sentimental education has not been careful enough. The meaning of certain refinements escapes me. I would steal a woman's purse rather than one of her old gloves or a dirty handkerchief, and if I threw myself at her feet in order to kiss them, I would embrace my fist in secret.

However, I do not forget to say to myself that my good friend is genteel, and adored. She has cut that lock with an excellent intention. It's almost a sacrifice on her part, and if I got a taste for it and asked for more she would soon have a bald spot. All well and good! But it's necessary for me to note my impression in all its vulgarity: those hairs disgust me! Just now I carried them, holding them at a distance, like something filthy, in a piece of paper. Now they're lying in the hollow of *Les Fleurs du Mal!* I shan't pick them up!

Instead of imagining the gracious movement of my good friend who cut them, the nice smile on her lips, the brilliance of her eyes, and the tender kiss that she added to that amicable souvenir for luck, I only see a comber of untidy hair from which hairs tumble in a light avalanche at each squeak of the scissors; hairs that curl up, agonizing, which are dead, which prick the neck and make cross-hatches in the ears.

Oh, I can't easily put one over my heart, me! Scruples wrinkle the end of my nose like fearful mice. My cat-mite repulsion dispels them.

Does my good friend hope that I'll enclose her lock of hair in a locket and wear it on my breast like the scapular of a Jesuits' pupil?

I regret not having thrown it negligently in the letter-box; a postman might have glorified it. Somewhere there must be collectors of hair. All tastes, etc. When I was at school I addressed my fingernail clippings in a screw of paper to a comrade who had the habit of biting his.

I could also make a little brush with a pot of glue.

Suddenly, precipitately, to put an end to it, I open my window and, raising the copy of *Les Fleurs du Mal* to chin-height, I blow on my good friend's hairs abruptly.

They have departed, sticking together, forming a tuft, winged, almost coming back to life, insects minus the sonorous buzz. They have flown away in a gust of wind!

Once they have disappeared, I immediately have the clear consciousness of having committed a petty infamy, and I kiss their place—yes, the place of the hair—very rapidly, on the sly, involuntarily, on the page where, by coincidence, the infernal poet exclaims, in lines that have stung me like a whiplash:

> *Ecstasy, to populate this evening the obscure alcove*
> *With the memories dormant in those tresses,*
> *I want to wave them in the air like a handkerchief!*

But it's very good of me to be chagrined; a head of hair is not a mere lock!

246

Glow-Worms

Dusk falls over the fatigued wood. The birds retreat and hide in the foliage that no longer has anything but the sound of their wings. They would like to be able to see something there, but the stars are too far away and the moon doesn't descend close enough. Besides which, the redness of hawthorn-berries and rose-hips is insufficient.

Suddenly, to illuminate their amours, expert in composing the scale of glimmers, the moss brothel ignites all its worms.

Grass

Full of dew, the grass shines, tender, green, almost transparent. A little stream runs through the blades. The grave man out for a walk is thirsty. Already, he is cupping his hands. But he fears lowering himself by bending down to drink.

Afterwards, the grave man is hungry. But his modesty prevents him—the pretentious fool—from offering himself, while on his knees, a nice dinner of fresh grass!

SAINT-POL-ROUX
(1861-1940)

"Saint-Pol-Roux" was the signature used in his later writings by Paul-Pierre Roux, a southerner born in Marseille and educated in Lyon. When he relocated to Paris he attended Stéphane Mallarmé's *mardis* and became an enthusiastic follower of the Symbolist creed. He was one of the early contributors to both the *Revue Blanche* (in the pages of which the items translated below appeared in 1892) and the *Mercure de France*, where he published both poetry and prose, especially in idiosyncratic combination, exhibiting a Neoplatonist philosophy he called "ideorealism." Much of it was assembled in a three-volume collection, *Les Reposoirs de la procession* (1904-07). Convinced of his genius, he became deeply embittered by the failure of others to share his conviction, and he left the capital in 1898, fleeing creditors. He settled in Bretagne, where he was eventually able to buy a house. He continued to write, but only published a small fraction of his endeavors. During the German invasion in 1940, a drunken soldier broke into the house and committed mayhem, rape, murder and arson; although the poet escaped immediate death, the trauma of his multiple losses—including the burning of his manuscripts—proved fatal, but his daughter Divine made Herculean efforts to rescue what she could of his work and to ensure that he was not forgotten.

Poplars

Blond halberdiers guard the souls of the valley.

"Let me visit the infinitely thin demoiselles of the emerald towers," I said

to the blond halberdiers guarding the souls of the valley.

In order to deck space with ample refusals, they gaze superbly from the orient to the occident, and then from the occident to the orient,

the blond halberdiers guarding the souls of the valley.

"But I am the Elect who has come to unfasten the mystery in which the eternal return of swallows smiles," I sang

to the blond halberdiers guarding the souls of the valley.

Sarcastically, they fanned me with phantasmal reverences,

the blond halberdiers guarding the souls of the valley.

Irritated, I cried: "I shall cut all of you, suzerain jets, in order that in epochs of sculpted water, your skeletons will rose-tint the livid days of beggars whose culottes remain in the jaws of dogs,

O blond halberdiers guarding the souls of the valley!"

Then, each population of leaves shivered like a frightened wing—without, however, opening the emerald towers and not daring to sever the firm legs

of the blond halberdiers guarding the souls of the valley.

Desolate, I fled; through haggard butterflies that were fluttering far from flowers in tragic brains, I fled

the blond halberdiers guarding the souls of the valley.

While I wept under a yew, many fingers frailer than the gazes of ancestors came to illuminate my brow; my pupils had unconsciously poured out the only ingenuous money that can hire

the blond halberdiers who guard the souls of the valley.

The Malign Statue

From the peak a sinister valley was visible where, among the debris of broken columns and caryatids with their feet in the air and upside-down frontons, those vines with bitter juice known as "tears of Judas" were entangled, twisted as if by remorse and planted in streams of extinct lava.

Effluvia of catastrophe rose up, like invisible bats, toward my fearful nostrils.

The guide, whose vine-branch arms had designated the precipice, said between his rare teeth: "Under that rubble down there the City of Felons lies."

Stimulated, his tongue, numb until now, stirred like a horsefly in the calyx of a putrid lily, and I heard this tragic tale:

"They were a simple people, faithful to the written maxims, whose prejudices were marble petals plucked from ardent bushes, credulous natures capable of being channeled to excess, and also susceptible of practicing a custom, good or bad—always good, in sum, if it emanated from a summit—provided that it was officially sanctioned. Are not all crowds similar? Insinuate to the multitude that bad is good, and you will immediately see the same conviction put into the culture of evil as the culture of good, without any afterthought, in a sincere hope of the final palm.

"The annals of annihilation prove that abundantly.

"Desirous of a little Christ to loom over their roofs, familial skulls, its inhabitants enquired one day about a statue that would depict in an exemplary fashion the worst human suffering.

"Each of them searched for the perfect icon, adequate to that task, but only ended up with images in which a blissful gaze blunted the expression of torments; it was important to select an expiatory victim in the entire splendor of agony.

"In the meantime, the pick-axes of a squad in the process of breaking up a mound, a cake of dust consolidated by the centuries, laid bare a bizarre bean,[1] a statue fulfilling the required conditions with so much suggestive craft that the massive pity of the city suddenly came running to lean over the work of the excavators.

"The extraordinary thing was that, during that kneeling enthusiasm, a legendary mummy with parchment cheeks opened by enchantment in a very ancient trunk informed them, in a virginally faded language, that on the precise spot to which the blows of the pick were addressed, a calvary had stood in archaic times.

"At that primitive bleating, they hastened to deliver the revenant of her bandages, and every soul acclaimed the annunciatrix, and all memories invited reflourishing old men into the best place in their gardens.

"A calvary, legend had affirmed?

"Marvelous!

"Those twisted legs carved in yew-wood, those sorb-berries crushed by way of eyes, that ruinous torso, that visage scored with grimaces, those drooping shoulders, that ensemble of horrors, that pell-mell of distress—in sum, that synthesis of dolor— could not be anything but the scrupulous effigy to the sublime torture-victim, Jesus!

"The opinion was treated as authoritative the moment it was put in doubt.

"Now, I will unveil the fact for you right away—which the people of the deplorable city never did—that the statue did be-

1 The reference is to the bean conventionally baked into the *gâteau de rois*, the cake served in France to guests at the feast of the Epiphany.

long to the ancient calvary, but that it represented the opposite of Jesus, Judas the Felon.

"Had the figures of Jesus and the eleven holy apostles been destroyed at length by the slow hail of the hours? Had devoted hands, disdainful of the *other*, collected them during the ages? Legend is silent on that point, and thinkers were far from caring about the crowd plunged in their scorn up to the neck.

"The solemnity was grandiose.

"A provision waving banners went to collect the 'miraculous' find, and the Judas was erected on this peak, exactly in the place of your stupor.

"From then on an ineluctable fascination operated on the victims of the filthy error, passing to strangeness . . .

"An abusive influence was emitted by the idol, which can be divined, and to which the surrounding souls were ingenuously submissive, as passive as lambs under the butcher's blade.

"With an extreme innocence, the previous confession was declared unhealthy; the mind had been inclined to the right, now it inclined to the left; affirmation became negation, and vice versa; henceforth the laws in vigor were interpreted in reverse, books of morality read backwards; it was even stipulated generally that the original virtue was treason, and vice the supreme wisdom.

"Immediately, professors taught paradox and sophism, priests invoked the seven deadly sins, and the aediles voted an expiatory column to the memory of historical rascalities.

"The fervor with which the new precepts were practiced was such that the least faithful soon had a soul of Judas, simply and with the best will in the world, in the name of salvation and truth. The rich threw their excrements to the poor imploring bread and water and built colored pyres in public squares; the pages of the gospel alimented cabinets of fundamental reading; jugglers of the balance sent rogues to the seat of honor and Vincent de Pauls to the pillory; instead of a necklace, a husband gave his wife a husbandman's tope; males sodomized males and females gomorrahized females; the disciple no longer gave his master anything but the kiss of Oliviers . . .

"In the meantime, nailed to his new cross—an octopus nailed to a main-mast—the Exemplar deployed his deadly snigger above the city, while unconscious victims of possession, their arms extended toward the peak, welcomed a smile of approval and begged for the promise of a salary.

"That abomination ended in terror.

"The same ardor that the pious brought to courting the reservoirs of Heaven, the impious brought involuntarily to provoking the craters of Hell. Novenas of filth succeeded macabre Lents in order to attract a blessing from below, a malediction from on high.

"Now, as events are the realizations of intense and numerous desires, the dissolute city received the infernal fire as truly as a sage hamlet received the celestial wave. Disaster arrived on the evening of a day when those lugubrious prayers had sprung forth with more ignominy than ever. A crevasse suddenly opened and the city felt a red hand rise from the bowels of the earth and grasp it.

"Oh, that last hour in Satan's left hand!

"Everything was overturned, twisted and crushed by the five reptiles.

"Then the iron fist was reintegrated with the entrails of mystery, with the accursed race between its darts, while the reproved without knowing it, a triumphant blasphemy on their lips, imagined that they were descending toward the coral of eternal joy.

"Ever since, the engulfed have been singing victoriously in Hell, in the belief that they are respiring the roses of the elect and savoring the strawberries of the blissful."

Once again I plunged the dual seal of my gaze into the hideous gulf; when I raised my eyes again, with difficultly, full of fear as they were, my guide had disappeared.

In the east, the wolves of the night were already sharpening their constellation jaws on the last angelus . . .

I descended from the peak as from a bad dream.

Half way down, having turned round, Lot's wife, whom my soul saw in the sector of the extended firmament, was scintillating thirty pieces of silver over the vanished City of Felons.

And my curiosity was changed into a rain of salt.

JEAN LORRAIN
(1855-1906)

"Jean Lorrain" was the pseudonym adopted by Paul Duval, at his father's request, to spare the family name from disgrace when he left his native Normandy to become a poet in Paris. Unfortunately, his apparently-wealthy father turned out to have been a wastrel, and he left his son penniless when he died, forcing him to make a living from his pen. Lorrain became a relentless journalist, capitalizing on a reputation he had already built up for scathing criticism. He befriended Joris-Karl Huysmans in his more turbulent days, and was powerfully influenced by *À rebours* and such studies of Parisian decay as "La Bièvre," He also affected an ostentatious dandyism, which earned him the sobriquet of "the last disciple of Barbey-d'Aurevilly." He began taking ether as a stimulant to maintain his literary output, and although he was soon forced to give it up, he mined the hallucinations it had visited upon him for inspiration, and built its legacy into his contrarian reputation as the ultimate model of *fin-de-siècle* decadence. When he reached the height of his fame in the 1890s he flaunted his homosexuality, while threatening to fight anyone who accused him of it. He decamped to the Midi for the sake of his failing health in 1901, but the damage inflicted on his gut by the ether proved irreparable; he eventually blasted a hole in his colon while self-administering an enema, and died of peritonitis.

Long before then Lorrain had begun to organize the *contes* and essays he supplied to *L'Écho de Paris* and *Le Journal* into loosely-knit series, or literary collages, including one titled *Astarté* in the paper and reprinted as *Monsieur de Phocas* (1901), which supplemented *À rebours* as a definitive description of a troubled decadent lifestyle. He had previously contributed a series of misogynistic character-studies to the *Écho* under the pseudonym "Raitif de la Bretonne" in homage to an earlier and equally perverse hero; the two examples translated below are taken from the 6 July 1890 and the 22 October 1892 issues; they are the least "poetic" of all the inclusions in the present assembly, but they typify one extreme of the spectrum of such works. Lorrain wrote many *contes* that are more decorative, including numerous fantasies akin to those of Catulle Mendès, most of which he collected in *Princesses d'ivoire et d'ivresse* (1902), translations from which are distributed in the collections *Nightmares of an Ether-Drinker, The Soul-Drinker, Masks In the Tapestry* and *Princesses of Darkness*); they qualify more obviously as poems in prose, but it seemed more useful in the context of the present ensemble to feature examples of his deliberately sleazy endeavors, which have affinities with other works reproduced herein that took their primary influence from Huysmans.

Flower of the Fortifes

A melancholy and ugly corner of an outlying district . . . waste ground, swollen here and there by plaster, rotten fruit and cinders; on the horizon, in the distance, the despairing sight of tanneries and factory chimneys; to the left, a round-path and the fortifes, the ramparts of Paris; outside, a poor suburban street comes to die, with houses decked with straw mattresses and undergarnents.

According to whether the horizon is swollen by the burnished gold of the dome of Les Invalides to the round ball, blurred and violet, of the paired cupolas of the Val-de-Grâce and the Panthéon, that countryside in rags is the plain of Grenelles, Gentilly or Vanves; it is the Bièvre and Bicêtre; on the other side of Paris it is the Route de la Révolte, the Quatre-Vents, Saint-Denis, a phantasmal site, a population of Limbo.; white quarries of marl, marl-diggers smeared with clay, with bleeding eyelids, equivocal beggars carrying barrel-organs; here and there, around the bastions, a soldier, a pitiful silhouette, carving a stick . . . a desolate and sick corner of nature with the breath of rotting manure, without any other vegetation than leprous grass where suspicious heaps of rags lie dormant,

254

workers devoid of work collapsed from fatigue, who wake up as surly pimps at nightfall.

From rickety shacks and tartaric buildings along the main road, the traces of which are blurred, and hovels with *Sautéd rabbits, beer and wine* painted in red, as if daubed with wine-lees, the prowlers of the fortifes emerge, selling amour and caresses at rock-bottom prices, descended to all obscene lusts, all infamous vices and all the follies wakened by the tempting shadows, like an opportunity for crime.

In excessively noxious white underskirts, creaking as she walks with a sound of dry leaves, she is the unhealthy flower, with a sickening reek of grease and pomade, of that flayed and weeping nature, the flower of prostitution on the dung-heap of rubble.

The daylight fades; lying in ambush on the round-path, her skirts raised over laddered stockings, a red carnation in her lips, she trots indolently, twisting her hips, enticing passers-by with a sudden flash of her knickers, in a swift thrust of her rump, shown and vanished.

There is a sly smile, a *psst psst*, a wink . . . if the client advances, the ditches are nearby, the bitch descends into them; if the man is a laborer, a faubourgian artisan, a tannery worker, bricklayer or well-digger, the filth is executed and the brutal idyll unfolds in the open air, groping in the shadows, on the side of a bank, but woe betide the client of the whore has sniffed loot and recognized a mark . . . a petty rentier drawn by avarice to land in the ambulant Cythera of the poor, or an anonymous student of vice drawn by curiosity, a louis in his pocket, in the ticklish anguish of danger; the long-haired whore will, if necessary, make his head ring on the road as she made the heel of her boot ring, enticingly, a little while ago. In the dark, before a full pocket, she will stab and rob, the prowler of the fortifes.

At the Porte de Bineau, the macabre heroine of the latest news of macabre gallantry knocks down an old man and summons *le Singe-Vert*. One morning, a fortnight ago, two blacksmiths were picked up at the Porte de Vanvers, belabored by blows, bleeding and cold because of her, unknown this time: the Venus of the

Morgue, the bloodthirsty and putrescent Siren of the puddles of the ditches.

From the circular path to the glacis of the ramparts, with or without accomplices, the fine work is never-ending for her, whore and murderess; she is almost the Herodias of that fair-ground Louvre, the criminal museum of ex-prefect Mace, almost the Gioconda of Jean Raffaëlli.[1]

Autumnal Souls

Oh, the first rains and the moist humidity of rotting leaves freeze her blood and chill her marrows; after the first days of October she no longer sets foot outside, no longer goes out; the sight of the defoliated avenues and the dirty passers-by saddens her too much; truly, that dilapidation of the sky and of objects sickens her, and the cold that penetrates her, and the yellow atmosphere in which one might think that chrysanthemums were snowing, if you believe that might cheer it up. She has a kind of mud in her brain and crushed ice in her veins; the heater is stoked up and great fires of crackling wood blaze in every room, in vain; she shivers, fearfully huddled up, and it is finished; she will not warm up again.

She no longer even comes down to the dining room; Monsieur takes his meals alone henceforth in the Henri II hall with the historic tapestries, admired by the All-Paris of newly-ennobled financiers, awaiting the catastrophe. No more appearances in the Acacias, no more visits to suppliers, no more interminable stations in the hairdressers' and the couturiers'. The little theatres and café-concerts, those of the exterior boulevard where she once liked to spend the autumnal evenings, here in railinged sections,

---

1 Gustave Mace (1835-1904) was the Head of the Sûreté durng the 1880s. The painter Jean Raffaëlli (1850-1924) was a painter who became famous for his images of the seamier side of Paris life, replacing the peasants depicted in his earlier paintings with the urban poor; Huysmans became one of his earliest champions.

there in the directorial box, in the company of clubmen, artistes and prominent journalists—her "gang"; Madame X's gang, as it was conventional to call them—are all finished too. So, no more forbidden theaters, no more café-concerts, no more boldly compromising promiscuities and no more little suppers, sometimes in a fashionable cabaret where one calls in for an hour after the theater, among passing "grand dukes" and the latest divette invented by Chincholle,[1] sometimes in a literary brasserie where handsome Merovingian poets battle with tribunal gestures, accompanied by muses with short-cropped hair and flat chests, Egerias of the Rat-Mort or Hebes of the Bon-Bock lingering outside Olympus over an oxtail salad.

Finished, all that . . . She is cold, cold in the heart and everywhere else, and, her hands numb in her long furry gloves, the soles of her feet icy under the hides of polar bears heaped around her, she spends plaintive days in the midst of the pink Turkish silk and Persian velvet cushions of her bedroom, her vast high-ceilinged Louis XVI bedroom draped with jonquil watered silk, the same brilliant artificial yellow as her dyed hair, a flower of discolored anemia, thin in the foaming undress of malines lined with padded silk, giving the impression, with the rosy patches of her cheeks rubbed with make-up, of an old Saxe figurine forgotten there and negligently thrown into the fabrics.

And in the high white marble fireplace, sandalwood blazes, bright and embalmed, and gauzes tinted with the colors of amber and dawn drape the windows, veiling the autumnal rust of the park and decomposes in reflections of daybreak the pluvious October atmosphere; and, completing the illusion, in a neighboring room, the light twitter of an aviary rises and vainly puts around the invalid the dream of fluttering wings and chattering nests.

She is cold, mortally cold, her lips almost blue under the perfumed muff that she applies to her mouth, without a drop of blood under the skin, and the undersides of her eyes bruised by

---

1 The famous journalist and playwright Charles Chincholle (1843-1902), author of *Les Survivants de la Commune* (1885) and the sensational novel *Les Jours d'Absinthe* (1887), among many others.

violet circles; she senses the hour, the agonizing and weakening hour, approaching. In vain her chambermaid sits on the edge of her chaise-longue, takes her poor icy feet, as if clenched by anguish in their mesh of mauve silk, between her hands and rubs them, trying to bring back the blood with incessant taps; a sharp sensation of fingernails scrapes her, to the point of filling her eyes with tears and making her even paler.

And she is bored, devoid of appetite for anything, and when the rain lashes the windows . . . Oh, it's then that her neurosis is augmented and that terrible Siberian cold makes her teeth chatter, and she blows on her fingers—her, the wife of a banker four times a millionaire, like a chimney-sweep in a Savoyard elegy; and there is no remedy. The Faculty can do nothing more, she has used up everything, tried everything: anesthetics, consoling and murderous poisons, no longer have any effect on her nervous system, distended and too lax; the sickening morphine and the once-adored ether frighten her; her intelligence, once so vivacious, no longer even sustains her; she has read with out interests the proofs sent to her of Bourget's next novel and the unpublished speeches of Renan;[1] in order to try to distract her, an aesthete duc has brought her the poet Verlaine all day long, and yesterday, again, installed before the Erard in her boudoir, next door, Gibert played for her the latest creations of Mademoiselle Guilbert and the spicy repertoire of Bruant.[2] Monsieur has thought momentarily about Réjane, and her sister-in-law about Péladan, but what would be the point?[3]

---

1 The references are to Paul Bourget (1852-1935), the most famous exponent of neo-Naturalist fiction, and Ernest Renan (1823-1892), a scholar who offened Churchmen with his skeptical studies of early Christianity, and many others with his fervent political support for France's colonial ventures.

2 Yvette Guilbert (1865-1944) was a popular café-concert singer who was a headline act at the Moulin Rouge when this story was written. Aristide Bruant (1851-1925) had been contracted to the Chat Noir before graiating to the Moulnin Rouge and his own cabaret, the Mirliton. Both were painted by Toulouse-Lautrec. "Gibert" was the name of a notable family of piano-makers.

3 The references are to the actress Gabrielle Réjane (1856-1920) and the art critic, novelist and lifestyle fantasist Joséphin Péladan (1858-1918).

And yet, one thing might soothe her, and perhaps cure her, one thing for which she has a mad desire but for which she can never decide to ask: to bring to her bedroom the gardener's assistant or one of the stable-boys, to make the fellow sit down beside her, unbutton his waistcoat and open his shirt, and then to plunge her poor frozen hands and shivering feet into the gap in the coarse cloth, into the hairy warmth of that rustic breast, to reanimate them with that human warmth, in that living moisture.

VICTOR REMOUCHAMPS
(1862-1907)

Victor Remouchamps was an associate of the Jeune Belgique who met Stéphane Mallarmé while the latter was briefly resident in Belgium. Remouchamps was highly praised for the metaphysical and stylistic aspects of his work by Remy de Gourmont, who wrote a brief obituary of him in the *Mercure de France* in 1907. He published two volumes, *Les Aspirations, poèmes en prose* (1893), from which the samples below are taken, and *Vers de l'âme* (1895), but he remained relatively obscure, although Paul Fort reprinted some of his work in 1906 in *Vers et prose*.

Of an Ideal Species

He was an eagle of an ideal species.

He required for his flight the vertiginous whiplash of tempests, a feverish sky to calm his pride.

He scarcely deigned to repose on terrestrial summits. He had glimpsed, higher than the bleak Himalayas, a virgin kingdom of such splendor that genius alone could have supported its ecstasy for long.

He was an eagle of an ideal species.

Everything seemed to him to be a lie except for the Dream. And when he descended over Life the eternal rancor of contingencies ignited, in the imperious soul of his eyes, the grim glory of two golden tears.

Frenzied desires sometimes seized him, to plunge into unfathomable mysteries, to exalt himself in an infinite flight that alone could arrest his agonies.

And every night his wing bled vast dolorous catastrophes, but he suffered more in his pride than in his wound.

When he finally understood that the chimerical regions retreated incessantly, that it was necessary to renounce the beyond and remain, after all, the slave of his mountain, he uttered a kind of mysterious bitter lament and gazed for a long time at the crepuscular Realities streaming the crimson of the sun . . .

He was an eagle of an ideal species.

My Soul is Poor

My soul is poor, my soul is gentle, my soul is alarming!

I have often recognized, even in the hours of their blossoming glory, the adolescents that death sets out to pursue. I see the pale and corrosive shadow floating over their celebration.

A strange instinct haunts me: to create pain and suffer therefrom.

As if Life lacked tears and blood I make the Dream bleed and weep.

My soul is poor, my soul is gentle, my soul is alarming!

And the unreal tortures file past, in intense frescoes, with hurricane fevers, before my frightened eyes:

Suns that blind; blizzards of snow in the Tropics; deluges of flame at the shivering Poles,

Entire cities fallen into lethargy; so many children guillotined; sepulchral resurrections suddenly appearing at the rare ball of human joys . . .

Or many invasions of black gods—the Omnipotents of Evil—flagellate the Virtues and torture the Chimera, and the sick insult the Pitiful, and then the Pitiful insult the sick . . .

And everywhere the splendor that dies away, the beauty that grows weary, the candor that is soiled . . .

Whence comes, O my soul, that clear vision of monstrous ideal calvaries?

Who knows?

Suffering bleeds further than the world, further than the red adieu of the setting sun, perhaps further than Reality.

Impression on Dreams

I believe that the entire shadow of slumber is delivered to Dreams, that all of that black silence is bursting with mysterious and profound sounds, and that the spiritual soul—finally free and serene in the annihilated flesh—scales the summits of the most monstrous fevers . . .

I have known fabulous frissons, fêtes of horror and splendor. It seems to me, in hours of waking, that all Thought and all Art came to live in me, with an intense and chimerical life.

Humanity is divinized in sleep. The soul, knowing itself to be quite alone, plays out its dramas and its féeries then like a very old and very great artiste—which, fundamentally, it is.

All the ideal regions are familiar to it. It becomes universal again in the reconquered clarity of its genius.

But as soon as the eyelid opens, the soul sometimes disdains to be recalled.

Perhaps, too, Dreams only exist for themselves and they dream alone, without our souls ever perceiving them then; and I also believe that they are more divine when more unconscious.

Of certain Dreams I have only perceived the conclusion, but I experience the sensation of having surprised that conclusion, as something I ought not to remember.

It has often happened to me to cry "No!" to a nightmare, or, more simply, to laugh without interrupting it.

My soul, spontaneous and conscious, pushed art as far as debauchery, played its tragedy with delight . . .

The Féeries of the Shadow

It was a superhuman dream . . . My eyes and my soul have retained its caressant ecstasy . . .

An infinite sea appeared, a heavy sea, fatigued and ill, a sea devoid of azure reflection; a strange sea that the sun—a golden intoxication in the dazzling sky—was not blessed by any light; a poor silent immensity, very old and dying, like Life . . .

The surface suddenly quivered; a lightning flash illuminated the abyss and slowly, the ideal and chaste forms were born, which the dream made sublime, of smiling gods and juvenile goddesses.

In that enormous fresco there was something of Michelangelo and Dante.

An entire mystical paganism was revealed to my ingenuous eyes.

I saw the Realm of white ecstasies flourish, where evil is unknown and Beauty was serenely resplendent, fraternal and pensive . . .

And good divinities, sprang forth incessantly, all pure and blinding flesh, like an evangelical flock of Chimeras . . .

Now, that sovereign florescence over the dolorous sea was the absolute symbol of my life and its aspirations . . .

And now that, with my poor fingers, I am recording the marvelous vision, with the hope of fixing its eternal frisson, I feel very miserable for having been able to contemplate such splendors . . .

But I work and I work, for I would like one day to merit my dreams . . .

262

Future Barbarities

Action radiated over the world, imperious, absolute and horrible. It was necessary to be human, uniquely human, and to renounce divinizing aspirations. All the subtle frissons that are the summit of life and the essential brightness of things, people wanted to abolish. The Ideal, consoling glory of the soul, was dying.

Every village had its Temple of Reason. Children worshiped the god Number there, and only believed in palpable verities. The earth sufficed for material ambitions. No marvelous atmosphere, no supernatural horizon, was required by that old globe of clay.

People only had faith in the immediate Real. Mystery was only accepted if it burst forth like lightning. It was an epoch of holy prosperity. Souls were unknown, but the flesh, sated with passions and meat, felt alive and infinitely joyful.

All splendor was suspect. The sun, however, was loved because its rays are as rich and fertile as gold. The moon and the stars were not tolerated.

Anything that had Beauty for a mission was annihilated, along with that which is simply grand, simply mild and simply just. Grotesque Hercules massacred Chimeras everywhere.

The most beautiful flowers had to perish, having no function except to be beautiful. Trees were depopulated of birds, and children threw stones at swans.

It was decreed that eagles, peacocks and lions are useless; and fanatics killed those indolent majesties, dutifully.

Dreamers, gripped by haughty pity for a world delivered to utilitarian delirium, wept or consoled themselves in death.

The rejected stars twinkled like tears.

Finally, hatred of the Ideal was exalted as far as crime.

Sometimes, strange little beings were born, their bodies sovereignly frail, with vast foreheads too heavy for Life and profound eyes, already wise, it seemed, and dolorous. The mothers saw red, cursing the infant geniuses.

A king, in his blind logic, had poets crucified, for he had thought about Christ, and religions were already dead. Then, on Golgothas, pensive heads crowned with palms were seen bleeding again, fantastic lyres in their nailed hands, ineffably pure beings whose death-throes were mocked. And young and fresh women celebrated the infinite shame of the Dream, dancing around the cross . . .

But the strolling players of Song, Vaudeville and Romance—all those who prostituted Art, aped Thought and violated candor—were fêted.

Diadems sparkled on low and wretched brows. The enormous Mud triumphed.

The black work was, however, aborted. Along the bloody Calvaries mysterious roses began to bloom, and birdsong flew with the death-rattles. A more profound hymn resonated in the branches, and lilies and doves seemed more divine. Nature protested with all its exasperated and rebellious poetry.

And then a mystical generation bloomed, amorous of all the old mocked Illusions—a poor folly that went to weep on the tombs of martyrs.

Enthusiasm, ardent and virginal, radiated again, for the gods of Dream can be crucified, but it sometimes only requires a spark of soul to spring forth for humanity entire to catch fire.

Then great winds of revelation traversed consciousness. Humans, more infantile and more emotional, smitten with stars and chimeras, wanted to live on the mountain, and loved the gentle sowers who enabled a little patch of sky to flourish in the misery of the terrestrial plains.

Now the world was happy for a time, for it believed in distant delights and blessed the lie of legends, naively.

But those who rocked it with their bitter charity—the eternal Wounded of Poetry—continued suffering silently, for they divined, in spite of everything, the foundation of things, and they knew that the splendor of their Art had to dazzle—and blind.

G. ALBERT AURIER
(1865-1892)

Gabriel-Albert Aurier contributed to Symbolist periodicals, including *Le Décadent* and the *Mercure de France*, before and after becoming the managing editor of *Le Moderniste ilustré* in 1890. In the pages of the *Mercure* he became an important propagandist for Vincent Van Gogh and Paul Gauguin. He died of an infection contracted on a trip to Marseille; his friends collected and published his *Oeuvres posthumes* (1895), which included his long prose poem (or short novel) "Ailleurs" (tr. with other material in *Elsewhere and Other Stories*) as well as the items translated below, the first of which had previously appeared in *Le Moderniste illustré* in 1890.

The Lover

When I returned from the Hindu lands, where I had loved the daughters and wives of rajahs as beautiful as simulacra of new bronze or cornelian in fabulous palaces with golden roofs, walls of jasper, paving stones of ruby, amethyst and chalcedony . . .

When I returned from the mysterious provinces of China, where, for a long time, I had caressed by moonlight, in a fantastic garden full of polycephalous statues, blue eucalypti, painted porcelain turrets and peach-blossom, the little princess with the turned-up eyes, the minuscule feet of a doll, the little princess who was none other than the precious and dear child of the Celestial Emperor . . .

When I had returned from Cytherean azures where, on a bed of pink roses, the divine Aphrodite, more dazzling than the genius of Praxiteles sculpted her, had offered herself to my kisses many times . . .

When I had returned to these sunless climes, obedient to the most bizarre of crazy fantasies, I wanted to choose, among all the women who are for sale, my mistress: very thin, very small, with big blue eyes bitten by the acid of old tears.

I wanted my mistress to have big blue eyes bitten by the acid of old tears, because such eyes are exceedingly diaphanous and I like to contemplate, in the depths of the limpid lake of my beloved's gaze, her soul, her woman's soul, a cloaca of all malevolence and all corruption.

I have chosen my very small mistress in order to give me the childish illusion of a more intimate and more entire possession, in order to be able to enfold her more completely in a single embrace, and to say to myself, infatuated with mad pride: Your arms are vast enough to embrace a universe of felony and egotism.

I have chosen my very thin mistress in order to feel, in the midst of our ardent kisses, the nails of her vertebrae and the trellis of her ribs, and thus to remind myself, in accomplishing the work of life, that the grimacing skeleton of death is lying in wait and watching, eternally hidden beneath our skin.

Thus I wanted to choose my lover, when I returned from the Hindu lands, where I had loved the daughters and wives of rajahs as beautiful as simulacra of new bronze or cornelian in fabulous palaces with golden roofs, walls of jasper, paving stones of ruby, amethyst and chalcedony.

Plutus

While the men of today hurl the honey of their hypocrisy toward Heaven, and, wallowing in the royal luxury of their houses, their hands bathed in the gold of coffers, priding themselves on their disinterest and scorn for vile riches;

While they spit ingrate blasphemies in your face, old Plutus, and clamor your infamy in the streets, and affect disdain for the presents with which you heap them;

Alone, my head held high, I will kneel publicly in your gold-en temple, a ragged vagabond, before your diamond idol.

Proudly, I will make you my humble prayer, unique conten-ter of human desire. Without deigning to listen to the mockery of the crowd, I will implore your divine blindness and I will kiss your feet, like an old beggar.

I will say to you: "Father of all joys and all virtues, sovereign effacer of crime and remorse, sole God of the world, be propi-tious to me. Let me draw gold and gems from the sumptuous and inexhaustible cellars of your mercy.

"Let your charity flow in my house like a Pactolus that never runs dry.

"Open to me the doors of hermetic caverns, enable me to possess piles of gold, silver, pearls, rubies, sapphires, amethyst, emeralds, topazes and diamonds as high as the Himalayas, that I might be rich enough to buy the universe!"

And if ever, eccentric idol, you grant my prayer, I will in-toxicate you with myrrh and incense, I will sing you marvelous hymns, I will immolate on your altars all innocences, all virtues, all grandeurs and all virginities; I will not be a shameful devotee; I will practice uniquely the cruel rites that please you, I will com-bat the angels with your golden sword. I will be your prophet, O divine corrupter!

I will live in a palace of dream. My palace will be full of distant music. Artistes will come to offer me the flowers of their hearts. Women will come, naked and perfumed, to present me with the flower of their bodies. Kings will be my valets. I shall buy amour from the queens of the night. And I will be a God, except for immortality.

While the men of today hurl the honey of their hypocrisy toward Heaven, and, wallowing in the royal luxury of their hous-es, their hands bathed in the gold of coffers, priding themselves on their disinterest and scorn for vile riches;

I will be your prophet, O divine suborner! I will be a poet. I will sing your glory loudly, your power and your goodness, I will say canticles of amour to you.

In order to sate your appetites as a corruptor god, I will make myself the great Sower of Evil. I will subsidize crime and treason. I will be the apostle of Vice, Depravity and Damnation. I will be a seducer, I will corrupt innocence, virtue and goodness.

I will make so much wealth flow over the earth that human-kind will soon starve to death in the midst of an immense desert of gold.

Old Plutus, father of all joys and all virtues, sovereign effacer of crime and remorse, only God of the word, be propitious to me!

The Blue Woman

As I searched for the supreme and unrealizable amour in the obscure maze of the shames of Paris, I arrived, weary and des-perate, on one of those lustful sepulchers where bare-breasted courtesans prowl.

And I was about to fall asleep in my desperation, as in a sin-ister catafalque, when I perceived, leaning on the white satin of a divan, the impossible woman once glimpsed in vague aspirations.

A cruel joy suddenly grew within me, and crazy frissons of desire burned my marrow, for I had before my eyes the beloved stranger, so long an object of hope, the unique, maddening, marvelous, monstrous, sublime, seraphic, divine phenomenon: the blue woman.

She let her satin chemise slide to the ground, and when she was naked, I saw that the flesh of her body had the pure and soft color of the pale azure skies of the morning.

Her large eyes shone like pure sapphires; her cheeks and the tips of her breasts had the joyful and vivid hue of cobalt.

Her hair was as fleecy over her celestial neck as the ultrama-rine of African seas, and her speech had the ineffable blue tint of forget-me-nots.

And when, on the satin of divans, I had embraced the blue woman for a long time, when I had learned from her monstrous kisses unknown on earth, I planted my trenchant teeth in her azure neck, in order that no one else would ever savor that superhuman sensuality; I saw the fuming indigo of her blood flowing over her flanks as caressant as the pale azure of a morning sky, and I saw her soul, as blue as the flame of sulfur, fly away toward the eternal blueness.

And since then I have wept, in the banal alcoves of white women, for the irredeemable loss of my life.

EPHRAÏM MIKHAËL
(1866-1890)

Ephraïm Mikhaël was the form of his name employed for publication by Georges-Ephraïm Michel. He was educated in his native Toulouse, where he formed a close friendship with Lazare Bernard, who signed his literary work Bernard Lazare, and who followed him to Paris, where the two became active in Symbolist circles. He wrote a lyric drama in collaboration with Catulle Mendès, who published his allegorical short story "Halyartes" in *La Vie populaire*, the literary supplement of *Le Petit Parisien*, but his career was cut short by tuberculosis, leaving other works, including those translated below, to be published posthumously in a collection of *Oeuvres de Ephraim Mikaël* (1890), from which the samples below are taken; some of the items had already appeared in translation in Stuart Merrill's *Pastels in Prose* (1890).

The Toy Shop

I do not recall, at present, either the time or the place, or whether it was a dream. Men and women were going back and forth on a long, sad promenade; I was going back and forth in the crowd, a rich crowd from which the perfume of women rose. And in spite of the mild splendor of furs and velvets that brushed me, in spite of the red smiles of fresh lips glimpsed under delicate veils, a vague ennui gripped me on seeing the monotonous strollers file past like that, to my right and my left.

On a bench, a man was looking at the crowd with strange eyes, and as I approached him I heard him sobbing. Then I asked him what he had to lament thus, and, raising his large feverish eyes toward me, the man who was weeping said: "I'm sad, you see, because I've been locked up here for many days in this toy shop. For many days and many years I've only seen puppets, and I'm tired of being the only living being. They're made of wood, but so marvelously fashioned that they move and talk like me. However, I know that they can only ever make the same movements and only ever say the same things.

"Those beautiful dolls, clad in velvet and furs, which leave behind them, trailing in the air, an enamoring odor of iris, are even better articulated. Their mechanisms are even more delicate than the others, and when one knows how to activate them, one has the illusion of life."

He fell silent for a moment; then, with the grave voice of those who remember, he said: "Once, I had taken one, delightfully frail, and I often held it in my arms in the evening. I had said so many very tender things to it that I had ended up believing that it understood them; and I had tried so hard to warm it up with kisses that I believed it to be alive. But I saw clearly, afterwards, that it too, like the others, was a doll full of bran.

"For a long time I hoped that one of the puppets might make a novel gesture, or pronounce a word that the others hadn't already said. Now, I'm weary of whispering my dreams to them. I'm bored, and I'd like to get out of this toy shop in which I've been locked. I beg you, if you can, take me outside, outside, where the living brings are . . ."

270

The Wake

On the jasper of the lake, an ebony junk with black sails, which is sailing without oarsmen, opens a long snowy wake. It is toward the Occident that it is going, slowly—oh, so slowly that one can scarcely hear the frisson of its sad wings. And yet, in the calm languor of the evening, I can now perceive an immaterial sound that is a cry exhaled by the soul of the junk.

The soul of the junk is moaning, and in that strange moan my mind recognizes—as the senses can separate two mingled odors—ennui and fear; because the junk, for hours, has wearied of seeing that wake, the color of shrouds, behind it. It would like to flee from it, in order to go and repose out there, near the magic palaces of red copper built by the setting sun, or stop silently, in order that the lake around it will no longer be anything but a plain of green marble.

But an imperious wind incessantly inflates its sails, and it hollows out itself, with its heavy keel, the wake that wearies and frightens it.

Then a voice, so mysterious and so intimate that I do not know whether it is coming from the junk or my soul, murmurs in the violet evening air: "Oh, no longer to see behind me, on the lake of Eternity, the implacable wake of Time!"

The Solitary

Anywhere out of the World[1]

In order to carry out the orders of a distant king, servants exposed the child in a place of forests and rocks. The abandoned infant was placed on a stone amid monstrous grass; harsh flowers around him opened their hostile red corollas like maws. But that

---

1 This epigraph is the title of one of Baudelaire's poems in prose, rendered in English in the original.

night the jubilee commenced, and the priests gathered in the forest perceived the child.

One of the hierophants, leaning over toward the stone, prophesied. "This one," he said, "is of noble race. He will be delivered from malevolent approaches."

The priests sang the customary hymns; then they all went together to confide the child to the king's pastors. A sounder of the conch preceded the procession; they were in mourning and, turning toward the plain, they made tumultuous and desperate plaints resound. But from the depths of the forests the buccina players in white robes responded with rich fanfares and the haughty straight clarions were seen rising in the dawn like golden lilies.

In the shepherds' village the child was named Stellus. He grew up wild and disdainful, and yet, there was a tenebrous tenderness in him. He opened his arms to children. He ran to mothers and hugged them filially. But he suddenly stopped, as if wounded by an unknown evil; he lowered his head and fled toward shadowed corners, toward the broad deserted highways. Other children threw stones at him and beat him with branches; the old men said: "They're right; you ought to play with your brothers."

Meekly, he then tried to follow those of his age when they went into gardens to steal fruit and pillage the beehives. But suddenly, without understanding, he had a desire to weep and to hide.

Often, he fled away from roads and villages, into the forest where he had once been found. A vast peace descended upon him; the friendly branches brushed him with welcome freshness, and it seemed to him that healing hands were being placed on his forehead. Silently, he sat down in a sunlit place, on the edge of a lake so profoundly impregnated with ancient light that it seemed to retain within its shores a marvelous liquid of cinnabar and gold.

Stellus stayed there, without a dream, without desire, intoxicating himself by listening to the wind. At first he heard nothing but a monotonous and confused noise spread over the entire country. Soon, he was able to distinguish the frisson of each wood, of every branch. Then he discerned unusual, supernatural sounds reminiscent of the songs of magical spinners and the sighs of celestial flutes.

And that rumor of the wind had a miraculous power. As he listened to it, Stellus sensed new thoughts surging within him. He understood, he knew and he saw the forest living; he saw the ineffable soul of the trees, the grass and the waters; and sounds fallen from the stars taught him divine things. He was not astonished, however. That revelation only seemed to him to be a recovered memory, and every idea that entered into him was like a returning exile. He listened placidly, and it seemed to him to be quite simple that the information was brought to him by the wind, like flowers plucked from the orchards of the night.

But when the breezes finally fell silent, an immense sadness grew in the child's soul. After the revelatory words that the wind brought him, he felt more prodigiously that he was a stranger. An imperious desire sometimes came to him to repeat to others what he had learned from the forest, but he divined that he would speak in vain, and he remained dolorously silent. When he returned to his companions, a strange malaise oppressed him. Every day he lingered for longer in the forest, in its unexplored sectors. For one entire summer, he lived among the trees. He stayed there, loving and savage, regretting his companions but not daring to return to them. Mist soiled the dusks; a long, sad quivering agitated the branches; the trees leaned backwards, frightened and tremulous, as if baulking fearfully before the approaching winter; the flocks in the short grass grew thin and bleated lamentably at the moon.

A man came from the village to enquire about the belated pastor. Stellus confided his dolor to him; he begged him to leave him in the forest. The man listened with an appearance of understanding. "I can see what you desire," he said, finally. "The priests have told you that you were of a noble race. That doubtless signifies that you are not made to be a herdsman. Go forth into the world in quest of glorious hazards. Be a soldier."

Stellus believed that man. *Yes,* he thought, *perhaps I will be better among soldiers.*

Having climbed a rock, he saw the troubled fires of a camp in the distance. He left the flocks and followed bitter paths toward battles. The calls of the sentinels on the hills guided his progress; trumpets sounded in the distance, as if to welcome the man that was coming.

His helmet crested by a bronze bird, his armor bristling with nails, Stellus fought with the ax and the sword. He served a conquering king whose army advanced triumphantly, odious to the nations. Such a hatred growled behind the invaders that they killed the wounded in order to spare them the expiatory tortures that the enemy would doubtless have inflicted upon them. And in order that no one would be captured alive, the soldiers were linked together in battle by chains. But a mysterious force pushed Stellus to fight alone.

He tried in vain to get closer to his brothers in arms; and an invisible power moved him away. On nights of alarm, he galloped alone toward perilous positions; he was the solitary torch-bearer who explored the barbaric woods; he was the unique defender of rearguards who was left behind like a martial offering to the gods of war during the flight of kings and captains. And yet, how he would have liked to mingle with his companions, to drink pillaged wine with them in stolen cups, and sing with them around the bivouacs! How he envied those who, on the eve of massacres, slept together fraternally under flapping tents. But he never had companions.

In the days of the first battles he thought: *Doubtless, being of a noble race, I cannot please myself among mercenaries; I would be happy if I were marching with the leaders.* He accomplished such exploits that the kings saluted him as their equal. He received the golden lance and banner and had his place among the princes of the army. But in the ardent cortege of young sovereigns, the ancient dolor surprised him again; in the squares of conquered capitals that he was given as a privilege, he sensed, as in the shepherd village, that he was a passing stranger.

As he was afflicted, an old captain who admired him said to

him: "I know what you desire. What you lack, Stellus, is amour. Go forth into the world in quest of some white princess. Be a lover."

Stellus believed the captain. He put ample branches of lilac into his saddle-bag; he rolled vine-branches and foliage around his lance and departed toward amour. Magical birds, dazzling the air with bright wings, fluttered around the cavalier; nuptial perfumes floated over the rivers and fields.

In a land of sunlight and fresh waters, Stellus found the white princess. She was standing beside a spring, drawing water in a silver pitcher; her pale and supple arms were leaning on the rim. The young woman began to laugh because the magical birds settled upon her abruptly, and sprayed bright droplets over her face as they folded their wings. When Stellus approached, she fled.

She ran into the country, and while she ran she laughed. At times she stopped, hastily picked red roses and white roses, and threw them at the cavalier, ironically. Her tawny hair was undone and spread over her shoulders like the mantle of a huntress fabricated from the pelt of a young lioness.

In the end Stellus overtook her, put his arms around her and pulled her up on to his horse. She was still laughing. "Drop the reins," she said. Gently, with caressant words, she guided the tamed charger. She conducted it along a pathway strewn with blue powder to her palace, and that night the sistra and tymbals announced a royal wedding.

The nuptial garlands had not yet faded on the palace balconies when Stellus came to sit down in the gardens, sobbing. He raised his plaintive arms toward the sky and murmured: "Who, then, will come to my aid? Who will advise me?"

Then he saw a tall old sacerdotal man who was listening to him. "Father," said Stellus, "if you are the savior sent to me, if you know hidden things, tell me why I am forever solitary. Tell me why, as a child, I was unable to play with the other children, why I was unable to reveal to young men the words of the wind, nor laugh with the soldiers, nor sleep voluptuously beside my wife?"

And in a supernatural voice, the old man replied: "Stellus, Stellus, since the enchantments of the kiss have not vanquished you, and since your incurably noble heart cannot be intoxicated by banal sensualities, I will speak. You are suffering, Stellus, because you are not similar to other men, because you cannot know their joys, nor their hopes, because you have obscure dreams within you, unnamed passions that you cannot express in words. But it is necessary that you know now that all men are, like you, solitary monsters.

"Do you remember, Stellus, when you were a small child, you could not distinguish he-goats from rams and ewes from she-goats. And when you heard bleating in the distanced, you said: 'It's the livestock moaning.' As the he-goat differs from the ram, one man differs from another. What is called humankind is only a disorderly flock of unknown and disparate beings.

"Stellus, the clairvoyant eyes of initiates perceive differences where vulgar eyes only see evident similarities. But men, ignoring the horrible, divine truth, believe themselves to be similar to one another. They speak to one another, the insensates, as if words could go from one soul to another. They look at one another as if they were not separated by insurmountable walls of darkness.

"You, Stellus, have understood obscurely that you are the only one of your race. It is for that reason, Stellus, that you have suffered. You appear to yourself to be different from other men, and you cannot resign yourself to your nobility. You fled into the forest because your companions were strangers to you, and you suffered in the forest because you no longer had companions. You loved solitude in the country because you suffered from being alone in crowds, and you have not been able to seek the deliverance promised by prophesies.

"Yes, the priests told the truth. You are of a noble race. But madly, like the others, you have searched for others of your race on earth. You have searched for them among soldiers and kings, and you thought you had found an equal when you had only encountered a lover. I have revealed secrets to you. Meditate, in order that you might one day, in accordance with what has been predicted, be delivered from the maleficent approaches of those you cannot believe to be your brothers."

Outside the gardens, outside the palace where his wife was asleep, Stellus drew away. He marched in stony plains; he climbed arid slopes; he followed the banks of funereal rivers. He came eventually into a land overhung by harsh mountains with sheer and smooth walls.

The inhabitants of the country that Stellus had entered were in affliction, because, from the heights of the mountains, a monstrous winged horse vomiting flames had fallen upon their houses. The hippogriff with diamond hooves shook the walls of the ancient houses with its resounding wings. It pawed the ground, tore up the sown grain, felled the oxen during the plowing; it abducted virgins, carrying them beyond the clouds. Then they were seen falling to earth, naked and bloody, like red and white flowers falling from the opening sky.

A great clamor had resounded at the advent of the monster, as imperious and loud as the voice of a herald, and prophetic words had been perceived. The victorious hippogriff would devastate the country until a man would voluntarily sit down between the scintillating wings and consent to go with the monster toward the stars.

Stellus arrived among those frightened people. He saw the monster from afar, and a hope rose up in his heart. Radiant, he went to find the village chiefs, and proclaimed that he would mount the hippogriff. The men saluted Stellus with long cries of admiration; the women embraced his knees and spread oils and balms over his feet.

The sages harangued the people. "See," they said, "the man who will sacrifice himself for you. He is young and glorious; he could live royal years, and yet he will quit the soft dusts on which we walk with joy; he will leave the natal mud, in which we delight; he will go toward the foreign stars, toward the sky at which prudent men do not like to look. Glory to the hero! Contemplate the man who loves us enough to flee the earth, the man who will be devoured for his fellows."

While they spoke, Stellus, seizing the resplendent mane with both hands, intoned a song of delight: "Hippogriff, liberator hippogriff, carry me higher than the sky. In order to obey the divine old man, we shall go, O monster, beyond the gates of the horizon. I shall ride above cities, above landscapes where I have suffered. If nothing awaits us above the worlds, let us wander forever in the desert of the constellations. You will spring from the earth through the night of joyful stars, and I shall be delivered; I shall no longer have to endure human beings, I shall no longer have to love human beings and I shall finally know, freely, among the mute stars, the voluptuousness of being born solitary. But if I have merited, O savior monster, discovering those who are of my race, carry me toward them. Winged horse, charger worthy of a noble cavalier, carry me at last to where my true brethren are. Hippogriff, liberator hippogriff, like a king returning from a battle, I shall reenter the realm of life, toward my high celestial dwelling."

Stellus caressed the colored mane of the winged horse. The astral vaults opened peacefully to their course; the breezes of the heavens murmured words of welcome; luminous blonde forms leaned over on the clouds and, through the mists of a strange dawn, the solitary finally saw, burning in the utmost distance of the skies, the light for which he had searched so long, the light of fraternal eyes.

BERNARD LAZARE
(1865-1903)

Bernard Lazare was the pseudonym of Lazare Bernard, who followed his friend George Michel, alias Ephraïm Mikhaël, to Paris from their native Toulouse and joined the literary clique of the "Moineaux francs" that had formed around him in Stéphane Mallarmé's salon, which included Rodolphe Darzens, Pierre Quillard and Saint-Pol-Roux. He contributed a good deal of short fiction to various periodicals, including Anarchist periodicals, and became intimately involved in the Dreyfus affair, originating the declaration "J'Accuse!" made famous by Émile Zola. His study of *L'Antisemitisme, son histoire et ses causes* (1894) led, absurdly, to his being accused of antisemitism himself, but he became an enthusiastic Zionist. He published three collections of hybrid *contes*: *Le Miroir des légendes* (1892; tr. as *The Mirror of Legends*), from which the items below are taken; *Les Porteurs des torches* (1897; tr. as *The Torch-Bearers*); which framed its individual inclusions within a propagandist Anarchist narrative; and *Les Portes d'Ivoire* (1898; tr. as *The Gates of Ivory*), but he died young.

The Garden

But my desire always goes toward the mystery,
Of marvelous lands where I have never set foot.
—Éphraïm Mikhaël.

The garden has not sealed mysterious Avalons and white Thules forever; the doors are not irredeemably closed.

You who, in the troubling pleasures of pale visions, flee the cities where you dragged your heart, your poor darkened heart; you who are weary of banal voices, quit the noisy crowds and sonorous voids and travel on roads detestable to you; you will find the garden of mysterious Avalons and white Thules.

If you are fond of abolished glories, if you have spat on the festivals in which, drunk on malign liquors, your brothers are feasting; if your dream is distant; if your desires are noble; extend your feeble hands even so; be fearless, and the magical beasts that guard the thresholds of fortunate countries will lick your feet and open the way for you to Thules and Avalons.

If your soul is pure, its own light will guide you, far from the borders that pollute the false pilgrims, through the bushes where large venomous flowers bloom for the impious, toward the bolted doors guarded by dragons, chimeras and wyverns, toward the doors of Avalons and Thules.

Then, behind rugged walls bristling with spikes, you will perceive the quivering crowns of friendly trees. The leaves of their branches sparkle, like candid enamels, and their gleam will be soft. The indulgent foliage will spread its subtle aromas over you; the scattered benevolent odors will lull all your senses, and the clement murmur of the soon-conquered forest will salute the new lover of Avalons and Thules.

And you will hear the song of virgins who walk in the shade of hasty rose-bushes, while invisible birds celebrate infallible joys in puerile cantilenas. Listen to the virgins who walk in the shade of hasty rose-bushes, the virgins of Thules and Avalons.

"Welcome, voyager, undervalued voyager! For you our fraternal voices have resonated, you have replied to our evocative appeal. You have groaned along evil paths; captive on the banks of enemy rivers, you have suffered. Our frail fingers have brushed your forehead with bright corollas, and those exiles have announced fabulous dreamlands to you. You are worn out, like a fawn tracked by hunters, and we read the customary apprehensions and fears in your still-obscure soul.

"Have no fear; you have already crossed the invisible porticos that the profane will never reach.

"Come to us, the revealers. You have left the impure gold, the sordid mire; henceforth you shall have unexperienced delights. You have disdained abject acclamations, and have rejected the buccinas of base triumphs; you have renounced the consecratory pedestals of unhealthy renown: you will contemplate your eternal and true image in the mirror of pure lakes.

"Come! Here the softness of lawns is starred with strange calices, the branches of orchards are hung with glistening fruits, melodious perfumes take flight, and rippling streams proffer unheard words.

"Come! An undulating and peaceful light will caress your eyes; look: it has the infantile candor of auroras, the attractive melancholy of dusks, the infinite gentleness of blue twilights.

"Come! You will know the eternity of the Word. The golden sistra are ready, the strings vibrate beneath the plectra, the air quivers with latent speech, rhythms are dormant in the wind, thoughts are huddled in the depths of grottoes.

"Enter, you will awaken the world that is waiting for you."

Thus you will hear the virginal spinners who tread the scattered moss beneath the blooming roses: the spinners of Avalons and Thules.

Touch, with your intrepid finger, the emerald that seals the heavy battens, and the battens will open. See, it is palpitating, the unpolluted gem; it is calling to you: "You whose soul is pure, aching heart, hear me! Hear me, new lover fond of abolished glories! The doors are not irredeemably closed; it is never closed, the garden of mysterious Avalons and white Thules."

The Forest

Listen; the forest, in the distance, out there, is stirring. . . .
—F. Vielé-Griffin.

Sad soul, disappointed heart, infatuated with divine chimeras that gallop in skies reddened by inviolate dawns or misted by tender dusks, you have crossed the threshold and your intrepid feet will not hesitate. The virginal and annunciatory virtues are summoning you, and you come, plaintive heart, weary soul.

You come, you enter, treading the parvis of sardonyx incrusted with magical carbuncles, and behind you, the door closes with an evocative sound. You feel distant from the hostile world, far from the unhealthy words that have afflicted your morose heart and your wounded soul excessively.

You believed yourself to be liberated, and, proud of your courage, you sang the paean in honor of the spinners who attracted you; but you searched for them in vain, with an emotional soul and an impatient heart. Alone, before you, the lugubrious forest extended, the forest saddened by the absence of familiar birds and sylvan nymphs, the bushy and empty forest, the forest filled with trees and strange flowers, the forest populated by imprisoned spirits.

The songs that incited you still resonated, but distant and vague, and one might have thought them a supernatural choir of virgins descending unperceived hills. Then, guided by the beloved sounds, you penetrated into the thickets to vanquish the unruly brambles, and, face and hands bloody, you advanced, heart resolute and soul strong.

Suddenly, the shroud of silence fell away, the wood became animated; your closed ears opened, you heard the murmur of the foliage, the clamor of oaks, the wailing of moss, the quivering of reeds, the rumor of privet and laurier-roses, the cantilena of giant lilies and bright jasmines. You heard the hymn uttered:

"Fraternal traveler expelled by the crowds, adventurous fugitive, we salute you. You have recognized the vanity of terrestrial glories; you have shamed the banal ambition of men, the ambition that conquers treasons and felonies dearly. Be saluted, hero! We welcome you at the entrance to your new dwellings, as faithful servants welcome an expected master, and also as hierophants seated on the steps of a temple to instruct ignorant mystes. Listen, we are the initiators.

"You have lived in the midst of barbarians, and the dream captive in your being, the dream remembering lost lands, rendered the roads familiar to all dolorous to you. While the nocturnal words of those who triumph rang in your ears you went forth, without hearing them; in the desert of your senses shone friendly torches, and you followed the dear scorned gleams. But you alone saw them and our friends accused you of folly, and our mother withdrew from you, and the indifferent sniggered, for you marched with your head held high, your lips speaking.

"One evening when, weary of insults, your face soiled with mud, your limbs bruised by stones, you had sat down on the edge of a ditch, you saw white phantoms coming toward you in the repopulated fields; they dressed you in rich fabrics, they sprinkled you with precious perfumes, they delighted you with specious and promising words, and you came toward the doors that closed the Avalons and the Thules. The guardian monsters crouched down, and the sigillary emerald, touched by fearless fingers, allowed you to enter the gardens that you believed to be pleasant.

"Now, here you are, pilgrim whose soul is shivering and whose heart is emotional. You await the forms that haunt you, the ideas, mothers and queens, that you want to conquer. Alas, they will flee, illusory princesses, and you will rediscover the rancor of former days. Eternal fugitive of appearances, you will always see them surging forth before your eyes, and the visions, which alone are real, will perpetually fly away, beyond your reach, mysterious doves escaping the grasp of the bird-catcher. Remain with us, do not continue your route; we will give you the only real wellbeing: the death of dreams. Stay. You will go to sleep in the serene peace of ignorance, in the delectable abolition of desires, and fervent roses will make you a bed of repose and forgetfulness."

As you once paused at the crossroads of cities, seduced by the sound of lyres scattered for you in the air, you pause here, persuaded by the insidious voices. The poisonous aroma of the trees penetrates you with weakness, your knees flex and, voluntarily, you are inclining toward the bunch of enticing corollas, when once again you perceive the fading chorus of spinning maidens:

"Hear us, undervalued of the world; beware of murderous lakes. Vanquisher of dragons and wyverns, beware of more subtle enemies."

At the supreme appeal the scales fall from your eyes. You see; you recognize those who are retaining you. The branches of the oaks are flourishing bitter hands, the boughs of the beeches are sharpening rigid claws, the calices of the flowers are stirring perverse mouths, their pistils capped with sly pupils, heavy tresses are agitating on the foreheads of elms, the willows are bending their trunks into redoubtable rumps, and the mosses are starry with white breasts and red fleeces.

"Recognize them," clamor the spinners. "The ancient adversaries, the false servants of the Word, the killers of the ideal, the lovers of vanities, the worshipers of the beast, the glorifiers of metal and flesh. They believe they have won reliable delights, and the living who salute them celebrate them as fortunate initiates. But even if they were able to cross the walls, as felons, the plains of mysterious Avalons and white Thules would be forever closed to them. Courage, O vagabond of mortal life; triumph over the last ambushes; come to us. The golden sistra are ready, the strings vibrating under the plectrum, the air quivering with latent words, rhythms are dormant in the wind, thoughts are gathering in the depths of grottoes. Come, you will waken this world, which is waiting for you."

And, reanimated by the divine sisters, you traverse the thickets with a firm tread. You extract yourself from the languorous lianas, the voluptuous appeal of the crimsoned rose-bushes, and you finally see the supernatural lawns shining, and the solemn lakes blossoming, beneath the purifying light of the revelatory sky.

HENRI DE RÉGNIER
(1864-1936)

Henri de Régnier moved to Paris from his native Honfleur in order to complete his education in law, but committed himself instead to literature, becoming one of the most prolific Symbolist poets of the *fin-de-siècle*. He was the second representative of that young generation to be elected to the Académie, his first candidature seemingly having been subverted by a cabal, in which the anti-votes cast against him had the probably-unintended consequence of electing Jean Richepin instead. He married Marie, the daughter of the poet José-Marie de Hérédia, annoying his friend Pierre Louÿs, who was very fond of her, but tried to make up for it by inviting Louÿs to accompany them on their honeymoon. Marie became a significant writer in her own right, under the pseudonym Gérard d'Houville. After the turn of the century Régnier's prose writings, including his novels, became more orthodox but his early *poèmes en prose* and hybrid *contes*, many of them assembled in the omnibus *La Canne de Jaspe* (1897; tr. in *A Surfeit of Mirrors*)—from which the samples below are taken—remain his most distinctive works.

Hermogenes

To Jean Lorrain

As I entered the forest I turned my head, and, with my hand on the dappled rump of my horse, I paused to gaze over my shoulder through the first trees at the land I had just passed through, in order to try to catch one more glimpse of the house of my master, Hermogenes.

It should have been at the extremity of the bleak, briny and boggy plain that displayed its checkered salt-marsh, flat and far and wide, where roseate puddles reflected and crystallized the rays of the setting sun. The sun blinded me, for it was straight in front of me, and the whole of that broken ground, traversed in the dampness of an autumnal afternoon, was no more, at that hour, than an expanse of gilded mist upon a glitter. The vapor and the glare outside the forest were reemphasized by the demi-obscurity slumbering in the interior of the covert.

Tall pines loomed up from a dull and felted ground, their slender trunks sunlit to mid-height, the shadow increasing as the sun descended over the sea. I could see the sea, smooth on the horizon, beyond the bare plain checkered by the pools in which, so brackish was their lukewarm water, my horse had refused to slake its thirst. It pawed the russet ground of the underwood with its hoof, causing the pine-cones with which it was strewn to roll gently down the slope.

They reminded me of those that were burning in the hearth of my master, Hermogenes, the other evening, the delicate scales of which, where tears of resin scintillated, I manipulated with my fingers, while my host, sitting beside me, told me his story, so quietly that his voice seemed to come from within myself, as if it were to the depths of my own being that he was speaking.

Oh, how often I had thought of him again while riding along the little crackling paths alongside the salty mash-waters. The dampness of the spongy air was so impregnated with salt that my tongue could taste it on my lips. Hermogenes' sadness could certainly not have been sharper or sourer. He had seemed to me to be retracing the path of his days and I told myself, as I resumed my route through the place that was already darkening; "May I be able to enter the twilight like him! May I be able to sit down at the spring, where there is a hearth for all the ashes of my dreams!"

I had arrived in a part of the forest where it appeared to me in its supreme autumnal beauty. There was a clearing between the tall trees. The foliage was red-brown and gilded, and even though the sun had disappeared, it seemed that a gleam continued in the treetops, where the illusion of its survival persisted by virtue of the tint of its presence. None of the leaves was moving and yet one of them, dull gold in color and already dry, or bright gold and still living, sometimes fell, as if the tiny melancholy sound of the spring in which their suspension was reflected had sufficed to determine, in the silent indifference of the atmosphere, the pretext for their fall.

I watched those which were falling into the pool of the spring. Two, then others, and one that I felt brush my hand. I shivered, for I was waiting, anxiously, in the silence, in order to continue my progress, for the cry of some bird to break the immobilizing spell. Everything fell silent, from tree to tree, to such a distance that I felt myself going pale, perhaps less because of the solitude than the caress of the leaf that had brushed my hand, lighter than a dream on the lips of memory itself.

I went closer to the water, instinctively, in order to look at my face in it, and, seeing it pale and perplexed, aged by all that a ripple can add to the nocturne of that which is mirrored within it, I thought of Hermogenes, of my master Hermogenes. I heard his voice again in the depths of my inner being, and it repeated the melancholy story that he had told me, the story that also began at a crossroads in a forest, near a spring in which he could see his face.

✳

"By what mysterious ways," Hermogenes said to me, "through what pitiless adventures must I have passed, only to have acquired the sentiment of a sadness so immense that it has veiled, by the excess of its bulk, the memory of its origin and the progress of its

286

estate. It oppresses me with the total oblivion of its causes and all the weight of its consistency.

"Nothing in that dark and secret past is illuminated. Golden blades among the cypresses, rings of joy and alliance lost in seductive waters, torches, on the threshold in the night-wind, smiles in the depths of twilight: nothing illuminates that invariable shadow from which I had come, by laborious paths, to the point at which, weary of a march of which fatigue alone caused me to feel the distance, lost in the forest, I sat down on the edge of a spring, as one rests next to a tomb.

"All that I had suffered was dead within me, and I breathed in the odor of the ashes that my memory exhaled. It was certainly mingled with flesh, flowers and tears, for I found therein a triple perfume of regret, melancholy and bitterness. There were echoes in the depths of that interior taciturnity, but they were torpid, and that formless and mysterious past surrounded me with its dolorous darkness. Without knowing its circumstances, I still felt regret, melancholy and bitterness. I would have liked its lips to murmur the cause in my dream; I would have liked to drink from its Lethean lake a memorial youthfulness, as in the water of that spring I perceived myself coming toward me, as silence comes to solitude, each with the desire to learn from the other the secret of their accord.

"Was nothing of myself going to appear in my face in the intermediary water, then? My hands reached out their wounded palms toward the reflection. *O my shadow, who appears to me thus, you seem nonetheless to have come from the depths of my past. You must know its ways, mysterious or ordinary, its adventures pitiless or otherwise. Speak! Smiles in the dusk! Golden blades among the cypresses, or perhaps the torch, or the rings . . .*

"A fallen stone had destroyed the mirror, and caused me to raise my eyes. They met those of the Stranger who had thus interrupted my reverie, and who seemed to be following her own, without perceiving my presence.

"She was standing in her torn and ash-stained dress, which surpassed the bare foot with which she had pushed the perturbatory stone. A singular curiosity led me to speak to the newcomer.

It seemed to me that I would only have to hear what she would say to me to remember. Our Destinies must have touched their lips and hands before separating for some inverse circuit in which they were finally meeting again at a point of their duration. They were two halves of a whole, and my sadness could only be the understanding of her silence.

"Yes, my son," Hermogenes continued, "she spoke to me. She told me why she had left the town. The life she had led there was loquacious, bombastic and frivolous; a futile slumber. The eve did not fructify any tomorrow therein, and the transient flowers of every day perished. The town was immense and populous. Its innumerable streets intercrossed in a thousand junctions, and all of them ended, via some that opened thereon, in a vast central square paved with marble.

"Odorant trees grew here and there between disjointed paving stones, and sculpted a delightful shade there; fresh water sprang forth there amid the moist silence in a crystalline atmosphere. But the square was always deserted; it was forbidden to pause there, and even to cross it. One would have been able to dream there under the trees, drink the water and confront the solitude, but the crowd had to wander incessantly through the labyrinth of dusty streets, between the tall stone houses with bronze doors, amid the different faces and the superfluous speeches.

"Oh, sad town! One wandered desperately there, in search of oneself—those, at least, who were not satisfied with arguing on the street-corners, making speeches on the boundary-markers, trafficking over the counters or dancing to the music of tambourines.

"The majority were content with that. They came and went without coming together save for the agreement of a bargain or the satisfaction of a desire. A few sages walked there, with mirrors in their hands. They looked at themselves obstinately, trying to be alone, but spiteful children smashed the evidential looking-glasses with thrown stones, and the crowd laughed, thus imposing the authority of its despotism . . .

"As she spoke, it seemed to me that the vision she evoked with disgust was reconstituted in me. I heard it, like a distant

288

interior buzz. It raised memorial and analogous rumors from my past, and I said again, as the Stranger had said: 'Let us leave the town, let us abandon the frivolous and vain life . . .'

"She had left one morning, weary of wandering amid the composite and uniform crowd, amid the dust of sandals and the sweat of faces. She passed others beneath the postern, who were coming from elsewhere to increase the number of those living there, and when she was outside the walls, she heard a bird singing in a tree. The pride of being alone exalted her, and she felt herself grow as she isolated herself further.

"The hem of her dress brushed flowers, while she descended by charming roads toward the sea. Sandy shores bordered it, roseate in the dawn, which melted into gold at midday and became violet in the dusk.

"Oh, dusk on that first day of dreams! Her shadow on the sand told her that she was alone, and that the residue of herself was no more than a phantom at her feet, and it was to her shadow that she sacrificed, thrown into the sea as night fell, the stones of her necklace, which tinkled more melodiously than tears. Her necklace was made up of three kinds of stones, all valuable, and the whole was inestimable. There was, all night, a star over the sea—a star over the sea, until morning!

"But I paid even closer attention to what the Stranger was telling me when she told me how the satyrs and fauns stripped her and left her naked in the forest. I understood that her actions and outcomes each represented my thoughts. I understood how I had lived the emblems of her adventures internally. They were what constituted my sadness.

"The satyrs had first surrounded her, dancing. The long lush grass had hid the lower halves of their bodies and their prancing bestiality, while their hands offered bunches of grapes, fruits and odorant apples—but their hands had soon become bolder.

"It was afterwards that she became a wanderer, entirely devoted to some mysterious and desperate quest: a philter to create souls within the hairy flesh of prowling goat-foots. She lifted up enormous stones with her frail hands but, instead of a balm or talisman, there were toads or stagnant water sleeping there. Snakes slithered under the dry leaves, hatched from golden eggs, which she believed to be those of peacocks or doves; a seething poison, where a remedy had been promised . . .

"My son," Hermogenes said to me, "I finally knew the origin and the substance of my sadness by virtue of all that the Stranger had told me. It was necessary for her to come to me for me to obtain, through her, consciousness of my misery. It had seemed immense and confused before; then I found it immeasurable—but, in seeing it more clearly, I recognized that I had deserved it.

"One can no longer find oneself once one is lost, and love does not return us to ourselves. Why had I not been one of those cautious sages, who walk about the town with a mirror in hand, in order to try to be alone, facing themselves because it is necessary to live in one's own presence?"

❋

Such was the tale of my master Hermogenes and his encounter with the Stranger. He had taken curious lessons from it, because his mind was rational, but he loved to invigorate his reason with allegories. Perhaps he had wanted to make more impact upon me by mingling a fable with his instruction.

His apologue was ingenious and certainly had not been fruitless, for I exclaimed: "Fortunate are those who, like Hermogenes, meet themselves on the path of life through the intermediary of a dream; more fortunate still are those who have never quit themselves, and for whom their own presence has taken the place of the world!"

Night had fallen; my horse was walking over the dry leaves and stumbling over roots. I did not know how to find my way out of the forest and searched the stars, through the trees, for the road to the dawn.

The Knight who Fell Asleep in the Snow

To Madame Judith Gautier

"I didn't know my father," he said to me, one evening. "Someone else took care of me in my childhood, but the first years of my youth were spent in the château that he inhabited and where he lived to old age, mad and hypochondriac, occupied with architectural and hydraulic schemes, the imagination of gardens, summer-houses and fountains. He ruined himself with the structures in question, and when he died, I came to establish myself in this room, which I have scarcely ever left since then. It's there, he added, that a man lived who had no adventures for having been too much a contemporary of a non-existent époque. Hence my solitude, and the appearance of being disdainful of the dictates of fate.

"The baseness of its offerings justifies the abstention in which I reserve my condescension. I rapidly limited my desire to certain objects that are more symbolic than material. I arrange flowers here and there. They have no other meaning than themselves, and I like them better for it. I also have a few items of crystalline and prophetic glassware on pedestals. One vase is not sufficient to evoke all the springs from which one has not drunk, although I can see through the windows the icy arabesque designs of shores on which I have not landed and forests in which I have not been lost.

"I also have this portrait on the wall. It is, behind an emblematic and dreamlike appearance, the face of a Destiny. It is in him that I see most profoundly into myself. He is the one who alerted me to myself and it is from the eloquence of his sadness that I have learned the lesson of my solitude. His voice has animated its silence; his hands have locked its doors with invisible keys. They are under the safeguard of his armed gesture and his peremptory eyes. Look at him as I have looked at him, and perhaps he will speak to you as he spoke to me. He is taciturn but he is not mute, for portraits speak, and if they do not express themselves by means of their painted lips, one hears them nonetheless. They are, in a mirror fashioned by the frame around their reflective glass, the almost-supernatural duration of someone who is behind us when we gaze at his appearance, who is perhaps within us, pale and a flower of dreams!

"For a long time I have scrutinized that bleak and naked face, that dolorous face with the sad eyes. The slightly-inflated lips are swollen by a grave sulkiness. It is a meditative face of desire and mortification, in accord with those hands, gripping their lassitude in the crucial hilt of the long sword. The feeble, melancholy hands will never lift it again. Their gesture of exhaustion has renounced twisting the torpid flash of metal that runs gently along the ridge of the triangular blade.

"There is no justification for the warrior costume whose breastplate stiffens that sickly torso. The shiny gleam of the polished armor seems to melt into long white tears, and beneath that bellicose clothing, beneath all that false appearance of continued strength, from the depths of being, life and destiny, one senses the suffocating moisture of a sob rising to that naked face, so much so that the hands on that superfluous sword manifest an attitude that is resigned not to persist in handling the useless burden any longer, heavier than strength and taller than the stature of the man who is measuring himself against it and succumbing thereto.

"For a long time I have thought about that face and that body, which is only still rigid because of its inflexible accoutrement of armor, only upright because of the sword on which it is leaning. Even his helmet, which lies beside him, demonstrates that at least he did not want to die behind the mask of its visor, giving passers-by the illusion, by means of his bearing, that he was what he seemed to be; that he did not want to die in that rigorous posture of iron, the lie of which he would have cast down had he not been too late in breaking its irreparable spell; that he did not want to die without revealing himself to everyone by means of the veridical nudity of his face!

"What was he, in his time, that authentic human being whose emblem survives in the appearance of what he had been? The old Chronicles cite his name and record his history: that of his deeds, which it is sufficient to interpret to have a sense of his soul. He lived in a century of violence and guile. He acted by means of speech and the sword. He sullied himself simply with all human actions, without being more avaricious or less brutal than those he robbed or vanquished. If defrauded or deceived, he altered the weight of the false balance. He employed himself in that which life demands of any man, to that which is called living, and the narrators of his deeds say, after having described and evaluated the epoch, that he died in consequence of languor for having, one cold night, in the mountains into which he had led his soldiers, lain down in the open air in the snow . . .

"O my brother of the olden days and the present, it is that night of your life on which I shall meditate forever, that night when you were the man who slept in the snow. It was then that you understood the meaning of your past, the ignominy of your desires and the opprobrium of your sad days.

"You have the face of someone who has looked himself in the face. The pure, cold and chaste snow taught you the regenerative lesson of its whiteness. It infiltrated the steel joints of your pride; it brought tears to the iron visage of your pride; it buried within you, beneath its shroud, the primitive and rugged mass of your faults as it leveled around you with its slow fall the facial cracks of old stones and the sharp blades of sterile grass.

"Woe betide the man who gambles his life on his desires. There are sometimes mysterious encounters in destiny; there are mirroring spaces beneath our footsteps in which we see ourselves entirely, instead of the dull disturbed marshes that were the color of our eyes; there are within us snowflakes of purity and dream, which extinguish the lukewarm ashes of the fires at which we warm our chilly and scabrous hands.

"Alas, pure knight, at the dawn of the night of redemption, you were unable to bear the intimate bounty, and before the all-white landscape, tranquil and purified, you shivered forever at your past; you trembled in the wan fever of that which you were, and felt growing within you, as on a supernatural tomb, the internal and funeral lily, whose evangelical sap your being could no longer nourish and whose stem extended its blossoming flower, visibly, outside your armor, in the morbid and desperate grace of your visage: its flower with the cold petals of your naked hands.

"It was then that, brought down again from the snow of the mortal summits and returning to the dead cities of your ancient dreams and the deserted palaces of your old desires, among the luxuries and vainglories of your former ideas, you languished for days in the slow death-throes compounded of the shame of that which you were no longer and regret for that which you could not be.

"Your pernicious past survived too well in you for any contrary future not to perish by the contagion of its contact, and you suffered thus, ensheathed by the base of brutal substance of your self, overcoming it nevertheless by means of the pure visage of your sadness.

"You were suffering thus when the painter represented on his anonymous canvas the emblem that you had become. It is that portrait which ornaments the wall of my room. It has alerted me to myself; it has spoken to my solitude the entire doctrine of its sadness. It is that which has instructed me not to adventure outside oneself—for all footsteps march over the snow, and are effaced there so quickly by the slightest wind that one cannot return to one's point of departure.

"So, when evening comes beyond the icy windows, in the arborescence of forests and the arabesques of imaginary shores, and an imperceptible regret saddens me, never to have landed there and never to have slept there, I gaze, while delicately handling the prophetic and empty glassware in which my dreams of thirst and philters amuse themselves, I gaze, at the wall above the flowers on the sideboard, at the taciturn antique portrait, upright in the icy arms of his frame of tortoiseshell and ebony, with his pale face and his sword, of the knight who went to sleep in the snow."

JEAN RICHEPIN
(1849-1926)

Jean Richepin was born in French Algeria and came to Paris to study at the École Normale Supérieure, but lived a rather turbulent existence there and thereafter, claiming to have been a sniper during the Franco-German War and leading a vagabond existence before publishing the first of his several volumes of provocative poetry, *La Chanson des gueux*, in 1876, which led to his being briefly imprisoned for outraging public morals—of which he was very proud. He had been one of the very few people who got along well with Arthur Rimbaud and had received one of the few printed copies of *Un Saison en enfer* in 1873 in compensation. In the 1880s he played the piano and sang his own songs at the Chat Noir, and wrote articles and fiction for several newspapers, including *Le Journal*, where the item below, advertised as a "*poème en prose strophée*," appeared in the 25 May 1896 issue. He took the lead in one of his plays when the actor hired to play the part fell ill, resulting in Sarah Bernhardt, who played opposite him, describing him admiringly as a bigger ham than she was. Later, he also appeared in silent movie adaptations of his work in the 1920s, but by then he had calmed down somewhat, and the novels he wrote after his surprising election to the Académie in 1908 are more earnestly philosophical than his earlier works.

Tomorrow
A Poem in Prose in stanzas

Sometimes, during an eclipse
I see such crazy phantasms
In which whirl the flocks
Of the moths of the Apocalypse
—Jehan de Moyouje[1]

---

1 The fictitious Jehan de Moyouje crops up in the epigraphs to several other newspaper pieces by Richepin, notably one in a sequence headed "Arlequins"

I do not know, and therefore cannot tell you, whether this was an enchantment of opium, a hallucination of fever, or a simple dream, whether asleep or awake; and I have no desire except to relate the thing as best I can, trying to employ a prose with somnambulistic cadences, in accordance with the spectral rhythm of magnetic passes, to the inflexible metronome of a gesture beating a hypnotizing and gradually evocative measure.

Without being in the least astonished, I found myself deploying my feet, fists and elbows in the densest part of a swarming crowd, on an enormous Champ de Mars, Babylonian and tumultuous, having come there is order to wallow in the brutal joys of a perpetual fair held there, always celebrated and presumably permanent, under the triumphant and derisory name of "the fair of tomorrow."

The din was horrific, of an entire orchestra unleashed tempestuously, in which the donkey-skins of tambours snored raucously and trombones trumpeted plangently, accompanying clarinets and the cannon-fire boom of big drums, while bells sobbed rapidly, recklessly and madly, as if to sound the tocsin and cry fire.

But what still dominated all that deafening, barking, trumpeting, roaring, drumming and howling racket, tearing the air and making the ears bleed, even more so than the instruments, were the innumerable loudhailers that were casting claptrap in all languages over the crowd, in uninterrupted downpours, torrents, cataracts, whirlwinds and cyclones, without the slightest pause or hesitation.

I understood all those tongues, and I did not believe myself for that to be a great clerk, having perceived from the outset that, in sum, those thousand-and-one appeals were only translating one another beneath the apparent luxury of their multiform vocabulary, with the real poverty of a single, unique patter announcing a single, unique and miserably identical thing.

That single, unique and identical thing had no need, moreover, to be announced with such a great reinforcement

in 1895.

296

of howling advertisements, and the braying of the loudhailers could very well have been more economical of drunken breath, probably-syphilitic saliva and cavernous lungs, which spat out indefatigable hurricanes of words at full volume over the imbecilic crowd drinking from the tin-plate vomitories.

In fact, even without being commented by any humbug at all, gestures would have sufficed to express to our gazes everything they wanted to suggest, and that uniform and imperious gesture, of a right hand striking the advertisement outside every tent—a painting promising the marvel offered inside for a truly infimal sum—with a long stick similar to an extended index finger.

For what was displayed on that painting, struck by the tip of the indicative stick, leaping to the eye with its explosive coloring, which solicited entry for two sous, was an immense figure of a coquecigrue,[1] which everyone recognized and at which everyone smiled.

And how could anyone not have recognized that amiable monster, how could anyone have been unable to recognize it, since a streamer was emerging from its mouth bearing a significative legend, endlessly repeated: *I am Tomorrow! Here is Tomorrow! Look at Tomorrow! Come see Tomorrow! Tomorrow in me, me, me! I am Tomorrow! Long live Tomorrow! Tomorrow! Tomorrow!*

And given that, it was quite unnecessary—was it not?—for the blowhards with the loudhailers to inflame their amygdalas, bloody their bronchi and make their jugulars explode yelling those inexhaustibly belched words into their tin-plate vomitories: *Come in! Come in! Come see Tomorrow, the famous Tomorrow, the celebrated Tomorrow, the beautiful Tomorrow, the one and only Tomorrow, the true Tomorrow! Tomorrow! Tomorrow! Tomorrow!*

But it is necessary to believe that those vomitories intoxicated the crowd, and also intoxicated the vociferators themselves, and intoxicated me like all the rest since, while judging the blowhards with loudhailers insupportable and the crowd that listened to them to be stupid, I soon excused the crowd for joining in chorus with them and I finally began to shout myself, with all my might, that doubtless magical word: *Tomorrow! Tomorrow! Tomorrow!*

---

1 *Coquecigrue* was a word improvised to indicate an imaginary creature, usually indescribable, symbolic of the ultimate in absurdity.

The worst thing was that people were still rushing into every tent with the same ardor, uttering the same frantic cries, after having heard the same fallacious patter, looked at the same lying painting and emerged from the previous one without having found the promised phenomenon resembling the coquecigrue painted on the outside, which everyone recognized and which smiled at everyone.

Nevertheless, you would certainly have been scalped by those mountebanks, and also by the crowd, if you had given the impression of putting in doubt the reality of what was there in the fair of Tomorrows, the suave Tomorrows, and implying that anyone could leave without having the Tomorrow at their convenience, and doubting that every tent possessed that Tomorrow, the famous Tomorrow, the celebrated Tomorrow, the beautiful Tomorrow, the one and only Tomorrow, the true Tomorrow!

That is why, my sudden temporary intoxication having evaporated, when reason gradually returned to me and whispered doubts to me, I was gripped by fear at the idea of those doubts, because had they been divined it might have put me in danger; and I had great difficulty extracting myself from the swarming crowd in order to head for the waste ground where the poor little tents of the most wretched mountebanks were pitched.

I arrived thus at the limits of the encampment, in a bare place where nothing flourished but bottle-tops and heaps of rubbish, among which dirty, snotty children in rags were swarming, also playing the Fair of Tomorrows, clarioning amid the broken bottles, drumming on the bottom of sardine-cans and shouting at the top of their voices to announce Tomorrow, Tomorrow! Tomorrow! Tomorrow!

And yet, out there, far out there, at the end of the road, in the rising dusk, proceeding with a very slow and heavy tread, was an old man who was carrying a formless infant in his arms, with the head of a calf, clad in multicolored and patched rags, and both of them vanished like the shadows at the moment when I understood that that vagabond was the one and only possessor of the truth, and of the sole true Tomorrow, the Tomorrow that is not at the Fair of Tomorrows.

MAY ARMAND BLANC
(1874-1904)

"May Armand Blanc" published work in the *Mercure de France*—whose associated press issued a small collection of her prose poems, *Minutes bibliques*, in 1902—and *La Vogue*, but the great majority of her short fiction was published in the feminist newspaper *La Fronde* in 1897-1903; all of it is translated in *The Last Rendezvous and Other Stories* (2021). She also published three novels. An obituary in *La Plume* written by her colleague in *La Fronde*, Judith Cladel, did not reveal her real name, but dropped hints allowing the deduction that she was the daughter of the writer Mathilde Saint-Vidal and the sculptor Francis de Saint-Vidal; the obituary did not identify the cause of her premature death after a long illness, to which she opposed the obsession of literary labor, but it was almost certainly tuberculosis.

Neurasthenia

In a sky like the face of a cadaver, the sky of a winter night in a lunar epoch—without a moon—a leaden sky dusted with rice powder and verdigris, in which the drool of the clouds spat flakes of ash and smoke, the lightning flashes at the zenith, tinting enormous roundels with sulfur and blue, seemed immaterial gemstones incrusted with reflections of nacre, snow and amber: vertiginous adornments that crowned the narrow wan brow of Neurasthenia. In that sky, after midnight, she surged forth, tall stretched and magnificent, queen and she-cat, ferocious and light, over the City, yawning her breath of pleasure through the stinking and perfumed mouths of theaters, splashing the sidewalk with a human foam. Wild beast and ballerina, with the backbone of a tiger and the sharp eyes, wearing little golden

299

bells attached to her thin ankles, with all the frills of follies that dance and swoon and pant and commit suicide, Neurasthenia pirouetted and leapt in a somersault that stirred the city and the sky with a convulsion of atrocious joy . . .

In eyes, she fixed her eyes, carved in metal and sculpted in flame, burning and brilliant; and nostrils sniffed the warm, humid air, the ambiguous air of the night, recognizing her passage by the strange reek of hatred and sweetness that she trailed after her, while she lifted her veil woven of rotten flowers, in order to freshen the streets—rivers of mud—and in tearing away the clouds she had carried away the stars, which fell into the gutter . . .

Select brains that passed that way under human appearances, picked up those stars in order to make works of them—art, poetry, beauty, happiness . . . and many, at that strong odor of putrescence and roses, at the delicate odor of decomposed flowers that marked her trail, panted in following her . . .

It was the abomination and the adoration of a people: prostitutes and princesses, perverse and vanquished in the soul, who sought her at the crossroads and in the ditches by the roadside for an embrace or a union.

They suffered in that imperious hour when she held them, Neurasthenia, but they knew that in the next hour she would sting them with a needle charged with a liquor surer than ether or morphine . . . a sweet poison that would slide into their flaccid soul a surge of energy, and into their empty veins the great flood of desire, the illusion of blood!

And for her court and her valets Neurasthenia shakes her little, short, thick mane the color of rust and hemp over her neck, of a delicacy to tempt the guillotine, and at moments that head tilts back with an abrupt shock like a broken corolla at the end of a stem devoid of sap—and then the entire body, the long, pale and sinuous body, agitates: a snake that does not want to die. That is because Neurasthenia, in her course, receives blows along with the kisses that attain her, snatching her like the bites of a rabid animal: a flagellation in the manner of the filthy and sublime parvenu who has climbed from the footlights all the way to pure thresholds . . .

Neurasthenia laughs like a child; she has a delightful and victorious laugh; dead chrysanthemums, lilies and irises exhale death and lust over her, in a shower of petals, while in her appearance as a fay who will play with a simple human creature, she extends her arms, which seem weak—so thin!—and stops . . .

One can approach her, touch her—take her, in sum, for what violations, or what triumphs, or what murders?—but her skin is so soft, so very soft . . . too soft, too fresh a flower, a flower splendid with divine pallor; it is silk the color of the moon, prestigious flesh of a fluid suppleness, flesh morbid with languor, flesh of caress and dream, to the point of not knowing what it imports from here or there . . . both doubtless, which pour out the same weakness—and thus escapes and flees again.

Neurasthenia . . .

Then, with a thrust of her crimson-tinted claw, she has departed to kiss the sky with the face of a cadaver . . . each of the nails of her narrow feet and her open hands—but filed like hallucinatory weapons—seems a jewel: pink rubies and red rubies . . . There she is, above the shiny roofs and the soot-colored reflection of blazing hearths, prodigious: a wild beast with a taut back, a ballerina scaling the clouds with an entrechat, Neurasthenia traverses the sky and reflects her disquieting and marvelous image in the moving mirror of the river; the river receives it with the silent and fugitive kiss of its bed . . .

And Neurasthenia finally snags her robe of putrid flowers, of beautiful deflowered blooms, on the new stones, the stones in domes, minarets, balusters, capitals, gables, pylons, stones that want to be of all ages, all epochs and all races—bastard styles coupled in deception and sham, in plaster and slapdash, in order to express to the crowds the immense adultery of time with hideousness and the lie: and that through the most magnificent effort of labor, Effort toward Beauty—who refuses herself.

Neurasthenia contemplates it, in the Field where the plowshare and the gesture of an invisible sower cause a new city to sprout from the bosom of the old city; and she sees that young city—which one might believe to be in ruins, given its disorder, so similarly chaotic are formation and destruction—already made up and ornamented like a whore for tomorrow: the spring of a young century . . .

A formidable hole—into which what remains of the palace of yesteryear will sink, and which seems the skeleton of a phantom vessel run aground, with its framework of scaffolding and ropes—will enlarge the horizon of the Élysée, where sumptuous life flows, above the bridge that will be made the color of gold and ash—what gold and for what conflagrations?—all the way to the Esplanade guarded by narrow mouths of bronze . . . They will be seen, from one bank to the other, those little round black mouths mounted like lorgnettes, which will have for targets . . . fêtes?

In the sky, Neurasthenia blinks, and seems to go to sleep—a repose . . .

The monstrous silence of the night, in which wakefulness seems an abnormal sin, is over the city . . . Neurasthenia sleeps . . . Whence comes that strange slumber, which does not put to sleep the smile of her teeth? Out there, toward the west, where a faint radiance indicates the undulation of little hills under frail winter woods carved in slate and drawn in blue ink under a timid moon, a delicate and white young woman places her fresh finger on her closed lips, takes refuge and disappears . . . That is the Beauty of the word, who has a savage and solitary caprice; she has escaped the new prisons in which some believed they had imprisoned her, so the lines remain graceless and the contours do not retain the prism of light and shadow . . .

However, because the exhausted crowd has fallen into the repose of drunkenness or agonizing pleasures, Neurasthenia raises her eyelids ringed with blue and mauve like crumpled petals . . .

It is the hour of mortal dawn, in which she throws to her own the fodder of bile and honey, the sickening nourishment that assassinates the appetite without satisfying the marrow . . . and Neurasthenia laughs again, because she knows full well that hunger will drive humans to carnage, and that, queen and she-cat, wild beast and ballerina, with the backbone and sharp eyes of a tiger, wearing little golden bells on her ankles and all the frills of follies that dance and swoon and commit suicide, she will be the mistress of the Universe, in the same Field where one believes that strong and virginal life is being grown, in which she sows the execrable seed, reeking of hatred and sweetness, while trailing her veil of corrupted flowers . . .

The Wedding of Time and Death
(A Black Tale)

It was beyond the leaves and the clouds, further away than the white horizons trembling in the light and the tender enchantments of the sky, on blue days.

It was *out there*.

Out there?

Up above? Under the ground?

Nowhere . . . perhaps . . .

But the sad eyes of the living and the calm eyes of the dead gaze at that ardent and unknown place—and wait.

Out there, Time and Death spoke: "O You! You go so quickly . . . so quickly, so quickly, do you know that your name on the lips of the sage cannot by 'present' but only 'past' or 'future' . . . stop . . ."

"O You, multiple and multiform, who run with a silent dread by the side of every living being, grimacing at his laughter, drinking his tears, and who finally tips him, on a whim, into the grave where you will have his spasm and his breath . . . listen to me . . ."

They stopped—a frightful thing! The motionless hours convulsed hearts, the infinity of agonies howled with terror.

Death neglected the living, Time neglected the open tombs of souls that only had hope in him.

It was the *duration* of the *moment*. Their imprecise form was affirmed. Who can tell the line of their appearance? Human folly has made a crude image of it: ugliness and old age.

Ugly? Death? The supreme administer of justice, the great dispenser carrying away, with a gesture invisible to the sighted, the nameless and priceless burden that makes the entire creature in a miserable body?

Old? Time? Time that had no commencement and will have no end . . .

They are not born. the eternal ephebes of primordial dawns, having been neither the seed not the embryo: *they were out there, once*—and remain, bearing in their features the grace and the color of an age unknown to humans.

Weary of their labor, then, the great laborers, they spoke.

"Are you not sated, O my Sister?"

"Are you not exhausted, my Brother?"

"All those who have gone to bed are afraid of you—for the attitude of slumber inclines to thoughts of you . . ."

"Yes, they are afraid—and I save them. They give me a strange name that I do not understand: *Death*? Thus they understand 'that,' non-existence. I know what 'atoms' are, for, being everywhere, I see everything . . . I know that pure delightful faces and all flowers are similar, that shivering bones and great trees bent under the tempest have the same cry; I know that, but *I don't exist*."

"Yes, they're mad; they say incredible things; I pass before their eyes and their hearts, always the same, but I never find the same eyes, the same hearts . . . other mirages shine there . . . and they say: Time . . . I am the immutable, the absolute, *I am not* . . ."

Then, silent, eyes riveted to eyes, they forgot the earth, human beings and human concerns.

They ignored the clamor that wanted them, wanted their caress, their cold and insatiable caress, which makes the heart light, the flesh heavy and icy: the accursed and redoubted caress—the unforgettable . . . They discovered one another—and loved one another. They loved one another, the Brother and the Sister, nameless, formless and ageless.

The human habit, they broke. He, having passed through so many amours, and She, having mingled her rattle with so many spasms, were subject to the avid contagion of desire and annihilation, and, on the far side of the clouds, they embraced in the light.

⁎

Then the leaves and the clouds, the trembling horizons and the great sky, so tender, sank into the primal Darkness, for, without Death and without Time, there could no longer be Life.

⁎

Is it a dream beneath the eyelids—or a shadow in the room . . . ?

Voluptuous and naked, she sleeps.

At the breath of her heart, her breast undulates, and under a pale light, her flesh is as silky as very clear water.

It is the terrible silence of the middle of the night—that unfathomable silence in which awakening seems an abnormal sin . . . Not a dream—and not a shadow either.

Time is upon us and Death before—unique certainty. What does it matter?

Thrown upon the beautiful and the fragile—the creature of an hour—I defy Time and Death . . .

It is necessary to drink, to drink, to drink . . .

Winter Heaths

The heath, as vast and changing as the sea, takes on all its beauty on winter mornings when it shivers, enveloped with the brilliant tulle of frost, melancholy and infinite, under the great pale sky in which the torn gauze of clouds fold up and deploy around the pale sun.

The russet ferns and the mauve heather give it a dappled adornment.

The clear atmosphere seems woven in crystal. The thickets, all thin branches and leafless twigs, are lacy and tremulous under a light wind that is scarcely perceptible as it passes. On the edge of the woods, on the hedges dotted with red berries, a population of birds takes flight with a rustle of silk and shrill cries.

A road cuts through the heath; that road is bordered by narrow ditches filled with stagnant water, and that water is half-frozen—not completely; all pink, all violet and all green, reflections of the earth and the branches, which give it their mirage like a kiss, that water resembles a mirror in broken fragments, a very ancient metallic mirror, tarnished by contact with too many faces—and those faces, annihilated a long time ago, it keeps forever: of their eyes, the extinct colors; of the fair or dark hair that veiled them, the veil of gold and shadow that trembles and still saddens its flat surface.

Who, then, has wanted to say that it is monotonous, the varied and magnificent heath?

It has no equal but the sea, and for having loved them as one loves animate and amorous creatures, one takes the rancor and horror of the monochrome landscapes of certain mountains that, like very beautiful women, seem to seize the pretext of that very beauty for the terrible insipidity of an invariable expression.

Here, there is an extreme grace in a detail of almost dry precision, apparently analogous to the delightful art of primitives in which all voluptuousness is dormant under the divinely calm harmony of lines.

A mysterious and magnetic beauty, which one pursues without wearying in order to adore and know all its roads, only marked by the double rut of heavy carts that hollow them out, roads that seem almost useless, dying who knows where, in the plain or the forest, where they are lost and rediscovered indefinitely in clumps of pines that cover them with an eternal shadow. Between the violet trunks of those trees, one can see the horizon scintillating like water.

Some of those roads, dulled by the gray of dried, ashy mud, intersect at crossroads where one would like to pause one's soul and one's life—in a dream, for those routes and that intersections seem to be chosen for the passage and the halt of a people of fays and witches. Oh, but very gentle witches of the woods, whose philters are devoid of poisons, and their incantations devoid of malefic spells. They must come on moonless nights, the queens of the trees and the plains, and dance silent rounds there, only illuminated by the whiteness of their interlaced hands. But those crossroads are deserted on winter mornings and solemn in silence.

The respiration of the world seems suspended here, and the heart is constricted as if before a beautiful dead woman one once loved.

That is because the land where one lived as child is alive with the individual and quivering life of an animate creature; it bears into the past the gilded hours of the joy of young mornings, and a little of the ingenuous and sacred alarm of evenings "when one was afraid!" Fear, a marvelous word, evocative of terrifying enchantments, the black sister of dusks dotted with stars when the lunar sky populates the earth with great dancing shadows!

Who has not traversed, in some evening of distant childhood, a large familiar garden, but which the night suddenly makes into a prodigious unknown, in order to search in the depth of pathways, behind the bushes, for some forgotten object? And who, that evening, at the blissful age when one sees further into the impossible than the real, has not sensed the irrational, mad and omnipotent fear that suddenly takes you by the throat and the legs, in order to prevent you from crying out or walking? And, with the eyes, peering into the obscurity, staring at horrible things that do not exist, and the ears filled with the sound of the ocean, whoever has known that fear has tasted a voluptuousness with a savor that the memory does not forget. They are the phantoms of evenings of old, of great, long summer evenings in which the light of the pink sky cannot die, but when that light remains suspended above the earth like a veil; it is them who populate the heath with their floating gait on this winter morning.

They emerge from beneath the clumps of russet furze and shake like feathers the frail little fir-trees what frost has made all rosy, fragile and implausible, like toys of spun glass. "It's us, it's us, don't you recognize us?" And they tell charming stories today to which one did not listen before when one sensed them palpitating in obscure thickets. They have the names of fays and beasts—how one would love, this evening, to see them again, with the same soul as of old, at the deserted crossroads . . .

But this will not be a summer evening—so soft that its blue pallor is less radiant than a pink dawn—this will be a winter evening when the wind will cry like a slaughtered beast in the branches, and skim the health with its mad gallop.

To see again this long-abandoned land where one was moved to puerile tenderness by details always identical—so that nothing seems to change here . . . In the old forest, trees have been felled and fires have eaten away entire kilometers of woodland with their ardent tongue—but on the corroded and rusted edges, an entire young forest is sprouting, thick and straight, and among the nascent plants are fir-trees so green that they seem artificially varnished; black and white herds in the far distance are like a game of dominoes symmetrically placed.

Yes, everything is immobile here—or seems so. The seasons, in passing, only change in eternal rhythm the color of the heath; autumn makes it pink with delicate heather with a thousand tightly-packed frail florets, and the golden gorse makes it all blonde in spring, with a river of flowers shaken in clusters, but it is less varied then than on a winter morning, when it is clad in the sumptuous grandeur of that which is placid and strong.

In traversing it, such as it is now, such as one loved it so much once, one senses how much the soul might be faithful to two various amours—for all the heart remains attached to the russet, melancholy and infinite heath; but because the enormous City that one has just quit holds you by all the senses, one cannot forget it even here—whereas within it, one forgets everything.

JACQUES FRÉHEL
(1861-1918)

"Jacques Fréhel" was the pseudonym of Alice Télot; the signature was used on five novels and three collections of short stories. She published in several periodicals before joining the stable assembled by Marguerite Durand to supply fiction to the feminist newspaper *La Fronde*, in imitation of *Le Journal*. She attempted to keep her identity secret but was "outed" by Abbé Louis Bethléem in his combative guide-book to *Romans à lire et romans à proscribe* [Books to be Read and Books that Ought to be Banned], first published in 1904 and reprinted several times. She did not want her literary work advertised because she was a senior social worker involved in political campaigns for the protection of children and feared the distracting effects of a literary reputation. After her death the Anarchist writer Han Rynner also revealed that, although married, she had been secretly his mistress for more than a decade. Much of her short fiction and hybrid prose poetry is translated in *The Inn of Tears: Stories and Prose Poems* (2021).

Last Light

The carriage had rolled along the quays and passed the bridges; very pale, with a crease on her forehead, the young woman sitting in the depths of the fiacre had said to the fat stranger placed heavily beside her: "Let's see, I no longer remember very clearly, my friend: where are we going?"

She passed her hand over her forehead with a strange gesture, as if to move veils aside, and a great tension was painted on her face, in her mobile and anxious eyes.

"You know very well, my little lady," the man replied, in a persuasive tone. "We're going to the Prefecture of Police to make a complaint against your neighbors, who are preventing you from sleeping."

He tried to soften his rough voice as he spoke, and crossing over his red hands, emerging from sleeves that were too short, he whistled as he looked through the window.

"Yes, yes, that's it," the lady had replied, in a very simple tone. "If necessary, I'll write to the Czar about it."

"Of course."

Another stranger was sitting on the seat. He was the one who had given the address to the coachman: three words whispered in the ear: "The depot infirmary."

A more sonorous rumble, the shadow of a vault, the ringing of a bell, bolts drawn, and then she had been pushed very gently into a profound and dimly-lit room, in the depths of which disquieting shadows were agitating. It resounded with shrill cries of torment, bursts of laughter, stifled ululations, and fearful and childish appeals: "Maman, help, I'm frightened!" Mute hand-to-hand struggles were perceptible, and in the muted light, the blue and black flutter of nuns' head-dresses.

Stupefied, shivering to the marrow, the young woman advanced meekly, brushing extraordinary beings with flamboyant eyes. Suddenly, a cell opened underfoot: walls, shadow, a bed. Then she jibbed, throwing herself backwards, clutching at the garments of the people holding her. But after a struggle devoid of violence she felt herself lifted up like a child by powerful hands and deposited in the bleak room, the door of which fell back with a cavernous sound, brutally evoking the idea of a definitive retrenchment.

In those surroundings everything became silence and immobility again.

Until those horrible minutes a sort of consciousness persisted in her: a frail tissue that would rip at the slightest shock. She felt mortally exhausted. However, her perceptions were sharpened morbidly; she counted the rustle of the habits and the gliding footfalls of the nuns, the buzz of distant voices and the infantile sobs of other wretches similar to her.

The following day, a cellular vehicle took her to a suburban asylum.

Again she found mental death floating there, crushing and invisible, and in the long days, the silence and the immobility of beings and things, broken by the abrupt audition of sonorous cries, projecting the horror of the inferno, and brief supplications.

"Help!"

"Quickly, quickly!"

"For the love of God!"

It was in those first days that the young woman felt her true name and her sane being decidedly detached from her, to make way for the vampire-madness that sucked her thought for such a long time.

The vampire howled with her voice, yapped for hours like a dog at the moon, scratched with her fingernails, bit with her teeth and pronounced base insults with her tongue. A padded cell had become her habitation, and the years passed without her perceiving their duration. No help descended upon her from the paternal bosom of Providence.

A kind of tragic beauty still floated over her dolorous pallor, around her bruised eyes and through her long, scattered hair.

Often, a word escaped her arid lips, and when she pronounced it, her voice became once again the melodious and passionate voice that had once enchanted those who loved her: *Before*.

Then she put her hands to her creased forehead in the effort of a profound and vain research; an expression of expectation was fixed on her features, and she remained standing, motionless, like a visitor behind a closed door. "Before" was lost for her, departed in the evening mist, via the dusty roads of the past, toward who knew what distant counties, from which it would never return.

It happened that she followed for long moments the fantastic play of the light on the wall; sometimes she thought she recognized cherished features there.

It was a grave profile of a thinker that interested her most of all, but she no longer had any idea who that profile resembled, nor what name to give that shadow.

It was in spring above all that she experienced the greatest troubles, when her soul of long ago lifted its broken wings of a dying dove. The buds of the trees glimpsed n the crowns through the bars appeared to her to enclose in their satiny sheaths familiar treasured mingled with impressions that had fled. As for flowers, by dint of considering them, she shed blinding, inexhaustible tears over their fate, so easy did it seem for them to be wounded and bruised, exactly like the virgin hearts of women.

One day, when the serene earth was delighting in the first enchantments of spring, when Ariel had wept in the morning and laughed at midday, when the vaporous air carried light perfumes of fecund humus, nascent lilies of the valley and partly-open wallflowers, the madwoman was sitting on the ground, gazing at the sky.

In the corridor, the ill-assured footsteps of a child were skipping, and a pleasant rising voice full of delight sang, stammering: "Quasimodo! Who broke the pots! Quasimodo, Quasimodo."[1]

The child, a little hospital attendant, never ceased repeating his refrain as he ran. When he drew away, the sonorous notes were mysteriously stifled, and then they returned, sounding richly in the young throat.

At first, for the insensate, they had only been syllables similar to others; then they struck her more forcibly, and in being assembled, acquired a complete meaning:

"Quasimodo! Quasimodo!"

Then she extended her infirm will and her suppliant hands toward the past, and, stammering with hope, she lay down in the dust, impotent to climb the giant steps that rose from her darkness toward the light and toward God.

However, her confused plaint found an echo somewhere in that vast universe, where, from tears and suffering, the prosperous seeds of pity emerge.

From all the obscure forms that populated her delirium, one was detached, and that phantom said, softly: "Oh, how was the memory of our amour lost?"

Overwhelmed by joy, she was only able to respond: "Beloved, oh, beloved!"

"Quasimodo!" sang the child. "Quasimodo!"

Yes, it was on such days, between flowery Easter and Trinity that she had lived the springtime of her amour.

O spring without rival, unparalleled flowers, violets on the edges of roads bathed by tears of pleasure, roses with burning calices, velvety palms, odorous mosses, diamond stars on the forehead, intoxicating vapors of the lost Eden: she sees you again and respires you again!

---

1 *La Fronde*'s readers would have been familiar with the name of Victor Hugo's legendary hunchback, but they would also have known what his name actually meant, being derived from the first words of the Introit of the mass sung on the Sunday after Easter: *Quasi modo geniti infantes* . . . [In the manner of new-born children . . .], taken from *Peter* 2:2, for which reason that Sunday was known as Quasimodo Sunday.

Her thought had become an enchantment again, and the past, emerging from the limbo of time and the abyss of her madness, enlaced her in a suave and strong contact.

She remembered, she revived their first embrace, when he had dared to take her hand, clasp her in his arms and kiss her face.

They had been very pure kisses, falling like rain upon her cheeks and hair, only brushing the lips by chance; they exchanged few words of amour, but they hugged for a long time, like two flowers of life sighing for another life . . .

Why had that sweet happiness not endured? Why, from the conquered Heaven had she fallen into this solitary Gehenna? That, that was what she could not comprehend.

But what did the ambiguity of reminiscences matter? The unknown had approached her and, as in the blessed days of happiness, he had clasped her to his bosom, brushed her face and hair with his lips, infusing her again with youth and beauty.

Thus he had rediscovered her; through the forest of sepulchral darkness, their wandering spirits finally found one another again . . . !

Before the past had reattached its impenetrable mask, she lived an hour of Paradise.

However, the vision glided toward the barred window, murmuring scarcely intelligible words, promising eternal reunions, an invisible bond stronger than terrestrial attachments . . .

As soon as the pensive phantom had disappeared, the chain of the madwoman's ideas was broken again; they fled in disorder like a crowd escaping through faintly lit doors.

All that survived in her was a formless aspiration toward the delectable repose of the tomb.

"Quasimodo! Quasimodo!" sang the child with the joyful voice.

Soon, everything fell silent, the sun sank, night descended, the bats flew through the ashen air, and the April rain, softer than the tears of human amour, streamed over the silent foliage . . .

Kemp Owyne[1]

Prelude

Can you see the scene again? Is the past hour present in its poetic rhythm? Is the light of our dreaming still shining in your soul?

. . . A golden evening in the Jardin des Plantes, the expressive language of strange animals; a continuous strident quarrel of winged beings; rare and superb trees, a beech with crimson leaves, higher up, a cedar extending its branches toward the city like noble prophetic arms. A slow ascension of the Belvedere: before us, Paris, like an immense gray canvas with dull bulges, a leprosy of banal houses; a few slender bell-towers, a few proud spires standing up like free individualities, rigid thinkers dominating sordid appetites with their arrogant will and vengeful scorn.

One divines the buzz of blind words and dolorous songs . . . A narrower enlacement brings us closer together. Our hands talk to our hearts; then one of us, with a smile: "Are we not contemplating that with the soul of a Rastignac?"[2]

"No, we're not experiencing any covetousness."

Over that height, the summits of our ideal shine with joy. What there is of the most noble in our minds combines.

You say to me: "Eve, magnified by dolor, incessantly chased from the paradise of thought by obscure torments, why are

---

1 "Kemp Owyne" is one of a set of English and Scottish ballads assembled by Francis James Child in the late nineteenth century, which attracted attention from fashionable Celtomaniacs. It tells the story of a young woman changed into a "worm"—i.e., a dragon—by her nasty stepmother, cursed to remain so until the king's son kisses her three times; different variants offer contrasted denouements. The ballad refers to the location of her torment as "Craigy's sea," perhaps a bay in the ancient district of Kyle where the modern parish of Craigie is located. The name of the male hero remains deeply enigmatic, although some speculators suggest that he is a borrowing of the Yvain of Arthurian legend. Adaptations of the ballad have been recorded by several modern "folk singers."

2 The ambitious social climber Eugène de Rastignac is one of the key characters in Balzac's *Comédie humaine*.

you weeping? Become devoid of sighs and tears. Do you not know that the spectacle of beauty is insupportable to ugliness and that the art of nature is creating monsters? What jealous furies would ignite inextinguishably if the human eye could contemplate the splendor of a heroic soul, that interior sky vibrant with stars of fire!

"Our soul, child, always encounters its cruel mother, the terror and despair of our uncertain wails. The torture is necessary, and also the wait for the one who will save us from the torture; persecutions and crimes border the route by which beauty rises from the flesh to the spirit!

"Do you know Ribera's *Prometheus*?[1] To become strong and sublime it is necessary to have been enchained. It is thus that wings are earned. Deliver, O deliver your captive deity."

But, puerile by virtue of amour, I said: "Next to yours, my soul is that of a child. If you want me to understand and accept, speak, speak again about liberating dolor."

"The repose of the day's end numbers the senses and throws a veil over real life. Listen; I shall search in legend, which describes its parabola through the centuries, for the profound symbol."

※

Once, on the coast of Scotland, there was a poor fisherman whose wife had just died. He had a daughter as beautiful as a nascent flower: the rosebud in her cheek had just opened; her face resembled an April morning.

When the dead woman was buried, the fisherman and his daughter remained alone, mourning the defunct. Moons succeeded moons, the eyes of the widower dried. Soon, he brought another woman into the cottage, the Megaera Margaret.

Isabel's beauty infuriated the new wife. When she spoke to her, it was as if one were seeing a dragon with flaming eyes crouching on her shoulders. As the soiled earth implores the rain of heaven, her hands needed to be washed in blood. Kill her! Kill her!

In sum, death appeared too mild an expiation for the crime of beauty, and one furious day, she dragged the child by her long

---

1 The striking painting by Jusepe de Ribera (1591-1652).

hair to the sheer rocks of the shore and threw her into the savage sea of Craigy, saying: "Stay there, dove Isabel, and let all my ennuis remain with you, until Kemp Owyne comes, traversing the sea, and redeems you with three kisses. But the world might elapse . . . oh, you'll never be delivered!"

The girl uttered plaints so resounding and sobs so profound that the seabirds, gulls, gannets and cormorants assembled, trying to console her, circling around her with compassionate cries; the sea serpents, like domesticated animals, licked her feet and enlaced her tenderly, but in a short time, her enchanting voice became loud and hoarse, and then frightful, like the bellowing of a savage monster.

The friendly birds were alarmed, crazed by fear, and then fled, and the inhabitants of the shore ran away. Their fearful stories reached all the way to Kemp Owyne, the hero who lived far away, beyond the seas.

His great black vessel arrived on the shores of Craigy at the solemn and mysterious hour when the night and the morning meet. The sandpiper began to sing and a smiling dawn was born, illuminated by rosy radiance.

The sun rose, setting the rippled nacre of the waters ablaze with crimson fire.

What became of Kemp Owyne when, instead of the savage beast that he was ready to combat, he saw, floating on the green mirror of the waves, a woman as beautiful as the agonizing Medusa, magnified by horror?

Her hair was undulating around her, tangled in curls; two of her long tresses wound three times around a tree. Her body like those of mermaids, was terminated by a fish's tail with ruby scales.

Isabel recognized the liberating hero and raising suppliant hands toward him.

"Save me," she said. "I can no longer live except in hope of you. Toward you I cried, like an eagle desperate at being unable to rise into the sky. Here you are! My God, how handsome you are! You seem to inhale light and spread it, O Kemp Owyne. Save me! I want to tread the land again with human feet and respire perfumed breezes. Will you enter into the sea of Craigy and give me a kiss?"

"I cannot obey you at the moment," replied Kemp. "I have my mission and cannot squander my actions. Perhaps I am separated from you by an insurmountable abyss. You do not know me, you do not know what I want. Your beautiful eyes contain the lightning of the soul or the vain intelligence of terrestrial desires. Speak! What have you to offer me? I am afraid of finding in you the stone that causes one to fall . . ."

Isabel replied, tremulously: "O Kemp Owyne, no gift is worthy of your celestial beauty and your power, but from the depths of the sapphire waves, the serpents have brought me for you a few of the treasures of the sea, which does not render any. Here is a royal ring in which a pearl radiates; so long as you wear it, you will be loved."

"I don't want a blind love obtained by magic," said Kemp Owyne.

"Accept, then," the child went on, "this royal baldric. So long as you wear it, you will reign over peoples."

"I have already reigned," pronounced Kemp Owyne.

"For pity's sake," begged Isabel, "don't disdain this sword enriched with diamonds; it renders one redoubtable to death; as long as you bear it on your thigh, you will live.

But Kemp Owyne said, not without disdain: "Gems are devoid of value, and I do not believe in death."

Then the girl threw the useless talismans back into the waves and started to weep.

And like a great black swan, the hero's vessel drew away.

With despair, her arms extended, Isabel saw it disappearing into the red sunset, and she said: "A kiss from you, Kemp Owyne! Ah, only one kiss from you and to remain enchained forever!"

That amorous thought loosened one of the long blonde tresses that attached her to the trunk of the tree near the shore of Craigy.

"Ah!" she said, again. "I can suffer now, resigned; I have seen you and I can think about you."

The acceptance of injustice and dolor untied another imprisoning tress.

She floated freely on the water.

"Let us stay," she said, "in the place to which the liberator came."

And, rocked by the waves, she went to sleep profoundly.

At the solemn hour when the night and the morning meet, the vessel bearing Kemp Owyne reappeared.

As soon as he could hear her, Isabel cried: "O beloved hero, don't abandon me today. Hear me, I sense that clarity is near. In me, a choir of immobile spirits is singing the ascension. Like a frail piece of wreckage I have been tossed by the waves, dragged into the torment, torn apart by the winds. Haggard, I have sunk into the gulf. Never has my life been so powerful as since it has communed with the abyss. Today I have thoughts as burning as veritable flames of dolor."

"They are what has liberated you, O beautiful infant soul," murmured the hero, pensively. "Peaceful, you can now quit the savage sea of Craigy."

Veiling her face with her long hair, Isabel sighed.

"Can I depart, O hero, without receiving the three kisses from you?"

"I'm beginning to understand," said Kemp Owyne. "Suffering has been for you victory; your feeble eyes are beginning to conceive the invisible. I will give you, with my amour, the kisses that deliver."

He took her in his arms, weak with joy, and carried her away in his black vessel, far beyond the seas.

HENRY KISTEMAECKERS
(1872-1938)

Henry Kistemaeckers was the son of a similarly-named Belgian publisher, whose ventures were often controversial, attracting the ire of would-be censors. The son made his reputation as a playwright, but in the early years of his career he was also a frequent contributor to Parisian periodicals, including *Le Journal*, where the item translated below appeared in the 17 August 1898 issue. He became a French citizen in 1900 when his plays began to achieve consistent success on the Parisian stage; many of them were filmed in France, and occasionally in Italy and Germany. He served a term as president of the Societé des gens de lettres.

The Hour of the Last Judgment

In the year 2000 of the Christian Era, at dawn on a day in April, a shrill and strident Theban fanfare quivered celestially above the old Earth and resounded indefinitely in the echoes of the younger stars, which scintillated, astonished, in spite of the incendiary flame of the dawn.

Immediately, the continents and their skies were overwhelmed by a strange phenomenon. From the ground and the clouds immense processions of beings surged forth, clad in their human insignia, the wave of which a fixed point in the Orient began to drink, in a powerful and continuous aspiration.

There was a vertigo.

Across the plains, on the rivers and the mountain slopes, under the ogives of the forests and the nave of the clouds, between the flanks of the valleys and in the glaucous or blue area of the oceans, innumerable armies extended, marching toward a star, miraculously animated by a dream-like velocity. The horizons were black with them and the lands stirred like stormy seas.

The cohorts were no less fantastic in their appearance than in their infinitude, for they were moving in homogeneous groups united by epochs and by castes—but all were flowing with heads bowed, their eyes turned toward the same cilice, and in a terrified silence.

Thus passed the humans of the first ages, gigantic rocs, and those of the decadence, pale florescences.

Thus passed tyrants in crimson togas, their mercenaries charged with swords, martyrs crowned with thorns, their black-clad judges and their torturers lit up with blood.

Thus passed vagabonds, priests, shepherds, navigators, cardinals, and then sages aged by doubt; thus passed naked negroes, antique pastors leaning on their crooks, kings filigreed with gold, and mousmés beribboned with changing silks.

And when they had passed, everything crumbled behind them that their will and their hands had edified. Nothing any longer remained in place but chaos or void. And the earth cooled again.

Out there in the bleak brush of Jericho, between the juvenile murmur of the Jordan and the harsh Judea of the Moab, God watched those immense pilgrimages hastening toward Nothingness. He had a sad smile as he espied a thousand twenty-year-old virgins swarming in the dazzling orb of his Tribunal, and his infinite eyes gazed pensively at the rising hour.

By midday, the monstrous battalions had already covered, like locusts, the sinister valleys of the Dead Sea, the hills of the Holy City, the neighboring desert and the rich countries of Syria, all the way to the plains of the Ark. But it was only as the daylight declined that the archangels ceased the terrifying appeals of their trumpets. All the tribes of creation, since the world was the world, were now there under the green sky, and the Hour had finally come.

Night descended, very cool, and the alarmed moon grew over the desert, drowning the darkness with a limpid, watery clarity.

Then the Eternal master rose to his feet.

And before the billions and billions of eyes darted at him in a mute and terrible harmony of anguish, he began the tragic trial of humankind. The lassitude, suffering and forgiveness of his voice ran in the wind like stellar music, and eternity remained suspended from his lips. There was no more Time; there was no more Space, and infinities of yeas went by in an atom of a second.

Thus the Voice had a sentence for every being. It was thus known that all men were bad, that all of them were egotists and liars, sacrilegious and criminal. The soul of the world was solemnly revealed, what it was in its grim hideousness, and it was like a wound open to the fearful face of other worlds, in order that they could contemplate it and meditate on all its horror.

Each verdict was a human vanishing in the ether. After having shown his Evil, God threw him into the Void, his molecules dismembered. And what had been an intelligence, a life and a force was effaced in a tiny blue flame.

In the nascent dawn, the fantastic myriads of the previous day had, therefore, evaporated. The entire devastated earth was now as bare as the plain of Jericho, as naked as a summer sky. A few fire-follets continued wandering toward the azure, where the planets were still waiting.

The master had only kept near him a few foolish young women having lived in tenderness and tears, a few prophets of various religions, a few blond children and a few saddened just men. Doubtless he would eventually make them the seeds of a new humankind.

In the meantime, he seemed, along with the prophets, to be looking pensively toward the rising sun, while the women cradled the infants and the just remained somber. Among them, sobbing silently, was the Christ.

Jesus sobbed . . .

Finally, he stammered: "Why, why, my Omnipotent Father did you create evil?"

"My Son," replied the Voice, softly, "it was for the pure charm of suffering and for the divine grace of tears—those things of which you are the image."

Having spoken thus, the Eternal rose up, surrounded by his own, toward the promised spheres, while a silvery dew engulfed the sympathetic planets. Then he made a gesture, and the Dead Earth, a furtive meteor, was squirted toward infinity. It was no longer anything in the universe but a shooting star.

Paul Margueritte

Paul Margueritte (1860-1918) was born in French Algeria, the son of the professional soldier Jean-Auguste Margueritte, who was subsequently promoted to general and led the charge of the Chasseurs d'Afrique in a doomed attempt to relieve the beleaguered French Army at the battle of Sedan in 1870—a circumstance that had a powerful effect on the work of his sons. Paul's younger brother Victor initially followed his father into the co-lonial army, but resigned in order to devote himself to literature; the brothers then shared a joint signature, apparently in imitation of "J.-H. Rosny," Paul's fellow-signatory of the *Manifeste de cinq* and fellow-member of the "Goncourt Academy." The two joined the stable of writers supplying material regularly to the *Écho de Paris*, remaining in it long after the majority of the other mem-bers decamped to *Le Journal.* Paul had launched his literary ca-reer with a pantomime, *Pierrot assassin de sa femme* (1881) before penning a number of Naturalist novels, and he wrote a series of similar works for the *Écho*, including the early one translated by Stuart Merrill in *Pastels en Prose* and the later one (7 September 1895) translated below; the series became increasingly surreal; the other sample is translated from the 29 February 1892 issue of the *Écho*. Both of his daughters, Ève and Lucie, with whom he briefly ran away to Algeria after his failure to obtain a divorce from his unfaithful wife, and whom he introduced into Parisian literary society at a tender age, became successful writers and translators; both married but the elder was swiftly widowed and the younger divorced, after which they lived together, both sign-ing their works with the improvised surname Paul-Margueritte.

Pierrot The Mormon

To the memory of the Hanlon-Lees.[1]

In Pierrot's absence, his three wives are receiving. Little soirée. Black coats and low-cut dresses. Pierrot's father-in-law and

1 The Hanlon-Lees were a troupe of acrobats formed in the 1840s by John Lees and the three Hanlon brothers (later joined by their three younger siblings) who performed in many vaudevilles on various Parisian stages, before touring extensively in Europe and America, being recruited by Phineas T. Barnum and being filmed by Thomas Edison; they pioneered the genre of "knockabout comedy" carried forward by the Marx brothers. They were greatly admired by Joris-Karl Huysmans, and their name was preserved long after the present story was written, most notably in the name of the Hanlon-Lees Action Theater founded in the USA in 1979 and still active at rodeos and "Renaissance fairs."

mother-in-law are at table with dignity before a tea-urn as stout as a barracks cooking-pot and a pile of sandwiches a meter high.

Pierrot's three golden-haired wives, Za, Cla and Lou,[1] are wearing similar pink dresses; their pale pink complexions are dazzling. They are coming and going, circulating, falling into armchairs, hanging on to the arms of dancers, radiating a gaiety that the absence of their husband renders significant.

Three flirters of preference captivate their attention. Major Bagstock,[2] as fat as a hogshead, oxblood red, with the eyes of a lobster, pleases Za. Cla is smiling at a gentleman planted so stiffly before her that he seems to be taking root in the ground. Lou charms most of all an unstable hunchback, curled up into a ball, with disquieting rubbery shoulders. At that moment a domestic with a tray of glasses bumps into the hunchback, who flies away like a balloon, pirouettes on his axis, collides with the ledge of the cupboard, rebounds on to the fireplace and, rolling with little bounces, returns to nestle against Lou, who does not seem unduly surprised by his disappearance.

Jerky and joyful music. Grave individuals are jigging energetically. An old lady is trampled. A negro in orange livery bounds on to the piano and treads the keys with his feet, like grapes. General enthusiasm, in the midst of which the negro disappears into the piano, the lid of which falls upon him with a bang.

Ladies are gossiping behind their fans. Whist players at a table are playing their cards, so absorbed that their wigs are catching fire on the candle-flames without them noticing. It is pointed out to them, but they continue playing imperturbably, their crania carbonized, their eyes revulsed in agony and their teeth grinding. Once bald, they extinguish one another.

In the meantime, the gentleman stiffly planted before Cla is stubborn in his deplorable rigidity. He is gradually becoming

---

1 It is probably not irrelevant to this nomenclature that one of Catulle Mendès series of stories in the *Écho* humorously detailing the immorality of contemporary Parisian society featured a trio of saucy young women named Jo, Lo and Zo.

2 Probably the character featured in Charles Dickens' novel *Dombey and Son* (1846), who pays court to Miss Tox.

green, turning into a tree. Imperceptible buds, and then little leaves, are growing at the ends of his arms and on top of his head. In a few minutes, growing visibly in the tropical heat of the chandeliers, it will be permissible to recognize him as a pear tree, of a firm and ligneous substance.

Major Bagstock prepares himself a grog of pure whisky, into which he squashes an egg and a pepper as large as a cucumber. He swallows it hot, without flinching. A little blue flame immediately pearls on his nose. A pragmatic Yankee leaps forward to light his cigar on that beacon. A magisterial punch followed by a catapulting kick precipitates him on to the elastic hunchback, bowling over Mistress Lou, who shows the color of her garters as she is upended. The hunchback-ball ricochets off the ceiling, flattening a gentleman like a pancake, and passes through the window of the gallery in a firework display of broken stained glass.

In the meantime, very calmly, Pierrot's father-in-law finishes reading the *New York Herald* and his mother-in-law finishes consuming the sandwiches and emptying the tea-urn. As she swallows, she swells; he, on the contrary, gets thinner. When he is no more than a skeleton, she continues swelling, and gradually, detached from the ground, oscillates and flies away through the window.

Universal joy. The father-in-law, liberated from a long slavery, plays a polka on his dental keyboard, with unusual talent. Only one diseased tooth, a false key, produces an intermittent and discordant B flat. The stiff gentleman is already bearing little pears, but they are not yet ripe. As his foliage is too much of a hindrance he is trimmed and pruned painlessly. Then gentlemen and ladies, holding hands, dance an epileptic conga around him.

Pierrot appears on the threshold, to the tune of the *De profundis*. A sad wind blows out the candles. The father-in-law's dental polka expires with a croak. All the lights dim. The dancers become pale—worse than that, livid—as if the white phophorescence of Pierrot's long glabrous face were extending a mortuary reflection over everyone. However, the round-dance continues, silently; at each circuit a link of the chain is detached and the dancer, of whichever sex, salutes Pierrot, who is immobile, like the specter of the Commander,[1] and exits, the women hopping and the men walking on their hands. The last to remain is a short young man whose nose Pierrot seizes; the young man picks his nose. Disgusted, Perrot grabs him with pincers and throws him into the street.

Za, Cla and Lou, meanwhile, surround him, heaping him with caresses, rummaging in his mastic overcoat and the pockets of his dinner-jacket. What gift has he brought them? He does not respond to their cajolery, intrigued by the presence of the arborescent gentleman, from whose elbow he picks a pear, which he peels and eats. It is exquisite. At his gesture, a harvest is made. Then, as the human pear tree is taking up too much room, Pierrot puts his arm around him, embraces him tightly, uproots him with a loud crack of the floorboards, and carries him away, his fibers severed and his roots dangling.

In his absence, Major Bagstock tumbles down the chimney and falls at Za's feet. A balloon squirted through the window knocks over the returning Pierrot and falls flat. It is the rubber hunchback, who is coming back to pay court to Lou. While Cla makes Pierrot respire salts, causing him to sneeze hundred-sou coins, Za and Lou, one pushed by Bagstock and the other by the hunchback, return to their bedrooms to the right and the left, traversing the doors as one might burst through paper hoops.

Pierrot does not show any gratitude for Cla's cares. Installed in his armchair, he invites her to undress, eyeing the sofa lustfully. She refuses, and he does not insist. Smiling, he puts his fingers around her neck and strangles her. She sticks out a tongue like that of a calf, her eyes bulging. He folds her in two and sticks her in a cupboard.

On to another! Before knocking on the door of Lou's bedroom he cocks an ear and looks through the keyhole. Horror! As expected! He resumes his impassivity and adopts a gracious air. Lou appears, in a corset and short skirt. He draws her to him, closes and bolts the door, and commences caressing her. Pretty leg, velvety arm. He points at the sofa. She refuses. He does not insist, and stabs her with his pen-knife. Punctured like a red target, he hides her behind the sofa.

1 In Mozart's opera *Don Giovanni* (1787).

Now for Za! He goes to the door, listens and looks. As expected! He knocks repeatedly, and negotiates through the keyhole. She appears in her chemise. He grabs her, draws her to him and guides her toward the sofa. She resists. He offers her a pastille of prussic acid, that she consents to take, without knowing what it is, without even saying yes, and dies.

Traversing the doors, Major Bagstock and the hunchback spring forth. They have seen everything. Violent reproaches. Briskly, Pierrot evades the blows that the clumsy major aims at him; as for the hunchback, his instability renders him innocuous. He leaps, rebounds, and finishes up smashing the chandeliers. Meanwhile, the phlegmatic Pierrot moves the sofa and opens the cupboard.

At the sight of the three dead women the major faints and the balloon man hides under a sideboard. Pierrot lights a cigar.

Courage and rage return to the major; he swallows a glass of whisky and a raw pepper, and wants to box. Pierrot extends his arms and touches his cigar to the other's lips. The major explodes, the balloon bursts, and the dead women resuscitate with a start. Pierrot smiles; everything collapses.

The Paradise of Horses

The skeletal mare writhed between the shafts of the fiacre, her hindquarters bleeding and her jocks ankylosed. The whip struck furious blows, not with the cord but with the hilt; and the exhausted animal, slipping on the black ice, saw her tumultuous life of lashes and the swarming of vehicles fleeing in a troubled pantomime dream. A soul of obscure suffering gave her wide dead eyes the sadness of a mirror, the fluid of which reflected the night. At a bend, she collapsed.

Oath and kicks in the belly could not lift her up; in vain humans hauled her like a boat; the animal lay there, her leg broken. Lying on her side, shaken by a breath of agony that ran along her projecting ribs, she awaited the knacker. Harsh voices buzzed around her, the hubbub of a gathering crowd, with interjections of pity from women. But the noise scattered gradually and no one any longer remained but the coachman, sitting on the sidewalk beside the mare, looking at her.

The beast and the man looked at one another, and for the first time, there was less hardness in the human eye, as if the malevolent brute who had abused the patient and obedient animal had begun to dream, confusedly, before the martyrdom which death was about to end. In the great black eyes of the quadruped a mist was already floating, and a sweat that the wind chilled was streaming from the coat of the skeleton. Suddenly, the lamentable beast felt someone manipulating her and trying to lift him to her feet. And suddenly, the sharp cold of a blade entered into her; great dolorous frissons shook her; she sensed great gouts of blood flowing away; what remained of her soul became vague, then vaguer still, and vanished.

But that liberated soul had not lost all consciousness and sensations persisted therein. It was thus that she felt herself lifted up, like an air bubble, far above the inferno of Paris, the rumble of the crowd and the slavery of the hundred thousand cab-horses. The equine soul flew toward the ether swarming with stars, passed over mountains and plains, saw the sea and skimmed the tips of the waves, far, far away, to land on the mysterious island discovered by the Englishman Gulliver in his voyages after Lilliput and Laputa, and which is, Swift assures us, the paradise of horses.

There, in the midst of the noble houyhnhums,[1] the kings of the land, their beautiful equine forms lustered by a gleam of health and strength, their white manes in the wind, the sad mare, resuscitated in the young immortal body of a houyhnhum, knew the sweetness of oats soaked in milk, exquisite repose, long slumbers and the love of a young houyhnhum, while the immemorial persecutors of horses, the filthy Yahoos with human faces, reduced to the humblest slavery, delivered themselves to the vile work of cultivation, vulgar and brutal slaves similar in their ignoble language to the Yahoo cab-drivers who had once rained blows and insults upon her, poor ambulant skeleton, in the horrible and swarming inferno of a vast city named Paris.

---

1 This is how the noun is rendered by the author, although it is not the way that Swift spelled it.

FRANCIS JAMMES
(1868-1938)

Francis Jammes spent most of his life in the Béarn region of the Midi, reputedly as a recluse, but he was acquainted with Stéphane Mallarmé and Henri de Régnier, and once visited Algeria with André Gide; while working as a notary's clerk he published work in the *Mercure de France*, whose associated press issued his early collection *De l'angelus de l'aube à l'angelus du soir* (1897), and he contributed to other Symbolist periodicals; he had a strong interest in nature similar to Jules Renard's, infused in its later manifestations by a quirky religious mysticism based in the Catholic faith, to which he reconverted in 1905. An enthusiastic hunter in his youth, he had also experienced a conversion in his attitude to animals, exhibited in some of his later works, including *Le Roman du lievre* (1903), in which the samples translated below were reprinted.

Paradise

The poet looked at his friends, his relatives, the priest, the doctor and the little dog, who were in the room, and died.

His name and age were written on a piece of paper. He was eighteen years old.

And, kissing his forehead, his friends and relatives observed that he was cold, but he did not feel their lips because he was in Heaven, and he did not wonder, as he had when he was on earth, whether Heaven was like this or like that. Since he was there, he had no need of anything else.

His mother and his father, who either had or had not died before him, came to meet him. They did not weep, any more than he did, for the three had never quit one another.

His mother said to him: "Put the wine to cool; we're going to dinner in a little while with the good God in an arbor in the garden of Paradise."

His father said to him: "You're going to pick fruits there. The trees will hold them out of their own accord, without their leaves of branches suffering, for they're inexhaustible,"

The poet was filled with joy, knowing that he had to obey his parents. When he had returned from the orchard and had plunged the carafes of wine into the water, he saw his old bitch, which had died before him, come running, wagging her tail. She licked his hands and he caressed her. She had with her all the animals he had loved on earth: a little brown cat, two little gray cats, two little white she-cats, a bullfinch and two goldfish;

And he saw the table laid at which the good God, his father and his mother were already seated, and a beautiful young girl whom he had loved down here; she had followed him to Heaven even though she was not dead.

He knew that the garden of Paradise was none other than that of the house in which he had been born, which is in the Hautes-Pyrénées on Earth, full of sheds, pomegranate trees and cabbages.

The good God had put his cane and his hat on the ground. He was dressed like the poor people of the highways, those who have a hunk of bread in their satchel and whom the local magistrates order to be arrested at the gates of towns and put in prison because they do not know how to make the sign of the cross. His hair and beard were white, and his eyes as rounded and black as the night. He said, in a soft voice:

"Let the angels come to serve us, since their joy is to serve."

Then, from all the corners of the celestial orchard, legions were seen running. They were the faithful domestics who, on Earth, had loved the poet and his family. There was old Jean, who had drowned saving a little boy, old Mare, who had died of sunstroke, Pierre the lame, Jeanne and another Jeanne.

Then the poet stood up to do them honor and said: "Sit down in my place; you ought to be near God."

And God smiled, knowing their response in advance.

"Our happiness is service; we're close to God like that. Don't leave your father and mother. Do they not serve the One who serves us?"

And suddenly, he saw that the table had expanded; new guests were sitting there. They were the fathers and mothers of his father and mother, and the generations hat had preceded them.

Dusk fell. The older ones went to sleep. The poet and his girlfriend loved one another. But God, whom they had welcomed, went on his way, like the paupers of the highway, those who have a hunk of bread in a satchel, and whom the local magistrates order to be arrested at the gates of towns because they do not know how to make the sign of the cross.

The Paradise of the Animals

A poor old horse, harnessed to a coupé, was asleep on a rainy night outside the door of a cheap restaurant where young men and women were laughing.

And the poor nag, its head hanging down and its legs weak, mortally sad, was waiting there until the whim of the debauchees finally permitted it to return to its stinking stable.

In its semi-slumber, the horse heard the vulgar remarks of the men and the women. It had been painfully accustomed to them for a long time. It understood, in its poor brain, that there is no difference between the ever-similar screech of turning wheels and the screech of prostitutes.

That evening, it was dreaming, vaguely, in the green grass, with its mother about the little colt it had once been, a rosy lawn on which it had frolicked with its mother, who was grazing it.

Suddenly, it fell dead on the sticky roadway.

It arrived at the gate of Heaven. A great scholar, who knew that Saint Peter would come to open the gate, said to the horse:

"What are you doing here? You don't have the right to enter Heaven. I have the right, because I was born of a woman."

And the poor nag replied: "My mother was a gentle mare. She died old, sucked by leeches,[1] I've come to ask the good God if she's here."

Then both battens of the gate of Heaven opened, and the Paradise of Animals appeared.

And the old horse recognized his mother, who recognized him.

And she did him honor by whinnying. And when they were both in the great divine meadow, the horse had a great joy in recognizing his old companions in misery, and seeing them happy forever.

There were some that had dragged stones while slipping on city roads, labored by blows, and had collapsed with the weight of carts on top of them; there were some that had circled, with their eyes blindfolded, for ten hours a day, pulling wooden horses, and mares that, during bullfights, had passed before young women, pink with joy, who watched them sweeping the hot sand of the arena with their intestines, dolorously. There were a great many more.

And they all passed through the great meadow of the tranquil divinity, eternally.

The other animals were happy too.

The cats, mysterious and delicate, no longer obeying anyone but the good God, who smiled at them, were amusing themselves with pieces of string, which they moved with light paws, with the sentiment of an importance that they did not want to explain.

The bitches, such good mothers, spent their time nursing their pups. Fish swam without any fear of anglers and birds flew without fearing hunters. And it was the same for all of them.

There were no humans in Paradise.

---

1 Worn-out horses were often killed in provincial France by forcing them into leech-infested ponds.

GABRIEL DE LAUTREC
(1867-1938)

Gabriel de Lautrec arrived in Paris from the Midi in 1889 and found employment as a schoolteacher while frequenting Le Chat Noir and other literary cafés in the evening. He contributed to various periodicals before publishing a notable collection of *Poems en prose* (1898; tr. in *The Vengeance of the Oval Portrait and Other Stories,* 2011 and *The Sacred Fire,* 2019), almost all of which, he claimed in "Le Sacré feu" (1903-04 in the occult periodical *L'Initiation*), were written under the influence of hashish, and from which all the samples below are taken. Resident in Passy, he established a salon there where his guests included Jean Lorrain—briefly a neighbor—the ubiquitous Paul Verlaine, Alfred Jarry and Oscar Wilde. As the Symbolist Movement faded out, after his flirtation with Occultism, Lautrec rebranded himself as a humorist in the vein of George Auriol and Alphonse Allais, and developed a quirky quasi-surrealist kind of comedy that was perhaps somewhat ahead of its time.

Sad Pride

For the woman on the sea shore

When I encountered you it was doubtless the same evening when I was to play the divine role of Hamlet; I already had the make-up of the impossible on my face and the flame of imaginary passion in my eyes, and it seems that I did not have the leisure that evening to love you, for an august ceremony was being celebrated in my soul with gold and chasubles, and you know that in the fêtes of the Intellectual, women's smiles are only admitted by candlelight.

That evening, however, was one of fatigued smiles and pale lips, with which I murmured to you what it would have been ungracious of you, Madame, not to take for the most delicate of confessions.

Very impertinently, I kissed your glove, and made the necessary compliment on the flower detached from my spray, which you had put in your hair. And truly, you appeared so charming and so rare that evening that in the music of the orchestra I believed that I recognized the voice of Ophelia, and I told you how much I loved it.

You loved me after that, you too; but beware: for loving art or the artist many have already died, and almost all the others have gone mad. Listen, this is what happens to those who ought never to love art.

Our amours have changed country and moon; we are the adorable adolescents of liturgical music and the servants of Eternal sensuality; but our voices die on our lips before we have disappeared, and we pass through real things as a troupe of actors and lovers that the old king of Bohemia is sending for his pleasure to his cousin the king of Thule passes through the picturesque streets of little towns, making the nocturnal pavement ring.

Moonlight

On the terrace paved with jade, like a dream more diaphanous than the gray wings of bats, the little princess advances fearfully under the pale rays of moonlight.

The moon marches, saddened, through the rapid clouds, illuminating the roofs of pensive pagodas and rendering the shadows of bushes sharper.

Along the terrace paved with jade, at the foot of which dragons with chimerical forms are asleep, the little princess advances, her silk dress rustling furtively.

Oh, in what path of dreams is she thinking of posing her delicate feet? What can her dark eyes, so strangely alarmed by kohl, distinguish in the obscurity?

Does she have exotic dreams of an unhealthy incoherence, the kind that come to us when we sense, in the depths of the soul, the evil of living in its full intensity? Is the musical charm of her gaze born of the bizarre sadness of her thoughts?

Above the bushes full of shadows, amid the frail and fine latticework of black branches and white flowers, the roofs of pagodas glisten.

Is she evoking, nostalgically, the distant landscapes of old Europe, where scenes of unknown amours are sketched under plane trees on the edge of great lakes?

It is a summer night, calm and scintillating. The profile of the princess is silhouetted delicately on the moonlit walls. A svelte golden butterfly, immortality, rises from her hair, and beneath her eyelids, irises full of an indecisive velvet have the charm of the night.

The water of pools, into which black leaves are falling, shines and plunges to infinity, and the memory of ancient things settles like a perfume on the calices of flowers, opening slightly to respire the shadow.

And, her soul full of the night and the vision of the impossible, with a silky rustle of her painted dress, the princess sits down on the jade steps, and, without knowing why, begins to weep.

Saddened, the moon marches through the rapid clouds.

The Mistresses of Poets

The mistresses of poets are thin; they are women with the bodies of children who, at dawn, while the beloved sleeps the heavy slumber of the ending night, get up in the crepuscular gleam. They go through the narrow bedroom, lighting the fire, disposing the white sheets that ought to collect the thought of the poet, and the dear books, too often read, that haunt his insomnias They are cold, in spite of the lighted fire, being among those who dream anxiously of being buried in the soft warmth of the bed and sleeping, sleeping forever, caressant and caressed, with

334

black hair, a pensive forehead and lips quivering with the fearful ignorance of everything that is not the kiss. And in the morning, soon risen, vigilant, but with heavy eyes, they come to lean over in bewilderment the closed eyes of the lover, like the page clad in black velvet in old German legends who watches over the lovesick page clad in white.

The mistresses of poets are ugly, but their ugliness is full of a charm to make one weep. Their eyes have a mystery and their lips the divine smile that humiliates beauty. And for the one that vulgar desires would scorn, the poet feels the source of his wounded heart opening; and the eternal song, as on the fragile strings of a sonorous violin, weeps its vibrant harmony in their desolate soul. O seductive and melancholy beloveds, what subtle and sad demon informs them of the dear secret of curing the disease of living by means of the disease of loving? Alas, it is of a disease that others might perhaps find strange that the poet is dying today, O sister of yore and poor pale child whose heart was so frail, her long black hair so caressant, and the frisson of whose eyes was unforgettable for such a long time.

The mistresses of poets are dead. During their terrestrial life, so brief, they were called Lilith, Antigone, Sperata—and it is them, who died of amour, whose kiss we seek on the lips of today. Oh, how eternal the wound is—to be unable to cure hat starry, futile and vain desire—and so dear!—Come the evening, which calms and lulls sick hearts, as one rocks unwise children who see frightening form in the night—And you put the soul of the poet to sleep with ethers and narcotics, so that he reposes in dreamless slumber where all dolor is annihilated. But before that somber dawn descends, he will go out under the moon, toward the tombs where the closed lips are and the eyes forever closed. And when he has confided to the magical quivering silence of the evening the secret of dear words, and luminous poems that no one but him will ever read, they will come, those of old, who alone will have listened; they will come, with caresses and their hair undone to murmur the amorous responses that he had never heard, and yet he recognized.

For a Demon

Are you now on the eve of disappearing before the phantom of naked life, you whose smile was the beacon of my yesteryear? Will the simple sensuousness of her hands of flame close her eyes habituated to mysteries? Shall I never see you again? Will you, the accursed whose ungraspable presence immortalized my anxieties, put on your face the color of my soul the new magical mask of being, in addition, the disappeared? I would like my prayers to be pagan, in order to praise you as much as I wish. The herald who came to search for us at birth, to summon us to play the role, wore a bracelet of black diamonds.

Your face was supple wind, and my words undulated toward you like the flame of a royal pyre. Your wings shadowed the morning twilight in which my violet sadness recognized itself, in the parks where, out there, above the haughty crowns of the trees, the dead gleams of the sunset came like the sound of horns. On the bosom of young men, in a beautiful tale of antiquity, a sculpted golden cicada sleeps, cradled by an amber necklace. A day arrives when it wakes up, listening to their hearts beating.

I know full well that I will die of your amour, one day or another, and that you will hold it against me. But, all decked in lace you strut, letting your languors flow from your long hands like waves of pearly opals, and your brothers in exile come in your wake in a great cortege, with torches, to gaze at me with their profound eyes. The poems they would recite if their lips were not sealed by the distant breath of seas would cause the old priors who, having risen at dawn, lean their foreheads worn by the light of cold cloisters over yellow missals, to pale with regret.

You are as beautiful as a sin, and your gaze is troubled, like eyes in which the divine spasm is playing. No one would weary of seeing you pass by. The supple grace of your body is a hymn to light gods. Sleeping in the hollow of your hand, all gestures disappear. You are also sadness. All other sensualities would wear the robe of censer-bearers before your young sensuality. If any-one named them, it would be a stray syllable of your name.

A memory, which bears your name, after what vanished generations and what furtive apparitions, in usual cities, of young women with beautiful breasts, will brighten the melancholy of adolescents, saddened by their heart in the future, like a dream lantern with colored glass that an unknown page clad in white will come to swing amid the black silhouettes of trees, through the real and lunar parks of their amorous youth.

The Invisible Soul

It is while turning pale over books that I have found the secret.

Enclosed in the pentagram, the formulae pronounced, I had enveloped myself in shadow like a cloak; my soul was invisible from then on and passed through the pathways of the garden bordered by immortal acacias. It went furtively toward the visible souls that it loved, and kissed them on the mouth.

At other times it leaned over the banks of rivers and was amused by not seeing its reflection.

Over the grass dampened by the night, it glided like a breath toward the tombs ornamented with Egyptian inscriptions.

But the thieves of souls have come. Their clenched hands raise a black cape all the way to the eyes; their footfalls are felted, their hearts have the hatred of the disappeared.

They had espied my soul and knew the route that it was following; with murmured words they whispered to one another that it was there, without seeing it.

They have groped in the darkness, gestures reaching forward, eyes closed, and their brushing fingers have encountered my wings, and the wings have appeared.

The entire body of my soul had been gradually revealed. Fallen from mystery, it has touched the ground strewn with black flowers. Now it is a natural thing, and forever sad.

FRÉDÉRIC BOUTET
(1874-1941)

Frédéric Boutet arrived a little late on the Parisian literary scene, but in time to hang out at Le Chat Noir and to encounter Oscar Wilde, whom he helped out of an awkward situation and befriended. His first collection of stories, *Contes de la nuit* (Chamuel 1898; second ed. 1903; tr. in *The Antisocial Man and Other Strange Stories*), many of which qualify as poems in prose and from which the sample below is taken, was set very solidly in the Decadent and Symbolist tradition, as were two collections of stories cast as horrific and melodramatic dialogues, *Drames baroques et melancholiques* (1899) and *Les Victims grimacent* (1900), but as the pressure of making a living forced his work to become more commercial the baroque aspects of his style and subject matter gradually faded away and he became a prolific producer of conventional newspaper fiction, much of it set during the Great War of 1914-18.

The Valley Named Solitude

> I shall give you
> The magic opal and the gold ring
> And what is worth more than glory or fortune,
> My robe woven with moonlight.
> —Leconte de Lisle, "The Elves."

A summer night, warm and moonlit.

The valley is slumbering in Solitude. And in the primitive majesty, the hills, covered with woods, hold up their immemorial peaks to the heavens.

To the west, a torrent surges from an elevated gorge, tumbling down the mountain-side. Framed by hanging draperies of ivy, singing with its harmonious voice, the steam runs over the shiny rocks and rebounds in crystal spray and vaporous foam. Masses of vegetation emerge and, seemingly floating in the middle of the water, mingle there in long filaments, which descend all the way to the lake bathing the foot of the hill.

The lake is sparkling with silver, thanks to the indolent waves softly agitating the rushes and water-lilies. Toward the middle, pale lacustrian plants extend their corollas, in soft or violent hues, and their fleshy leaves. The banks are covered in fresh grass speckled with asphodels. Large trees shade the base of the mountain.

The most beautiful flowers grow in multitudes in the valley, where woods of myrtle and ebony mingle with holm-oaks, whose old mossy trunks welcome virgin vines, honeysuckle, jasmine and wild roses. Great white rocks loom up in the clearings, along with grass banks that are reminiscent of altars or tombs. No animate being appears to inhabit the valley.

The full moon, bathing the valley with its magical light, adds a romantic prestige to everything. On their obscure slopes, the high hills conceal mysteries and apparitions; white vapors visit the profound woods and linger in the shadows cut out on the water; at a distance, the flowers seem as far away as the nebulous stars, swaying the harmony of their embalmed heads; the reeds stirring in the silvery undulation of the lake seem to be listening to distant voices responding to the voice of the cascade, which is expanding into the silence and vibrating languorously.

And in the enchanted purity, Night reigns over the Solitude.

Now, two human creatures appear, emerging from the wood: a man and a woman. They are young, walking side by side, wearing cotton tunics.

Beneath her black hair, covered by a white veil, the woman's face seems possessed of a passionate, troubling and triumphant beauty. With her large blue eyes she contemplates the valley, and sometimes glances at her companion, who remains taciturn.

Both move toward the lake. They stop by the cascade, on the grassy bank where the waves die indolently at their feet.

After a moment, the man, extending his arm, calls three times to the Enchantress whose same is Solitude, or Chimera, but whom no one knows.

And the face of the Enchantress rises from the lake. She looms up in the midst of the flowers, in the middle of the waters, which seem to form transparent draperies, as light as rays of moonlight, streaming with iridescent pearls, dressing her with long pleats. Heavy tresses, glaucous and amber, fall over her shoulders. Her eyes, luminous and changing, are like the sky or the sea. Her smiling mouth is melancholy. Above her forehead, large droplets form a crown, scintillating like diamonds, while others form a necklace at her throat and bracelets round her bare arms. And the beauty of the Enchantress spreads an invincible charm, and there seems to be an indefinable allusion within her to the beauty of the young woman who is contemplating her, standing on the banks where asphodels flower.

The man's eyes are lowered, and he stands there silent and tremulous. Finally, his voice rises up, hesitantly, in the harmonious music of the cascade.

"Solitude," he says, "Chimera, Unreality, whatever your name is, whom I have loved uniquely in the past, I am abandoning you because I want to give myself, with no return, to the woman beside me—to this woman, love for whom has arisen before my disgust for the real world to make me adore everything real in her person. She has entrapped me with light bonds stronger than any chain. Her smile is now my life, her body is my universe, and I am the slave of her eyes.

"Adieu, you who are the multiple, adorable and deceitful soul of the valley named Solitude! Adieu. My hours will no longer be your hours. Charms stronger than yours have enchanted me, for living lips have educated me in love . . ."

He falls silent.

The Enchantress cries: "You want to leave me, then, for a woman! Have you lost the memory of the dreams in which I have cradled you for so many nights, the immense joys that you have known in me and the marvels I have created for your pleasure? With me, you have possessed all things by means of thought, and is that not the true possession? Have I not given you all splendors and all voluptuousness? We have built magical palaces in the sumptuous domains of our caprice. In the gardens of our fantasies we have extended rivers and lakes beneath the setting sun, magic mirrors through which our visions have passed. We have made the most beautiful flowers grow, more perfumed than the flowers of the earth, and the breeze has engendered heady religious effluvia and unforgettable harmonies in the embalmed branches.

"Our dreams have sailed over seas of amethyst, emerald and topaz, beneath skies of unknown purity, beneath clouds as pompous as fêtes. For ourselves alone we have brought all centuries, all civilizations and all barbarisms to life again. Every city and every nation of times past and present has offered itself to us, without ever causing us to know disillusionment, since their décor reproduces our very dreams.

"You have known all glories and all triumphs. You have been an invincible conqueror, made peoples tremble with the hoofbeats of your horse. You have been a philosopher and a scholar; masters of science throughout the world have bowed down before your genius. You have been an artist whose divine works were adored by generations. You have possessed perfect beauty allied with irresistible force and universal intelligence!

What women have I refused you? Empresses celebrated for their charm, the priestesses of every cult, the most famous courtesans, all women, in their various beauty, have been delivered in turn to you with passion, with terror and with pride, in accordance with your caprice. You have descended the tenebrous roads of vice, horror and blood. You have known corruption, theft, murder and sacrilege. You have known the proud abasement of supreme debauches and the delights of cowardly ferocities. You have enjoyed tears that you have caused to flow. You have enjoyed supplications and impotent rages, broken by your will!

"Have you not lived all lives, savored the bitterness and charm of all joys and all misfortunes, all strengths and all weaknesses? Have you not possessed all human things completely, and have you not raised your proud desire toward things that are not of the earth, toward unknown paradises, supreme delights?

"Come back—you do not know what earthly loves are, in which sensuality engenders dolor and death!

"Come back, come back—I have the secret of every dream, the key to every door, and my kiss is immortal . . ."

Thus speaks the Enchantress—but the rival voice of the living woman rises up and replies to her: "No, you are not immortal, and you are not anything at all. In you there is nothing true, and the joys you invoke are not your own. You see them in the distance and cannot attain them . . . as water flees the thirst of the damned. In vain you try to entice them, in vain you strive in exhausting struggle; your imposture cannot deceive entirely, and your voice is false, to which you provide the reply yourself . . .

"A man cannot believe you, he cannot love you; you have prostituted, in your impotence, the very identity of his desire, to which you have given birth without satisfying it, of which you are the reflection without ever being the image.

"You are within him, and too much within him. He lacks in you the unforeseen that is present in others, which is the personal soul of a living creature whose will, taste and desire, acting out of free choice, gives the pride and joy of having been chosen.

"You are an automatic figure, whose mechanism always acts in the same way. Like the actor of an overly familiar play, you know the intrigue before it is knotted, and the vain simulacrum of the anticipated denouement, only suggesting the joy that it would give if everything were sincere. And your kisses give themselves to the void, and your arms open to embrace a fugitive shadow . . .

"That is the Paradise you promise to your lovers. It is by means of that bait of lies that you want to vanquish me, who is soul and flesh—who possesses, for the enjoyment of pensive tenderness, the enigmatic profundity of my eyes, the mysterious softness of my passionate words and the expression of love that extends over my beauty, like the caress of a spring evening over a garden; who possesses, for sensual pleasure, the irresistible attractions of my naked flesh, the transport of my embrace and the intoxication of my kiss . . .

"I am the dream and the reality; I am the divine flower that is uniquely capable of intoxicating the body and the mind! I am the One who is stronger than the World! And all joys without

342

me are nothing, and all misfortunes with me are nothing. A single one of my loving glances can send the bitterest dolor to sleep, and render all pride and enjoyment to my lover, in disdain for those who are not loved.

"When a man drowns his eyes in mine, he forgets earth and heaven; when my lips are on his lips, he faints, scorning everything else; when voluptuousness turns him upside-down on my quivering breast, from which perfumes of love rise, I am his triumph and his God!

"Don't try to fight me; I abandon to you those of whom cruel destiny has made objects of horror, disgust and pity, and who only have your exaltations to deceive the desires of their flesh that real kisses will never calm. They are granted to you in advance and no one will compete with you for them, but my lover, in his youth and beauty, is not destined to that puerile pursuit of an ungraspable mirage. He was created for sincere embraces, for living caresses, for all the seductions of human passion! I love him and he loves me, and for our marvelous amours the days and nights unfurl their enchanted future . . ."

She has seized her lover's hand, and gazes proudly at the Enchantress named Solitude or Chimera, but who is unknown. Now the poignant voice of the enchantress rises up again, to the accompaniment of the rhythmic resonance of the water.

"Oh," she said, "your reproach is unjust! The soul of a man cannot be content with the world; it always seeks the impossible here. Borne by my wings, with me, the Chimera, it launches toward the great sky, where its dreams search madly for their incarnation . . .

"A man soars into the sky with me, his Chimera . . . and if he is able to give himself to me completely, I envelop him with unparalleled joys. If he does not ask himself whether he is dreaming or not, the dream will not deceive him and will give his mind unequaled voluptuousness, and even give him voluptuousness in the flesh. However, the majority cannot; they want to attach me to the earth and search around them for the realization of that which cannot be realized.

"It is the cruel dementia of this man that wants to abandon me; that is his damnation, for what he loves in you, poor creature whose attractions will wither tomorrow, what he loves unconsciously in you, is me: the Enchantress named Chimera. With his dreams, his hopes and his sense of beauty has woven a magical cloak of seduction and harmony, which he has thrown over you. As he has made up the appearances of your body cosmetically, with his illusions, he has fashioned another soul for you, a companion of his own soul. He has created you in the image of his desire, and has so much desire that you should be thus that he truly believes that you are . . .

"What he loves in you is the reflection of his dreams of me! You are the road guiding him toward the goal, you are the opium that procures intoxication, but you are not the goal and you are not the intoxication; you are merely the mask of the phantom he adores, which he embraces recklessly upon your lips, to which he addresses his passionate plaints and all the delirious ardors of his soul: the redoubtable phantom that makes you shiver when you see its shadow passing in your lover's eyes; the phantom that, on earth, is known as the Ideal.

"O Ideal, eternal enemy, eternal benefactor, it is for you that the prodigious efforts are accomplished of solitary martyrs, the destined suffers of torment whose Hell and redemption you are. It is because of you that the happiness attained is poisoned by disillusionment and the worst dolors are soothed. It is because of you that there are supplicant triumphs and agonies full of ecstasy, for you are glory and misfortune, and the true God!

"Be careful, O Daughter of Men, for I tell you this: it is the Ideal that your lover always thinks that he has found in you, and will find until the moment he sees you for what you are: an imperfect human creature a thousand times inferior to his dream. Then he will weep all the tears of dolor and shame, and you will suffer a distress more atrocious than any other, for he will scorn you, and that will be unjust . . .

"And in the reality that you possess, the horizons of the dream will be effaced forever, definitively, and you will be condemned to veritable life, to the horror of monotonous days of bitterness and hatred, to the intolerable unhappiness of having lost faith in the Chimera . . . and that is the unavoidable Future."

The young woman, leaning toward her lover, smiles, and, plunging her eyes into his, intoxicates him with her breath, which has the scent of jasmine, murmurs: "Come, my love, it is the nuptial hour; the night is enchanted and I am mad with love. Come—our first kiss will give us the Ideal."

They both quit the bank where the waves died near the asphodels, going toward the woods of flowering myrtles, toward voluptuousness, toward real life . . .

They walk, enlaced together, madly in love, without seeing the tenacious shadows that attach themselves to their heels: the shadows named Disillusionment, Lassitude and Disgust; those named Jealousy, Deception and Hatred; and without seeing, in front of them, seizing each of their seconds in order to make it the prey of the past, the hideous Old Age that oppresses, ever more cruelly, and the fear of Death.

And the Enchantress named Solitude, named Chimera, but who is unknown, remains in the middle of the waters, weeping crystal tears, raising her bare, writhing arms toward the heavens, as if to implore or curse the enchanted Moon.

ALFRED JARRY
(1873-1907)

Alfred Jarry was educated in Rennes before moving to Paris in 1890, where he became closely associated with the Symbolist Movement. Always something of an *enfant terrible*, he caused a minor scandal by turning up at Mallarmé's funeral in bicycle shorts and a pair of yellow shoes borrowed from Rachilde. A prolific journalist, he also collaborated with his friend Remy de Gourmont on the *avant garde* art periodical *L'Ymagier* (1894-95), initially trailed in the *Mercure de France*. He achieved a spectacular *succès de scandale* with the only performance of his play *Ubu roi* (1896), greatly admired by Jean Lorrain. His later work pioneered "pataphysical" fiction, pataphysics being a mock-science concerned with the exceptional rather than the invariable; the Parisian *Collège de 'Pataphysique* is still thriving. His "novel" *Gestes et Opinions du Docteur Faustroll, pataphysicein* (written 1898; published 1911), from which the excerpts translated below are taken, is actually a collage of vignettes detailing the exploits of the eponymous character. Jarry's brand of absurdism was an important precursor of surrealism.

The Amorphous Isle

To Franc-Nohain[1]

This island is similar to soft coral, ameboid and protoplasmic; its trees are little different from snails that show us the horns. Its government is oligarchical. One of its kings, as indicated by the height of his pschent, lives on the devotion of his seraglio; to escape the justice of his Parliament, which proceeds solely by envy, he has climbed via the drainpipes to the underside of the monolith in the grand plaza, and has gnawed it until only a crust two fingers deep remains. Thus he is two fingers from the gibbet. Like Simeon Stylites he isolates himself in that hollow column, for it is fashionable today only to lodge on the platform of the capitals of statues, which are the best caryatids in bad weather. He works, sleeps, makes love and drinks on the verticality of a great ladder, and has no other lamp for his vigils than the pallor of his merrymaking. One of his least discoveries is the invention of the tandem, which extends to quadrupeds the benefits of the pedal.

Another, versed in halieutics, flourishes his circular railway lines, comparable to river-beds. But the trains, whose age is

---

1 "Franc-Nohain" was the pseudonym of the librettist Maurice Legrand, who allegedly published poetry alongside André Gide and Pierre Louÿs, in *Potache-Revue*, and also in *Le Chat Noir*. He founded a Theatre des Pantins with Jarry, and subsequently edited the satirical periodical *Le Canard sauvage*.

pitiless, drive the fish before them or crush in their bellies the embryo of bites.

A third king has rediscovered the paradisal language, even intelligible to the animals, and perfected a few of the latter. He has fabricated electric dragonflies and counted the innumerable ants by means of the number 3.

Another, remarkable for his hairless face, taught us precious artifices, enabled us to utilize our wasted evenings, consolidate our dead-drunk credits and obtain, without squandering our merits, the recompenses of the Académie française.

One mimes human thoughts by means of characters in whom he only conserves the upper part of the body, in order that there should be nothing impure in them.

Another is compiling a large book in order to tabulate the qualities of the French, who are, he ventures, no less brave than gallant and no less gallant than witty; in order to devote himself entirely to that labor, he took advantage of a moment of the inattention of his young posterity to lose her in a forest during a provincial excursion. And while we banqueted in his company, and that of other kings, on the various steps of the great ladder, Bosse-de-Nage being charged with wedging the foot, the cries on the magic square of newspaper-vendors informed us that his nephews were enquiring desperately under the quincunxes, that day as on previous ones, about the venerable missing person.

The Fragrant Isle

To Paul Gauguin

The fragrant isle is very sensitive, and fortified by madrepores that retract at our approach into their carline refuges. The mooring-rope of the ace was wrapped around a great tree, swaying in the wind like a parrot swinging in the sunlight.

The king of the isle was naked in a boat, his loins girded by a white and blue diadem. He was also draped by the sky and verdure, like the chariot-race of a Caesar, and russet, as on a pedestal.

We enabled him to reason with fermented liqueurs in vegetal hemispheres.

His function is to safeguard for his people the image of their Gods. He fixed one of them to the mast of his boat with three nails, and it was like a triangular sail, or the equilateral gold of a dried fish brought back from the north. Above the dwelling of his women he enchained the swoons and torsions of amour with a divine cement. Outside the interlacements of young breasts and rumps, sibyls have established the formula of happiness, which is twofold: *Be amorous*, and *Be mysterious*.

He also possesses a cithara, which has seven strings of seven colors, which are the eternal ones, and a lamp in his palace alimented by the odorous springs of the earth. When the king sings along the shore to his cithara, which is pruned with an ax of images of living wood, the growth of which disfigures the resemblance of the gods, his wolves nestle in the hollows of beds, the weight having fallen on their loins of the fear of the gaze of the watcher of the Spirit of the Dead, and of the perfumed porcelain of the eye of the great lamp.

As the ace overflowed the reefs we saw the king's wives expel from the island a little legless man, covered like an old crab with seaweed; a fairground wrestler's leotard on his dwarfish torso aped the nudity of the king. He was hopping on his gauntleted fists and the creaking castors of his base tried to follow and climb on to the platform of the Corinth Omnibus, which crossed our path; but such a bound is only possible for a few, and he fell miserably, cracking his posterior bowl with a fissure less obscene than risible.

The Ise of Ptyx

To Stéphane Mallarmé

The isle of Ptyx is a single block of the stone of that name, which is inestimable because it is only seen in that island, which is composed entirely of it.

348

It has the serene transparency of white sapphire and it is the sole gem contact with which does not become tedious, but whose fire enters and spreads out, like the digestion of wine. Other stones are as cold as the cry of trumpets, whereas it has the precipitate warmth of a drum-skin. We can easily approach it, because it is carved into a table, and can set foot on it under a sunlight purged of opaque and excessively shiny particles, like ancient ardent lamps. One no longer perceives the accidents of things there, but the substance of the universe, and that is why were not anxious as to whether the irreproachable surface was a liquid equilibrated in accordance with eternal laws or a diamond, impenetrable save for light falling vertically.

The lord of the island came to meet us in a vessel; the funnel sounded out blue aureoles behind his head, amplifying the smoke of his pipe and imprinting it on the sky. In an alternating movement, his rocking chair punctuated his gestures of welcome.

He took four eggs with painted shells from beneath his plaid, which he handed to Doctor Faustroll after drinking, by the flames of our punch, oval seeds germinated on the shore of the isle; two distant columns, isolated by two prismatic trinities of pipes of Pan, expanded from their corniches quadridigital handfuls of quatrains of sonnets, and our ace swung its hammock in the new-born reflection of a triumphal arch. Dispersing the hairy curiosity of fauns and the incarnadine of nymphs woken up by the melodious creation, the bright and mechanical vessel coiled its blue-tinted breath back toward the horizon of the island, and the gasping chair saluted an adieu.[1]

---

1 Author's note: "Since this book was written the current around the island has become a mortuary wreath."

The Isle of Her, the Cyclops and the Great Crystal Swan

To Henri de Régnier

The isle of Her, like the isle of Ptyx, is a single gem, framed by octagonal fortifications and similar to the basin of a jasper fountain. The map registers it as the isle of Herm, because it is pagan and consecrated to Mercury, and the local people call it Hort because of its magnificent gardens. Faustroll informed me that it is unnecessary to read in its name anything but its ancient and authentic root, which is the syllable *her*, as in a genealogical tree, which is equivalent to saying *Seingneuriale*.

The surface of the isle (it was natural that islands appeared to us as lakes in our navigation of firm ground) is formed of immobile water, like a mirror, and one cannot imagine that a boat could glide over it, except as a skimming ricochet, for that mirror does not reflect wrinkles, even its own. Nevertheless, a great swan floats thereon, with the candor of a powder-puff, and sometimes, without interrupting the ambient silence, it flaps its wings. When the flight of the fan is rapid enough, the entire isle is discoverable through its transparency, and it expands as a sheet of water fans out.

There is no example of the gardeners of the isle allowing a jet of water to fall back on the basin, the surface of which it would depolish; the bushes extend, at a certain height, a horizontal sheet, like the clouds, and the two parallel mirrors of the ground and the sky secure their reciprocal vacuity like two lovers face-to-face.

The habitude of the island is entirely solemn, as in an abolished century where that word signified *customary*.

The seigneur of the isle is a Cyclops, but we had no need to renew the stratagems of Ulysses. Before his frontal eye was suspended the metalwork of two silvered mirrors back-to-back in a Janus frame, Faustroll calculated that the double silvering was exactly 1.5×10^{-8} centimeters thick. He reflected the light toward us like the carbuncle of a wyvern, ad the seigneur of the isle, the

350

doctor told me, could clearly discern through it the ultra-violet things forbidden to us.

He advanced on tiptoe through a double hedge of reeds, which were carved at his order in accordance with the obsolete hierarchy of the syrinx; his majordomos served us sugar and quarters of poncire.

His wives, whose robes spread out like the ocelli of a peacock's tail, gave us the diversion of dances on the vitreous lawns of the isle, but when they lifted their trains in order to walk on the grass, less glaucous than the water, as Balkis, when summoned from Sheba by Solomon revealed her donkey's feet in the room parqueted with crystal, seized by alarm at the sight of capriped hooves and skirts of fleece, we threw ourselves into the ace at the foot of the jasper perron, and I pulled the oars.

Bosse-de-Nage translated the common stupor. "Ha ha!" he said, but fear doubtless cut off his speech.

And I recoiled from the isle, perpendicularly enough, for as long as Faustroll's head was able to hide me from me the gaze of the seigneur of Her and the artificial eye in its brown orbit, like a semaphore watchman's reflecting telescope.

HUGUES REBELL
(1867-1905)

"Hugues Rebell" was the best-known pseudonym of Georges Grassal de Choffat. He is now remembered primarily for the erotic elements of his novels, including the soft pornography he penned under other pseudonyms, but his perverse religiosity and Nietzsche-influenced philosophy are far more intriguing; he wrote a robust defense of Oscar Wilde for the *Mercure de France* in 1896. His collection of Symbolist poems and prose poems *Les Chants de la pluie et du soleil* (1894) is stylistically innovative and extravagant, somewhat reminiscent of Saint-Pol-Roux's work, and he was greatly admired by Paul Fort, who reprinted a number of his prose poems, including the samples below, in his periodical *Vers et prose*, alongside similar work of his own and adventurous endeavors by Paul Leclecrq (which could not be sampled herein because they are not yet in the public domain.) Prolific while his career lasted, but always struggling financially, Rebell died penniless in wretched circumstances, of peritonitis.

Successive Deaths

Oh, why are my eyes not like good hunting dogs, which bring back all the game killed by their master, why are they not similar to jailers who do not let anyone escape from prison?

In these sunsets, these thousand gray, pink, crimson and orange tints, and the soft sky and fresh verdure that veil the evening, will all these marvels, then, collapse like an enchanted castle, in an instant?

Glorious clouds, pathways in the plain, the noise of cicadas in the warm air, and that moist kiss and those beautiful eyes that are staring at me, will nothing remain of them? Nothing?

I would like to perceive all the beauty, all the beauties, and every scintillation of a wave, every odor and every nuance, and jealously conserve within me the treasure of things; but in immense life I am but a little fleeting mirror, a wavelet in which a particle of the Universe is reflected momentarily.

I rejoice, however, in the forms that have just been mirrored in me. So many images succeed so many images! I want to think about those that are yet to come; I even want to think about future mirrors.

The Virile Robe

I want to be a man; that alone is important to me.

I have been endowed not with eternity but with life, and I want to live.

The right to life is in strength, intelligence and beauty. If I do not possess any of those qualities, well, I shall resign myself to dying, but as long as I am handsome, strong or intelligent I shall triumph; I know that.

Alive! If you understand the word, if you sense its grandeur, how proud you will be of all the divine activities that are in you! How you will have neither pain, nor dread, nor anger.

For myself, I am neither Christian nor pagan, I am simply human, and I am proud of it.

I have no consciousness of sin; I do not know what a crime is; my only concern is living.

My hair, let the wind make you unkempt, let the sea breeze caress you.

My eyes, rejoice in the variety of things, in the changeability of the sky, days gray with rain, days of yellow and violet clouds, blue and golden days of sun.

My ears, hear everything: the babble of springs and the rustle of leaves, birdsong and the songs of men.

My mouth, receive the meat and wine that my hand brings, the meat that dispenses vigor and courage to the whole body, the wine that awakens the drowsy instincts and teaches us joy.

You, hands, be laborious nobles, create human happiness; do you not have your recompense in the caress?

My feet, go without fear of pebbles and brambles through mountains and valleys.

You that fecundates, marvelous liqueur, spread liberally in your embraces.

And you, queen-soul for whom all the limbs of the body strive, associate yourself with its pleasures; do not be enemies but companions; march fraternally on the great highway of the World.

My soul is not a German damsel with blue spectacles who thinks about paradise, blushes at everything and wants to depart for "elsewhere."

My soul is infatuated with the beauty of the Universe; nothing that is human shocks it or afflicts it.

Its domain (how vast it is!) is cities and the countryside, the thought that ferments in intelligence and the grape that ripens on the hillside.

My soul, proud among its peers, is not before that of the World.

And that is why, when I have worked, loved, enjoyed, lived in every fashion, I shall simply die without murmurs, like wood that burns and turns to ash, like the leaf, green all summer, that dries out in autumn.

The Noble Pauper

The noble pauper stands up in the sky of flames; he has waited to show himself for the evening light, in order that things should be in harmony with the proud ruin of his body.

He is a former soldier in the African army, and his hands have been reddened a hundred times by the blood of barbarians. He has gasped for breath and howled in battle; he has loved war like a mistress under the burning sun and in the infinite sadness of tropical nights.

And now, a shadow of a being whose past, still unknown, was glorious, he goes along the highways, trailing his wooden leg and his rags, but without falling, disdainful of inspiring a ridiculous pity in the passers-by.

Why is he still attached to life, when he no longer has its activity? A semi-broken-down machine that is being destroyed completely, he does not utter a plaint.

But he does not want to soil the triumphant combatant that he remembers having been, and to that face, which has had so many victories, he will not give a humiliated and vanquished expression.

Thus, when I pass close to him and see that beautiful head, on which ancient ardors still shine and an entire tumultuous life is agitating, I say:

"Take this, my good man, take this purse of gold, which you have not solicited, but which you need. Above all, do not have any gratitude for me, for, perceiving your gaze so magnificent with pride, your gaze that ill-fortune has not been able to lower,

I ought to forget my personality before yours and proclaim your grandeur.

"O poor man whose hand is not held out, it is not your poverty with which I sympathize. Poverty disgusts me, and if I saw you submissive to it I would turn my eyes away. But I want to glorify your superb beauty and thank you for having made such a splendid phantom shine before me!"

The soldier accepted my offering, as he had accepted the medal attached to his garment, without astonishment and without baseness, and he headed for the village, dominating with his tall stature the sparse groups that formed in his passage, while surprised by respectful whispers celebrating the venerability of the tranquil hero.

GUILLAUME APOLLINAIRE
(1880-1918)

"Guillaume Apollinaire" was the name adopted by Wilhelm Apolinary Kostrowicki, born in Rome of Polish descent, following his emigration to France in his teens. As an avant-garde artist he is said to have coined the term Cubism and was painted by the Cubist Jean Metzinger with his friend André Salmon, who shared his radical socialist views. Their journalism helped to popularize the term. As a writer he became one of the great precursors of surrealism, initially in the collections *L'Enchanteir pourissant* (1909) *L'Hérèsuarque et Cie* (1910) and *Alcools* (1911), the third of which reprinted the item translated below. As a critic he helped to reignite interest in the works of the Marquis de Sade and wrote pornographic novels of his own, although circulation of the most famous, *Les Onze mille verges* (1907) was clandestine until 1970. He died of influenza, after being severely weakened by the after-effects of a wound sustained in action during the Great War. (André Salmon was also wounded but survived to serve as an unruly war correspondent in World War II.)

Poem Read at the Wedding of André Salmon on 13 July 1909

On seeing flags this morning I did not say to myself:
    Behold the rich garments of poor people.
    Nor: Democratic modesty would like me to veil its dolor;
    Nor: Liberty in honor enables us now to imitate foliage, O vegetal liberty, O sole terrestrial liberty!
    Nor: The houses are aflame, because people are leaving never to return;
    Nor: Those agitated hands will work tomorrow for us all;
    Not even: Those who did not know how to profit from life have been hanged;
    Nor even: The world is renewed by the retaking of the Bastille.
    Of renewals I only know those founded in poetry.
    Paris has been decked with flags because my friend André Salmon is getting married.

✳

We encountered one another in an accursed cellar
    In the time of our youth
    Both smoking and badly dressed, awaiting the dawn,
    Smitten, smitten with the same words, of which it was necessary to change the meaning,
    Deceived, deceived, poor mites, and no longer knowing how to laugh
    The table and the two glasses became a dying man, who cast the final gaze of Orpheus at us.
    The glasses fell and broke
    And we learned to laugh.
    And we departed then, pilgrims of perdition
    Through the streets, through the countryside, through reason.
    I can still see the river on which Ophelia was floating,
    Who is still floating whitely among the water-lilies.
    Going in the midst of wan Hamlets
    To the flute playing the tunes of madness.
    I can still see him gazing at a bear dancing and getting drunk
    In order to give me a design of liberty.

I can still see him, next to a dying muzjik, counting blessings
And admiring the snow, similar to naked women.

I can still see him doing this and that in honor of the same words
Which change the faces of children, and I am saying all these things
Memory and future, because my friend André Salmon is getting married.

※

Let us rejoice, not because our friend has been the river that has fertilized us,
Riverside terrain whose abundance is the nourishment for which all hope,
Nor because our glasses are casting at us once again the gaze of dying Orpheus,
Nor because we have grown so much that many people might confound our eyes and the stars,
Nor because flags are flapping at the windows of citizens who have been content for a hundred years to have life and meager things to defend,
Nor because we can weep without ridicule, and because we know how to laugh,
Nor because we are smoking and drinking as of old.
Let us rejoice because the Director of fire and poets,
The amour that fills like light
All the solid space between the stars and planets,
Amour, wishes that today my friend André Salmon is getting married.

RENÉE VIVIEN
(1877-1909)

"Renee Vivien" was the pseudonym of Pauline Mary Tarn (1877-1909), the daughter of a wealthy English playboy and an American mother, who was educated in Paris and returned there when she came of age, becoming a key member of the coterie of female poets gathered around her lover, Natalie Barney. Their relationship was troubled and Vivien eventually became involved with Baroness Hélén van Zuylen van Nijevelt, née Rothschild; the two published a number of books together, some of them under the pseudonym Paule Riversdale and some under a Frenchified version of van Zuylen's name, although it is generally believed that Vivien wrote almost all the material therein. Vivien's early *poèmes en prose* were collected in *Brumes de fjords* (1902), from which the first two samples below are taken, and *Du vert au violet* (1903), in which the others appeared. She also contributed work to the feminist newspaper *La Fronde* and wrote two significantly different versions of an autobiographical *roman à clef, Une Femme m'apparut* (1904 and 1905; both tr. as *A Woman Appeared to Me*). Her neighbor during the final years of her life, Colette, wrote an affectionate memoir of her in *Le Pur et l'impur* (1932), the detail of which was hotly contested by Natalie Barney. Most of her prose poems and short stories, including some signed by van Zuylen, are translated in the collections *Lilith's Legacy* (2018) and *Faustina and Other Stories* (2019).

The Black Swan

Over the heavy waves, a flock of bright swans floated.

They left a silver reflection in their wake.

Seen from afar, they resembled undulating snow.

But one day they perceived a black swan, whose strange aspect destroyed the harmony of their assembled whiteness.

It had a plumage of mourning and its beak was a bloody red.

The swans were frightened by their singular companion.

Their terror became hatred, and they attacked the black swan so furiously that it nearly died.

And the black swan said to itself: "I am weary of the cruelty of my fellows, who are not my peers.

"I am weary of sly intimations and declared angers.

"I shall flee forever through the vast solitudes.

"I shall take off and I shall fly toward the sea,

"I shall know the taste of the bitter breezes of the open sea and the sensualities of the tempest.

"The tumultuous waves will lull my sleep, and I shall repose in the storm.

"The lightning will be my mysterious sister and the thunder my beloved brother."

It took off and flew toward the sea.

The peace of the fjords did not retain it, and it was not slowed down by the unreal reflections of trees and grass in the water; it disdained the austere immobility of the mountains.

It heard the distant rhythm of the waves.

But one day, a storm surprised it, brought it down and broke its wings.

The black swan understood obscurely that it was going to die without having seen the sea.

And yet, it scented the odor of the sea in the air.

The wind brought it a taste of salt and the aphrodisiac perfume of algae . . .

Its broken wings lifted it up in one last surge of amour.

And the wind carried its cadaver toward the sea.

The Dead

I plucked the mysterious flower that takes root in the hearts of the dead.

I took away the funereal lamp that burns on tombs, and I penetrated all the way to the domain of the Dead, in order to obtain from them the secret of their forgetfulness of things, and of their enviable peace.

A virgin was asleep in an ivory coffin.

She was asleep in a poor slumber, which was not traversed by the shadow of a dream. She was asleep, very white, in an ivory coffin. I touched her lips with the mysterious flower that takes root in the hearts of the dead, and the dead woman spoke in a languid voice:

"I am sleeping dreamlessly under the perfumed earth, because I have not known amour."

And her lips fell silent, smiling.

A king was buried in a golden coffin. I touched his lips with the mysterious flower, and the king replied to me:

"I am sleeping happily under the earth. I have known the din of assaults, the sonority of clarions and battle cries, the tread of armies, the ardent anguish of conflicts and the glory of victory; I have known omnipotence, pride and limitless splendor, and the glory of a crown.

"But I have not known amour, and that is why I am sleeping without regret under the earth."

A prophet was asleep in an ebony coffin. I touched his lips with the mysterious flower, and the prophet replied to me:

"I am sleeping peacefully under the earth. I know the secret of spaces and numbers, oceans and dawns. I have interrogated the stars and the silence, I have sounded the frightful universe resolutely, I have confronted the horror of the unknown, I have leaned over abysms and I have plunged into darkness.

"But today I am sleeping peacefully under the earth, for I have not known amour."

And I saw the tortured face of a dead man who was only half-asleep, oppressed by a nightmare. I touched his lips with the mysterious flower.

He groaned, in a pain-racked voice:

"I do not know warm slumber under the earth. The Dead, my neighbors, sleep divinely. Sometimes, they turn over on their serene couches. The soil that covers them is like perfumed velvet. They listen obscurely to the veiled sounds of the existence that no longer afflicts them.

"They sense the effort of plants germinating, sprouting, growing and flowering toward the distant sun. They divine the breath of the wind in the grass, and the odor of violets in the shade, and the melancholy clarities of evening slip all the way to their solitude and mingle with their dream . . .

"The Dead, my neighbors, sleep happily. But I am eternally unquiet, for I have known amour . . .

"I am suffering from the beauty of a woman. I have hated her voluptuously and loved her bitterly. Her caresses had the charm of a peril and the inadmissible attraction of a treason. Because of her, I have known intoxication and dolor.

"The Dead, my neighbors, sleep happily, but I am eternally unquiet, because I have known amour."

Lilith
(A Hebrew Legend)

> Fundamentally, believe me,
> woman has only ever loved the serpent.
> —Villiers de l'Isle Adam[1]

Lilith was created before Eve.

She was more beautiful than the Mother of the human race. She was not drawn from the flesh of the man but born from a breath of the dawn.

Her crimson hair set the dusk ablaze and her eyes reflected the beauty of the universe.

When he created Lilith, God destined her to smile at the man. But she considered the man and found him coarse in essence and inferior to herself.

And she turned her eyes away from Adam.

One evening, while she was wandering in the triumphal gardens of Eden, she saw the ineffably dolorous gaze of Satan posed upon her.

He had put on the undulating and supple form of the Serpent, and his eyes were sparkling like pale emeralds.

He said to the woman: "You do not know the mystery of Amour.

"You are wrong to scorn your disgraceful companion, for you can teach him and learn from him unknown joys."

---

1 The quotation is from the drama *Morgane* (1866).

Lilith contemplated the strange eyes, like two pale emeralds.

And she replied to him: "You're lying, and you're tempting me with the vulgar bait of pleasures devoid of beauty.

"You also know the secrets of subtle sensuality that resemble the Infinite.

"You, who are tempting me with amorous words, be my mystical lover.

"I shall not conceive and I shall not give birth under the ardor of your embrace.

"But our dreams will populate the earth, and our chimeras will be incarnate in the Future."

There was a vibrant silence between them.

And from the intercourse of Lilith and the Serpent were born the perverse dreams, the maleficent perfumes and the poisons of revolt and lust that haunt the human spirit and render the human soul similar to the sad and dangerous soul of Angels of Evil.

The Forest

Come into the forest, come into the fraternal darkness. Come, I shall collect for you the flowers that resemble you, the nocturnal flowers that harbor subtle poisons.

I shall ornament your lunar tresses with aconite, foxglove and belladonna . . .

Are you not frightened to be alone with me, in the nocturnal forest that loves me and which hates you?

I should like to flee from your bright eyes, as penetrating as mortal steel; I should like to flee from you and draw you to me.

The branches of the trees incline toward you like long menacing arms that stifle in an embrace of hateful amour.

They might strangle you, but they are impotent against me, because I am the being of silence and solitude.

The entire nocturnal forest menaces you and hates you; it has seen the lie in your eyes, and the peril of your voice, and the cruelty of your caress.

But I love you, while wanting to flee from you, and I will protect you against the forest and against myself.

Tender and true things are begging me to abandon you and flee—the foliage and the ivy, and the moss and the beloved violets.

Only the fervent serpents and the moon rejoice and encourage our amour.

Oh, how sinister the voice of the owls is!

The owls are advising me to abandon you and to flee.

The bats with blue wings go astray, tormented by the weight of their bodies and the impotence of their wings.

Their soul is similar to my soul. They collide with one another stupidly, and the desire for infinity is in their blind eyes.

I feel, cruelly, the desire to soar . . .

If I could fly, I might perhaps be able to escape you, O incarnation of my desire.

And if I dared to love you, I would kill you, in accordance with the desire of the nocturnal forest, which would bury you under the foliage and under the branches.

I would stifle your last gasp with my kisses . . . Oh, your last gasp in the night! I would stifle you with embraces and caresses, and you would die of my lips . . .

For I am the Lover who cannot love without hate, and whose covetousness is made of bitterness and melancholy.

And you, you are the Evil Mistress who exasperates fevers and intensifies the malady.

Do you not sense the danger around you?

The odor of Death is in the air and is intoxicating me strangely . . .

Oh, how sinister the voice of the owls is!

"The Moon is laughing, the Moon is laughing . . ."

MAURICE MAGRE
(1877-1941)

Maurice Magre was a native of Toulouse who went to Paris in 1897 in order to become a Symbolist poet and Bohemian; he associated with Stuart Merrill's coterie and published several collections of Symbolist verse before directing the bulk of his effort into prose, eventually becoming a successful novelist and essayist. All of his work—much of it infused with a fervent eroticism and equally-fervent mysticism—retained very strong Symbolist and Decadent influences well into the twentieth century. Almost all of his prose fiction, which commenced publication with the stories reprinted in *Histoire merveilleux de Claire d'Amour suivue d'autres contes merveilleux* (1903), is available in translation in a twelve-volume set from Black Coat Press issued in 2017; the samples below are taken from his collection of Buddhist *poèmes en prose, Le Livre des lotus entr'ouvertes* (1926; tr. as "Lotus Blossoms" in *The Poison of Goa*).

The Black Serpent that Brings Luck

Dawn is rising. Thank the God who has enabled you to discover in his gilded court the black serpent that brings luck to the house.

It is necessary to bring him milk in a flat earthenware bowl and put dry foliage alongside in order that he may repose there.

No face of evil augury will appear at the door today, no sad thought will stand on the threshold of the soul.

An entire day of good fortune, with no quarrel among the servants, no bitter memory to trouble the purity of your gaze!

O black serpent, I shall put milk in the flat bowl every day and I shall prepare the dry foliage, back serpent who visits me so rarely!

364

The Emperor of China and the Emperor of Japan

The Emperor of China and the Emperor of Japan met one beautiful evening on the calm sea. Two flag-decked ships advanced solemnly from either side of the horizon, and thousands of junks, with their colored lanterns, were motionless on the waves, like as many great stars, while countless stars were motionless in the sky, like as many minuscule junks.

The Emperor of China and the Emperor of Japan sat facing one another under a silk parasol with a golden handle, and beside them there were a Chinese dwarf with a square bonnet and a Japanese dwarf with a miter of peacock feathers, who presented them with tea in a hollow block of crystal. The two emperors drank a few mouthfuls of it and gazed at one another in silence. Their robes were streaming with precious stones and they resembled two timid gods who dare not engage in conversation.

The courtiers on the decks of the ships formed a respectful circle of embroideries and armor. There were mandarins there of the nine different ranks, from the Tai Fou who wears a red stone to the Tai Tchao who wears a golden globule. The Shogun was there, surrounded by the Lords of the Earth, and certain religious functionaries bent double by the discipline of rites, radiating veneration as a lamp radiates light. And on the shores of China and Japan the peoples were amassed, gazing at the calm sea.

The two emperors were going to discuss the imminent invasion of the Tartars, and the potency of the epidemics that had fallen mysteriously on certain provinces. They were going to seek together means of making rice circulate rapidly over land and sea, in order to remedy famines; they were going to study the causes of the fabulous typhoons that, in certain epochs, raised up the sea. They were going to enter into communication with the Spirits, listen to the voices of the ancestors. From their meting the lightning would spring forth that enables the Gods to descend.

The Emperor of China, the more resolute, spoke first, and the conversation was rather animated. They were both great lovers of lacquer and were astonished that a certain shade of violet could not be obtained.

"The polishers of Canton do not bring as much care to their work as before. The colcothar is too calcined. One no longer finds absolutely pure cinnabar. As for the rose, it's even more terrible. The cultivation of safflower has been abandoned. The secret of the ancient masters is lost. In truth, the world is in decadence."

The two emperors were very unhappy, and when the conversation was concluded, they almost wept, bowed down behind their fans, while the two ships drew away solemnly over the calm sea.

The God of Benevolent Intelligence

O god of benevolent intelligence, who is depicted with the large bare forehead of a mature man, the ingenuous gaze of a child and the creased mouth of an old man, you who hold a crystal ball and a closed Lotus, you who are motionless, you who see, you who know.

O god of benevolent intelligence put on my face the smile that comprehends, enable my hand to make the gesture that excuses, give all my attitudes the agility that daily indulgence brings to the body.

Take away from me the anger that blinds and envelops us with a red mist, do not permit frantic desire to possess me, for it forces a man to walk on all fours in the manner of beasts.

Give me the measure with which one weighs one's actions like black pebbles, the measure with which one weighs one's thoughts like grains of luminous wheat.

Give me the judgment by means of which the truth is discerned from error and the clairvoyance that enables one to know that a man is good even beneath a vulgar or unpleasant appearance.

Enable me to stand up between good and evil as one stands up between two enemy brothers. Show me the part of the lie that the mildness of the white mask hides and the part of human necessity that there is beneath the grimace of the black mask.

Do not make me laugh because of the pleasing character of pain, nor make me weep because of the spiritual emotion that beauty procures, and permit me to understand death, that entry into the land of immaterial humans, subtle landscapes and delicate vibrations.

Give my mind an inexhaustible thirst for knowledge, my heart an unlimited faculty of cherishing the various forms of creation, and permit me to climb with the agility of a runner the steps of knowledge that lead to the portal of amour, O god of benevolent intelligence!

HÉLÈNE PICARD
(1873-1945)

Hélène Picard was, like several of the other authors represented in this book, a "career invalid" who suffered recurrent bouts of illness all her life. As with most of the others, it was suggested to her that her symptoms were due to "neurasthenia," a vague term expressing an inability on the part of the medical profession to find a discernible cause. Suspected neurasthetics are often drawn to poetry, including poetry in prose, because such works lend themselves to composition in short bursts of feverish creativity between periods of relative incapacity. Sufferers also tend to develop a rather downbeat attitude to life, reflected in their work. Hélène Picard published half a dozen volumes of poetry before obtaining a position briefly as Colette's secretary while the latter was assisting the editors of the newspaper *Le Matin* to fill the daily fiction slot introduced into the newspaper in imitation of the *Contes du Journal* featured in its principal rival. Colette encouraged her to write a novel, and arranged for its publication, although it is less a novel than a collage of prose poems, which qualifies as one of the culminating works of the great French tradition of literary Satanism launched by Alfred de Vigny's "Eloa" (1824) and continued by Baudelaire's "Les Litanies de Satan" in *Les Fleurs du Mal,* the influence of which Picard's *Sabbat* (1923) readily cites. It was not quite her last published work but she produced little thereafter, the attrition of her condition forcing her to live as a virtual recluse, keeping in touch with Colette and other friends, including Marcel Schwob's widow, the actress Marguerite Moreno, by mail. The translation below introduces the section of the work titled "Satan."

Invocation

Appear to me, Satan, belly open and digesting—O Gigantic!—the lust of an entire destroyed kingdom. Have in your eyes the implacable and desperate bestiality that makes you the supreme Brute. Drive before you, Satan, in the cry of penitent Egypts and the silence of burned Sodoms, the tribes of Jehovah that made Moses despair, but show that sad foundation of power that it is you who animate the brazen wand, and that you bear the tables of the Law on your formidable breast.

Let Hell emerge from the gaps in your hood, Monk who casts a shadow over cilices and the cross, and since you are the goat, O Satan, fornicate before me simultaneously with four witches coiffed with fire follets and the laughter of the accursed dead.

I await ten thousand cats weeping sulfur, as many owls with wings lined with phosphorus; and in the midst of that lugubrious militia, inquisitors advancing breathlessly—for the cross with which they stun their victims is now across their throats.

I want to see the seven deadly sins in the form of carrion transpierced by dancing pins, or butterflies that have the souls of Sardanapalus and Balthazar for wings, or madwomen with eyes of precious stone.

Show me the serpent of sin coupling with the dove of salvation, and around that sacrilegious symbol the round of your imps, all inflating with their hideous laughter a bellows with the pustules of a toad.

I summon those reprobates whose sacerdotal and preciously anointed elegance is so dear to my exasperated Catholicism, and among them, I will salute the one I love: the red Prince of the Church whose leprosy is masked in black.

I summon the accursed, of whom I am one. One has a fiery slipper sealed to her heel of an excessively chaste dancer, another a ruby necklace planted like a dagger in her neck of a seductress who always says no, and among them I rediscover the Lady of Quality whose lover died while possessing her and who hides her culpable hand in a velvet glove stigmatized by a bite.

Spread around me, Satan, the icy nights of whistling and forever-tempted penitence, the sinister blue of impious concupiscences, the frightful red of crimes committed in the entrails of mothers, the blanching yellow of catastrophic skies when, to the melodious metallic song of wars, hatred, rape and wolves hurl themselves upon the same prey. I want to see, simultaneously, the violet of chasubles and that of mental debauchery, the white of the worst soilings and that of the doves that nourish the eternity of poets. Enable me to know the green of all putrefactios: that of the drowned dog, that of the cadaver that perhaps experiences the sensuality of the caress of larvae, and that of Jehovah, who ends up, so many of those he has invented, being devoured by locusts . . .

⁂

I beg you for that, Satan! Let me satisfy absolutely the detestable love that I have for the presence of poison. Enable me to sense and touch them all, in their thousand thinking cells, and enable venomous flowers, daughters of the sun and death, to incline one by one over my lips with the hissing of drunken vipers.

Open for me, Satan, the stables where the decadence of Empires wallows when, weary of anxieties and blasphemies, Nabuchodonosors rejoice in only bringing the carcass of a hog to annihilation and putrefaction . . .

Offer me, Satan, as so many Hells, the hearts that I have paved with the furnaces of my desire and throw, finally, into my arms the Being that I refused myself until now because he and I were not yet worthy of the number and splendor of my sins. Let my eyelid flutter at him like the wing of a baleful owl, and let him come, Satan, let him come, for the great Salvation is to be damned together!

"Is that really you who is speaking? I was sleeping on the blonde sheaf of my lightning bolts, and dreaming once again that the azure was mine."

"Pardon me, but I have not yet given the Devil anything but lyricism."

"Well, what more do I have, then, my naïve daughter? Why would you, a poet, make of me another being than the Genius, the musical damned soul? Why should I not remain, for you, above all, the skimmer of unreal seas who has divine pillage and fortunate shipwreck in his breast, and the death that leaps toward the stars with powder-kegs in revolt and thunderous laughter in his heart?

"Satan is what all humans have within them of the most alive and the most involuntary. Get a grip on yourself, my fervent she-demon, and continue your work by opening the wings of sacred dementia further and further. The sabbat of the spirit is far more terrible than the other, and much more sumptuous, my daughter. Dishonoring oneself with a few filthy devils when the night reeks of the priest and the witch and the rags of the shameful accursed is a game in bad taste, quite obsolete, and not worth a thrust of my horns.

"But to recreate Satan is something else. All great poetry is infernal because it has my two powerful virtues: revolt and pride. What have you done until now except free yourself and hope? Hope in the most immense pride, child of my heart.

"Let my puerile alchemy simmer in the crucibles of rudimentary Fausts. Let my frightful and ridiculous imagery continue to pervert abulic adolescents who nourish their rebel anemia, and priests who, in the fanatical sadism of Catholic fears, believe themselves already skewered by my fairground theater demons because they sometimes have fire under their soutanes.

"Child, child, I have no commerce with the horn of the young ram whose throat is cut under the navel of witches in art, or the viscera of snakes surprised by the hatchet in the moment of amour. My traffic is more serious. I am the smuggler who passes souls of pure metal from one world to the other. Already, I have lifted you in my arms; soon I will load you on to my back. My mark, on your forehead, is not a patch of soot; it is a trail of stars, and, since you invoke Satan, merit him.

"But I know you; you are playing with knucklebones in the tempest . . ."

"But then, I never have enough diamonds to break the hoops. I also need the golden fists of the sun."

"I know. You've just invoked me with such astonishing candor! How you thought you were saying abominations!"

"Yes."

"Ha ha! You're not unaware, however, that damnation is elsewhere, and that sniffing a rose is the greatest torment for a poet, and thus the greatest sin. My thousand devouring temptations only surround persons who dream with arms folded over their linen garments, and one visits Hell—I swear it!—in the robe of Beatrice and crowned with laurels. As for the chapter that you're consecrating to me, what is in it?"

"O my radiant Archangel, you have seen that I was counting, in order to nourish it, on dirty magic, the somber kabbala, horrible inverted masses, the filthy witches that come to crouch around the moon while Belzébuth, hound of darkness, howls in the silence of the dead . . ."

"Fool!"

"Why?"

"Sacred tribe of poets! They suspect nothing, and how right they are! 'What about your book? When will you give it to us?' they ask. 'My book? I've almost finished it . . . hmm . . . yes, finished . . .' They only have the title. But what spirits do not flutter around the title of a poet's book, above all when it is yet to be written? The spirits form its pages of their own accord, and since you have wanted to name the second part of your poem *Satan*, my daughter, well, by Satan I'll help you!"

"What luck! But I expected it."

"Oh, divine false innocence of poets! Charming perversities, delightful accursed. I'll come to fetch you tomorrow, at midnight."

"Where will you take me?"

"Hush! But, by Satan, my daughter, I want to prove to you that Hell is much more subtle, mysterious, delicate and . . . infernal than one imagines via the catechism and Lent sermons. Consequently, I shall put you in the presence of a few more of my possessed. You have known them all, in any case.

"Tomorrow, at midnight."

A PARTIAL LIST OF SNUGGLY BOOKS

ETHEL ARCHER *The Hieroglyph*
ETHEL ARCHER *Phantasy and Other Poems*
ETHEL ARCHER *The Whirlpool*
G. ALBERT AURIER *Elsewhere and Other Stories*
CHARLES BARBARA *My Lunatic Asylum*
CHARLES BARBARA *Stirring Stories*
JULES-AMÉDÉE BARBEY D'AUREVILLY *Hannibal's Ring*
NATALIE CLIFFORD BARNEY *The One Who is Legion*
S. HENRY BERTHOUD *Misanthropic Tales*
MAY ARMAND BLANC *The Last Rendezvous*
LÉON BLOY *The Tarantulas' Parlor and Other Unkind Tales*
PETRUS BOREL *The Treasure of the Arcueil Cavern*
ÉLÉMIR BOURGES *The Twilight of the Gods*
ADA BUISSON *The Baron's Coffin*
CYRIEL BUYSSE *The Aunts*
KAREL ČAPEK *Krakatit*
BERNARDO COUTO CASTILLO *Asphodels*
JAMES CHAMPAGNE *Harlem Smoke*
FÉLICIEN CHAMPSAUR
  The Emerald Princess and Other Decadent Fantasies
FÉLICIEN CHAMPSAUR *The Latin Orgy*
ARMAND CHARPENTIER *Claustrophobic Madness*
BRENDAN CONNELL *Unofficial History of Pi Wei*
BRENDAN CONNELL (editor) *The Zaffre Book of Occult Fiction*
BRENDAN CONNELL (editor) *The Zinzolin Book of Occult Fiction*
RAFAELA CONTRERAS *The Turquoise Ring and Other Stories*
DANIEL CORRICK (editor)
  Ghosts and Robbers: An Anthology of German Gothic Fiction
ADOLFO COUVE *When I Think of My Missing Head*
RENÉ CREVEL *Are You All Crazy?*
QUENTIN S. CRISP *Aiaigasa*
QUENTIN S. CRISP *Graves*
LUCIE DELARUE-MARDRUS *Amanit*
LUCIE DELARUE-MARDRUS *The Last Siren and Other Stories*
LADY DILKE *The Outcast Spirit and Other Stories*
CATHERINE DOUSTEYSSIER-KHOZE *The Beauty of the Death Cap*
ÉDOUARD DUJARDIN *Hauntings*
BERIT ELLINGSEN *Now We Can See the Moon*
ERCKMANN-CHATRIAN *A Malediction*
ALPHONSE ESQUIROS *The Enchanted Castle*
ZDRAVKA EVTIMOVA *Laura and Other Stories*
ENRIQUE GÓMEZ CARRILLO *Sentimental Stories*
DELPHI FABRICE *Flowers of Ether*
DELPHI FABRICE *The Red Sorcerer*
DELPHI FABRICE *The Red Spider*
BENJAMIN GASTINEAU *The Reign of Satan*
GUSTAVE GEFFROY *Decadent Tapestries*
EDMOND AND JULES DE GONCOURT *Manette Salomon*
REMY DE GOURMONT *From a Faraway Land*
REMY DE GOURMONT *Morose Vignettes*
GUIDO GOZZANO *Alcina and Other Stories*
LUIGI GUALDO *Narcisa and Other Stories*
GUSTAVE GUICHES *The Modesty of Sodom*
ALTHEA GYLES *A Woman Without a Soul and Other Writings*
EDWARD HERON-ALLEN *The Complete Shorter Fiction*
EDWARD HERON-ALLEN *Three Ghost-Written Novels*
RHYS HUGHES *Cloud Farming in Wales*

J.-K. HUYSMANS *The Crowds of Lourdes*
J.-K. HUYSMANS *Knapsacks*
COLIN INSOLE *Valerie and Other Stories*
JUSTIN ISIS *Pleasant Tales II*
JULES JANIN *The Dead Donkey and the Guillotined Woman*
LIONEL JOHNSON *The Complete Winchester Letters*
VICTOR JOLY *The Unknown Collaborator and Other Legendary Tales*
GUSTAVE KAHN *The Mad King*
KLABUND *Spook*
MARIE KRYSINSKA *The Path of Amour*
BERNARD LAZARE *The Gate of Ivory*
BERNARD LAZARE *The Mirror of Legends*
BERNARD LAZARE *The Torch-Bearers*
JULES LERMINA *Human Life*
MAURICE LEVEL *The Shadow*
JEAN LORRAIN *Errant Vice*
JEAN LORRAIN *Fards and Poisons*
JEAN LORRAIN *Masks in the Tapestry*
JEAN LORRAIN *Monsieur de Bougrelon and Other Stories*
JEAN LORRAIN *Nightmares of an Ether Drinker*
JEAN LORRAIN *Princesses of Darkness and Other Exotica*
JEAN LORRAIN *The Soul Drinker and Other Decadent Fantasies*
JEAN LORRAIN *The Turkish Lady and Other Writings*
GEORGES DE LYS *An Idyll in Sodom*
GEORGES DE LYS *Penthesilea*
ARTHUR MACHEN *N*
ARTHUR MACHEN *Ornaments in Jade*
PAUL MARGUERITTE *Pantomimes and Other Surreal Tales*
HENRI MARTIN *Isuren*
CAMILLE MAUCLAIR *The Frail Soul and Other Stories*
CATULLE MENDÈS *Bluebirds*
CATULLE MENDÈS *For Reading in the Bath*
CATULLE MENDÈS *Mephistophela*
OSCAR MÉTÉNIER *Three Decadent Stories*
ÉPHRAÏM MIKHAËL *Halyartes and Other Poems in Prose*
LUIS DE MIRANDA *Paridaiza*
LUIS DE MIRANDA *Who Killed the Poet?*
OCTAVE MIRBEAU *The 628-E8*
OCTAVE MIRBEAU *The Death of Balzac*
GAURAV MONGA *Costumes of the Living*
RICHARD O'MONROY *The Last Waltz and Other Stories*
CHARLES MORICE *Babels, Balloons and Innocent Eyes*
MANUEL MAGALLANES MOURE *What is Love*
MONTESQUIEU *The Temple of Gnide*
GABRIEL MOUREY *Monada*
DAMIAN MURPHY *The Acephalic Imperial*
DAMIAN MURPHY *The Star of Gnosia*
KRISTINE ONG MUSLIM *Butterfly Dream*
OSSIT *Ilse*
PHILOTHÉE O'NEDDY *The Enchanted Ring*
CHARLES NODIER *Jean Sbogar and Other Stories*
CHARLES NODIER *The Memoirs of Maxime Odin*
CHARLES NODIER *Outlaws and Sorrows*
CHARLES NODIER *The Story of the King of Bohemia and his Seven Castles*
HERSH DOVID NOMBERG *A Cheerful Soul and Other Stories*
HERSH DOVID NOMBERG *Happiness and Other Fiction*
EDITH OLIVIER *Horror! Horror! Horror!*
GEORGES DE PEYREBRUNE *A Decadent Woman*
HÉLÈNE PICARD *Sabbat*

URSULA PFLUG *Down From*
JEAN PRINTEMPS *Whimsical Tales*
RACHILDE *The Demon of the Absurd*
RACHILDE *The Blood-Guzzler and Other Stories*
RACHILDE *The Princess of Darkness*
JEREMY REED *Bad Boys*
JEREMY REED *Surrender to a Stranger*
ADOLPHE RETTÉ *Misty Thule*
JEAN RICHEPIN *The Bull-Man and the Grasshopper*
FREDERICK ROLFE (Baron Corvo) *Amico di Sandro*
FREDERICK ROLFE (Baron Corvo)
  An Ossuary of the North Lagoon and Other Stories
JASON ROLFE *An Archive of Human Nonsense*
ARNAUD RYKNER *The Last Train*
WILLIAM SEABROOK
  Astounding Secrets of the Devil Worshippers' Mystic Love Cult
ROBERT SCHEFFER *Prince Narcissus and Other Stories*
ROBERT SCHEFFER *The Green Fly and Other Stories*
MARCEL SCHWOB *The Assassins and Other Stories*
MARCEL SCHWOB *Double Heart*
COLBY SMITH *The Ironic Skeletons*
SIMEON SOLOMON *Collected Writings*
CHRISTIAN HEINRICH SPIESS *The Dwarf of Westerbourg*
BRIAN STABLEFORD (editor) *The Snuggly Satyricon*
BRIAN STABLEFORD (editor) *The Snuggly Satanicon*
BRIAN STABLEFORD *Spirits of the Vasty Deep*
COUNT ERIC STENBOCK *Love, Sleep and Dreams*
COUNT ERIC STENBOCK *Myrtle, Rue and Cypress*
COUNT ERIC STENBOCK *The Shadow of Death*
COUNT ERIC STENBOCK *Studies of Death*
MONTAGUE SUMMERS *The Bride of Christ and Other Fictions*
MONTAGUE SUMMERS *Six Ghost Stories*
ALICE TÉLOT *The Inn of Tears*
GILBERT-AUGUSTIN THIERRY *The Blonde Tress and The Mask*
GILBERT-AUGUSTIN THIERRY *Reincarnation and Redemption*
GILBERT-AUGUSTIN THIERRY *Stigma and The Pompeiian Fresco*
DOUGLAS THOMPSON *The Fallen West*
FELIX TIMMERMANS *A Peasant Farmer's Psalm*
TOADHOUSE *What Makes the Wave Break?*
LÉO TRÉZENIK *The Confession of a Madman*
LÉO TRÉZENIK *Decadent Prose Pieces*
ANNA JANE VARDILL *The Secrets of Cabalism*
RUGGERO VASARI *Raun*
ROGER VAN DE VELDE *Crackling Skulls*
JANE DE LA VAUDÈRE *The Demi-Sexes and The Androgynes*
JANE DE LA VAUDÈRE *The Double Star and Other Occult Fantasies*
JANE DE LA VAUDÈRE *The Mystery of Kama and Brahma's Courtesans*
JANE DE LA VAUDÈRE *Three Flowers and The King of Siam's Amazon*
JANE DE LA VAUDÈRE *The Witch of Ecbatana and The Virgin of Israel*
AUGUSTE VILLIERS DE L'ISLE-ADAM *Isis*
RENÉE VIVIEN *Lilith's Legacy*
RENÉE VIVIEN *A Woman Appeared to Me*
RENÉE VIVIEN AND HÉLÈNE DE ZUYLEN DE NYEVELT
  Faustina and Other Stories
ILARIE VORONCA *The Confession of a False Soul*
ILARIE VORONCA *The Key to Reality*
TERESA WILMS MONTT *In the Stillness of Marble*
TERESA WILMS MONTT *Sentimental Doubts*
KAREL VAN DE WOESTIJNE *The Dying Peasant*

www.ingramcontent.com/pod-product-compliance
Lightning Source LLC
Chambersburg PA
CBHW020524110726